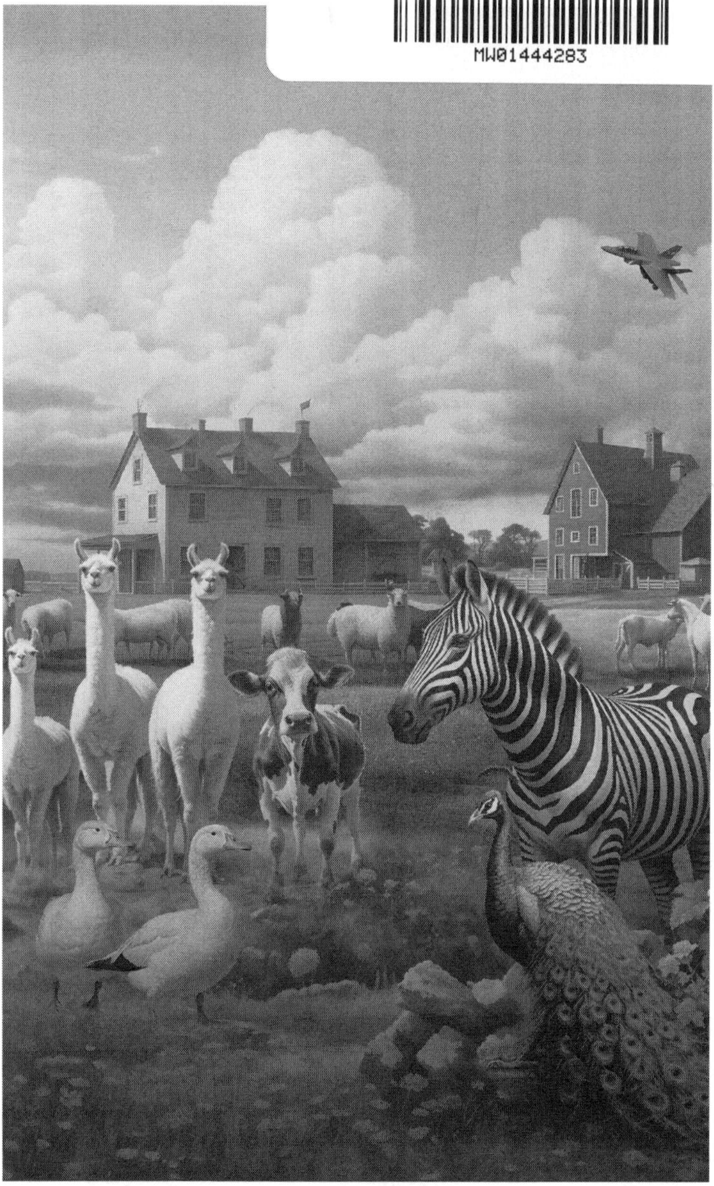

TWOPENCE PRESS books are published by
Twopence Press, LLC
P.O. Box 1753
Leonardtown, Maryland 20650

TWOPENCE PRESS
www.twopencepress.com

Copyright © 2024 by Christine Trent

All rights reserved. Except for use in any review, the reproduction or utilization of this work in whole or in part in any form by any electronic, mechanical or other means, now known or hereinafter invented, including xerography, photocopying and recording, or in any information storage or retrieval system, is forbidden without the written permission of the publisher.

This is a work of fiction. Names, characters, places and incidents are either the product of the author's imagination or are used fictitiously, and any resemblance to actual persons, living or dead, business establishments, events or locales is entirely coincidental.

All Twopence Press titles are available at special quantity discounts for bulk purchases for sales promotion, premiums, fund-raising, educational, or institutional use.

Cover Design and Interior Format by
The Killion Group, Inc.

THREE NOTCH SAFARI

HEART *of* ST. MARY'S COUNTY
✥ BOOK TWO ✥

CHRISTINE TRENT

For Sarah Copsey
Inspiration, friend, and menagerie keeper. Who never keeps it simple, except in her love for animals and family.

"Courage is being scared to death
but saddling up anyway."
— *John Wayne (1907-1979), actor*

CHAPTER 1

"**M**ORE WINE, MISS?" The server held the bottle of Quinta do Noval port in her hands. Her gaze was sympathetic, which made me irrationally annoyed although I knew my situation wasn't her fault.

"Thanks, no, just the check." As she nodded and moved away, I glanced at my watch for the hundredth time. Once again, Mark hadn't shown up. He couldn't even be thoughtful on our 22nd wedding anniversary.

The glorious, late bottled vintage port soured inside my empty stomach, adding to my nausea. I had waited so long for Mark, rejecting offers of bread and crackers, that the wine had first gone straight to my head and then settled badly in my gut. Now I was just irate.

I knew Mark was a reliability risk, so why had I chosen to have a fancy drink—one he had introduced me to long ago—while waiting?

I shook my head and pressed my lips so tightly together I could feel the blood draining away from them.

It was always like this with Mark, as of late. A promise made casually and then just as casually broken. Always an unbelievable excuse later but accompanied by a gorgeous smile and sparkling blue eyes framed with curling black hair, so I somehow always managed to forgive him.

I wondered once more if there wasn't another woman behind his thoughtlessness. Or maybe more than one woman, given how long he had been like this. It was so sickening to think of that I always swallowed the idea, trying to convince myself that such a thing wasn't possible.

I wiped an unbidden tear from my eye. It was as hot on my skin as the rage was inside my body.

Yet nothing had ever changed with my husband. He was handsome, charming, and careless.

I paid the check and fled the restaurant. I had sat there so long that the sun had already set, leaving just a thin ribbon of orange in the sky. I was soon back behind the wheel of my truck which, truth be told, probably needed a good vacuum and shampoo given that it smelled of dog, goat, and hay.

I drummed my fingers on the steering wheel while waiting for my fury to abate. It hadn't started this way. We initially had a nice marriage — romantic even, with a child, a dog, and a modest but comfortable home. Why was Mark now so unable to just be a normal husband? How many more years did I have to endure my husband's fecklessness?

You don't have to endure it, Becca.

I stilled as that unbidden thought entered my mind. My heart began beating rapidly as I let the notion bloom.

Fifteen minutes later, I pulled out of the parking lot, ready to confront Mark and give him an ultimatum. *You're on probation, pal. One more slip-up and we're through.*

I never got the chance to verbally blast him, though. As I made the turn down our road and approached the house in the darkness, I saw bright lights everywhere, then realized those lights were attached to several big, black SUVs.

My rage instantly turned to dread and fear. What was going on? Was April in trouble? Had criminals broken into the house? Did—

I maneuvered around the intimidating-looking vehicles and jumped out of my own, the engine still running.

Before I could reach the front door of my little farmhouse, it opened. Out came Mark, his hands behind his back, with men as large as gorillas on either side, marching him across the porch and down the concrete steps.

I was paralyzed with fear. What was happening?

Mark caught sight of me. "Becca! This isn't what it looks like!"

I had no idea exactly what it looked like.

"I didn't do anything. They've got the wrong guy. I didn't do it. You've got to believe me."

That was the last thing Mark said before he was unceremoniously tossed into the back of the largest of the SUVs.

CHAPTER 2

"YOU WANT TO do *what?*" I dropped my pail of horse feed to the ground. The metal container full of tiny, dark pellets landed in a freshly laid pile of John Wayne's particularly mountainous evening droppings, but that was the least of my problems.

"C'mon, Reb, don't be like that," Mark pled, offering that winsome gaze that had once made my knees buckle but now made me want to reach for the crap-covered pail and swing it at his head. Everyone calls me Becca, but Mark whipped out "Reb" when he wanted to cajole me into something.

Mark had been released from confinement remarkably quickly. The government had decided he was not the one responsible for stealing high-tech secrets from his company to give to another company. Whoever had done it had thrown a multi-million-dollar procurement into chaos and lawsuits.

Instead, they had verbally patted him on the head and dropped him off at home, stating that their investigation had led them in another direction.

After that, it had seemed churlish to tell Mark off. Besides, he had been quiet and introspective in the month since then, so I'd thought maybe the arrest had been what he'd needed to examine his life and change his ways.

As usual, I was wrong where Mark was concerned. He wasn't that deep.

"Like what?" I demanded, narrowing my eyes. "You

mean, don't be like a wife whose husband is the biggest idiot in the county—which is really saying something given all of your relatives—and who decides to step it up a notch by doing this on *my birthday?*"

Mark flashed the smile that also used to give me the tremors. "You always know how to make me laugh," he said. "Anyway, you know I've always been a beach bum, not a barn dweller."

I didn't appreciate my husband sucking up to me at the same moment he was announcing that he was leaving.

"Besides," he continued. "It's just temporary. I think. To clear my head. After all, I've been through a lot."

"You think going to Florida to pursue your heretofore completely unmentioned dream of being a surfing instructor is a *temporary* situation?" I spat the words like an ill-tempered llama whose feeding was late. Which reminded me that if I didn't get Doodlebug and the rest of the llama squad fed soon, I was in for trouble.

Yet I was rooted to my spot as a million images rose unbidden in my mind. Mark complaining about the cold winters in Southern Maryland, which are cold only by Southern standards. Mark always wanting to take beach vacations and glorifying the surf and sun of the Outer Banks. Mark's collection of longboards in the garage and his insistence that they were going to be valuable one day. Mark's head being shoved into the back of an SUV. My brother, Bear, shaking his head and saying that Mark was a few burgers short of a barbecue.

Dear Lord, wait until Bear heard what Mark had planned. Bear had begged me not to marry Mark but I had dismissed his concerns. At the time, I was a mature woman of twenty, so what could my seventeen-year-old brother have said that was of any value?

Since then, Bear had always privately mocked Mark in subtle ways. Upon Mark's arrest, Bear had been uncharacteristically silent, but hearing this news would turn my brother into a full-fledged comedian with a two-hour routine on it.

I cringed at the thought.

Shaking that off, I realized Mark was in his own routine, a combination of flattery and whining that only he could pull off.

"...You know that these animals were your idea, not mine. And you're at your happiest when you're left alone with them on your little hobby farm. Why shouldn't I have an opportunity to be happy, too?" He reached out a supplicating hand to me.

I stepped backward out of his reach. Twenty-two years of marriage had at least taught me when I was being played. To think that I had let that hand touch me in intimate ways not two nights ago.

I narrowed my gaze at him. "When did you make this decision?" I asked quietly.

Mark's expression grew anxious. Over two decades of marriage also taught him that when I was deadly quiet, I was at my most dangerous.

"Well, you know, I've been thinking about it for a while. On and off for a few months. Since before I was unjustly accused of stealing secrets." He laughed nervously. I'd asked him why they would have even suspected him out of all of the company's employees. *What* could have drawn the authorities to him? Of course, he fed me enough twaddle to both satisfy me and leave doubt. His bottom line was that he was innocent. End. Of. Story.

"Where are you staying in Florida?" I kept my tone even.

"I appreciate you being concerned for me," Mark said.

Idiot.

"I talked to Jake about it," he added.

Jake was Mark's younger brother. Last I had heard, he was on his third marriage to some art gallery manager.

Jake had always had a way with women. And their bank accounts.

Maybe Jake and Mark were too much alike for comfort.

"He says I can stay with him in his condo in Cocoa Beach until I get on my feet. He's even made some contacts for me at the Ron Jon shop. You know how rideable the waves are there."

No, I really didn't. I was a little too busy with life to contemplate how good the surfing was along Florida's Atlantic coastline.

But Mark was warming up to his topic and I guess my silence implied that I was approving the stream of inanity coming from him.

"If I could win at the Florida State Surfing Championship, that would really help my business. And you could come visit when you have time. Cape Canaveral is there. So is the Wizard of Oz museum. You like that kind of stuff."

Sarcastic questions whizzed through my mind like a comet and I regretted that I only had but one pail within reach to bang some sense into him. "Sure," I said. "I'll just walk away from Mom and the farm so I can fly down to see some rockets and glittery red shoes while you paddle away in the Atlantic. Mark, what is *wrong* with you? You should be telling me about your plans for my birthday dinner, not your cockamamie ideas to relive your youth. Not that I expect you would actually show up to my birthday dinner."

Naturally, Mark seemed offended by my response. He lashed back. "I've only been in Southern Maryland this long because of you. I should have left once I graduated from St. Mary's College, but then we got married, and then had April, and then it seemed like I was stuck here. But now she's twenty and you can get a job to support yourself, so there's no reason for me to stay."

I stared at him in disbelief for several long moments. In the background, John Wayne snorted his irritation that dinner was not forthcoming. Subconsciously, I began comparing my husband to my horse. John Wayne was far less complicated and far less stupid. I also had a deeper emotional connection to him.

I bent down and picked up the pail, shaking some of the excrement from it. I thought back to my resolve when I left the restaurant six weeks ago. This was Mark's "one more slip-up." I was officially done.

"You know what?" I said, gazing steadily at him. "You're right, there's no reason for you to stay. You should leave right now."

With that, I stalked off to replace the feed pail with a clean one so I could take care of John Wayne and all my other animals, none of whom would ever behave as foolishly as my forty-five-year-old husband.

CHAPTER 3

BY THE NEXT morning, I wondered if the previous evening had been a freakish nightmare. But no, Mark's side of the bed was untouched. And I was still roiling with anger. I stumbled out to the kitchen in my fluffy cheetah-print robe. Mark hated the robe, which I loved because it was so warm. Today I was glad I had never listened to his insistence that I toss it out and had, instead, kept it. It seemed like a moral victory over him.

I glanced up at the clock on the wall. Crap, already six o'clock. The critters would be getting anxious soon. Daisy, my border collie, sat panting next to the door. I let her out, started a pot of coffee, then went back to my room to change, careful not to wake my mother, who slept in what had once been April's room. Mom would be up soon enough and when she came out for breakfast, I'd have to tell her what had happened yesterday. Thank God she'd been in her room with the television volume up to an ungodly level, so she hadn't heard what had transpired between Mark and me as we had carried our argument from the barn to our bedroom.

It was the first time I had been glad that Mom absolutely refused to wear her hearing aids. "I don't need them," she would insist, then constantly parrot, "What? What? What?" all day long.

Don't get mad at Mom for Mark's stupidity.

I took a deep breath as I slid into my favorite pair of torn work jeans and my grimy boots. Both got washed regularly but they always smelled faintly of hay and manure.

I slid as quietly out the kitchen door as I could so as not to wake my mother, although it was unlikely that she would hear a tornado racing up Three Notch Road, much less the door creaking open and clicking shut.

I clucked my tongue and Daisy came running. She liked nothing better than to "help" me feed my critters, although her help often took the form of nipping at heels or racing up on an unsuspecting goat to terrorize it. Such a brat.

The morning was already warm and sunny. Hopefully, it wouldn't be a scorcher. Late August could be iffy; most of it was brutal but it could be interspersed with some balmy days. I went to the feed shed and decided to start the morning with the goats. I opened their metal trash can full of pellets, and scooped a quantity into a pail. Which reminded me that the poopy pail still sat outside the shed, waiting to be cleaned.

I carefully secured the metal lid back down on the garbage can. I had initially tried using heavy plastic bins to store feed. Big mistake. Squirrels and mice can get into anything like that and all you're left with is a chewed-up bin with no feed left.

The goats all anxiously ran to their fence to greet me. I'd like to think that it was because they had such great affection for me, but I knew their little horizontal pupils really gazed longingly at what I carried in my hand.

"Okay, babies, breakfast time," I said. I fed my six goats in individual metal dishes set up in a row, with each dish set about two feet apart. I'm sure I made quite the scene as I dumped feed into one bowl and then ran down the line dumping some into each subsequent dish.

Right on schedule, all the goats crowded at the first dish, then all but one ran to the second dish, then to the next and the next, until finally there was just one goat bellying up to the sixth dish of feed. "Piglets," I murmured affectionately.

Daisy assisted by running up and down the line like a maniac, as though by doing so she was getting them to eat faster.

I returned the pail to the feed shed and hefted a bale of hay from the stack I had just purchased two days earlier. Had I known what Mark was about to do to me, would I have done anything differently this week?

I shrugged to myself. Except for horses, farm animals don't care about your emotional problems. They need to be fed, watered, groomed, and cleaned up after, on time every day.

Dumping the hay into a wheelbarrow I keep right outside the feed shed, I took the hay to the goats' hay station, one of the few contraptions Mark had been willing to build for me. Constructed about three feet off the ground between two trees, it had wide slots so that the goats could easily eat hay from it yet it kept the hay off the ground to prevent it from getting moldy. Goats don't like eating from the ground. Their penned area had trees completely devoid of vegetation from about three feet off the ground.

I lifted the hay and tossed it into the hay station with a grunt, then spent another thirty minutes taking care of the horses and llamas.

When Daisy and I returned to the house, her panting and me a little smelly and a lot sweaty, I found Mom sitting in the kitchen with a cup of the coffee I had brewed. In front of her was an open box of Krispy Kreme doughnuts I had purchased yesterday morning before Mark had turned into a complete wanker, as the British would say.

Without a good morning, she set the cup into her saucer and said, "I need to get my pie plate back from Betty Ann."

I sighed. "Mom," I explained patiently as I retrieved Daisy's food bucket from under the sink, "Betty Ann dropped the pie plate off last week."

"She did?" Mom looked at me quizzically.

I nodded and poured some of the chow into Daisy's bowl on the floor. "She did. Listen, I need to tell you what happened last—"

"I don't remember her coming. When was she here?" Mom had that faraway look she got when she was reaching futilely backward, grasping at wispy memories.

Whenever I got a little irritated by Mom's wandering mind, I reminded myself of the woman she once was and that I could very well end up in the same situation. Except I wouldn't have someone solid like me to take care of me. I would have my daughter, April.

I shuddered at the thought. I would never understand how April had become the opposite of me. Although, truth be told, wasn't I the opposite of my own mother?

Georgina Denise LaMotte Manigault had been raised in Charleston, South Carolina, to be the quintessential southern belle. She had taken that duty seriously. Mom could verbally slice you in half with a captivating smile on her face as she handed you a homemade pecan pie.

Dad had been a sailor posted at Naval Weapons Station Charleston when he met Mom at a dance. Fireworks ensued and soon we were a typical Navy family traveling from duty station to duty station. Naval Air Station Patuxent River had been Dad's last posting, so they had retired in St. Mary's County.

Mom had never lost her status as belle of the ball with Dad, but it did sort of morph into her being a grande dame of St. Mary's County for many years. Until now, with dad gone and her mind existing in a sort of mental urban area, where some days were sunny but most were smoggy and overcast.

I realized that Mom needed a moment, and it wasn't time to tell my story. I poured my own cup of coffee and sat down across from her, selecting a particularly gooey glazed doughnut from the box and taking a hefty bite. It wasn't completely fresh but it still oozed with caloric goodness.

Feeding animals makes a girl hungry, right?

"Betty Ann stopped by last Friday. She invited you to the Ladies with Hats summer social at Pier 450 in two weeks," I said.

Betty Ann was Mom's church friend. A veritable social force of nature, Betty Ann had started a club for elderly women who didn't get out much anymore. They all primped up in their Sunday best clothing, gathered their curled-and-set hair under hats, and went to lunch or tea together. Betty Ann rounded everyone up in an old van she had and then dropped everyone off at the conclusion of the events which took place roughly five or six times a year.

God bless that woman. Mom's spirits were always lifted when she saw that dusty old gray van pull into my long driveway.

"WHAT?" Mom said, cupping one ear. "Betty Ann stole two sheets?"

I repeated myself, only louder.

"Oh!" Mom exclaimed, brightening. "I'll need to pick out what to wear. The netting on my blue hat is a little frayed and needs fixing. Can you call Betty Ann and tell her to bring back my pie plate when she comes?"

I swallowed the last bit of melty deliciousness and said, "Sure, Mom. Now, I need to tell you what happened yesterday between Mark and me."

A half-hour later, with multiple 'WHATs?' behind me, Mom had the gist of what had happened.

"Oh, sweetheart, and after he was caught being a spy," she said, reaching out to pat me.

"Mom, they decided he wasn't guilty of anything, remember? And it wasn't for spying, anyway."

My mother patted my hand again. "Your father would be so disappointed in Mark."

My father, Marlon Taylor, had had a special talent for only seeing the best in people. He had treated Mark like a son. And Mom like a queen, despite her sometimes sharp and biting comments. "Georgie," he would say to her as he fired up the riding lawn mower to make perfect little rows in their two acres of front yard, "you're in charge." Then he would stay outside for many hours beyond what it took to mow the lawn. I always thought that all that time outside gave him the intestinal fortitude to deal with whatever life was throwing at him.

Usually, it was Mom throwing the difficulties.

Returning to the house, he would say to Mom, "What would you like to do this evening? Anything you want."

As Dad's heart grew weaker, Mom's sarcasm grew stronger. "Marlon, stop sleeping," she would insist, shaking his shoulder to wake him from his recliner. "It's too early in the day to sleep."

"Yes, Georgie."

"Marlon, I keep telling you not to pace the floors at night."

"Yes, Georgie."

"Marlon, I'll drive us to the store. You drive too slow."

"Yes, Georgie."

Yes, Georgina Taylor had enjoyed being the center of Dad's world, but I think her subtle snipes had made him sort of glad to go when he had died five years ago of congestive heart failure.

"On the bright side," Mom said, "Mark was always a bit tedious, wasn't he?"

She wrinkled her nose and added in as deep a voice as she could muster, "C'mon Reb, you don't mean that."

I couldn't help it. Despite my anger and anxiety over

everything that had happened, I laughed. Mom still retained her ability to verbally cut you so deeply that you were dying on the floor before you realized she had pulled a knife on you.

When it wasn't directed at you, it could be pretty funny.

Mom laughed too, which got me laughing even harder, and pretty soon we sounded like two teenage girls as we mocked my husband. Even Mom constantly asking me to repeat myself didn't dissolve the brief uplift to my spirits.

It felt great.

Then my phone rang.

CHAPTER 4

"Hey, Becca, I'm headed over. Donna's got a ton of vegetables from the garden she doesn't know what to do with. Says you should have 'em." It was Bear.

I told him I was home and to come on by. I now had about twenty minutes until he arrived from his house in Chaptico.

Telling Mom that Bear was on his way over, I quickly transferred dishes to the sink, hopped into the shower to rinse off animal and feed odors, then changed into a clean pair of jeans and a "Jet Noise: The Sound of Freedom" t-shirt, the first thing my hand touched inside my shirt drawer.

Feeling more presentable, I headed outside to wait for my "baby" brother so I could talk to him in private about what had happened with Mark.

Bear came roaring up in his twenty-year-old Chevy truck, Brown Betty. She was once a deep chocolate color but over the years the truck had seen so many repairs and body part replacements that I now thought of her as Calico Betty. Bear believed you drove a vehicle until parts were falling off as you rode down the highway. Which was sure to happen soon, given that my brother drove like a demon wherever he went.

That said, my brother, a master carpenter by trade, was the sunniest human being on the planet.

"G'mornin', sis," he said, opening the driver's side door and jumping down onto my gravel driveway wearing shorts, a roomy t-shirt to fit his immense frame, and his signature orange Stihl baseball cap. Calico—I mean Brown—Betty groaned loudly at having her door opened, but I admit she still sounded solid when he slammed the door shut.

Bear was carrying a paper grocery bag, filled with tomatoes, cucumbers, and jalapeño peppers. I was already envisioning the salsa I might make with that. Which made me start to think about a cold beer to go with it. Which unfortunately led to my thinking about throwing the bottle at Mark.

I shook my head like a human Etch-a-Sketch to clear my thoughts.

Taking the bag from Bear, I said quietly, "Hey, listen, I need to talk to you about something. Yesterday evening—"

But Bear was already distracted. "Mom's at her bedroom window, waving. I better pop in real quick to say hello. Be right back." He tipped his cap at me as he moved toward the house.

"Bear, no. I should talk to you first before you see Mom. I—"

But he had already hopped up the kitchen steps on the side of my long rambler and pulled open the storm door. "Hey, Mama," I heard before he disappeared inside.

Oh boy.

Rather than go inside and try to referee anything Mom told him and knowing that it would take Bear at least a half hour to extricate himself from Mom's presence, I went to the horse stable to visit John Wayne. I tried to not play favorites with the animals, but it was difficult when it came to him. He had come with the house fifteen ago. Mark and I showed up that day after signing settlement papers and saw the horse standing in the one fenced pasture that existed on the property at the time.

A quick and frantic phone call to the seller had resulted

in his telling me, "Oh yeah, I couldn't take the horse with me. He's yours."

I had ridden horses in the past but never owned one, so I had had about five seconds to figure out how to care for one.

As I stroked my Morgan's chestnut-colored muzzle, I murmured to him the story of how my husband had left me for the stupidest reason in the world after I had been the stupidest woman in the world for continuing to tolerate him. John Wayne huffed his way through the story, and when I finally said, "So what do I do now?" my horse shook his ebony mane and I swear he gazed at me with deep understanding and nodded as if to tell me all would be well.

Horses are like that.

Suddenly, I found myself feeling very small and sorry for myself, so I buried my face against his left jowl and put my arms around his solid neck. Silent tears came in that private moment between my horse and me. The comforting odor of hay enveloped me as I clung to my big beast as if he were an equine life preserver.

I hung out with John Wayne until I heard my brother calling my name. I quickly wiped my eyes but before I could leave the stable, Bear found me. Reaching up to rub my horse's shoulder, he said, "What's this I hear about Mark leaving town for a private vacation? What the hell, Becca?"

I rolled my eyes. "You know Mom can't keep a story straight. However, it is true Mark left last night." I outlined the story for my brother as I had just done for John Wayne. I had released a lot of pain now that I had shared it with the horse, so I explained it all calmly and without emotion.

Then I waited for the explosion. It didn't take Bear long.

"That dumb, stupid horse's ass—sorry for the

comparison, John Wayne—is one sorry excuse for a human being. You know I never liked that guy. I bet he really was stealing company secrets but managed to charm his way out of it with the feds." Bear shook his head in disgust.

"I knew he would find another way to end up a fool, Becca, but I didn't think he would do anything quite this moronic. I should drive to Florida right now and beat him to death with his surfboard. No, I should shove it up his—"

"Bear, stop," I said. My brother was working himself into quite a lather. He was the most affable guy on the planet until you messed with the women in his life. Then he was scary.

Bear stood a hair over six feet tall, and he was built as solidly as Brown Betty. He was really named Edward, but his name had gotten abbreviated to Ted and then affectionately to Teddy by the time he was a young child. Donna, his wife, had nicknamed him Bear when they were dating, and it was so apropos of his size and his lovable demeanor that turned ill-tempered when his den was threatened that we all immediately started using the name.

"I know you don't like Mark, but you can complain about him later. I'm in some trouble here," I said, ready to voice my deepest fears. "What am I going to do for money?"

Bear looked at me quizzically. "Go back to your contracting job on base? I'm sure they'd take you back in a second."

I tamped down my impatience. "Really? I'm going to leave Mom, as well as all of my animals, alone for eight hours or more a day for a job?"

Bear considered this. "Hire a daily caregiver for Mom and a farm sitter for the animals?" he suggested.

"Really?" I repeated. "Do you know how much

caregivers and farm sitters cost per hour? I'd be handing them half my paycheck."

John Wayne huffed in agreement.

"Plus, you know how Mom is. She would have a caregiver verbally beaten into a bowl of lumpy oatmeal the first day."

"Yeah, I guess that's true." He removed his cap and scratched over one ear, a tell-tale sign that he was thinking furiously.

"Well, maybe Mark needs to pony up some money," Bear said. "With all due respect," he added, glancing at John Wayne again.

I had already thought about that, too. "I assume he's halfway to Florida by now. Within days he will be a completely broke beach waif. How am I going to get money from him? It would be like squeezing blood out of a turnip, as they say. Want to help me with the llamas?"

I gave John Wayne a final pat. "I'll be back later to muck you guys," I said to him, walking over to Annie Oakley's stall and stroking her jowl. "I mean you, too, lady."

I stopped at three other small stalls, saying goodbye and promising to return soon to each of my miniature horses, Randy, Reba, and Kenny.

Bear followed me to the feed shed where I filled a pail with llama treats. I handed it to Bear so he could offer the treats up to them. He loved the llamas. Everyone loves the llamas.

At their fenced enclosure, Cuddlebug, Doodlebug, and Ladybug came running to greet me. Okay, they came sauntering to greet me.

I must admit, Cuddlebug was my favorite of all my animals. Next to John Wayne, of course.

"Kisses," I said to Cuddlebug, who pressed his nose

against mine and blew hot breath through his nostrils at me for several moments.

"Maybe you could sell the llamas' fur," Bear suggested as I continued to nuzzle Cuddlebug.

"It's not fur, it's hair," I said, pulling back from the llama so that Bear could grab treats from the pail and hold them out individually to the llamas. They were usually polite to one another and waited to be offered treats in turn, but on some days, Ladybug would decide she was Queen Llama and try to bully her way in to get them all.

I was relieved that today she was on her best behavior.

"Whatever," Bear said. "Don't they use the stuff to make high-end sweaters?"

I shook my head. "No, alpacas have the premium hair for sweaters and blankets. Llama hair is a lesser product. If I could get five dollars a pound for llama hair, I'd be lucky. And a pound of llama hair is a mountain of it."

Bear frowned as he handed out the last treat to Doodlebug. "Then that won't work unless you have a thousand llamas."

"And I'm not going to have a thousand llamas."

I noticed something protruding from Doodlebug's jaw. "Not again with you," I said, moving to where he stood, gazing at me with his perpetually goofy look. Poor Doodlebug had a deformity that caused him to have a buck-toothed underbite. It didn't impact his life much except that all kinds of stuff seemed to get lodged in his mouth.

I gently cupped his jaw and pulled out a clump of straw mixed with dirt. I dropped the clump to the ground and told the llama, "You've got to be a little neater, my man. You're going to get an infection."

Doodlebug was forever getting infections, which meant expensive vet visits. Was I going to have to give him up? Was I going to have to give up everything?

I turned to say something to Bear, but he was standing there staring at me with a devilish grin. "What is wrong with you?" I asked.

"I, the best brother in the world, have just come up with the best idea in the world. You are going to be the number one attraction in St. Mary's County. You are going to make lots of money and, of course, you will remember your brother when that happens."

Bear explained the idea.

I wasn't sure if he was brilliant or certifiably insane.

CHAPTER 5

"...AND YOU COULD also have a shop where you sell fun stuff for the kids, like cowboy hats and neckerchiefs. Maybe you could come up with a logo for the farm and sell branded items for the adults. You could even have various themed kits for kids' parties and sell them out of your shop." Bear was really warming up to his idea as we walked back toward his truck.

I wasn't so sure. "You think I could make money on a petting zoo? How much would people pay to let their kids pet a llama?"

"Are you kidding me?" Bear said. "There's nothing like it anywhere near here. You'll be a unique creation. And the money will be in the private parties."

Things were happening too fast. Mark had left me less than twenty-four hours ago, and now I was to become the proprietress of a petting zoo and party palace. It was a little too much of a zig-zag at the moment. I threw up roadblocks to fend off my enthusiastic brother.

"Wouldn't I need to have ponies to ride?" I asked as we stopped next to Brown Betty's driver's side door. "I just have the two standard horses, three mini horses, the llamas, and the goats."

"Get ponies later. Your llamas and goats are very tame. Kids will love 'em."

"I don't know the first thing about starting a shop." My brother was freaking me out a little with his overwhelming fervor.

"No one knows the first thing about starting a shop when they start one. Go talk to a shop owner. Go to Marie and Nash or Cecil's Country Store, they're full of stuff that flies off the shelves." Bear opened up the door and Brown Betty groaned in protest.

"You know about the popularity of these shops?" I asked. How was it possible that my brother, whose primary loves were his wife, his children, and car racing, knew anything about local shops that sold home decor and unusual gifts?

"I'm not a Neanderthal," he said, firing up his truck's engine. Brown Betty still roared to life on command, even if she showed her great age in every other respect. "Besides, Donna makes me go with her Christmas shopping every year so I can haul bags to the car. I know those places very well."

Bear shut the door and pressed a button to roll down the window. Brown Betty wasn't too happy about that, either, and shrieked against the action.

Ignoring Brown Betty's pain in favor of my own, I asked, "What about Mom? Wouldn't it freak her out to have a bunch of people running around the property?" I had thirty acres, but that might get small in short order with a lot of children running around high on candy and soda.

Bear shrugged. "Becca, you have more serious matters to contend with than Mom's discomfort at a lot of visitors. You have to do whatever is necessary to survive and put food on the table, and that includes food for Mom. Besides, you never know. She might actually get a kick out of the whole thing."

I offered a final, desperate volley. "What about April? If I was busy with this business venture, how would I have time for her?"

"Maybe April could run the shop," Bear suggested. He tossed his ball cap onto the seat next to him, pulled down an old red handkerchief tied to his rearview mirror, and wiped his sweaty brow.

I offered him an incredulous look. "April?" I questioned. "I'm sorry, have you met my daughter?"

April had just left her teenage years behind and was trying to live her best life, as the modern philosophers like to say. I really wished she would just come back to church on Sundays and live her best life there. Anyway, April's version of that best life was a series of odd jobs—picking vegetables at a local organic farm, groundskeeping at a Quaker meeting house, long-term pet sitting—that somehow landed her with spartan but free temporary living situations. These jobs also provided her with lots of free time to think up other unprofitable things to do.

It occurred to me that April had quite a bit of her dad in her.

Bear laughed. "Okay, maybe not April. I bet Donna would help out, though, on her days off. I can pitch in on weekends. You've got friends. Becca, I think you could make it work."

He saluted and put Brown Betty in reverse. I stared after him as he backed all the way up to my road, pulled out, and headed toward Three Notch Road, officially State Route 235, which was one of St. Mary's County's two main thoroughfares. I was far enough away from the road to not hear traffic noise except in the winter, but close enough to get anywhere I wanted, what with my central location in Hollywood.

I stood there, thinking, until his truck was out of sight. I *could* put a sign up on Three Notch Road to advertise the petting zoo. Everyone in the county would drive by it at some point. Didn't the local radio station morning duo, T-Bone and Heather, do live appearances to promote grand openings? Maybe the local school system would be interested.

Was my brother right? Could I actually make a business out of my motley collection of animals?

———∽∾∽———

"WHAT? Bear wants you to have animal parties in the house?" Mom cupped her hand around her right ear again as she sat at the kitchen table while I chopped Donna's vegetables for salsa. I do love a fresh salsa, full of chunky veggies and not very saucy at all. I was happy to find a nice red onion in my veggie bin to go in it.

"Mom," I said, as patiently as I could, putting down my butcher's knife, "will you *please* put your hearing aid in?"

"I don't know where it is," she said, waving her other hand. "Just say it again."

I closed my eyes. I was forever "saying it again" because of my mother's obstinance over her hearing aid, which I knew was sitting in its case on her nightstand, in pristine condition because she absolutely refused to wear it and instead played her television loud enough to be heard all the way up on the commercial jets that crisscrossed St. Mary's County's skies all day long on their journeys up and down the east coast. I had no doubt that my mother viewed the hearing aid as an affront to her status as an elegant lady, despite the fact that you could hardly see it even when her ears were showing beneath her snowy-white hair.

I did hope my hair would be that gorgeous at her age.

I acquiesced and repeated Bear's idea to her. After the usual round of 'WHATs?' and misinterpretations, she finally understood the plan.

Mom shook her head. "I don't like it. Not at all."

Not surprising. Mom was growing increasingly opposed to most things. She had even groused when I changed butter brands on a recent shopping trip because it was on sale.

"Why don't you like it?" I dared ask, preparing myself for a litany of complaints. Would it be the number of strangers on the property? The potential for increased farm animal smells?

"It will take too much of your time. You won't be able to take me to get my hair done. Or drive me to church. Or take me to see...to see..."

Mom was clouding up again.

"I'm sure I'll have free time to help you out," I said, although I wondered if what she said was true. Would the idea make me bound to my property night and day as if I were a bed and breakfast owner? "After all, I will want to get *my* hair done and go to church and see other people, right?"

"Humph." My mother crossed her arms.

"And I'm already grocery shopping and managing a bunch of animals. What's a few more?"

"WHAT? You were once a Seymour? I don't know that family. When were you a Seymour?"

"I said, what's a—" I stopped. Sometimes the constant repetition became too much, especially since my mother was belligerent about her hearing aid. I picked up the knife and began chopping again. "I just said that I'll take care of it myself."

"Humph," Mom repeated. "Won't be able to. Mark wasn't good for much but he could at least manage to pick up a dozen eggs when you told him to. You—*we*—won't have that now. No, I don't like this one bit."

I clamped down on some snark, given that I really had no idea what I was doing. For Pete's sake, Bear had just given me the idea this morning and it wasn't a completely formed plan. Still, I resented Mom pooh-poohing it out of the gate.

Not to mention her implication that I couldn't do it without Mark. Who was rather tedious. And, also, no longer on the premises.

CHAPTER 6

I DECIDED TO FOLLOW up on Bear's idea of visiting the Marie and Nash store on Leonardtown Square. It was a fun place to wander through even without my mission so I looked forward to my visit.

There was some sort of late summer festival occurring. Colorful banners were hanging from the multitude of light posts lining the main thoroughfare. Near Marie and Nash was a grassy area surrounded on nearly all sides by shops and restaurants from which Leonardtown Square got its name.

People in shorts, t-shirts, flip-flops, and baseball hats were gathered in the square, many in folding canvas chairs, listening to a local band enthusiastically playing golden oldies on a small stage.

I managed to parallel park along the square without scraping my tires and without it turning into a fiasco of pulling in and pulling out while drivers waited impatiently for me to finish the job. Mark always said I was the worst parker in the world.

"Not so bad at it with you gone, right?" I muttered to myself.

I opened the car door and the music's joyous racket rolled over me like a love letter to summertime. I realized it was Friday and thus was First Friday in Leonardtown, which explained the festive atmosphere. I resolved to walk around and visit shops when I was done at Marie and Nash.

Opening the door to the shop was like opening into

another world, full of lush scents and unusual goods from local artisans. I browsed around a while and picked up some scented goat milk soaps, which I frequently washed with after a day of working with the animals. Goat milk soap seemed to keep my skin softer than regular soap so I liked using it.

As I checked out with the employee behind the counter, I asked for either Angie or Tyler. To my surprise, both came out to greet me. I explained that I was considering opening a petting zoo and shop on my farm but wasn't sure where to start.

The mother-daughter team was enthusiastic and full of suggestions. I quickly felt stupid for not having brought along a notepad to record every gem of advice as I stood across from them at their white marble counter.

Angie, Tyler's mother, waved her hand. "Don't worry, you can come back anytime. Now, as I was saying, you really need a fundraiser event for your grand opening. That will get the community involved. Is there a charity of which you're fond?"

I thought about this. "I'd probably want to raise money for an animal charity."

Tyler nodded. "A good fit for your business. And there are plenty of good ones. Also, do you need a special license for your petting zoo?"

That hadn't occurred to me. I understood animals, not zoos. "I don't know."

"You should start with planning and zoning about it," Tyler suggested. "You might need special licensing from both the county and the state for a petting zoo."

Before I could respond, Angie asked, "What kind of insurance will you need to cover your unusual business?"

"I don't know."

"I'll give you contact info for our insurance agent, she'll help you out with the right type of policy. You've potentially got a lot of liability."

"Okay." My head was beginning to swim. Was I going to have to cash in my retirement savings to make this happen? I didn't have that much to begin with and could hardly afford to empty it.

"Oh, I have an idea," Tyler said, turning her attention to her mother. The two women were unmistakably related, with their dark hair and placid demeanors. "Mom, remember that artisan who brought in those wild animal purses? What if we did a sponsorship? Like..." Tyler looked upward as she contemplated for a moment. "Like what if we offered a donation to Becca's charity for each bag sold?"

Angie pursed her lips. "Okay, but how does that help the actual event? We should offer to do the donation *and* have Becca give us some complimentary tickets to the event, which we would give away with each purse sold."

The two nodded their heads in agreement and Angie pulled a paper pad from under the counter and began scribbling notes on it.

Tyler snapped her fingers. "You need promotion. You should contact the radio station and have a commercial made."

Angie agreed. "Get it on the morning program. In fact, see if you can get T-Bone and Heather to cut a commercial for you to play during drive time. Put up signs and posters wherever you can."

"About my farm shop..." I started.

"Oh, right!" Tyler replied. "I can offer you three pieces of advice. First, get the highest quality merchandise you can afford and brand as much as you can to your farm. Second, give your visitors a lot of value for what they purchase. Third, don't do consignment deals, buy products outright. Finally, purchase in small quantities and then in larger quantities once you figure out what sells or not. I can give you a list of some local artisans we like."

All of it made total sense and I was grateful for Bear's suggestion that I talk to these shopkeepers.

"You also need to decide on your payment system." Tyler rattled off multiple options.

I needed to create a grand opening event, generate tickets, blast the county with news about the event, set up a shop, get insurance, and, oh yeah, make sure the county was going to allow me to do this in the first place. Bear's instinct about Marie and Nash was spot on, but I was beginning to wonder about the genius of my brother's initial idea for the petting zoo. Was I competent enough for it?

With Tyler's list of artisans in my hand, I decided to head out into the square to relax and listen to the band. But there was more waiting for me outside.

Someone had just vacated a park bench, so I quickly slid onto it to listen to the oldies music and peruse Tyler's list of local artisans. It was an impressive list and I was certain I couldn't afford anything from any of them.

When I reached the end of the list, I closed my eyes to free my mind of everything that had happened in the past twenty-four hours. The day was sunny, warm, and breezy, and the temptation to take a nap was strong, even if I would have to do it sitting up.

The four-man band was crooning a Beach Boys tune, telling me that I shouldn't worry, baby, everything would turn out fine.

From where I sat, it didn't seem likely, but maybe I—

"Becca? Is that you?" came a female voice from in front of me.

My eyes flew open. "Meesh!" I said, jumping up to hug my friend.

Michelle and I had been friends for years, first as co-workers and then as moms with girls the same age.

We had both long ago quit our boring jobs, but Michelle had picked up photography as a hobby-turned-business, while I had started collecting animals as, well...as just an expensive hobby.

"Let's have lunch and catch up," Michelle said. "But first let me get rid of all this stuff." Her arms were indeed full of bags.

I walked with her to her car so she could toss the bags inside. "The photography business must be treating you well," I said, observing her late-model luxury car in a statement-making aqua blue.

Michelle shrugged. "I'm always driving to location shoots. I figure it helps me be a better photographer if I'm comfortable. Now, where do you want to go? Sweet Bay? The Rex? The Front Porch?"

I considered the options. All were good, but I preferred to move away from the music if we were going to talk. "Let's go to the Front Porch. I haven't had their roasted red pepper soup in forever."

Once we were seated, with mason jar glasses of iced tea in front of us, Michelle said, "So tell me what's happening with you."

Where to begin? "If we were having this conversation two days ago, I would have told you, 'same old, same old'. But you won't believe what's happened in less than forty-eight hours."

I spilled all regarding Mark's departure and found myself dabbing at my eyes with the restaurant's folded black cloth napkin. As mad as I was at Mark for being an idiot, and as much as Mom was right about him being tedious—damn, we had been married for two decades. That's not easily cast aside.

Michelle nodded in sympathy, her salt and pepper pixie cut bobbing with the movement. Michelle had been the first among my friends to completely give up coloring her hair and "embrace the gray," as they say. It worked well on her. I wasn't so sure it would work on me.

"I'm not sure whether to tell you how sorry I am or to congratulate you," she said, as the server put down bowls of soup and plates of the restaurant's signature house salads before us.

"Congratulate me?" I asked as I dipped my spoon into the thick, pumpkin-hued red pepper soup.

"Yes. I must agree with your mother about Mark being a bit tedious. Not exactly the description I would have used, but good enough. That supposedly false arrest never sat well with me, either. I *wondered* if he had gotten away with something. Plus, in all the years of your marriage, that man never spoke more than a sentence to me, did you know that?"

I was shocked. "Really? He didn't talk to you?"

"Rarely. It was as if his head was always somewhere else. I realize now it was always hovering over the Florida coastline. You'll be fine without him, I promise."

Easy enough for someone who hasn't just been abandoned to say. Also, despite Michelle giving her hair over to its natural aging state, the rest of her looked like she was barely thirty years old. Her green eyes sparkled luminously, her skin was flawless, and I was certain she still shopped off petite racks.

"How's Jack?" I ventured to ask.

"Good. Still working on base, still going on hunting trips every chance he gets."

Jack Knott was as hard working as Mark was a dreamer. He frequently stayed late to complete engineering projects and his staff loved him because he was tough, fair, and full of dumb dad jokes. His only obsession was in bagging deer, wild turkeys, and sometimes rabbits, as often as he could manage. The Knott freezer was perpetually overflowing with meat and their house overflowed with joy. Meesh was fortunate.

I sighed aloud.

She misunderstood my wistfulness. "I don't mind him doing it. There are far worse habits he could have."

I mumbled something in agreement and changed the subject by telling her about Bear's idea for a petting zoo.

Michelle listened without interrupting to what my brother's suggestion had been, as well as to a recounting of my visit with the owners of Marie and Nash. I concluded my story just as she took her last bite of her Front Porch salad lightly covered in a raspberry vinaigrette. A lone spiced pecan remained on her plate as she placed her fork neatly across the plate.

"Dessert before we talk more?" she suggested.

How could I say no?

Within minutes we were each diving into deep dishes of bread pudding soaked in a luscious custard sauce. I was going to have to jog around the horse pasture ten times to make up for what I was happily shoveling into my mouth.

"Here's what I think," Michelle began.

I braced myself. Usually, when someone opened with that line, you knew you were about to be bludgeoned with a proverbial two-by-four board. Well, if it was a lousy idea, I knew I could rely on Michelle to tell me and save me from a huge mistake. She was originally from Massachusetts and there's no sugar-coating anything with a New Englander.

"I think it's a great idea and has the potential to put your little farm on the map," she said, licking the back of her spoon and dropping it into her half-eaten dessert.

"You do?" I tried not to sound overly surprised.

"Yes." Michelle nodded resolutely. "Not only does it keep you from having to go back to a regular nine-to-five nightmare—" Meesh shuddered for effect. "—but it would be an opportunity to earn money at something you love. And I have another idea for you."

Other than Mom, other people seemed to be very enthusiastic about the idea. I felt the warmth from a flicker of confidence spreading throughout my torso. "Sure, I need all of the ideas I can get."

"You know I have my little studio here in Leonardtown and I also go out to customer locations—homes, parks, waterfront venues, and so on." Michelle picked up her spoon and dug into the bread pudding again, having apparently found room in her tiny frame for polishing it off.

"What if we made your farm a photo shoot location and I pay you a fee for each session? I can only imagine how many parents would just love to have their wee ones photographed with the Bugs." Michelle could never memorize each llama's name so she just referred to them collectively as "the Bugs."

"In fact," she said, pointing her custard-streaked spoon at me, "we could create some fun backdrops. Or put fancy collars on the llamas. Or place floral garlands on their heads. Wouldn't that be the sweetest thing? Oh, I have another idea!" Meesh was really warming up.

"For your grand opening, we can schedule a two-hour period for impromptu photos for a fee and we split the money. No, you can just have the money. I'll make plenty on subsequent photo shoots." The spoon went back into the bread pudding dish with a clatter. Michelle was apparently too excited with her own thoughts to finish off the sugary goodness.

As for me, I was quite overwhelmed by her rapid-fire thoughts but agreed to everything she suggested.

Michelle was really warming up. "I'll get right to work on it. Let's make some money together, my friend. The only thing is…and I hesitate to even suggest it…" She paused and my stomach sank again. Didn't she realize I was as fragile as a crystal butterfly right now?

"The only thing is that I'm not sure you have enough

animals. Nor the right kinds of animals." Michelle looked up as the server approached our table with the check and took it before I could even open my mouth. "Nope, this is on me," she said, her tone brooking no opposition.

Now my stomach was residing somewhere around my kneecaps. "The right kinds? What do you think I need?" Animals were not cheap to purchase, unless they were rescues, and rescues frequently cost a lot of money nursing them back to health or putting weight on them.

"Remind me again what you already have," Meesh said as she laid several green bills on top of the check.

"Well, there's John Wayne and Annie Oakley, of course," I began.

"Your horses are too big for a petting zoo. They will just look good in the field as people approach your place. Which reminds me, you need a sign out on Three Notch Road."

I'd already had that thought, but I added "road sign" to my mental list, which had swollen to the point that I was pretty sure things were leaking out of my ears.

"Then there are the llamas, Doodlebug, Cuddlebug, and Ladybug."

Meesh nodded. "The stars of the show."

"And the mini-horses, Kenny, Randy, and Reba."

More nodding. "Kids will love them. Although, I recall that Randy poops his own weight every day. He'll need watching."

I smiled at the thought. Yes, Randy was a prolific pooper. "Then there are the goats. I'm up to six of them."

"What are their fancy names?"

I shook my head. "I don't name the goats."

She gave me an incredulous look. "Really? Why not?"

I wasn't quite sure why. "I guess because everything

else I have in twos and threes so they're easy to name. The goat collection came about so quickly that, I don't know, I just viewed them as a collection."

We stood and left the restaurant, then walked down the sidewalk back toward the square. The music had ended, and people had dispersed to wander in and out of shops. We returned to the bench where Michelle had found to me to continue our discussion in the quiet created by the band's departure.

"So, you've essentially got three llamas, three miniature horses, and some goats for petting," Michelle said. "Do you think children could ride the miniature horses?"

I frowned. "I don't think so. I'd need ponies."

"If you could add rides, that would probably make it more attractive. So, in summary, we have llamas for photo shoots and petting, plus miniature horses and goats for petting."

I bit my lip. "The goats might need to be petted from behind their enclosure. A couple of them can be real butt-heads. Literally. But they certainly don't bite."

Michelle nodded. "It's a great start, but I think you need other exotics. Something to make people say, 'Wow, we have to visit that petting zoo because they have a giraffe'."

"A giraffe!" I exclaimed. "You can't own a giraffe in Maryland without being a zoo."

She rolled her eyes. "Okay, not a giraffe. You can figure out what you can own in Maryland that children can interact with on the farm. But make sure it's unusual."

I also had to make sure it wouldn't financially break me. I felt a catch in my throat as I realized I was going to need a loan to make this all happen. What bank was going to loan money to someone with no income who was saddled with caring for an expensive farm and her ailing mother? No financial institution was going to take that risk. I wouldn't blame them, either. What guarantee could I make that I could pay a loan back?

I would have to put the farm up as collateral. I might end up homeless.

That bleak realization made me want to run into the barn and bury myself under John Wayne's hay bale.

Meanwhile, Michelle chattered on next to me about the framed animal photos I could merchandise in my as-yet non-existent shop.

My anxiety was so great that it was a relief when my cell phone rang to interrupt the conversation. I pulled it out of my purse. It was April, her voice frantic.

"Mom, quick. You've got to get home right away. *Please.*"

CHAPTER 7

I NEARLY WENT AIRBORNE getting home, clutching the rosary beads that usually hung from my rear-view mirror and earnestly praying until I turned off Three Notch Road onto my long road. I skidded sideways as I stopped at the top of the pea gravel driveway, then stumbled as I fell out of my truck in my haste to get into the house. I vaguely noticed a dusty old hatchback parked in the yard. As I crunched through the gravel and into the carport, my mind's eye was filled with images of April in all sorts of serious situations—injured, heartbroken, homeless.

Dear God, please don't let her be injured, heartbroken, or homeless.

Daisy stood in the yard next to the house, wagging her tail as if she might explode from the joy of seeing me. "Sorry, girl, not now," I said as I raced to the kitchen door. Daisy ignored my admonishment and was hot on my heels.

I threw the door open so hard it banged against the wall, causing the occupants sitting around the kitchen table to jump.

Daisy and I came to a complete stop as I took in the scene. At the round table, using tortilla chips to gobble up my guacamole from a large ceramic bowl were my mother, April, and...who was this scruffy-haired young man?

"Mom!" April jumped up and rubbed her hands

together against a napkin, releasing the chip dust from her fingers. She was all smiles as she came out from the back side of the table to give me a hug.

"Is everything…okay?" I asked, uncertain as to what the emergency was. I didn't see blood anywhere and no one was unconscious. My mother was unusually silent, but she probably couldn't hear anything and hadn't wanted to shout 'WHAT?!' in front of a stranger.

"Oh, sure, we're fine. Mom, I wanted you to meet—"

"Is something wrong with the animals? Is there a vet on the way? Did your father—" Crap. Had Mark gotten to April before I could?

"I don't think so. I just wanted to introduce you to Jimmy." April sat down again and gazed at the young man in adoration.

"Jimmy," I repeated, dumbfounded. I had risked an expensive speeding ticket to meet someone named Jimmy?

I took a deep breath. I seemed to be doing that a lot these days.

"Is this why you sent out a distress signal?" I asked as calmly as my rising blood pressure would allow. As if realizing my anxiety, Daisy licked my hand. I absentmindedly reached down and scratched her behind both ears.

April didn't seem to notice. "Yes. Jimmy has a meeting with Wal-Mart in a little while and I wanted him to meet you before he has to leave. Jimmy's an entrepreneur."

My daughter said this as though that explained everything.

"Yo." Jimmy nodded his head at me without standing to shake my hand, instead reaching back into the bag for another chip.

Please, God, not another one of April's weirdo boyfriends.

Realizing that what was done was done, I left Daisy and sat down at the table with everyone. The dog whined and disappeared elsewhere into the house, most likely to the foot of my bed.

"We're having your guacamole," my mother offered.

"Yes, so I see," I said.

Jimmy mumbled something around a mouthful of food. I presumed he was complimenting the dip, but who knew?

Okay, April wanted me to know Jimmy, so I needed to assess what we had here. Jimmy was cadaverously thin and wore torn jeans, a metal-head t-shirt, and flip-flops. It looked as though a razor might have grazed his face a week or so ago, but it appeared as though scissors hadn't touched the caramel-colored shrubbery on his head in the past decade.

His gaze assessed me right back and he was clearly unimpressed. I didn't like that he found me to be of no consequence. If only Mark were here to—

I held back my sigh. Great, now I had to be both mom *and* dad.

"So, Jimmy," I began, "what is your business that requires a meeting with Wal-Mart?" I couldn't imagine the retail giant's management having an executive meeting with Jimmy.

"I'm an entrepreneur," he said, repeating April, who was clearly besotted with him for some reason I could not possibly fathom.

This was going to be a very long conversation.

"Yes, an entrepreneur doing what?" I replied patiently. I was going to need some tequila to go with the chips and guacamole if this went on for too long.

"Oh, yeah, I have an invention." Jimmy took a swig from an open soda can in front of him.

An invention? I knew I hadn't misheard what he had said as his mouth was finally clear of chips and dip.

"Mom, it's so cool. It's going to revolutionize everyone's health. Wait until you hear about it. Jimmy, tell Mom what you have." April's enthusiasm was infectious. Was I reading Jimmy wrong? Was there something to him?

I waited expectantly and he finally spoke up. "Yeah, you see, all these people, they don't sleep good because they snore. What I have takes care of that."

He had my attention. If he had a cure-all for snoring that didn't involve surgery or alien machines attached to the face, the boy might really have something. Wal-Mart would only be the first stop in its sales.

Jimmy leaned back and dug around in his jeans pocket. He triumphantly produced the anti-snoring device and held it in the air for me to see.

It was a rubber bracelet. The kind you get at fairs and sporting events that are all manner of color and are typically emblazoned with a team name or a pithy saying—"Stronger Together" or whatever.

I set my lips firmly together to refrain from saying something that would anger April. Jimmy clearly expected a reaction from me so I gave him one, holding my hand out so that he would drop the bracelet into my hand.

"So, what is this?" I asked as I examined the circular, navy blue piece of rubber. It had no logo or saying on it.

"It's a Snore-a-Gone wristband," he said proudly.

"Okay," I said. "How does it work?"

Jimmy pointed at it. "It's blue."

Good Lord, this boy was as dumb as a box of rocks. "Does 'blue' have curative properties?"

He frowned at me and shook his head.

I tried again. "What about it being blue makes it cure snoring?"

Jimmy looked at me in pity. "Everyone knows that blue is the most peaceful color. The internet says so. Blue paint on walls in doctor's offices keeps sick people calm." He took the band away from me and put it on his wrist. "Keeping blue nearby will cause people to relax and get good sleep."

Jimmy was making Mark look like a Nobel Prize candidate. "So…people will gaze at the strip of blue and it will hypnotize them into good sleep?" I asked.

"Hypno—" Jimmy shook his head. "No, it will just work on their brains to make them *want* to sleep good."

Yup, this was another one of April's weirdo boyfriends. Well, I had to try to guide him.

"Jimmy," I said patiently, "I think the success of your product might only be wishful thinking. Gazing at a color does not cure illness or chronic conditions."

Jimmy glanced at April. "Just like my parents," he said with a heavy touch of disgust.

April immediately reacted to Jimmy's displeasure. "Mom!" she chastised me. "We need to support Jimmy. He's got a very important meeting with the local store manager to see about carrying Snore-a-Gone. If he gets it into the St. Mary's market, he can expand throughout Southern Maryland, then the entire state, then it will go national. It will sell millions."

I was quiet for several long moments. Then I gave up. I had far too many of my own problems to worry about what Jimmy—of apparently no last name—was doing. Moreover, I needed to talk seriously to April and there was no point in her being worked up at me when I told her about Mark and the farm idea.

"You're right," I told April. "I wish you well," I said to Jimmy. "Please let me know how it goes."

Jimmy seemed satisfied with that, thus April settled right down.

"Gotta run, babe," he said to April as he stood up to leave.

April escorted him out through the front door. When she returned, her mouth was opening and I knew it was to gush about the entrepreneurial genius known as Jimmy. I stopped her with, "We have to talk. It's important and I need your help."

April nodded and sat back down at the table. My mother, who had been silent through the previous conversation, had perked up and tilted her head to one side in anticipation.

"Maybe we can go take a walk along Three Notch Trail," I suggested.

"Why?" she said. "What's so important that Gram can't know?"

I braced myself for what I knew was coming next.

"WHAT? You're putting me in the snow?" my mother said, once again cupping an ear as if that would help her hear.

Why did April have to do this? I had no desire for my mother to start complaining about Mark in front of his daughter.

"Fine. We'll talk here. Fair warning, though, we are going to talk about your latest tattoos."

April was very careful not to let her grandmother know about any of her body artwork, lest she be the recipient of my mother's barbed comments about them.

"April made ratatouille?" Mom asked. "Let's have it for dinner."

April gave me her patented death stare. It had long ago ceased to work on me. "Okay, okay, let's go to the trail," she said.

It was nice when I occasionally won.

By the time we were done with our walk and I had spilled everything, my head was spinning from April's response.

———∞∞∞———

We hit the asphalt at Three Notch Trail at a brisk pace. A hefty trek at thirteen miles long from Mechanicsville to Charlotte Hall, I doubted we would complete it, but

I imagined we would at least make it the short distance to Morganza-Turner Road before wanting to turn back.

The trail ran parallel to Three Notch Road and had been carved through a series of old residential properties. It was bordered on both sides by woods and the occasional house, driveway, and barn or garage. It gave the sense of total serenity, yet it was always vaguely discomfiting to know that these once peaceful properties were now subject to bikers, hikers, and joggers traipsing through them from dawn to dusk.

Once we were underway, I told April about her father leaving. It was hard to believe that Mark had just made his announcement yesterday. It felt like ages had passed already.

"So Dad's gone? Just like that? He didn't come see me first?" I couldn't tell if April was exceedingly upset or just irritated.

I shrugged. What comfort could I offer? Her father had indeed gone "just like that."

We walked along in silence for a while. As we approached a split rail wood fence around a tiny farm property, a little gray cat with white paws ran onto the trail from under the fence to greet us.

"Hey, Squirt," I said, reaching down to scratch him behind the ears. The cat's ears had nicks and crusty patches on them, demonstrating that he was not exactly the dominant male of the neighborhood. He rubbed against my legs in appreciation, so I knelt to get a better reach on my ministrations to him.

"Mom," April said in exasperation, "let's keep going." She had never inherited my love of animals. Sure, she liked them, but she didn't have my passion for them. A shame.

I rose and kept walking with April, occasionally looking back at the cat. He followed us for a short distance but then seemingly got bored and hopped off into the woods on the other side of the trail from the fence.

I changed the subject away from Mark and broached the idea of the petting zoo. I explained Bear's suggestion for both it and the shop.

April was again quiet as we continued walking. I realized how humid it was when a bead of sweat trickled down my back, causing me to involuntarily shiver.

Finally, she spoke. "It's not a terrible idea. It's in line with your creature obsession."

High praise from my daughter. I bit my tongue on asking whether it was as good an idea as a rubber snoring bracelet.

"I wouldn't say I'm obsessed with animals," I said, stopping on the trail. "I just like them. They bring me joy."

April nodded slowly, deep understanding in her expression. "One man's obsession is another man's joy," she said. "Anyway, this will bring in some money until Dad comes back, and it will be something you enjoy. You're gonna need help, though."

I swear, one minute April was bringing home stray puppies she called men, the next she was gazing into my soul and picking my psyche apart like it was tar-soaked oakum.

I had no desire to discuss the fact that I had no intention of welcoming Mark back, but she had certainly opened the door to something else.

"Would you like to help me?" I asked tentatively.

April wrinkled her nose so tightly that I almost didn't continue. It was like a giant raisin had landed in the middle of her face. However, being a mother meant nothing if not a constant stream of rejection from your child, so I plowed on.

"I was thinking that maybe you could move back

home for a while to help me get launched." April was a consummate couch-bouncer, staying with one friend for a while, then drifting off to another friend's house. I could not for the life of me understand such a vagabond lifestyle, but she seemed to find it perfectly natural.

"Move back home?" April started walking again and I fell into step with her.

"Just so you're on hand for the startup. Where I could really use someone is in this shop your Uncle Bear thinks I should have."

"Will it be an environmentally sensitive petting zoo?" April asked.

"What the hell is that?" Sometimes my daughter asked the strangest questions. "If you're asking if the animals will poop natural turds that can be made into compost, the answer to that is an emphatic yes."

"Mom." April rolled her eyes and held up a hand that had at least one silver ring on each finger. "I mean, will your shop carry only organic products? And your party supplies should be made from recycled paper. If you sell animal treats, they should be made from non-GMO ingredients." April ticked these items off on her fingers in front of her.

My mind was swirling with these considerable requirements. "I need all of this?"

"If you want to cater to today's consumer, of course you do."

I guess I had been locked away on my farm for so long that I didn't realize how particular today's consumers would be.

"Okay," I said slowly. "You can advise me on products."

We had reached the gate that served as a cautionary pedestrian barrier at Morganza-Turner Road and I suggested we turn around. "Hungry? We can stop at the pizza place at the beginning of the trail."

"Mom, you know I can't eat that stuff. I'll have a

bottled water while you poison yourself with that unnatural product they call food."

"For Pete's sake, April, it's bread, cheese, and tomato sauce. Mankind has been eating it for hundreds of years."

"Hmmm. It's up to you. But I do have some thoughts about your petting zoo."

At least if she was sharing ideas while I ate, she wouldn't be focused on criticizing my food choices.

"I also have one really important observation to make about you," April said.

I mentally rolled my eyes. I could hardly wait.

CHAPTER 8

WE SAT AT a picnic table outside the restaurant with our purchases. True to her word, April settled for a bottle of water, while I had a gigantic slice of New York-style pepperoni pizza. April glanced at it as if I had selected a barbecued rat for lunch but exhibited enough grace to keep her opinion to herself.

How had I produced this kid? This part of her was all Mark's fault, I was sure.

"So, what are your thoughts about the petting zoo?" I asked, twirling a long string of mozzarella cheese around the narrow end of a pizza slice. Was it just me or was the very first bite of pizza always the tastiest, with every subsequent bite a little bit more of a letdown until you got down to the dry, inedible crust?

"I have an idea for the name of it," April told me. "And it's awesome."

I braced myself. "I'm listening."

"You should call it Celestial Paws and Hooves. Because the customer experience is out of this world!" my daughter exclaimed triumphantly.

I put down my half-eaten slice of pizza. I couldn't for the life of me imagine such a name working in St. Mary's County. "Isn't that name a bit…ethereal?"

"Of course it is! The county could use some shaking up. It's a great name."

"Mmmm." I was dubious and shoved the pizza back into my mouth so I wouldn't have to directly respond. A petting zoo name should give the impression that families will have fun there, I thought, not that they will be attending seances.

April rolled her eyes at me. "At least think about it," she said. "Especially if I'm going to be helping you out with the shop."

I nodded as I swallowed. "I promise to think about it. So, what's your important observation about me?" I figured I might as well get that over with.

April took another swig from her bottle of water, the contents of which had no doubt been sprung from the finest of underground sources. She stared hard at my facial features, making me uncomfortable and causing me to put down the last of my pizza. I was almost at the crust, anyway.

"Mom, you've got a bit of a skunk stripe forming up there," April said, pointing to my head.

I reflexively reached up to my hairline. How long had it been since I had colored my hair? Sometimes I got busy between my mother and the animals, and I forgot to go to the salon. My hair, originally dark brown but faded some with time, was frequently bundled up under a ball cap, so no one was likely to notice me much.

"I suppose that might be true," I said.

"You're never going to catch a man that way."

I gasped. "April! I'm still married to your father, remember?"

She rolled her eyes again. I would have thought that was strictly a teenager move, but apparently it was in use well into a daughter's twenties.

"Dad's being a butthead. And the gray hair makes you look old."

"Thank you for such an incisive observation," I said drily. "Is there anything else you'd like to criticize?"

"Mom, I'm being serious. You're very pretty with those long-lashed, caramel-colored eyes and you can still fill out a pair of jeans just right, but lately, you've been letting yourself go. If you're going to be a businesswoman, even if it's the running of a petting zoo, you need to look the part. Go to the salon and get your hair done, buy some makeup, and get some snazzy new pants and tops. It wouldn't kill you to get some new boots, either." There went the nose wrinkling again.

Was my daughter right? Had I become frumpy? Maybe that was the real reason why Mark had left.

The pizza began churning in my stomach as I thought about all of my suspicions about his behavior over the years.

It roiled even more as I realized that Mark was likely in Cocoa Beach by now, begging for a meager-paying job at Ron Jon surf shop and not caring at all about the grenade he had thrown into our marriage.

Which reminded me that I was in financial peril thanks to Mark. The pepperoni threatened to come back up and I swallowed hard to keep it down.

"I'll call the salon tomorrow for an appointment," I agreed. "And maybe I'll do a little online shopping for clothes."

"And makeup," April insisted. "At least get a little blush and eyeliner on that face."

Now it was my turn to roll my eyes, but I tried to not be as dramatic about it. "Okay, okay. On another note, how did you meet Jimmy?"

April's expression lightened. "Oh, we were both attending a conscious living expo."

"I see. And so he has this…invention…that he wants to sell to Wal-Mart."

"Yes." April glanced down at her pink-banded smartwatch. "I should be hearing from him anytime. Once Wal-Mart buys his Snore-a-Gone wristbands, the sky's the limit. Every big box store will want them."

I nodded slowly. "Um, April, what if Wal-Mart has no interest in them? I'm sure they are selecting among thousands of products every day for what they will carry on their shelves."

She stared at me, uncomprehending. "Jimmy says it's a surefire way for him to get rich. He plans to be a millionaire by this time next year. Can you imagine?"

"Not really," I said.

She ignored me. "He says that when he becomes rich, he's going to take me on exotic vacations. My first stop will be Egypt, so I can commune with the ancients inside the pyramids."

"Those are some pretty big plans," I ventured noncommittally.

"Yes, and then eventually we will return to America and establish an organic restaurant where all the food is produced behind the building. A farm-to-table concept except no products will come from anywhere else except the restaurant's garden. It will be famous and people will come from all over the world to visit."

I was silent, having no comparable lofty plans. I just needed to be able to make next month's mortgage payment while juggling all of my responsibilities.

But April was full of dreams. "Hey! I know. How about if Jimmy provides you with some of his Snore-a-Gone product for the petting zoo shop? I'm sure he would give them to you for a great discount. People will love them." She was clearly in love with this notion and I didn't have the heart to tell her exactly what I thought of Jimmy and his immature ideas.

"Maybe Jimmy would like to earn a little money working at the petting zoo shop with you until he strikes it rich," I offered.

April considered this. "I don't know. He's going to be pretty busy with his financial deals once he really gets going with placing his product in stores. And he has other ideas, too."

How was April so insightful when it came to me, but

utterly snowed when it came to Jimmy? I guess that's what infatuation does to a person. Certainly, it had done so to me when I had met Mark.

Nuts, maybe April was more like me than I realized.

CHAPTER 9

I DROPPED APRIL OFF at Wal-Mart, where a dejected-looking Jimmy was waiting outside near the cart return. Having no desire to be involved in *that* conversation, I kissed my daughter's cheek and told her I'd call soon, leaving her to console her boyfriend.

Was it terrible to have a glimmer of hope in that moment that perhaps Jimmy wasn't destined to be a permanent fixture in the family?

As I turned north onto Three Notch Road from Wal-Mart, I realized that the only real decision that had come from my discussion with April was that I was not going to call my petting zoo Celestial Paws and Hooves.

I supposed my next step was to figure out what I needed to buy so that I could—*gulp*—see about a loan at the credit union. Might as well go see Bear and get his thoughts on what Marie and Nash's owners, as well as Meesh, had suggested.

I turned left at the light at Loveville Road on my way toward Chaptico. Loveville was Amish country, so I drove much more carefully to avoid a bad encounter with a horse and buggy. Every once in a while, there was a horrific crash when modern technology, piloted by someone hasty and oblivious, barreled into the old ways. The Amish carriage always came out on the losing end of those collisions and it was devastating for all involved. I had no desire to have a dangerous, and unnecessary, run-in with the gentle Amish, who were good neighbors within the county.

I reached Chaptico and pulled into Bear's driveway, beginning the quarter-mile trek to his house. Bear and Donna lived much more remotely than I did, and their ill-maintained dirt-and-gravel road rattled my teeth as I dipped into every rut along the way. Despite her advanced age, Brown Betty could handle such a rough roadway better than my truck.

Nevertheless, five jarring minutes later I reached their white clapboard farmhouse, a cloud of dust billowing around my vehicle.

Their home was older but much larger than mine. They had done little in upgrades over the years, so it felt like stepping back in time as I crossed onto the old wide pine floor planks into their kitchen, which still had an old wringer washer in one corner, unused except as a place to pile up winter coats.

However, where Bear's talents had been put to use was in the reclaimed-wood kitchen cabinets, which were sanded and stained to perfection.

The hospitality at my brother's was always good and I was soon seated on their screened-in back porch with them, sipping sweet tea. Donna made it with enough sugar that a spoon could stand up in it, which is exactly how I like it, so I smacked my lips in an unladylike fashion to show my appreciation for her culinary talents.

After pleasantries about how their three boys, all of whom were off at some sort of after-school sporting camp, as well as my description of April's latest boyfriend—and really, I did try to keep the eye-rolling to a minimum—we settled down to what I wanted to discuss.

I outlined everything that had happened since I'd talked to Bear and the two of them listened intently. I was happy for Bear in his marriage to Donna but admittedly I was a little jealous. They were so attuned to one another. Two peas in a pod, as they say. Donna could finish Bear's sentences before he ever even opened his mouth. And they did things together. Not just vacations, but hiking, fishing, and going to target practice at a local shooting range.

When had Mark and I last done something together?

While Donna responded in animation to what I had told them regarding the nascent plan, Bear briefly left the room. He returned with a pad of paper and a pencil.

"Seems to me you need a list of purchases if you're going to go talk to the credit union. Do you have a list?" he asked, holding up the pencil. It was a yellow number 2 that looked as though he had sharpened it with an ax, so blunt were the edges of the lead.

"I have one in my head," I said defensively.

My brother nodded. "Let's get that list out of your head."

We sped through the obvious, like a small shop building, a cash register, inventory management software, signage, marketing, insurance, and the like.

Bear even addressed details like the logistics of the public coming to the farm. "You need parking, but that can just be blue chip gravel, you don't need asphalt to start."

I nodded at everything he said.

"What this really boils down to, Becca, is that most of this is just icing on the cake. The cake is your stable of animals, and you need more of them."

"How about a small monkey?" Donna asked. "I've read that they are highly trainable."

I shook my head. "I can't have primates. There are certain types of animals that you cannot own in Maryland without special licensing," I said, holding up a hand to tick them off my fingers. "Can't have patently wild animals, like lions and tigers and bears."

Donna nodded. "Oh my."

"Basically, you can't have anything that would be

deemed dangerous to public safety. Unless you're a zoo."

I was glad that I knew this information already, which had been gleaned while procuring my llamas.

"Hey! What about a bird enclosure?" Donna asked. "You know, one of those things where a person walks down a center aisle and there are giant cages on either side that extend over your head and are full of birds."

"An aviary," I replied.

Bear nodded. "You could have a trained parrot and have shows. Have it say funny things and fly around taking people's hats off."

I knew little about birds, particularly enormous ones with large beaks and talons from the Amazon. "I'd have to find a trainer."

"Sure," Bear said breezily as if that would be the easiest thing in the world. "Get the trainer to make the birds tame enough for a child to hold. Speaking of training birds, how about a bald eagle show? Maybe the trainer sends the eagle off to catch a mouse and bring it back or something."

I shook my head again. "You can't easily have birds of prey. There's licensing for it and lots of limitations."

Bear frowned. "This is going to require more thought, but I would think that for your initial discussion with the bank, you'll want to focus on your infrastructure and the acquisition of a few animals—a couple of parrots, maybe a pair of peacocks—you can have a peacock, right?—and maybe a hedgehog and some guinea pigs. That would be cute. Oh! What about an ostrich? That's not a bird of prey, is it?"

I wasn't sure about the legality of owning an ostrich.

Donna rose from her chair and walked to the kitchen to pour more tea. Her voice carried from where she was standing in front of the open refrigerator. "Maybe a rabbit hutch? Kids love rabbits and they're cheap. Hell, Bear can trap a few of them for you here."

I laughed without mirth. Wild rabbits were everywhere in Southern Maryland. "Believe me, I have plenty of my own. But I probably shouldn't just trap untamed rabbits. I should buy more exotic breeds that have been raised by hand and will be used to being handled."

Bear made more notes. I hoped that list wasn't getting ridiculously long.

"The county fair will be coming up soon," he said. "I bet you could buy a bunch of rabbits that way. In addition to other exotics."

Donna returned with refilled glasses and I drank from mine again while I thought about that. Bear was right. The county fair would be a great place to collect animals. But there were also animal auctions in St. Mary's and counties beyond.

"Here's an idea," Donna said. "How about a part of your zoo with animals that kids would know from animated movies and books? Like a pig to represent Wilbur in *Charlotte's Web*? Or—"

"Rabbits that you would name Flopsy, Mopsy, and Peter Cottontail." Bear laughed, jumping in on the idea and making notes.

I liked it. We continued twirling out the possibilities for a while, then Bear made another suggestion. "Hey, how about a raccoon? They're cute."

"It's not legal to own a pet raccoon in Maryland. At least, not to trap a wild one. I think you can get a permit for one if you've brought it up from a cub. Although strangely, you *can* have an opossum." I shrugged. I didn't want either one of them. Raccoons could carry rabies and while opossums rarely had rabies, they just had an unnerving look to them. I couldn't imagine children wanting to pet an opossum, which looked to me like a giant rat.

But Bear wasn't done with the topic. "Wasn't there a case of some guy in northern Maryland who had tamed a raccoon and it was house trained and basically a lap animal, but some neighbor complained and he was forced to get rid of it? That had to have been terrible to be told you have to get rid of your pet because your neighbors don't like it."

I remembered the incident. Of course, there was no telling what the entire story was. Maybe the raccoon was getting into everyone's trash or entering houses through dog doors. Raccoons might be cute little masked bandits, but they really could be pests.

Bear and Donna continued suggesting more animals—foxes, sloths, and ocelots—none of which were allowable under state law.

Bear expressed his frustration. "Well, this was a lot about what you can't own and very little about what you can own. I think maybe you need to investigate whatever permit is required to step up your game on exotics, Becca. Meanwhile, with the creatures we've discussed thrown in with what you already own, you've probably got a good start."

From there, we drew up some rough numbers as to how much I needed to borrow to get started, given that I had no idea what an ostrich or a peacock might cost. My mind wandered off wondering whether there was such a thing as an exotic bird rescue where I might be able to pick up one or two of each, even if they required some nursing or rehabilitation.

"Becca!" Bear raised his voice, startling back to what he was saying. "I think you will have to put up your house for collateral and even then, it might be tight. You need a *lot* of money for this, but it will be worth it." He held up a piece of paper full of numbers with one number—containing too many zeroes and commas—circled at the bottom.

My vision dimmed as my heart hammered away. Bear must have sensed my panic, for he said to Donna, "What do you think, should we invest in the project? Enough to get the bank to say yes?"

Donna nodded in agreement. "This is going to be great, Becca," she said, and I knew it was to encourage me.

It did nothing to alleviate my anxiety, as owing my brother and sister-in-law money was only going to add to the pressure.

Before I could open my mouth to say anything, I heard a deafening noise, as though a weapon had just been fired into the house.

CHAPTER 10

I JUMPED IN MY seat at the sound, but quickly realized it was just the front door banging open loudly against the wall.

Spilling into the house were their three boys returning home from practice in sweaty, dirty football uniforms. Bear Jr., Bobby, and Billy had all been born in rapid succession, thus Bear Jr. was seventeen while Bobby and Billy were fifteen and fourteen. All three were in high school together for the first time this year.

"...and you should have seen me take down Richie Tennyson!" Bear Jr. crowed.

Bobby gave him a brotherly shove. "Yeah, big man taking down someone who broke his arm over the summer."

Bear Jr. glowered at his brother. "Says the jerk who let an easy pass slip through his fingers in the third quarter of jayvee practice."

"Y'all are too serious about the game. It's just for fun," Billy said, grabbing an apple from the kitchen counter and biting deeply into it. Juice dribbled down his chin and he wiped at it carelessly with the back of one hand, smearing dirt on his face.

Billy was the youngest Taylor but by far the most handsome. And he knew it because all of the young teenage girls he encountered were already making it abundantly clear. My brother was quite proud of his youngest son's easy charm, but Donna fretted constantly over the possibility of her youngest bringing home a grandbaby way too soon.

"How ya doin', Aunt Becca?" Billy asked, taking another bite of his apple and sitting near me. "Haven't seen you in a while."

That was part of Billy's charm. Only fourteen years old and considerate of his elders. I just hoped it was genuine and he wasn't turning into one of those Eddie Haskell-type of kids.

Before I could answer, Bear spoke. "Your Aunt Becca is going to have a petting zoo for kids. Doesn't that sound cool?"

Billy chewed as he considered this while Bear Jr. and Bobby argued and shoved their way upstairs to their rooms.

"Sounds interesting," he said, gazing steadily at me. What a diplomat. "But *why* are you going to have a petting zoo?"

Now it was my turn to pause. I decided at that moment that he was old enough to hear the truth. "Well, as it turns out, your Uncle Mark has decided to…live elsewhere. I need money and your dad thinks I might have some success turning my farm into a petting zoo and shop. We were just discussing how much that might cost."

"So it would be like what we saw when Mom and Dad took us to that place in Virginia last year? Ponies and goats and stuff?" He took a final bite from the apple and placed the browning core on an end table.

"Billy!" his mother exclaimed. "Really? Pick that thing up! You'll stain the wood." Donna pointed at the apple remains.

Billy looked down at the apple core, his expression confused, then he picked it up and put it in his lap.

I almost laughed at his typical teenage boy cluelessness.

Donna rolled her eyes and threw up a hand in exasperation.

"Yes," I said, glad for the amusement that broke my tension. "Animals like that."

Billy nodded. "Yeah, that sounds fun. When will it be open?"

I shrugged. "As soon as I can do so. A month from now? Two months?"

That sounded like an impossible timeline but a bridge had been built over the Potomac River, from Newburg to Dahlgren, in about a year, so perhaps I had a chance.

"I can come over after school some days to help if you want. When I don't have practice. I'll make Bear Jr. and Bobby come with me. I don't mind wrassling some goats for you," Billy said, flexing his arm muscles for me.

"You're on," I said, still amused by my nephew.

"One thing, though," he said, as he stood up, letting the apple core fall to the ground and eliciting a sigh from Donna.

"What's that?" I asked.

"You gotta get some sugar gliders. They're cool." With that, Billy stepped over the apple core and left the room, presumably in pursuit of his brothers.

Where was I supposed to find gliding possums, which admittedly were far cuter than regular possums?

The next morning, I sat in front of the balding loan officer inside his black-and-glass furnished modern office at the credit union the next day. Bear had offered to come with me, but I wanted to do this myself and not have my brother going to bat for me.

The process was as brutal as I could have imagined. Once Mr. Rowan Everett was done frowning and tut-tutting his way through my loan application, he looked at me with great curiosity. "I'm not quite sure how this makes money."

I certainly couldn't admit that was my own question, as well, so I tried to dig in with all I had. "It will be unique here in Southern Mary—" I began, but the loan officer cut me off.

"Every business owner thinks that, Ms. Garvey. But being unique doesn't necessarily translate into profit. How will the credit union earn back its investment? And you have a promissory note from Mr. and Mrs. Taylor. How will they get a return?"

Mr. Everett did not wear glasses, but I still envisioned him pushing little wire rims up his nose while he examined me as if I were a common insect.

I tried again, and this time I didn't give him room to interrupt me.

"My plan is to create a special place for children and their families to not only have an opportunity to pet the animals and directly interact with them, but to enjoy experiences with them. A birthday party with a couple of my llamas hanging out with the kids, for example. And a bouncy house—no animals in there, of course. And arts and crafts for them. And…and…catered fun food for the tykes."

I was still a distasteful little bug, lying on my back flailing all my feelers in the air while Mr. Everett was deciding whether or not to squash me with his shoe.

"Also, the farm store will sell branded items like puzzles and games and clothes for both kids and adults. Oh yes, and I'll have a photo studio. And—"

Mr. Everett held up a hand. "Thank you, Ms. Garvey, I think I've heard enough. I must say that I do not see a path to profitability in the short term for your idea. But I will also admit that your idea actually is unique to the county, and we can always use a tourist draw down here."

I realized I was holding my breath, but I couldn't quite let it go. I hoped I wouldn't embarrass myself while passing out cold on his multi-colored, geometrically patterned carpet while waiting for him to finish.

"I'm going to recommend you for a loan." He gathered up my loan papers into a pile and neatly returned them to a file folder with my name on the label.

I expelled my breath in a great whoosh and covered it with a cough. "Thank you, sir, you won't regret it."

He looked doubtful. "Perhaps. But I'm certainly interested in bringing my grandkids to see it, so I'll expect you to be up and running soon and I'll want to see that the credit union has spent its money wisely."

An hour later, with the loan waiting formal approval and a small deposit made in a newly opened business account, I walked outside, gulped air, and lifted my face to the bright sun in relief as I walked to my car. It was now early September, but Maryland tended to stay quite warm through the month.

I slid into the seat and started giggling uncontrollably. How the hell had Becca Garvey ended up in a bank requesting a fantastically large business loan just after her husband had walked out on her?

I was glad that I had those few minutes of comic relief to myself, because by the next day, the world as I knew it had morphed into something completely unrecognizable.

CHAPTER 11

IN THE MORNING, I woke up slowly, my brain registering that something was wrong, but I couldn't quite figure out what it was.

I was on my back and rolled over to my left side throwing out an arm. It was still just me in the bed.

I murmured a few choice expletives before bolting up in bed in terror, realizing what was wrong.

There was daylight streaming into the room, which meant I was very late in taking care of my critters.

Now more vocal in my expletives, not just toward Mark but toward myself, I ran to the bathroom to empty my bladder, brush my teeth, and rip a brush through my hair for a few strokes before diving into my grubbies to feed the animals.

I slipped outside with Daisy without waking my mother and started my rounds. John Wayne eyed me suspiciously and then turned his head away from me when I tried to stroke his cheek. I could hide less from him than I could from most humans.

Feeling a bit ridiculous, I spent time explaining to him what I was planning to do.

"And so," I finished, "you'll have to be on your best behavior when people are here. I'm not going to let anyone ride you, but at least be decent and greet visitors at the fence."

John Wayne snorted and dipped his head into his feed.

Annie Oakley didn't seem to care much one way or the other, she was just hungry.

I watched the two of them nuzzle their feed for a few moments, thinking about how many ponies I needed and how to stable them.

Daisy grew impatient, licking my hand, then gently head-butting the back of my legs.

"Hey, I'm not one of your critters to keep in line, missy," I said to her, although I couldn't stay mad at her any more than I could stay mad at any of my animals. The dog at least had the courtesy to sit back down quietly.

One pony to start, I decided. I was glad I had had the foresight to build a stable with multiple stalls so I could easily clear out one of the extra stalls containing hay bales on the ground and riding equipment hung on hooks on the back wall. All of that could be easily moved.

Proud of myself for making a solid decision, I clucked at Daisy and continued my rounds to the goats and the llamas.

It wasn't nearly as warm this morning as it had been yesterday. That was the other thing with Southern Maryland weather. A good hot streak could be obliterated overnight for no explicable reason.

At least there wasn't frost on the ground. We shouldn't experience that until at least January. I hoped.

By the time I returned to the house, I was definitely ready for some morning coffee. Maybe I would make some French Toast, too.

My mother was already up and seated at the kitchen table with her arms crossed when I came in.

Uh oh, had I done something?

"I need to go to the grocery store," she said flatly. "Why are you preventing me from shopping for my groceries? I'm close to starving to death. Even prisoners get a tray of food each day." She held up a list of at least twenty items jotted down in shaky handwriting.

Sometimes Mom slipped into paranoia and that meant lashing out at the nearest object of that delusion, usually me. I'd learned not to argue with her—after all, I kept the pantry filled to the brim and there was always some sort of ready-made in the refrigerator and on the table, but to point that out was useless.

"Sure, Mom, sorry. Would you like to go to Harris Teeter today?"

She cupped her hand to her ear. "WHAT?"

"HARRIS TEETER. DO YOU WANT TO GO TO HARRIS TEETER?"

"Yes, I'll go get my purse." Mom sprang up from the table like a woman half her age.

I guess this meant I was going to have to work my mother through the grocery store, which would require at least two hours. I just hoped I could get some work done today. I quickly made coffee as I thought through my to-do list. I had animals to buy, building plans to research, contractors to contact—

"Ready!" Mom had her purse over her shoulder and wore mismatched sneakers. She was properly wearing a left one and a right one, so I let it go at that.

At the store, I yanked a cart out of the row. Why was it always so difficult to dislodge carts? Was there no technology that could just dispense one out to you when you pushed a button?

I invited Mom to push the cart since that kept her nice and steady. Thus began the great grocery shopping ordeal.

With Mom, the grocery list had to be purchased in order. So, if she had written down, say, tomatoes, milk, and cucumbers, you had to go from produce on one side of the store to dairy on the other, and then back to produce.

There was no deviation from it, no suggesting that

perhaps *all* the produce on the list could be picked up at once. That's why it always took two hours.

We moved up and down the aisles, with Mom getting distracted by products on the shelves and then getting distracted again when we went past the same items for the second or third time.

I loved my mother, but I must admit that these shopping trips drove me quite close to insanity.

As we stood in front of the pasta section, my mother enamored of all the different forms durum wheat could take, I was startled by a woman's voice. "Becca Garvey?"

I turned. Before me was a woman about my age who, though slim, was considerably more…bosomy, shall we say, than me. She was also heavily made up. Or maybe in my sparse look—after all, I still hadn't even showered yet for the day—I didn't have a good perspective on others' appearances.

"Yes?" I hoped I didn't look too confused if I was indeed supposed to recognize her.

She tucked a tress of beautiful auburn hair behind one ear and I thought about my skunk stripe. This woman's hair stylist probably spent hours a month on that head and my entire salon experience was going to be an encounter this weekend with a box of L'Oreal. Because I'm worth it, of course.

"I can see you don't recognize me." The woman laughed prettily. "I'm Deanna Boone. Most people call me Dee Dee. We met at Globotechnico's holiday party, what, two years ago, I think."

Globotechnico was Mark's employer, whom he had presumably told he wasn't coming back to until he had hit the perfect wave. To its credit, Globo had stood behind Mark after his arrest, publicly stating they believed in his innocence and taking him right back after his release.

It was coming back to me. "Right. Your husband's name is John. He home brews beer and you…" I had to think about it. "…you were taking sailing lessons up in Annapolis."

Dee Dee smiled. I must have remembered correctly.

"What are you up to these days?" she asked.

Here was an opportunity to talk about the petting zoo with someone completely unconnected to me. I briefly described my plans to her.

"How fun!" she exclaimed. "I can't wait to bring my nieces and nephews. I doubt any of them have ever even seen a llama before. What a blast it will be."

I admit, I felt warmed by her words.

"WHAT? What did you say? Who's doing a fast?" Dee Dee and I had distracted mom from her fascination with spaghetti, macaroni, and lasagna noodles. "Who are you, dear?" Mom asked.

"Mom, this is Dee Dee Boone. She works with Mark."

My mother frowned. "Humph," was her response. "He was always a bit tedi—"

"Dee Dee is an engineer at Globotechnico," I said, cutting my mother off from the awful thing she was about to say.

It worked. She wandered away with the cart to look at the spaghetti sauce jars, which were as plentiful and varied as the noodles were.

"I quit Globo a while ago," Dee Dee said. "John and I called it quits and I decided I needed a complete life overhaul. I took the realtor's exam and now I'm selling houses for a living. I'm hoping to eventually buy my own sailboat, maybe even live on it. I've even met someone. His name is Jason."

That was one heck of a life change. I wasn't sure whether or not to tell her what had happened with Mark but she took the decision away from me.

"How's Mark doing these days? Still climbing the corporate ladder? So sad how he was falsely accused of secret stealing. It must have been hard on you."

Now it was my turn to harumph. Was I already turning into my mother? What a thought.

"Mark isn't here anymore. He left for Florida." I hoped Dee Dee wasn't one of those types who would go blabbing it all over the county, but odds were she would. Gossip traveled faster than lightning down here.

"What do you mean?" Dee Dee asked, tilting her head to one side. "Is he on extended travel for work?"

I took a deep breath and briefly told Mark's ex co-worker how my husband had gone to Florida for his own selfish pursuits.

Dee Dee reached out a perfectly manicured hand and squeezed my shoulder. "Oh, my dear, I am so sorry. What a terrible time for you. But...surely this didn't come as a surprise?"

I extricated myself from her gentle grasp. "I'm sorry?" I said. "What do you mean?"

Dee Dee reddened as though she had perhaps revealed a confidence. "Oh. Ummm...well, I just thought... Mark always told us...I didn't think he..."

She was flailing with whatever it was she was trying to tell me. I felt my insides grinding in dread and wasn't sure whether to encourage her to talk or to just walk away and accompany my mother on a fourth trip to the produce section.

Dee Dee seemed to find her courage. "Mark always talked about his dreams of leaving Maryland for a warmer climate near the beach. But he said he would never go there alone. So, if *you* haven't gone there with him then..."

She let the words dangle as I turned to complete ice inside. As had happened when Mark first let his verbal bomb drop on me, I found myself numb.

"It was a pleasure to see you again, Dee Dee. Best wishes on your real estate career."

I walked away before she could say anything else sympathetic and before my head blew off my shoulders.

CHAPTER 12

MOM WAS FULL of questions and 'WHAT's' that I ignored to the best of my ability as we checked out and I loaded her three meager bags into my car. All of that walking back and forth for fifteen items.

"I need to make another stop," I told her as I started the car.

"WHAT? You need to find a local cop?" Mom said, her purse propped up in her lap.

I tapped my forehead to the steering wheel. "No, Mom." I raised my head as well as my voice. "I need to go to Mr. Stauffer's. I'm running out of goat feed and llama chow."

Visiting the Amish feed mill would be a nice distraction and I really did need to replenish my feed.

Mom talked non-stop from Harris Teeter to the feed mill in Loveville. "Who was that woman at the store? Is she a friend of yours? I didn't like her hair. She knows Mark? He was always so tedious. Does she know how tedious he is? I thought—"

On and on it went until I pulled into the long gravel drive leading up to the mill's shop.

The feed mill property was large, consisting of a shop, a barn where feed was dispensed, and various outbuildings that stored hay, straw, and other goods. The entire front acreage was an expansive grassy area offering animal pens, watering troughs, and the like.

I loved this place. If I had come by myself, I would have spent an hour or more wandering around. As it was, I needed to get my business done before Mom got tired or irritated. Or likely both.

I helped Mom out of the car and into the shop, where Mr. Stauffer greeted us personally. "Good afternoon to you, Mrs. Garvey. And to you, too, Mrs. Taylor. You're looking well." The Amish farmer and businessman was as gentle as he was kind. He reminded me of someone's sweet uncle, the one who always remembered your birthday and knew what your favorite color was.

Mr. Stauffer pushed his silver, wire-rimmed glasses up his nose as he stood behind the old oak counter in the middle of the cluttered shop. "What can I help you with today? How did Daisy fare with the new kibble? Did it agree with her stomach?"

This is what I meant. I had purchased new food for Daisy a couple of months ago because she was experiencing an upset stomach and throwing up everywhere. Mr. Stauffer remembered it.

"Yes, sir, she's much better now, thank you. I need both goat and llama chow."

"How much?" he asked, pulling out his ordering pad. "Fifty pounds each?"

I was about to tell him I wanted seventy-five-pound bags but realized there was no longer anyone at home who could haul it all into the shed. I would have to do with something lighter.

"Fifty pounds sounds good. I also need six bales of hay and four straw bales."

Mr. Stauffer nodded as he jotted down my requests. He figured up the order by hand and showed me the total.

Two large black labradors came wandering through the shop. One was clearly much older than the other, with a gray muzzle and a thick body causing him to waddle more than walk. These were Mr. Stauffer's dogs and typically roamed freely in and out of the shop. Presumably, they chased off verminous critters throughout the property, but I doubted the older one could capture a dead rat, much less one that was on the move.

The shop owner looked over the top rim of his glasses as he tore the order sheet from the pad. "Boys, leave the ladies alone."

Completely ignoring him, the labs both walked up to Mom, wagging their tails.

To my surprise, she seemed enamored of the dogs, bending down and baby-talking them. The two pooches ate it up.

I watched in amazement as my southern belle mother allowed the two dogs to slobber all over her and rub up against her, transferring their fur to her pants.

Mr. Stauffer must have understood my surprise, for he said, "Dogs are perceptive, Mrs. Garvey. They see things in people that other people don't. Your mother is good with animals."

I wasn't sure what to make of that. Mom tolerated Daisy but seemed disgusted by the farm animals. She was good with certain pets, sure, but animals in general?

He waved over a dark-haired young man wearing black pants and suspenders over a navy blue shirt. "Need some feed and bales loaded," Mr. Stauffer said, handing over the order sheet.

The other man nodded wordlessly and left with the sheet.

Mr. Stauffer's words made me think of something else. "Speaking of good with animals," I said, counting out cash for the mill owner. "I'm starting a petting zoo on my farm and am interested in finding some animals."

That got the shopkeeper's undivided attention. "A petting zoo? Never understood those myself. Animals are for working, not petting. Well, except for those two ingrates." He nodded toward the black labs.

"Yes, well…" I cleared my throat. "I find myself in need of…additional income…and I want to put my farm to good use as a place for people to come and spend money. Not just a petting zoo, but a shop, a place for kids to have parties, and so on."

My typically deaf mother must have heard every word, for she bobbed up from the dogs to say, "Did she tell you why she needs income? It was that Mark. He left her. He left *us*. He was always so very ted—"

"Ahem." I cleared my throat again and felt my face redden under Mr. Stauffer's sympathetic gaze. This was not how I wanted this conversation to go.

Bless Mr. Stauffer, for he kept his face schooled to neutral.

"So anyway," I continued, "I need to buy some animals. Do you know where I might be able to find some unusual ones? Maybe some interesting birds and the like? Or perhaps a calf or lamb that kids could bottle feed?"

But Mr. Stauffer wasn't quite done offering his opinion on the idea itself.

"You know there are other petting zoos around, Mrs. Garvey? And many of them are mobile. They'll bring the animals right to the child's party." He scratched behind one ear and shook his head. "Be hard to compete with that." His smile was kind but suggested I was perhaps out of my mind.

Not that I needed to be informed of that likelihood.

But I had the bank's approval, so forward we would go.

"My petting zoo will be different," I said. "We will have photo shoots with my critters, who are pretty tame. And most of them just have ponies, goats, llamas, and maybe some piglets. I will have more exotic animals. Maybe some birds." I thought about Donna's suggestion for an avian enclosure.

Mr. Stauffer smiled kindly again. "Right you are, then. So, there is a monthly auction up off Route 6 in Charlotte Hall that you English can attend. Lots of animals there, although they might not be as exotic as you want. It's sort of hit or miss each month. Might want to give that a try. The next one is, let me see…"

He referred to a wall calendar nailed to a post at one end of the counter. The calendar, emblazoned with the logo of a local farm supply company, sported a shiny red tractor as the September picture.

"Actually, it's next Wednesday. They have food and baked goods for sale, too, so go there hungry." He tapped the date of the auction for emphasis.

I wondered how good an option the auction might be for me. The Amish did not typically keep animals as pets. Everything, from horses to cats, had purpose in the world and all animals and humans were expected to help keep the world running smoothly. I definitely would not be finding a fat, lazy pony there. But the Amish were fair and square in their business affairs and I might be able to find some good deals there.

"I think Jacob will have your feed ready by now if you want to pull around," Mr. Stauffer said.

I nodded as I mentally made a note to attend next week's Amish auction. "Mom, ready to go?"

"Are the puppies coming with us?" she asked. Each lab had taken a position on either side of mom, flanking her like a pair of statues.

"Afraid not. Besides, we have Daisy, remember?"

Mom frowned in consternation. Daisy was a herder, which I'm sure wasn't nearly as much fun as two dogs who just wanted to be loved on.

I helped Mom back into my truck and drove around to the big barn-shaped mill building. I backed up to the loading dock and got out to watch as Jacob shut off the release to one of the big chutes that fed into my sack.

Jacob effortlessly tied off the sack, picked it up, and tossed it into my truck bed. He signaled to me to drive over to one of the other buildings for hay and straw to be loaded into the back.

Once there, I again got out to watch, amazed at how agile and muscular the men were. It seemed they could jump over, climb up, and lift just about anything.

With everything loaded up, I got back into the driver's seat.

My mother wasn't in the vehicle. *What the hell?*

I jumped back out. "Mom?" I shouted, cupping my hands around my mouth, knowing she likely couldn't hear me. My number one concern was that she could wander out to busy Route 5 and be struck by a car.

I kept shouting as I ran around the property looking for her. After several minutes I nearly collided with my mother, who was hidden by weeds as she bent over an animal trough, examining it.

"Mom!" I exclaimed, flooded with that weird combination of relief and total anger you get when you were certain something cataclysmic had happened and you're both glad it hadn't and mad that someone had put you through worry.

Mom looked up at my approach. "There you are," she said as if *I* had been the one who had wandered off. "Look." She pointed down at the trough.

Inside the metal "V" of the feeding trough was a tiny young calico cat, looking barely out of kittenhood herself but swollen with pregnancy. She was likely a barn cat for Mr. Stauffer whose job it was to keep vermin out of hay and feed.

"Should we take her home?" my mother asked.

Wow, ten minutes with Mr. Stauffer's dogs and Mom was suddenly Dr. Doolittle.

"She belongs to Mr. Stauffer," I said, gently putting

my hand on her elbow to guide her away. "She has to chase mice for him."

"She's pretty," Mom said, a pout emerging on her features. I didn't like where this was headed. With Mom's Alzheimer's, once she got an idea in her head, it could be very difficult to dislodge it.

However, the kitty did me a solid. She stood up and stretched, then hopped out of the trough. As if to prove my point, she revealed that she had a dead mouse in her mouth and waddled off with it.

"Oh. Yuck," Mom said, allowing me to lead her back to the vehicle.

WITH MOM HOME and quickly asleep in front of her blaring television—it had been a pretty big outing for her already—I unloaded my purchases into their respective storage locations, distributed a few treats to the goats and llamas, then, inspired by Dee Dee Boone and my own daughter's comments, I decided it was time to rid myself of my gray hairline.

After all, I was going to be a businesswoman now and needed to put my best farm boot forward.

Fortunately, I had a couple of boxes of hair color in the linen closet, so no need to make an expensive salon appointment. I stared at the model on the box of 'chic auburn brown', a color I had picked up on clearance a few months ago. Was I really going to have gorgeously healthy, windswept hair like hers when I was done?

The box promised me rich, luminous, fade-defying color and a new and improved floral fragrance.

Mark used to refer to me as his "Brunette Barbie," but I think I was more like a Cabbage Patch doll: not professionally put together but cute in a homey sort of way. At least, that's what the unremarkable brown eyes and light sprinkling of freckles that reflected back to me in the mirror said.

I sort of doubted I'd be that much improved, despite L'oreal's promises, but I had to start somewhere, and April had made a valid point that sprucing up my hair was a good place to start.

I was almost done applying the product when my cell phone buzzed on the bathroom counter next to me. Quickly shedding my gloves, I picked it up and answered before bothering to see who was calling, a move I instantly regretted.

CHAPTER 13

"HEY, REB, HOW are you?"

It sounds ridiculous, but I was vastly irritated that I looked a mess while Mark was on the other end of the line. I know he couldn't see me, but the old saying is that the best revenge is living well and my gloopy hair didn't come close to representing that.

I put him on speaker. Again, it was ridiculous, but I didn't want his voice up against my ear.

"I'm fine," I said flatly. "Today I—"

"Good, good," Mark replied perfunctorily. "Thought you'd like to know that I'm thinking about finding a new place, although Jake says I can stay with him as long as I like. He and Jessica are on the outs right now and she's staying with her best friend, so we're like a couple of old bachelors hanging out together."

I reached into a drawer and grabbed a rat-tail comb to scratch an itch on my head. Hair color could be really irritating to the skin. Almost as irritating as my wayward husband.

"Okay," I said. Was he expecting me to congratulate him?

"I'm interviewing with Ron Jon tomorrow. I'm already making friends, too. Jake is introducing me around."

Yes, I was sure he was making all kinds of friends. I decided to hit things head-on. "Who did you go down there with?"

There was a moment of silence. "What?" he squeaked.

"Who did you travel to Florida with?" I repeated.

But by then Mark had recovered. "Honey, no one. I'm here by myself. I'm surprised you could even think that. How could three people fit in Jake's condo anyway?"

Very cozily, no doubt.

I plowed forward. "I ran into Dee Dee Boone earlier at the grocery store. She told me you've been cooking this plan up for quite some time and that you had every intention of fleeing to Florida with someone else." Not exactly what she said but I was going for shock value.

He was silent for several moments. "Dee Dee said that? Surely you can't believe such a ridiculous lie, Reb. I always thought she had a crush on me, anyway. She was just trying to rile you up."

Uh-huh.

I checked my phone. My color processing time would be done soon. "Anything else?" I asked, ready to be finished with this pointless call.

"Yeah. I need you to send me my birth certificate from the safe. Also, can you cash in the CD we bought last year in your name and transfer the money to an account number I'll give you?" He started to read some digits at me.

Was the man serious? He expected me to assist him in his foolishness?

I cut him off. "No, I'm not doing either one of those things. I need to go."

"Becca! You're my wife and I need your help. You've had the opportunity to live your dream with all of your farm animals and I never stood in your way. Now I want to spend some time in my dream. Don't stand in my way."

Was he wheedling me or threatening me?

Now that I thought about it, he hadn't asked me a single question about me other than a perfunctory 'how ya doin'?' For Pete's sake, I had a massive operation about to open at the farm. Had he always been this narcissistic without my realizing it?

But he had done even worse than abandoning me. I changed the subject on him. "You didn't even bother telling April. I was stuck with doing that."

More silence. "Well, I just hadn't had a chance to do so yet. She's a sensitive girl and I needed to find my moment. I was planning to invite her down here for a visit once I got my own place."

I had to give him credit for thinking quickly on his feet.

"If you really thought she was sensitive, you would have sat her down before leaving."

"Sweetheart, you know all of that psycho-babble stuff is your thing, not mine."

"*Psycho-babble?* Telling your daughter you are leaving her to go a thousand miles away for who knows how long for a completely stupid idea amounts to psycho-babble? Mark, what is *wrong* with you?" I could hear the hysterical note in my voice. Mom was right. He was a tedious human being.

"C'mon, Reb, you know what I mean. I'm just not good at goodbyes."

I didn't realize I was capable of getting as furious as I was at that moment. I resolved then and there not to tell him about the petting zoo.

I also determined that there was no way I was going to pave his path with sunshine and unicorns. "Well, here's what *I'm* good at: self-preservation. Not only am I not cashing in the CD, I'm not sending you your birth certificate. You want it so badly, you can drive back up here and get it yourself."

"Reb..." Mark started wheedling again. I had a lot of four-letter words in my head and was proud that I was managing to keep them to myself as I listened to him in silence.

As he droned on, I thought about that CD. Perhaps I should cash it in. It wasn't worth much, but I could use it for the first few months of loan repayment. Hmmm.

Then my conscience twisted a knife in me. *Rebecca Garvey, you must give Mark half of that CD.*

I frowned at my hair color-sodden image in the bathroom mirror. Sometimes a conscience could be a real pain in the butt.

Before I could even concede the CD to him, I heard an ear-piercing screech coming from somewhere. It was so loud and sharp that it literally blocked my hearing for several moments.

Which at least saved me from a few seconds of listening to my husband.

"I gotta go," I said, ending the call while Mark was in mid-sentence and running toward the front door to see what the cause of the screeching was.

It was my mother.

Mom stood at the open front door, trembling. The storm door was still closed, letting warmth and sunlight into the living room.

"Mom, what in heaven's name is wrong?" My heart was pounding from a combination of terror and mind-numbing conversation.

Mom raised her shaking hand like the ghost of Christmas past and pointed out the glass storm door.

At first, I couldn't see what she was pointing toward. John Wayne and Annie Oakley were in the front field, grazing. Daisy was also out there, sniffing along the fence line closest to the house and—

Oh.

Mom was actually pointing down at the front porch. There was a dead bird there. Not just any bird, though, but a hawk. A goshawk, if I wasn't mistaken, based upon the poor thing's pale underbelly overlaid by a dark back and wings.

"I was watching TV in my room when I heard a loud bang and rushed out here and found...it." Mom lowered her arm and tucked it around mine.

I must have been arguing too loudly with Mark to have even heard the bird slam into the storm door.

Lots of small birds bang into windows, unable to see the glass as they race through the air. But for a large raptor like this to have done so was strange. Particularly, because you don't tend to see them too often this far south, despite "goshawk" being the name of a U.S. Navy training aircraft used at nearby Patuxent River Naval Air Station's test pilot school.

It was also ironic. If my high school science class served me well, I recalled that goshawks remain monogamous to one another for life. This bird's mate was now as alone as I was.

"Do you think it's an omen?" my mother asked, still clutching my arm and trembling. "Maybe you shouldn't start your petting zoo."

I caught her glance slyly at me. Leave it to Georgie Taylor to turn a poor bird's kamikaze death into a reason for me to not expand the farm.

I might be hesitant about it myself, but I didn't want anyone else telling me I couldn't do it. I was juvenile like that, I suppose.

"Well, Mom," I said, disengaging from her, "the only way to eliminate an omen is to literally remove it."

I reached for the brass storm door handle but stopped at my mother *tsk-tsking* me.

"What?" I asked as patiently as I could.

"My dear, you can't go outside looking like that." She pointed at my gloppy head, which was no doubt well beyond its processing expiration time.

I glanced at my watch, then through the glass storm door at the bird, trying to make a decision.

I muttered a curse under my breath and stomped back to the bathroom to rinse my hair.

When I was finally in possession of a clean and unstriped—if still wet—head, I went outside and worked up a sweat burying the poor bird in the pet graveyard I kept deep in the woods of my property.

An animal that large makes you feel like you're burying a pet, not just some random little sparrow. The poor thing.

Actually, poor me. My mother wandered out of the house and found me as I was smoothing dirt and leaves over the bird's makeshift grave with a shovel.

"Rebecca, I think you should give up on this idea of your petting zoo. They say that when a bird flies inside a house, it foretells an important message, and if the bird dies, it foretells *death*. That poor bird was trying to tell you something about your petting zoo being bad luck."

I slid the blade into the ground next to the grave and leaned against the handle.

"Mom, that's a little dramatic. Besides, the goshawk didn't get into the house. He just accidentally hit the door. You wouldn't be as worked up if it had been a little cardinal or a blue jay, it's just upsetting because the bird was so large."

My mother apparently heard what I said because she compressed her lips into a thin line and shook her head at me.

"As a matter of fact, Mom, I'm going to get even more birds. Bear and Donna think I should do an aviary, something where people can walk through sort of a tunnel and see exotic birds above and next to them.

"WHAT? You're going to funnel turds? Why in the world would you do that? Is that some strange new animal care routine?" Mom looked at me expectantly.

I understood the vanity that went along with a refusal of older people to wear hearing aids or use canes—and

I was sure I would join their ranks one day—but at the moment it sure was aggravating.

"No, Mom, I'm building a TUNNEL through the BIRDS."

"Oh, I see." Frowning in confusion, she clearly hadn't understood, but she seemed fixed on her own point. "Your plans are too large. You won't have time to do it all and take care of your family. That's what the bird's omen was. You risk neglecting your family."

My mother was guilting me, and drat it all, I felt a pinprick in my innards over it. But there was nothing to be done for it. Mark was in Florida doing stupid things and I had to make money.

"Mom, doing this ensures I *won't* neglect my family because I will be working here at the farm instead of going into an office. It will all be fine, I promise." I hoped I sounded confident.

"Okay." My mother's shoulders sagged and she turned away from me to return to the house. As bad as her hearing was, Mom was quite spry for her age. She didn't move fast, but she was steady.

As soon as my mother had trudged out of sight, I scurried back to the bathroom to blow dry some style into my hair. I reflected on my finished image in the mirror. A little bit of attention to my looks really had made an improvement. April was right, I had let myself go for too long, but I wouldn't do so anymore.

What I would also no longer do was try to take on everything by myself.

I pulled my cell phone from my pocket and dialed Michelle.

I needed help.

CHAPTER 14

MICHELLE CAME THROUGH and agreed to meet me at the Amish animal auction the following week.

The auction house was just an enormous metal barn with metal bleachers on opposite sides of its long walls. Meesh and I made our way to places in the middle of a row on one side of the seating, placing ourselves about a third of the way up the bleachers.

Interestingly, very few buyers appeared to be Amish but instead were English like us.

At one end, the auctioneer staff sat behind a table on a platform. On the other end, which was open to the outside and let in both light and air on a humid day, were stacks of cages and crates. Chickens, turkeys, baby goats, rabbits, lambs, and other animals filled them. An odorous mélange of hay, straw, animal hides, and feces wafted through the room. I didn't find it offensive at all, and clearly neither did anyone else.

Well, perhaps Michelle did, based on her wrinkled nose and expression of distaste. It made me laugh.

I soon learned that the cages I saw represented only a fraction of the animals up for auction. Amish men would disappear out the open end of the auction house and return with more containers of animals as soon as other animals were sold.

One man served as an animal handler while another man and a young boy worked as spotters. The auction was conducted with amazing precision in what seemed at first glance to be an informal and almost chaotic environment.

The animal handler went to a cage, set it on a table to one side of his open space, and lifted out a pair of chickens, tucking one under each arm and walking around so that the bidders could see them.

Then the auctioneer, introducing himself as Ronnie Farrell, began, speaking so rapidly that it was almost impossible to hear what the opening bid was. Others must have been much more experienced at it, for they seemed to completely understand the rapid-fire stream coming from Mr. Farrell and would raise their hands at certain points.

The spotters would whoop and point when a bidder raised his or her hand, alerting Mr. Farrell to the bid. The auctioneer would nod and up the bidding at a rapid-fire pace. "Twenty-twenty-twenty-I've-got-twenty-do-I-have-twenty-two-twenty-two-twenty-two? Twenty-two-in-the-top-row-do-I-have-twenty-five-twenty-five-twenty-five?"

It was a beautifully orchestrated, if rustic, dance of buying and selling between Amish and English cultures. I was absolutely fascinated.

Once animals were won, they were tucked back into their containers and carried around behind the auctioneer staff then through a curtain to some sort of staging area beyond.

After an hour of watching the action, Michelle leaned over to me. "See anything that interests you?" She pulled a tissue from her purse and wiped her brow. I had almost forgotten how hot it was in my fascination with the proceedings.

"Not yet. I saw a couple of sweet little La Mancha kids. They're docile, friendly goats, but they don't have outer ears and I think it might freak out children."

"You mean those two gray goats with holes where

their floppy ears should be? I remember that. Very strange looking." Michelle mopped at her face again.

"Yes. I wouldn't want people to think I've lopped off my animals' ears. Maybe I should—"

But at that moment the heavens opened, warm sunshine seemed to pour down on me and angels started singing in my ear.

The handler briefly held up a cage like the kind you'd keep hamsters in. He lowered it down to the top of the table and unlatched a door on one end.

Were those what I thought they were?

He reached in a hand and pulled out one little bundle then another. Holding one in each hand, the handler held up two tiny hedgehogs.

"Look up what hedgehogs eat, how to tame them, and what sicknesses they are susceptible to," I hissed to Michelle. "Oh, and do they require specialty vets?"

She looked at me wide-eyed for a moment but obediently got out her phone and began tapping away.

I should have waited for answers before bidding, but I was already smitten and fully prepared to do something rash.

The bidding began at a dollar for the hedgehogs. At first, I thought I was the only one interested in them, but then a young boy engaged in bidding, encouraged by what appeared to be his father next to him.

I'm not proud to say that I was cutthroat with a ten-year-old, but I knew those hedgehogs would be a fun part of the petting zoo. I ended up winning them at fifteen dollars each.

The cage was whisked away through the parted curtain.

As the auction continued without any animals coming up that interested me, Meesh regaled me with hedgehog care tips and tricks. "Looks like you can feed them cat kibble, but you need to supplement with insects. They like crickets. Ick. Oh, you can buy them freeze-dried... who knew? Their main health concern is obesity. Hey! Just like us."

Michelle carried on, seemingly delighted with what she had learned. "You can give them canned cat or dog food, too. And hard-boiled egg. And...ewww. You can feed them pinky mice. Do you know what pinky mice are?" She looked like she had swallowed a bug.

I nodded, bemused at her reaction. "Newborns."

Michelle shuddered. "Don't feed them pinky mice." She continued scrolling through her phone. "You need to put a piece of your clothing in their cage so they get used to your smell. Looks like they can become quite tame."

That was what I had thought was true of hedgehogs, so I was glad for the confirmation. They were also so darned cute.

Once the auction was over and Mr. Farrell made announcements about other upcoming auctions for animals, farm equipment, and quilts, buyers were instructed to pay for their purchases at the teller window near the entrance.

Once that was done, Michelle and I went to retrieve my purchase from behind the auctioneer stand.

Back behind the curtain, the myriad of cages was stacked around haphazardly. There were also stalls containing the larger animals—sheep, goats, and the like—that had been won.

Standing next to the hedgehogs was the boy who had lost. He looked so crestfallen as he wiggled his fingers between the cage wires at the little bundles of quills that I wanted to hug him.

"Hey," I said, walking up to him. "I'm sorry you didn't win, but guess what? You can visit these hedgehogs."

The boy looked at me suspiciously.

"Seriously. I'm going to have a petting zoo in

Hollywood and you can come whenever you want to visit them."

"Christopher, let's go," came a male voice from behind me. I turned to see the man who had been helping the boy bid.

"Sorry I took the hedgehogs," I began again. "I was just telling your son—Christopher, is it?—that I'm starting a petting zoo and he can come visit whenever he wants." Maybe I was securing at least one customer.

The man stopped and put a hand on Christopher's shoulder. "A petting zoo? Like ponies and rabbits and stuff?"

"Yes," I said. "I'll also have a shop and photogra—"

"I guess you'll also have my son's hedgehogs." I couldn't tell whether he was being serious or not, what with his intense stare.

"Umm—" Why did I suddenly feel like the world's worst person?

"I'm kidding. I brought Christopher here to learn about animals. The hedgehogs were just an impulse desire. Radar, our golden retriever, would probably snuffle them to death. I'm Danny Copsey." The man held out a hand.

I held out my own, suddenly noticing he had eyes the color of freshly cut Timothy grass as he warmly grasped my palm. Annie Oakley's favorite hay was Timothy grass. She always got excited and jumpy as soon as I brought it close enough for her to smell it.

Michelle cleared her throat next to me. "Hi, I'm Michelle Knott, Rebecca's best friend," she said, holding out her hand to be shaken.

"So your name is Rebecca," Danny said, still looking my way while shaking Meesh's hand. "Rebecca the Rodent Thief."

"They aren't rodents," I said. "I think they are more

related to shrews than to—oh, you're joking again." Was I blushing from embarrassment? I mentally crossed myself for having thought to color my hair.

He nodded and smiled. "Yeah, I'm joking. Christopher's birthday is in November. Maybe I'll bring him to your petting zoo so he can visit his hedgehogs. How do I reach you?"

"Ahhhh..." I had no business cards, no website, nothing. I didn't even have a name for the petting zoo.

Meesh jumped in. "She's in the middle of printing business materials. Do you have a card? Becca can call you in a couple of days to set up your son's birthday party."

"Sure." Danny reached into his jeans pocket and retrieved a well-worn black leather wallet, from which he pulled out a business card and handed it to me.

"'Copsey's Critters,'" I read aloud. "Do you have a pet store?"

He flashed a great smile. I quickly admonished myself for noticing his smile and his eyes. I was a married woman, after all. For now.

"Hardly. I work on base, but I do taxidermy part-time. Started off doing it for some of my own trophies, then friends started asking me to take care of some of theirs, and it just grew from there. It's not enough to make a living, but folks appreciate it and I enjoy doing it."

Meesh looked like she had swallowed a bug again, which was strange given that Jack was always dragging home some dead thing.

Although, now that I thought about it, maybe he field-dressed his kills and hauled them straight to a processor, returning home with neatly wrapped and taped packages of meat.

I thought of the goshawk I had just buried. "Too bad

we didn't meet yesterday. A goshawk slammed into my storm door and died. I buried it, but it might have been better if it had been preserved by you."

He smiled again, likely due to my recognition of his hobby. "Maybe next time. Look forward to hearing from you about my son's party. C'mon, Christopher," he said, turning away from me and to his boy. I tucked his card into my denim pants pocket as they left the barn, which was now filling up with buyers picking up cages and loading crates onto wagons, I noticed that both father and son had dark hair curling at their napes. Christopher even had the same stride as his father, albeit in a much slower fashion.

"Hey! Cinderella!" I was jolted out of my sinful reverie by Michelle. "Let's get these little quill balls to your house and plan the next auction. It's going to take you forever to amass a petting zoo collection if you're going to do it two hedgehogs at a time."

The Amish spotter came up to us, carrying a clipboard. He checked off my bidder number and offered to carry the cage to my car. I thanked him but declined, carrying it myself.

Michelle walked with me to my truck. I loaded the cage onto the rear seat and turned to say my goodbyes, but she cut me off. "I'm serious, girlfriend. You will run out of money quickly. You should plan to be operational within the next sixty days so you can start recouping money and begin paying the bank back. You need animals and you need promotion. It's time to start calling in the big guns..."

She raised an eyebrow at me. "And I don't just mean the ones on that Danny Copsey."

CHAPTER 15

I COULDN'T HAVE IMAGINED that by "big guns," Michelle meant her own husband, who soon arrived at my doorstep full of advice, phone numbers, and catalogs.

Jack had some good ideas, but I was exhausted by the time he left. I had scribbled pages of notes from his visit but quickly decided that I couldn't move forward unless it was my way.

"Sorry, Meesh," I murmured, crumpling the pages and dropping them into the kitchen trash can.

Jack's enthusiasm had been such that my mother stayed hidden in her room until he was gone. She now crept out to talk to me.

"Who was that?" she asked as she made her way to the kitchen table.

"That was Jack Knott, my friend Michelle's husband."

My mother frowned as she sat down, reaching through her mental database for who Jack was. While she did that, I opened the kitchen door to let in Daisy, who was whining and pawing at it.

"Is Michelle the little one? That's a loud man for such a tiny girl." Mom started digging into the fruit bowl in the center of the table.

Daisy briefly snuffled around in her food dish and, finding nothing there, moved over to my mother and laid her head in my mother's lap. Mom slipped her a chunk of banana.

Thirty minutes with Mr. Stauffer's labs and suddenly my mother was a dog lover.

Daisy seemed quite happy about her newfound status as a beloved creature. She gulped another chunk of banana.

My mother noticed the cage on the counter. "What is that?" she asked, pointing.

I picked up the cage and brought it over to my mother so she could see the little hedgehogs, who were curled up into tightly sleeping balls on top of their bedding of wood shavings.

"Are they baby porcupines?"

I explained that they were hedgehogs and were to be part of the petting zoo. She quickly lost interest and returned to feeding banana to the dog.

Didn't Michelle say hedgehogs could eat fruit? I grabbed another banana and cut half of it up into tiny chunks and put it on a small paper plate. I opened the cage door and slid the plate inside. The hedgehogs woke slowly, blinking and yawning.

Holy crap, their yawning was adorable. Okay, I would take care of setting them up in the morning. As I contemplated obtaining more animals, I realized that I had to be ready to house them all. But I didn't know what kind of structures needed to be built without knowing what animals I would have. My application to the bank just listed everything I thought I needed but didn't really spell out in what order I intended to do everything.

I would have to do everything all at once and the two tiny balls here in the kitchen were a minor start, as Michelle had pointed out today.

With Mom occupied by Daisy, I retreated to my room. I prepped for an early bedtime and sat up in bed with my laptop. I started scouring the internet for other local animal auctions but soon expanded that search into Virginia and North Carolina, marking several for consideration. I also noted the county fair's dates on my calendar. It was just two weeks away.

I looked up all the local and state requirements for my petting zoo. No sense running afoul of the law.

My fingers tapped away as I began more serious planning than anything I had done with my brother. A vision arose in my mind of what my farm would look like. Overlaid on that vision were dollar signs.

I hoped what the bank had given me would be enough.

I decided I would ask Mr. Stauffer to point me to some Amish builders who could erect barns and sheds for me.

I also thought about something Jack had given me. Putting my laptop aside, I went to the kitchen to retrieve the flyer for prefab, metal farm structures from the trash can.

Mom had gone to bed so the kitchen was quiet. Daisy didn't come to greet me so I assumed she was snuggled up with my mother. I turned out all but one light and glanced at the hedgehog cage again.

I need to visit Southern States up in Charlotte Hall tomorrow, I thought. All these new animals would require specialty feeds. Hedgehogs, for example, might be able to eat cat food, but I was sure there were purpose-made pellets for them.

I went back to bed and, sitting up again, continued working on my computer. Staying busy made it easier to forget that I was now alone in this bed.

As I contemplated what actions to take tomorrow besides going to Southern States, I heard a banging on the front storm door, causing me to jump. I looked at the time on my computer. It was nearly nine o'clock.

Putting the laptop down for a second time, I grabbed a robe and threw it on as I went to the front door. I could hear Daisy softly woof twice from my mother's room, trying to do her job as a guard dog without disturbing her comfortable resting place.

It was Dee Dee Boone, Mark's old coworker, looking just as put together as she had when I ran into her at the grocery store. Meanwhile, I was in ratty pajamas and a mismatched robe.

But I had hair that was all one color, so there was that.

"I had a heck of a time finding you but finally figured out where you lived from a friend at Globo," she said. "Sorry to just show up like this and to do it so late, but I've been thinking about your petting zoo plan and, well, I'd like to volunteer my services."

Intrigued, I invited her into the living room to sit down. Dee chose one end of the blue chenille couch. I sat on the opposite end from her, worried that Daisy may have spent too much time where Dee Dee was and that the woman was going to end up with a hairy patch of black and white fur on her rear end.

"I thought about your…situation…and felt terrible about any part I may have played in making you feel bad."

I shook my head. "No need for you to feel bad for anything whatsoever. You aren't responsible for Mark's behavior."

"Still. It seems to me that I have a skill to offer you for your launch event. You're going to have a launch event, right?"

"Yes. But I have a long way to go before I'm ready to open up. All I've really done is get a loan and buy a couple of hedgehogs." I realized how pathetic that sounded.

Dee Dee waved a hand. "Take your time. As you know, I'm in real estate now. I help people stage their homes to make them ready for sale and I'm good at it, if I do say so myself. I can help you stage the farm to be attractive to visitors. I also know how to advertise properties and I think that experience can translate into helping you promote the farm. What do you think about a billboard?"

She looked at me expectantly.

I had discussed radio ads with Angie and Tyler but I knew nothing about billboards. Weren't they the preferred medium for lawyers and drug clinics? "I guess I don't have an opinion one way or another on billboards," I said. "Why?"

"I'm seeing a series of billboards along Route 5 from Waldorf to Mechanicsville, sort of like what is done along Interstate 95 going to South of the Border." Dee Dee waved a hand in the air as if brush stroking it into my imagination. "Do you know what I mean?"

I did. The tourist spot was located just over the border into South Carolina from North Carolina, hence "South of the Border." With its kitschy Mexican theme, the attraction sold fireworks, cheap gifts, gas, and offered both a restaurant and a motel. Billboards dotted the highway for many miles prior to the place, presumably to build up excitement for a car's occupants to get them to stop and spend money.

"Yes, you want to build anticipation for people driving down Route 5 on their way to my farm." It wasn't a terrible idea.

Dee Dee bobbed her head up and down. "Exactly. I think we can also do quite a bit of online marketing. Do you have a website yet?"

I wanted to tell her she was getting too far ahead of me, but hadn't I just decided that I needed to do everything at once? "I don't, but I also haven't decided on a name for it yet."

Dee Dee shook her head in disbelief. "Girl, that is your next order of business. Without a name for your petting zoo, you have nothing."

So many things were important all at one time. "My

daughter suggested Celestial Paws, but I don't think that's what I want."

Dee Dee's expression told me she agreed with my decision. "Definitely not. You need a name that's catchy and screams 'fun for the whole family.' Seriously, call me as soon as you decide on it."

Both Dee Dee and Meesh were saying "seriously" to me as if I weren't. However, they both seemed to have my best interest at heart.

"I promise to get right to work on a good name and will call you tomorrow with it." I accepted the business card Dee Dee proffered me.

I never called Dee Dee—nor Danny Copsey—the next day, though, for a crisis struck my household, obliterating all thoughts of my petting zoo.

CHAPTER 16

IN THE MORNING, I started working through my to-do list, first visiting Southern States. I admit that I started there because I liked visiting the place, so it was fun task. I spent an enjoyable hour chatting up a worker about the various types of feeds available for exotic animals, including my new hedgehogs. I was invited to put up a flyer for the zoo, which drove home to me that Dee Dee was right, I needed a name, pronto.

Following that, I drove to the credit union to close out the CD and transfer money to Mark. It was both exhilarating and a relief to do it, as if it put me one step closer to being rid of Mark's dead weight.

I returned home, whistled for Daisy, and together we started pacing around the property, envisioning what the possibilities were and mentally planning what would go where.

"The shop should go near the entrance, right, Daisy?" I asked the dog, who stayed close to me, ready to herd me back into line if I wandered away from her. I continued talking to Daisy as if she could answer. "All good tourist spots have their gift shops at the entrance or exit."

There was an opening in a grove of trees that would be good for an avian enclosure. I could incorporate some of the trees inside the enclosure so the birds would have natural roosting spots.

Using the same principle of creating an enclosure, I decided to carve out part of the llama field and use it for small animals—the hedgehogs, rabbits, Billy's sugar gliders, and whatever else I could find. I would need to keep them separate from one another but accessible to visitors, as well as provide the animals a way to retreat when they were overwhelmed.

Larger animals would need to be kept near their respective stables or pens. Hmmm, maybe I could teach kids how to take care of farm animals so they would understand what a serious undertaking animal husbandry was. I could even have a summer program for it. Maybe the local 4-H club would want to partner with me.

I was getting excited about the future.

I heard the crunching of gravel and saw the billowing of dust as a vehicle came up my driveway. "C'mon," I said to Daisy as I crossed one of the fields to see who had arrived.

The driver waved to me from outside the vehicle. "Hiya, Becca!"

It was Mom's friend, Betty Ann. "Came to pick up Georgie for this afternoon's event at Pier 450."

Ah, had that much time passed that another Ladies with Hats day had rolled around? Betty Ann wore a straw hat laden with lime green and amber artificial flowers and adorned with a chocolate brown bow with tails. It was...something.

I escorted Betty Ann to the kitchen door, intending to call out for my mother, but she opened the door herself, ready to go. Mom's hat was a little more subdued, a little purple pillbox with a pearl pin in the shape of a parrot attached to one side. She carried a purple clutch purse I'd never noticed before.

"You ladies look fetching," I said. "You'll be fighting off the waiters and busboys."

"WHAT?" my mother said.

Betty Ann jumped in. "You look lovely," she said

loudly, taking Mom by the elbow and guiding her to the car. "Be back in a few hours," she said over her shoulder.

I watched them leave, then returned to my planning. After another hour or so, I decided it was time for the evening feeding. I started with my miniature horses, who were in the field with John Wayne and Annie Oakley. They shared the same barn as the larger horses but had smaller stalls.

As I approached the fence, I saw plenty of poop piles that needed to be scooped and tossed into my fertilizer bin. I knew a few folks who liked to periodically come by and take portions of it for their gardens. I probably should have been charging them for the valuable fertilizer, but it just seemed a neighborly thing to do.

That might have to change with the implementation of the petting zoo. I couldn't have people wandering in and scooping poop in the middle of a children's birthday party. I mentally added it to my list of things to manage.

I clucked my tongue and Randy came trotting over to me, swinging his head so that his luxurious mane flowed around him. Randy was buff-colored with a white mane. The top of his head was at my shoulder, making him the size and shape of a very large dog.

"You think you're handsome, don't you?" I asked him as I opened the gate and entered the field, Daisy hot at my heels.

People often confused ponies and miniature horses. Ponies are usually stocky with short legs, whereas minis are perfect replicas of a horse's build, just smaller.

Unfortunately, minis couldn't be ridden the way the more sturdily built ponies could. So, Kenny, Randy, and Reba wouldn't be able to have children ride them. However, the three of them could certainly do duty pulling something.

That gave me an idea for little wagons that a couple

of small children could get in and be pulled around by one of the minis.

Kenny and Reba soon joined Randy in following me to the barn. Reba, who tended to be bossy with everyone around her, even got behind me and pushed me with her nose. "Hey!" I said, stopping and turning around to her. "Don't rush me."

The horse barged right past me and stood at a door in the barn, behind which I kept their feed. She was white with black splotches, appearing as if someone had tossed an open can of paint her way.

Sliding open the door, I reached to a shelf and pulled down a bag of horse treats. I opened it and fed each of the minis a treat to keep them happy while I assembled their food dishes.

I removed the lid from the plastic feed container and scooped a strictly measured amount of pellets into their dishes. Like the big horses, the minis required a balanced diet of grass, hay, oats, and other grains. However, the minis were much more prone to becoming overweight if I didn't keep a close eye on them.

I left them there to eat while I mucked their stalls.

With the minis fed and their stalls cleaned, I then went to the equipment shed and jumped on my tractor, which had a flat trailer attached to it. The trailer was covered with a plastic tarp. I drove back to the field and scooped the big manure piles from the field, pitching them onto the back of the trailer and then driving it all off to the area—a low area back in the woods—I had set aside for people who wanted to collect it. Jumping back off my small tractor, I dragged the tarp off the trailer and shook the poop off, watching it roll down the small hill.

I wiped my forehead with the back of my arm. It was still hot even though the sun would be down soon. My tiny farm was hard, sweaty work to manage alone, but I did love it. The smell of hay, the feel of a llama greeting me by pressing his nose against mine, the sight of my horses trotting around the field, the sensation of pleasant exhaustion at the end of a day...it all felt rewarding in an indescribable way. Like I was one with the nature around me—a nature environment that I had myself assembled.

Mark didn't understand that and I realized he would never understand it.

I continued my rounds with John Wayne and Annie Oakley, then the Bugs, and finished up with the goats. Daisy stayed at my side the entire time, nipping at the heels of one of the goats who tried to make an escape through the gate when I went into their pen to replenish their hay bale.

"Good girl," I said to the dog. "You deserve a little something, too."

Inside the house, I went straight to the bathroom for a quick shower and clothing change before feeding the hedgehogs and Daisy. I was reaching into the dog treat jar when my phone buzzed on the kitchen counter. I flipped the treat to Daisy without asking her to do a trick first and reached for my phone.

"This is Dr. Lily Dunaway at St. Mary's Hospital. I'm the emergency room doctor today. Is this Rebecca Garvey?"

I felt the color drain from my face. It was never good news when the hospital called you. "Yes."

"Your mother, Georgina Taylor, is here. She has had an accident. Can you come right away?"

As with the time I thought something had happened to April, I likely broke multiple laws as I screamed south on Three Notch Road. The traffic light was in my favor at Sotterley Road, so I was able to easily turn right and reach the hospital in a time that would have made a NASCAR driver proud.

I raced through the automatic sliding doors at the

emergency room entrance and breathlessly presented myself to the clerk on duty. Fortunately, the ER wasn't crowded and I was quickly buzzed back through the locked entry into the emergency room cubicles.

My mother was sitting up in bed, wearing a beautiful faux fur-edged bed robe in a gorgeous shade of mauve, over a hospital gown, with multiple wires running from her to various beeping machines.

"Hello, dear. I think I had a heart attack," she said calmly.

CHAPTER 17

MY MOTHER WAS useless in helping me ascertain exactly what had happened, so I ran out to the busy nurses' station, around which all the ER cubicles were positioned.

Everyone behind the station was wearing scrubs, but they were all different colors. Which of these people was actually a nurse?

There was a pictorial guide on the wall explaining the rainbow of various scrub colors and what they meant. Specific colors referred to specific disciplines, such as nurse, technician, or other health care worker, then it was further broken down by discipline—emergency room, surgery, obstetrics, and so forth.

How could anyone memorize this? I finally just approached a woman wearing blue scrubs, as that seemed the most prevalent color within the hive, and inquired about my mother.

The woman, whose badge dangling from a lanyard around her neck read, *Angie Thompson, RN*, tapped at a computer and then said, "Yes, your mother was admitted with chest pains. I'll ask Dr. Barnes to come see you."

She refused to say more, which sent my anxiety through the roof. How bad was it if the nurse wouldn't say anything?

Mom was dozing when, to my pleasant surprise, Dr. Barnes appeared in Mom's cubicle a few minutes later. He was tall with graying hair at the temples of his mahogany skin and he carried himself with total assurance. My mind was instantly set at ease.

"Your mother had an episode at the restaurant where she was eating. One of her dining partners drove her here and the tests we've run so far don't indicate anything amiss. She's quite boring, medically speaking, other than her obvious dementia and hearing loss. It may have been a panic attack of some sort or maybe even some serious heartburn. We're going to keep her overnight for observation and let her go in the morning. I'm just waiting for a room upstairs to open up so we can move her."

Mom had awakened during his visit and now glanced back and forth between us, clearly not registering what was being said against the background noise of machines, bells, and buzzers, but likely too vain to shout 'WHAT?' in front of the physician.

I exhaled loudly. Okay, presumably nothing serious.

"I need something to eat," Mom demanded. "I'm starving."

The doctor winked at me. "That's a good sign." Turning to my mother he said, "I'll talk to the nurses about having food services bring you something."

That satisfied my mother so he left.

"Where did you get the bed jacket?" I asked.

My mother patted one mauve sleeve. "Betty Ann had it in her car when she drove me here. She said she keeps them on hand for when there's a little nip in the air."

It wasn't even officially fall yet and nowhere near cold. Leave it to an elderly woman to carry around a bedjacket as if it were a pair of jumper cables or a tire pump.

But I had to be grateful to Betty Ann for getting my mother to the hospital promptly. The drive from Pier 450 had to have taken at least forty minutes.

"Did the doctor tell you I had a heart attack?" Mom

asked, seemingly quite pleased with her dramatic self-diagnosis.

"Looks like you may have just had a bout of indigestion." I raised my voice so I wouldn't have to repeat it. "You're going to spend the night while they make sure it isn't more serious."

I swear Mom looked deflated at the news that it wasn't a heart attack.

A plate containing a grilled cheese sandwich, jello, and macaroni and cheese appeared a few minutes later and I left Mom to eat while I called April to come to the hospital.

April apparently doesn't feel the urgency that I do when receiving emergency-type calls, for she showed up ninety minutes later once Mom had been moved to a room on the second floor of the hospital.

Mom was glad to see her granddaughter, so I told myself that was all that mattered. April's appearance at her bedside, combined with being fortified by a grilled cheese sandwich, seemed to have given my mother a fighting spirit.

"April, honey, I'm glad you're here. I had a heart attack!" Mom exclaimed brightly.

I stopped her. "No, Mom, you likely just had some heartburn or indiges—"

"Sit down, lovey," Mom continued, patting the covers next to her. "Your mother doesn't listen but I know you will."

April obediently sat down on the side of the bed.

"I've been telling your mother that her idea for this ridiculous petting zoo is doomed."

"Why, Gram?" It disturbed me that April seemed poised to believe whatever my mother was about to say.

Mom loosely clasped one of April's hands in her own. My mother's hand had an IV needled taped down to the back of it. "We've had omens," she whispered dramatically.

I was impressed that Mom could even successfully whisper, given her typical need for volume.

Gram was talking April's language. "Omens?" my daughter repeated, adopting the same hushed tone. "What have you seen?"

I sat down on the blue-patterned loveseat under the room's window, which overlooked the front parking lot. I swung my legs around so I could stretch out against the sofa's arm and look out the window.

A sheriff's deputy pulled up to the curb and helped someone out of the back of his car. It was a young woman, probably no older than April, cuffed and in an orange jumpsuit. The prisoner moved slowly toward the hospital entrance and was obviously in great pain.

The deputy and his charge disappeared from view and I shivered. I hoped that girl wasn't in prison with some serious—or even fatal—disease.

I glanced back at April, who was in rapt attention to what her grandmother was saying. Did that poor prisoner have a mama like me somewhere, fretting for her daughter's life night and day?

I couldn't bear to think of it.

"A hawk!" April was exclaiming. "How terrible. You must have been so scared, Gram."

"Oh no, not me. I knew it was an omen, though, and I called out to your mother to show her and prove it to her. Terrible things are going to happen, just you wait and see," Mom intoned. "A dead bird and your nearly-died Gram are just the beginning. Why, honey, the whole farm might burn down. Becca needs to just forget the whole idea and do something else. Maybe she could be a cashier at Walmart."

April murmured something that I couldn't hear and hugged her grandmother.

I rolled my eyes and stretched out to pull my cell phone from my pants pocket. The inanities of the internet had to be better than where this conversation was going so I figured I would immerse myself in stupidity while half paying attention to my mother and daughter and completely forgetting about the sight of the deputy and prisoner.

"I think Mom can make it work, Gram."

I had hardly opened up social media when I was distracted again, this time by the shock of April actually taking my side in the petting zoo.

"Besides, I get feelings about things and I'm sure Mom has to do this to fulfill her cosmic requirement."

"My what?" I asked, but April paid no attention to me.

"I've also given Mom some good ideas for it, Gram, including the name. She's going to call it 'Celestial Paws,'" April said.

I had never committed to that. "No, I'm not. I'm—"

My mother's expression turned stormy. "You shouldn't be leading your mother on like that."

April's expression was one of shock. "But I'm not. I truly think Mom can do it."

"She cannot." My mother's lips were set in a grim line. "This is madness and it must be stopped. I will do what I can to make her see the light."

Why was my mother so inflamed over this? I realized the goshawk against the window may have been upsetting, but things like that happen, especially on a farm. And her episode at the restaurant was also just an accident.

Mom was like a terrier with a bone on this, growling and unable to let go. I had to be able to calm her down or she would become completely obsessed. A couple of years ago she had gotten it in her head that Dad hadn't died but had gone to live with an old friend of hers who lived in North Carolina. For months she talked about how Regina had stolen Marlon away from her and she needed to go to North Carolina to get him back. She had sometimes even followed me to my car and insisted that I drive her to North Carolina that instant. I don't remember what eventually moved Mom off the topic, I just remember being relieved that I no longer had to try and convince her that her husband was dead and buried.

I didn't want the petting zoo to turn into some uncomfortable obsession with Mom.

I felt the familiar gnawing in my gut that I got when I had the feeling that I was going to have to do something unpleasant to keep the peace. It was like having a goat obsessively picking you clean, nibbling and chewing repeatedly in the same location until you were raw.

Becca Garvey, you are the only person permitted to be scared about this venture. No one else.

I realized April was looking at me helplessly.

"Mom," I said, seeing a nurse enter the room from the corner of my vision, "I don't need to see the light. I'm going to proceed with the petting zoo no matter what 'omens' occur."

"WHAT? You agree that you had a fright?" I swear I thought I saw a smile curving on Mom's face.

The nurse checked my mother's vitals, then beckoned me to follow her outside the room.

"Your mother could use hearing aids," the nurse said.

I blinked slowly at her. "No kidding. She has them, won't use them."

The nurse nodded. "Ah, yes. That's common. I'm so sorry."

Not as sorry as I was for everything that had happened over the past few weeks. Nor as sorry as I was going to be at the St. Mary's County Fair.

CHAPTER 18

MOM WAS HOME and settled back into the house the following afternoon, with the doctor having diagnosed her as having had a case of dyspepsia and sending her home with a few antacids tablets and an admonishment to eat more slowly.

A bullet dodged, as they say.

However, Mom didn't seem to have forgotten that omens were lurking everywhere.

Some Amish men arrived in three buggies to do an estimate for the outbuildings. They were all dressed identically in their dark pants, shirts, suspenders, and straw hats, and they all even had the same facial hair.

Only one of them spoke to me. He introduced himself as Hiram. As I traversed the property with the group, I noticed my mother venture out onto the front porch to watch us, arms crossed tightly in front of her.

I ignored her as best I could, but it proved difficult to concentrate with her watching like a hawk––forgive the pun.

When I had finished showing Hiram and his friends what the job entailed, they went off into a huddle to discuss the project. Sounds of their guttural German carried over to me as I occupied myself by paying attention to Kenny, Randy, and Reba, who had also been following the action, albeit with far more pleasant expressions on their faces.

After several minutes, Hiram sought me out to offer me a reasonable price. I readily agreed and the verbal contract was entered. They would start in a couple of days and be finished in a few days. Once the Amish started a job, they worked with limitless energy until the project was done and then they immediately went to their next job with the same gusto.

I waved goodbye as they returned to their single horse-and-buggy vehicles and lit the lamps at their carriage corners before hopping in. It wasn't close to dark yet, but they would have a long journey at the horse's pace, and it would be dusky by the time they got all the way back to Loveville, for sure.

I avoided Mom the rest of the week by spending time with my animals and working on a makeshift enclosure for the hedgehogs until such time that my permanent structure for small animals was built. I worked on training the hedgehogs to go potty in a small tissue box with a bit of litter in it that I put in their cage, surprised by how quickly they picked up what to do.

I also performed the important task of naming the hedgehogs, deciding on Pip and Pop. I had no idea what sex they were and researched how to figure it out, but the internet disappointed me by offering only vague ways to determine sex, with the male hedgehog having a "bump" on his abdomen. I figured "Pip" and "Pop" could work no matter what each turned out to be.

The weekend approaching was the third weekend in September and thus the county fair was going to be in full swing. I decided to go early Saturday morning to attend the livestock show. I invited my mother to go with me and was relieved when she declined.

I was going to have to concentrate intently during the auction and it might be hard to do with Mom next to me, depending upon her mood. Plus, she was already cranky with me for moving forward despite her "evidence" that the project was doomed.

On a whim, though, I called April and was both surprised and happy that she agreed to meet me at the fairgrounds.

I hooked up my horse trailer to my truck in case I made a great find, then headed off to Leonardtown. The fair always opened on Thursday evening and ran through Sunday. It was commonly held lore that it *always* rained on fair weekend, but the past few days had been near perfect and today was also promising to be gorgeous.

I arrived at the fairgrounds well before eight o'clock, but the parking lot was already filling up. Workers guided vehicles onto the grassy field to park and I ended up not too far away from the entrance. I stayed in my truck until April texted me that she, too, had arrived, then walked to the entry gate to meet her.

I paid the ten-dollar admission for both of us, took the proffered fair guide, and entered the grounds, which were already coming alive with music and vendors hawking their wares. I turned almost immediately to the left to get to the open-air livestock auction building, with April silently following me. The familiar odor of beast and manure told me we had reached the correct location.

The auction was close to starting as we climbed up into the bleachers. I was immediately reminded of what the Amish auction had looked like.

The auctioning began, starting with small animals. First was a parade of rabbits in an unimaginable array of size, fur length, and markings. Some had ribbons attached to their cages for having won prizes in whatever bunny categories they had been entered in for the fair.

"'Prize-winning rabbits' has a good ring to it for the petting zoo, Mom," April urged, so I bid on and won several of them, pleased that April was taking an interest in the auction.

Following the rabbits were other small animals, none of which interested me at all until another cage was brought out that made my heart soar.

Presented to us were three sugar gliders, just like my nephew Billy had requested. I was shocked to see them come up in a fair auction.

I bid on—and won—those, too.

Larger animals came and went. I considered some sheep but wasn't sure I could do anything with them until the Amish were done with my outbuildings.

It was with the next auction lot that I lost my heart completely.

Up for bid were three small calves. Not regular calves, mind you, but miniature cow calves. They would grow to be about as big as German Shepherds. Or maybe Great Danes.

Two were red and white, and I believed them to be Hereford meat cows, while the third was black and white, suggesting it was a milk-producing Holstein.

I had to have them.

"Mom, you're not actually thinking of buying all three, are you?" April glanced at me suspiciously. "That's crazy."

In the moment, I was like an obsessed gambler, completely ignoring my daughter's conscientious buzzing in my ear.

A woman across the arena must have also fallen in love with the tiny bovines, for we got into an intense bidding war. I prevailed but had spent enough that I decided I would stop for the day, especially since April was giving me her death stare.

I was told to come back in another hour or so once the livestock had all been sold to pick up my sweet little female cows as well as the rabbits and sugar gliders.

Pleased with my purchases and feeling a little hungry from the intense activity, I suggested that we peruse the food trucks for a snack. It seemed we had a choice of anything we wanted, as long as it was fried. Poor April.

She turned up her nose while I settled on deep-fried stuffed ham eggrolls with dipping sauce and ate them from a little red and white checkered cardboard tray as we walked around the fair checking out the various vendors and entertainment.

We stopped and watched for a few minutes as a local dance school troupe of children tap-danced their way across the fair's auditorium stage to an old musical number. From there, we toured the commercial buildings which contained the usual blend of local businesses, artists, and political candidates. With the two egg rolls devoured, we went outside so I could seek out one of the many trash cans on the fairgrounds. It was already overflowing with the usual fair detritus—drink cups, funnel cake, wrappers, and kettle corn bags.

With my trash added to it, we walked back toward the front of the fairgrounds to collect my new critters. I stopped when I saw a parked van with the local radio station's logo emblazoned across it. Next to the side of the van, a man and woman sat at a table with tabletop microphones and a soundboard in front of them.

"That must be T-Bone and Heather, the local morning show personalities," I told April. "The owner of Marie and Nash said I should get them to cut a commercial for me or do live spots."

I suddenly realized I could hear Heather's distinctive voice through the loudspeaker system, as she announced the winner of a year's worth of free car washes from a local car dealership to the fair's attendees and presumably her listening audience.

They were broadcasting live from the fair.

"Let's go meet them, then," April urged as I stood there waffling.

We approached their table but I hung back while they

continued their broadcast, wishing I had another egg roll to keep me and my stomach occupied in the meantime.

As soon as they moved away from their microphones, April practically pushed me forward. I went up and introduced myself, explaining the plan for my petting zoo and that I had been encouraged to seek them out.

They were gracious and began asking me questions about the zoo. T-Bone, in particular, seemed very interested in what I was doing.

"So, is it just for children's parties, or is it for adults, too?" he asked. "Will you be open year-round? Can people feed the animals? What kind of animals will you have?"

I fielded his questions as best I could. "I would say it's for families in general," I said. "I just purchased some mini-cows, which I think adults will enjoy as much as the kids will. I will have treat bags people can buy for most of the animals."

I'd have to watch out for the porky little hedgehogs, though. Probably no treat bags for them.

"Treats will be sold in the gift shop, run by my daughter. This is April." Instead of shaking hands with the radio personalities, April did some sort of strange bowing-praying stance that I didn't understand. The duo took it in stride.

"I'll probably shut down in the winter months," I continued, having no idea if that were true or not. "The weather will be too messy for visitors." I went on to describe the animals I had and what I was currently planning to buy.

Their interest was flattering, given that they surely met hundreds of business owners each month.

"And how do people visit? Is there a mapped-out route or can they just wander from enclosure to enclosure?" T-Bone wanted to know.

An excellent question. "Well…although I don't want

anyone to feel like they are on a theme park ride, so to speak, I also want to ensure they see everything, so I guess—"

"You need golf carts," T-Bone said.

Heather nodded. "Great idea, T."

"Golf carts?" I repeated.

"Yes. Let people go up and down paths and through your enclosures on golf carts."

I instantly warmed to the idea. Golf cart pickup and return could be next to the gift shop.

"Mom, you need to consider a renewable energy source to power the golf carts," April said.

I bit my tongue and replied as gently as I could. "Honey, golf carts don't run on gas, they have rechargeable batteries."

"Oh."

Heather snapped the fingers of her right hand. "And put your logo on the side of the carts. What's the name of the zoo?"

"Well…" I started again. "I haven't figured out—"

"I suggested that she call it Celestial Paws and Hoo—" April began.

"What you've really got here isn't a petting zoo," T-Bone said to me. "You're creating a cuddly creature safari. Where is it?"

"Off Three Notch Road in Hollywood," I said. "It's a long driveway back to it but easily accessible from the road."

T-Bone nodded. "Call it Three Notch Safari. People will love it."

My jaw dropped at how easily the disc jockey had come up with the perfect name for it. I was so speechless I forgot what I wanted to ask next.

April shrugged. "That name is so-so. It doesn't really have the panache of Celestial Paws—"

"Here's another idea," T-Bone said, as effortlessly

as if he just sat around all day having brilliant ideas. "Have you thought about putting on plays involving the animals? Such as a western skit involving your new mini cows? Hey! If you need someone to be the bad guy in the play, I'm your man. I've always wanted to be the bad guy." He grinned, and I couldn't imagine him ever being a bad guy.

Heather laughed. "The ad copy writes itself."

Right, advertising was what I wanted to know about. I inquired about having them cut a commercial for me and they gave me information for reaching out to the radio station's sales staff.

"How about this in the meantime?" Heather said, pulling her microphone toward her and speaking into it. "We're back live at the St. Mary's County Fair. T-Bone, have you heard about the new zoo coming to St. Mary's County?"

The other deejay pulled his own microphone toward him and jumped right in. "Don't you mean the new safari? Conveniently located in Hollywood, Maryland?"

"Yes!" Heather exclaimed. "It's going to be the biggest thing in the tri-county area if not the state."

"When does it open?" T-Bone asked Heather, then turning and raising an eyebrow at me.

I thought fast. Could I get everything done in a month? "November first," I mouthed.

April sucked in her breath next to me.

"I hear it's opening the first of November," Heather said.

If I were to open it in November, I couldn't very well shut it down two months later for winter, could I?

The two of them joked back and forth about the zoo—oops, safari—for nearly a minute, and they sounded almost as if they had already visited a fully functional tourist spot.

"I might be making a special appearance there," T-Bone announced.

"Is that right? How so?" Heather asked. It was amazing how these two could just roll with each other.

"There's going to be a western skit with some of the animals and I'm going to be the bad guy." He thumped his chest.

Heather rolled her eyes exaggeratedly at her husband. Too bad the listening audience couldn't see it. "T, nobody is going to be afraid of a teddy bear like you."

Her statement made me realize that T-Bone, a large but gentle human, reminded me a lot of my brother.

They bantered a little bit more, then announced the times for the remaining fair activities for the day and cut over to commercials.

"Let's put that safari on the map of St. Mary's County must-see attractions, Becca," Heather said, standing and shaking my hand warmly and nodding to April.

T-Bone also rose to shake my hand. "Don't forget that you need to build a stage. We thespians need our space."

Heather rolled her eyes again.

As for me, I had just received some invaluable free marketing. How could I ever repay them? "A stage it is!" I assured him, mentally adding to my impossibly expanding task list.

As I walked away, I was overcome by what had just transpired with the two radio personalities. For one brief moment, I was on top of the world.

Then we ran into April's boyfriend.

CHAPTER 19

"HI, SWEETIE," MY daughter said to Jimmy, now clinging to his scrawny arm as if he was a life preserver she was scared would float away. Jimmy carried a big clear plastic cup of lemonade. Chunks of lemons floated in the cup.

"Hey, what are you doing here? Oh, I bet you're looking for animals." Jimmy took a sip from the exhaust pipe-sized red straw stuck in his drink, his bored gaze not seeming to land on either me or April.

I nodded. "That and food. I had some stuffed ham egg rolls but I'm now thinking about a hot dog. With chili. And cheese. Want to join me?"

My growling tummy couldn't have cared less that it was only ten o'clock in the morning and way too early for that much caloric intake. The stomach wants what the stomach wants.

April looked at her boyfriend questioningly. "I'm sure we can find something better than chili dogs." He shrugged and nodded at April without acknowledging me.

Sigh.

I bought all of us hot dogs—with theirs being plant-based, of course—and French fries, although I seemed to be the only one who wanted mine loaded with heartburn-inducing extras.

We found an empty picnic table within the eating area and sat down with our food. After the first bite, I had chili dribbling down my chin.

Swiping at my face with a napkin, I asked Jimmy, "So, how go sales of your Snore-a-Gone bracelets?" I tried to sound interested and not caustic, which was becoming harder and harder for me since Mark's abrupt announcement.

Jimmy swallowed a huge bite of his hot dog, which was smothered in mustard. He was so thin that I could almost see it traveling down his throat. "Oh, that. Yeah, I'm not doing that anymore." He took a long sip from his lemonade, which seemed to push the hot dog further down his gullet.

I was hardly surprised that Snore-a-Gone wasn't working but was a little taken aback that April hadn't mentioned it. "Oh really?" I asked as innocently as possible. "What happened?"

April jumped in before Jimmy could respond to me. "Wal-Mart just didn't understand the value of the product. Can you believe it? They didn't buy *anything*, not even a few pieces to just try out at the local store. Wal-Mart doesn't know what it's missing." April gazed adoringly at Jimmy.

"Yeah," her boyfriend added.

I dabbed at my chin, hoping I didn't have any more chili or cheese sauce dribbling down it. "I'm sure that's very disappointing," I said evenly.

"'S okay," Jimmy added, sipping more lemonade. Was there a more eloquent speaker than April's boyfriend?

I guess he didn't need to be well-spoken, for April was willing to take on the task for him.

"We realized that Wal-Mart just isn't visionary. They're just buying the same old products over and over, so it was near impossible to introduce them to something new and revolutionary."

I knew it was of no use to tell them that Wal-Mart was a retailer and likely constantly in search of new and revolutionary items consumers would love.

Instead, I tried to push Jimmy in a different direction. "You know, I could use some help at the zoo starting soon." I went on to explain the direction where the zoo—I mean, safari—was headed.

"I'll have lots of opportunities for both of you. April is going to run the gift shop." I nodded at my daughter. "I'll also need help feeding and cleaning up after the animals, grooming them, assisting with photography, keeping golf carts in running order, grounds maintenance, answering visitor questions…" I continued listing jobs as I thought of them.

Jimmy stared at me blankly. "Can't do it. Have another invention. It's an even better idea than Snore-a-Gone."

I tossed the remainder of my gooey hot dog onto the paper plate. My previously voracious appetite was gone.

"Yeah, Mom," April said enthusiastically, nibbling like a mouse at her mushroom-tofu-wheat grass-whatever hot dog. She put it down before continuing. "The Wal-Mart rejection was really a blessing in disguise because Jimmy's new idea is actually way better than Snore-a-Gone."

I braced myself. "Really? What is it?"

Jimmy didn't pick up the ball and run with it, so April did. "You won't believe how unique it is. He's developing the best car air fresheners. You know, the kind that hang from the rearview mirror."

Jimmy nodded modestly.

"But there are many varieties of car air fresheners," I said slowly. "Kinds that attach to air vents, that plug into car power, that tuck under your seat, and that also hang from rearview mirrors. So, for the idea to be unique would require quite a spin on them."

April gave Jimmy another worshipful glance. "That's just it, Mom. They *are* different. Jimmy is making fast-food fragranced air fresheners!"

The only thing missing was a dramatic arm sweep.

This was such a difficult thing. Telling your kid how ridiculous an idea was without blowing your kid's self-confidence and optimism.

"That's certainly an interesting idea," I began. "How did you determine there was demand for such a product?"

Truly, why would people want the aroma of a greasy burger and fries lingering in their cars?

Jimmy looked at me incredulously. "Everyone likes fast food. Or at least everyone likes the *smell* of fast food." He nodded in April's direction as if it explained how vegetarians would also like his product.

"I see. How do you capture these aromas in an air freshener? What's the manufacturing process?" I surreptitiously checked my watch. I would need to pick up my animals soon.

Jimmy airily waved a hand. "You hire that part out. I just have to tell them what I want and they make it for me."

They? Who was *they?*

He continued, uttering more words in a single sentence than I'd ever heard before. "And I won't let Wal-Mart have a crack at them, I can tell you that. I'll put them at car washes and dealerships. They will be a big hit. And they won't cost a lot to produce so my profit margin will be really high. I should be a millionaire by this time next year."

Ah, the arrogance of youth. I couldn't burst the bubble, so I tried a different approach. "The offer is still open for you to come work at the safari. It might provide you with money to carry you until you become a millionaire."

He looked at me as if I'd offered him a dead rat. "That's dirty work. Manual labor."

"Mom," April said with exaggerated patience. "Jimmy

has to focus on his invention. Having a job at the same time will just make the process take longer."

Righto. Had April picked someone just like her father? If so, how could I complain? After all, I had picked her father.

As if reading my mind, April changed the subject to Mark. "By the way, Dad called me and said he was looking for his birth certificate. I went to the house, got it out of the safe, and sent it to him."

My daughter had the combination to my safe? That would require further discussion later.

"I didn't ask you in advance because I know you're mad at him—I am, too, what with his stupid arrest and then leaving us—but he has a right to the document."

I bit my tongue on what I thought of April's sudden imperiousness, particularly considering what I had done myself for Mark. "That's OK, I also sent him half the proceeds of a joint financial account."

Mark was getting his way with both wife and daughter without putting out much effort, it seemed.

With our meals finished, I said my goodbyes as April had decided to visit the carnival portion of the fair with the esteemed Jimmy. I retrieved my new animals, loading them by cage and rope into my trailer. I was beginning to think the beady-eyed rabbits were smarter than my daughter's boyfriend.

Turns out the bunnies were also better behaved than some of my neighbors, who soon rose up and threatened to destroy me.

CHAPTER 20

I WENT INTO OVERDRIVE getting the new Three Notch Safari ready to open. I was amazed by how much there was to do and found myself up before dawn to feed animals and not going to bed until nearly midnight every night.

The farm was a flurry of activity with an excavator clearing trees for new buildings, the Amish banging and sawing from dawn to dusk, a paving contractor creating a blue-chip parking lot and golf cart paths, and a fencing company erecting new pastures and enclosures for me.

Some of the neighbors wandered over to watch the progress, with most of them eyeing everything suspiciously. I can't say as I blamed them. I already had an inordinate number of animals, then we'd had Mark's arrest drama, and now intense construction suggesting I was perhaps building a new town in my neighborhood.

I was as polite as possible with my neighbors, but I was so consumed with everything going on it was difficult to spend much time assuaging them that Three Notch Safari would be a benefit to the neighborhood.

Among other activities, I registered the business name with the state and county, ordered checks, and found a designer to build a website. I also hired a graphic artist to make business cards and flyers.

"What sort of background do you want?" Lisa, the graphic artist, asked me.

I thought on it. "Can you make a collage of animals

against a farmhouse backdrop? Llamas, miniature cows, and goats?"

I considered my previous conversation with Bear and Donna about what I might buy in the future. "And maybe a sheep. And a peacock."

Lisa frowned. "That's a lot of animals, but okay."

"Oh, and a fighter jet in the corner. This is St. Mary's County so it needs a fighter jet on it."

Lisa seemed doubtful but went on to design a fantastic logo and other materials that I passed on to the website designer for inspiration.

Now I was starting to feel a little prepared.

I tackled having a road sign made and designing branded materials for the shop.

Porta-potties and other supplies were delivered. I received word that my ten golf carts were ready for delivery and I instructed that they be delivered to the custom car wrap company so that the new Three Notch Safari logo could be placed on all of them.

It was all nerve-wracking and exhilarating at the same time. My stomach did perpetual somersaults and I could never decide if it was fear or excitement causing them.

As for her part, Mom was subtly sharing her irritation with me at every opportunity. I truly didn't want her to feel bad about what I was doing, yet I was also irritated that she wouldn't support me.

I also realized her dementia impacted her thought processes and I couldn't stay mad at her.

Mom sat on a porch rocking chair one storm-threatening morning, arms crossed as she watched me directing a multitude of contractors and delivery people. I noticed a man walking up my driveway from out of nowhere. I was hardly presentable, with my hair falling out of hastily placed clips and my jeans and boots filthy from walking through construction debris.

It was Dickie Walker, one of my neighbors who lived

further past me on the road. I waved. "Hey, Dickie. Come to see my progress?"

As he neared, I saw that Dickie was scowling and had a bulge in his lower right jaw. He wore his customary light blue denim dungarees over a short-sleeved plaid shirt and his head was topped with a John Deere baseball cap. The only fashion change I ever saw Dickie make was to switch out a short-sleeved plaid shirt for long sleeves around the end of October.

Dickie and his wife, Nancy, lived in a tiny rambler on about twenty wooded acres and had enough 'trespassers will be shot' signs posted on it to scare even the most intrepid intruder.

"Heard about you on the radio and been hearing you ever since," he opened, throwing out an arm to indicate the beehive of activity on my property.

Uh-oh.

"Sorry about that," I replied, feeling genuinely contrite that I hadn't taken my neighbors' feelings more seriously. "It will be completed soon, within the next couple of weeks."

Dickie crossed his arms in front of him. Now I had both him and my mother in aggressive stances. "And you think that fixes it for everyone, young lady?"

It had been a long time since anyone had called me young lady, but I didn't think that in this instance it was flattery.

"The noise won't be anything more than the bleating, neighing, and huffing my animals have always done," I said.

"You must think I am stupid, Miz Garvey. You are dropping a tourist attraction right here in the middle of Hollywood. Are you out of your mind? I'll have to tolerate carloads of families coming up and down the road, whooping and hollering over your animals?"

I was quickly growing uncomfortable. "Mr. Walker, I

hardly think there will be that kind of commotion. Just a few people here and there riding on quiet golf carts through my property to visit and feed animals."

Dickie Walker's response was to spit a particularly nasty bit of tobacco juice from his jaw to the ground. I tried not to shudder.

"That's not how it's going to be and you know it. These visitors—and I bet a lot of them won't even be from the county—will be tearing up the road, throwing garbage out their windows, and their kids will be screeching up a storm." He was working himself up into a fury. However, he did have a point about the road.

"I assure you that I will take care of re-paving our main road every three years. Would that help?" Did every three years even make sense? I made a mental note to check this with my paving company.

"No!" he stormed. "What would make it better is if you abandoned this foolish idea. I find it insulting that you didn't even consult your neighbors before pushing forward with it. It's rude and intolerable. I assure you that everyone else on the road feels the same way."

I tried a different approach, one that I hoped would garner his sympathy. "Mr. Walker, my husband recently left, and I find myself needing to support not just my home, but my aging mother." I waved back toward where Mom still sat on the porch, only now her arms weren't crossed, she was instead leaning forward as if hoping to hear my conversation from that far away.

Dickie Walker did not thaw at all at the news. "Why'd he leave you? Didja deserve it? Maybe he was tired of your animals."

The man wasn't entirely wrong but I wasn't about to let him know that.

"Regardless, I am in a financially precarious position and this safari I am building will help me stay afloat. Surely you can appreciate that." I tried to make my expression winsome but that's not really something I'm good at.

He stared at me stonily so I tried something else. "I would be happy to offer you and your wife—in fact, everyone along the road—permanent complimentary admission to the safari. It would be a great place to bring children and grandchildren for their birthdays." Who could refuse a nice offer like that?

"I don't want free admission to your dadgum safari," he shot back. "I don't even want it to exist; why the hell would I want free admission to it? Let me tell you, you better rethink what you're doing here."

With that, Mr. Walker turned and stomped off back toward his property.

Now I had not just my mother, but the entire neighborhood against me.

Which was nothing compared to the county coming after me.

CHAPTER 21

I RESOLVED TO ASSUAGE my neighbors by delivering flyers to each doorstep, offering them permanent complimentary access to the farm and also assuring them that I would take care of keeping the road in pristine condition.

I had no idea if I could even afford that much paving, but what else could I do?

I also offered my phone number in case anyone wanted to talk to me about it. None of the neighbors responded at all, so I had to move forward as though Mr. Walker was just a singularly disgruntled man and I didn't have anything over which to worry.

As everything came together, I still needed to quickly stock the safari with more animals. Fortunately, I had much more barn and stable space now.

I made a run to the Calvert County Fair and bought several lambs, praying I wouldn't come to regret it. Sheep needed a lot of work to keep them clean and groomed.

To my surprise, T-Bone and Heather were set up at this fair, too. I waved to them and they called me over, inquiring about the status of Three Notch Safari.

When I told them I was nearly prepared for the November first opening, I was shocked when T-Bone turned his microphone toward me, plopped his headphones over my ears, and Heather began interviewing me live on the air.

It was terrifying, but Heather gently guided me

through some easy questions about the safari, and pretty soon I warmed up to talking about it. In fact, I couldn't *stop* talking about my safari.

The disc jockey let me ramble a bit, then interrupted to tell the audience to be sure to attend my grand opening on November first.

November first. The date was coming at me like a freight train.

I hustled the sheep home and was on my computer looking for exotic animal auctions when I heard the doorbell ring, which of course set Daisy off. That was strange because people—even strangers—rarely rang the bell, they typically just banged on the storm door.

And people I knew well often just walked in, an act that irritated me. I always cautioned people that they risked getting a hole blown through them that way, but no one paid any attention to me.

I reluctantly got up from what I was doing and found a petite woman in a lime green pantsuit at the door. I mean, the color was blinding. I almost missed the thick-soled, white sneakers she wore with them. The rectangular badge pinned to her upper right chest announced her name as Leslie Alexander from the Farms and Festivals Department. In her hand was an old-fashioned clipboard with multiple pages attached beneath the metal clip.

"I'm here to inspect your agricultural tourism business prior to opening," she said without preamble as I greeted her.

Daisy stepped outside to perform her own greeting, namely sniffing intently at one garishly green leg.

"Oh," I said. "But I'm not quite ready to open yet. I'm still purchasing animals and I'm sure you can see that my buildings are still under construction."

I guessed the woman standing on the porch to be a little older than me. Her hair, which I imagined was once a vibrant red, was now faded and heavily streaked with gray. She wore it back tightly in a bun. I wondered if she had a headache.

Leslie nodded impatiently as if I were offering an excuse. Or maybe her headache was bothering her. "Consider this an interim inspection. Please show me around."

I shrugged. "Suit yourself." I stepped outside to join her on the porch and led the way down. Never one to be left out, Daisy loped behind us and stayed close on our heels.

I showed Ms. Alexander around, much as I had the Amish crew. In this case, however, I wasn't working with someone cooperative.

"I don't like the way you've done the fencing. People won't be able to get close enough to the birds to see them," Leslie said as we approached the half-constructed avian enclosure.

Her attitude felt like sandpaper against my skin. "I see. Are you telling me I am violating county rules?"

Leslie frowned. "No, I suppose not." She seemed disappointed. "It's just not what I would have done. I also think it isn't going to be a good environment for hawks. If you plan to apply for permits for any, I mean."

I showed the inspector the goats, the llamas, and my two adorable mini-cows.

To my delight, I noticed that Clarabelle was seemingly chewing on nothing. "Do you see that?" I asked, pointing and refraining from jumping up and down with excitement.

"See what?"

"Clarabelle. My cow. I think she's re-digesting. That means she's growing up!" Leslie looked askance at me. Clearly, she had no bovine experience. Yet here she was, inspecting my operation.

As cows mature, they digest their food, then re-digest

it again. It's like a two-fer on their meals. It was a signal to me that my cows, tiny as they were, were reaching another stage of development.

I also showed Leslie the horses, inviting her into all the structures, both existing and half-finished, and explaining how the golf cart trail would work.

"Your golf cart charging station is too far away from your gift shop," she said.

"No one will be able to see the large animals from the road," she said.

"It's going to be too inconvenient for people to have to go into the gift shop to buy animal treats," she said.

On and on it went. The inspector seemed to hate everything.

What had I done to annoy her? I wasn't a total stranger to inspectors since I had had a couple of barns and other outbuildings constructed in the past. They could sometimes be very particular, but I had rarely experienced one so outright hostile.

As we returned to the house, I decided I wasn't inviting her in, but instead walked her to her car. "I understand your concerns," I said. I didn't. "But am I doing anything *illegal*?"

At first, Leslie seemed uncomfortable, but then it was as if she gathered strength and was mad.

"Ms. Garvey, please understand that the county is here to *protect you*." Leslie opened her driver's side car door, tossed the clipboard across to the passenger seat, and reached down to the driver's side floor, producing a pair of tan sandals that were a much better match to her pantsuit.

She sat sideways in the driver's seat with her legs out of the car as she switched shoes.

"You're fortunate that you have *me* conducting your inspection, as I myself have opened an alpaca farm and can advise you better than almost anyone else."

Leslie wiggled her toes inside the first sandal placed on her right foot. Her toenails were carefully sculpted and painted bright orange. What a combo with the pantsuit.

"I'm afraid I'm going to have to fail you," she said as she put on the second sandal. That done, she stood back up out of the car. "So sorry. But you will need to plant some trees and bushes to replace some of the vegetation you have mowed over. I can come back and inspect again."

Leslie Alexander did not seem sorry at all. I swear it seemed to give her joy.

She reached back into the car, grabbed the clipboard, and began scratching furiously on the top sheet of paper. That done, she pulled it out and handed it to me.

She had scrawled a list of the number of trees and shrubs I would be required to plant. It was a ridiculous number of them and I had not budgeted for it.

"Ms. Alexander, my safari is opening up in days," I explained, holding up the paper in disbelief.

"I certainly didn't complain about planting a few things here and there for my alpaca farm," Leslie replied with a sniff. "I did what I had to do. Perhaps you aren't ready for 'prime time,' as they say."

I took a deep breath. Getting into an argument with a local official was not going to help the situation.

"I am ready," I said slowly. "I just wasn't expecting to have to do some ridic—I just didn't expect that I would have the expense of tree planting when they don't seem to matter to the safari's operation."

"Is that so?" Leslie said. "Well, they do. You'll have to get it done before you can open. I will, of course, be back to inspect again and hopefully, I won't find anything else wrong." She slid into the driver's seat and started her engine.

As it roared to life, a realization hit me. I rapped on the window and she lowered it. I leaned my elbow on the open ledge of the door. "Ms. Alexander, do you by any chance have plans for your own property beyond that of just an alpaca farm?"

She reddened. "I'm not sure what you're implying, Ms. Garvey, but I don't like it. But I can tell you that in looking around here, it's obvious that your so-called 'safari' is never going to make it here in St. Mary's County."

With that, she pushed a button to roll up the window, forcing me to step back. She backed all the way down my driveway and tore down the road toward Three Notch Road.

As Leslie Alexander drove away, I saw her pull aside to let a long, flatbed trailer go past her. The trailer contained my gorgeously finished golf carts.

All with the name of the safari misspelled.

Everything seemed to go completely haywire at that point. I rejected the cart delivery and got on the phone with the car wrap people, who reluctantly agreed to take them back and fix them.

I then ran around like a chicken with its head cut off ordering birds for the aviary.

Ha, a chicken…an aviary. I kill me sometimes. If only everyone around me had a sense of humor.

I found a hatchery in Missouri that stated they had peafowl available June through August. A quick call to them snagged me a male and a female, leftovers that hadn't sold.

I knew peacocks could be noisy and the hatchery spent considerable time emphasizing that fact to me. Despite knowing that Dickie Walker was probably going to be even more riled up, I still ordered the chicks. The male would be gorgeous parading around and letting kids watch babies being hatched would be educational and fun for them, even if it would take the female two years to begin laying eggs.

I also found multiple breeders offering large parrots, like macaws and cockatoos, as well as an aviary in Maryland that had gorgeous, strikingly colored smaller birds from Australia, Africa, and South America.

Thank goodness, all of them offered great tips on setting up my aviary as they assured me I would receive birds safely and quickly.

Did I have enough to start? I hoped so.

The Amish were true to their word and finished in record time. I was particularly impressed with the barn-red painted gift shop, which wasn't huge, but not only had plenty of built-in shelf space, but room in the center for tables and chairs so that I could host indoor parties.

Trimmed out with black shutters and white doors, it was a welcoming sight to visitors.

April had jumped right in to help me order products for it, in addition to tables, chairs, a counter, and decor. For as much as my kid could drive me crazy, there were times when I just wanted to plant kisses all over her face.

Friends and neighbors started showing up unannounced, all expecting tours. As busy as I was, I figured it was all good publicity so I always dropped whatever I was going to show people around.

An unexpected benefit was that it helped me hone my visitor speech.

"Welcome to Three Notch Safari. We have a variety of animals for you to see and touch. You can either walk the paths or take a golf cart through our thirty acres of grounds. Photographers can capture your special moment..."

I was feeling nearly ecstatic over how everything was proceeding as I drove home one day from Southern States, my truck loaded with various bags of animal feed.

I clicked the turn signal and made my way onto my road, slowing in disbelief as I approached the farm.

My gorgeous gift shop had been covered in graffiti in multiple colors with a single message.

YOUR SAFARI NOT WANTED. STOP OR ELSE.

CHAPTER 22

I TREMBLED AS I sat in my car, drumming my fingers against the steering wheel as I stared at the defacement. Who the hell had done this?

The wording was accompanied by a crude spray painting of what appeared to be a lion.

In my troubled state, I considered how the vandal had no idea that it was illegal to own a lion in Maryland unless you were an actual zoo. And that made the vandal stupid. So there.

It had to have been Dickie Walker. Was he really that angry about what I was doing?

I guess my conciliatory flyer hadn't budged him in his opinion one bit. Come to think of it, he had not been among the myriad of people stopping by to look at what I was doing.

I would have to deal with Dickie, but first I had to get the building cleaned.

I put the car in reverse and drove to see Hiram, calling the insurance company on the way to report the vandalism. Hiram agreed to send a couple of men to re-paint the building right away and I promised to pay him as soon as the insurance company paid me.

While I was out, I went to Zimmerman's on Route 5 to pick out some trees to satisfy the county's planting requirement. What, was there not enough foliage in St. Mary's County that I had to buy a bunch of expensive specimen trees for my largely wooded property?

I sighed. It wasn't the worst thing that had happened

to me and if that made it so I would pass inspection, so be it.

An Amish gentleman helped me pick out a few tulip trees, some red maples, and even a couple of magnolia trees. He heaved them all into the back of my truck. The weight had me driving cautiously from Loveville to Hollywood through Amish country and down Three Notch Road.

Once home, I called Bear and asked if he and the boys could help plant them. He agreed to come the next day.

Finally, things were coming together.

Except that there were more angry people ready to do battle with me.

Lisa, the graphics artist, designed an amazing, full-color roadside sign for me, with a row of whimsical animals running along the bottom and "Three Notch Safari, Turn Here" above it. A sign company installed the large steel piece between two sturdy posts, adding a metal placard stating, *Opening November 1st!* The placard dangled via hooks at the bottom so that I could replace it with other future temporary announcements.

I stood in front of the sign now, admiring it as traffic whizzed by me on Three Notch Road. A few people honked and waved. I waved back, happy that people were noticing it.

Pleased that there were at least a few members of the community excited about the safari, I started walking back down the road toward my house.

A car came roaring up behind me, startling me and forcing me to jump onto the culvert to avoid it.

The car stopped suddenly next to me, sending a cloud of gravel dust into the air. I coughed as I made my way out of the culvert, intent on telling whatever teenager was driving to be more careful.

However, it was another of my neighbors, Mrs. Lomax, who lived further up the road near Dickie Walker. We didn't see her very often, since she only left her house to buy tequila or cigarettes at the Early Bird store. No one knew much about Carrie Lomax—whom everyone referred to by the honorific of Mrs. Lomax—except that she frequently raised her windows to yell at children, cats, and the occasional chirping bird.

When she did venture out, it was unsteadily on a cane. She also drove like she walked—all over the place.

Rumor had it that she had been married at least three—but maybe four—times, and twice to the same man, although she appeared to live alone now. It was also local gossip that she had been quite wild in her youth.

I guess we are all products of our own decision-making.

Mrs. Lomax rolled down her window, seemingly oblivious to the fact that she had nearly run me over and then sent me into a cloud of choking dust.

"What's that sign out on the main road?" she demanded without preamble.

I walked around to the passenger side of the car so that I had actual road to stand on. Mrs. Lomax was clearly irritated with having to roll down a second window.

"Well?" she said, glowering at me. I wasn't sure how old Carrie Lomax was, but her desiccated skin made her look like she had been born two centuries ago. Her long hair was gathered in a snowy braid down her back, schoolgirl-style, an odd juxtaposition against her skin.

I leaned over the car door, much as I had done with the county inspector, crossing my arms on the door ledge. "Is there a problem?" I asked.

"I seen all of the buildings you're putting up and the animals you got coming in on trailers. You can't have a zoo back here. Ain't right. These people will be blocking the road. I hafta be able to get in out for my—my—for my groceries. I tell you what, there are others who are going to be up in arms over it, too." She was getting quite worked up at the moment, a fleck of spittle appearing on her lips.

Maybe Carrie was worked up on her own, maybe she wasn't.

"Have you been talking to Dickie Walker by any chance?" I asked, keeping my tone neutral.

She flushed. "Maybe. That don't matter as I was planning to talk to you anyway. You ain't being neighborly, I can tell you that. First, it's animals, then it's cops, then it's big buildings."

That sent a pang into my stomach. Was I truly being a bad neighbor? I was doing everything in my power to keep the fuss to a minimum for the few neighbors that I had.

"Did you see the flyer I left in your door?" I asked.

She frowned. "What flyer? 'Deed I didn't. Did you put it at my front door? Everyone knows I always go out the back door. Only a fool would put it at the front door. I don't—"

Mrs. Lomax was lathering up again. I had to interrupt her train of thought. "My apologies, Mrs. Lomax. I want you to know that I am having our neighborhood road paved at my own expense, and I'm offering lifetime free admission to everyone on our road. Bring a friend or relative."

Mrs. Lomax sniffed at me, but it wasn't with her earlier vitriol. "Why would I attend some ding-danged event for snot-nosed kids? Why would any of us living back here want that?"

I noticed that Mrs. Lomax had a narrow brown paper bag and two packs of smokes in the passenger seat. I suspected that she simply didn't want anyone bothering her, and I was willing to bet that Dickie was bothering her daily far more than my safari was.

"I understand," I said, attempting to be conciliatory. "I'll do everything in my power to make the safari as peaceful and non-intrusive as possible."

"Yeah, okay," she said, glancing down at the passenger seat. She was probably anxious to get home with her purchases at this point, but I needed another moment of her time.

"By the way, did you notice that someone vandalized my new gift shop building?" I asked.

She shook her head in silence and shifted her gaze away from me.

Liar.

But I knew it wasn't rational to think that Carrie Lomax could have physically painted up the building. She could probably barely get from her car door to her front door. I mean, her back door.

My money was still on Dickie Walker as being the embedded burr under my saddle. I had no idea what to do about him, but I couldn't worry about it for the moment, for I was close to throwing open the proverbial doors to Three Notch Safari and an enormous surprise awaited me during the grand opening.

CHAPTER 23

I HARDLY SLEPT AFTER my encounter with Carrie Lomax. Every single day was consumed with animal husbandry, ordering animals and other supplies, and just generally getting ready.

April not only helped me with setting up the gift shop but also became my right hand. In fact, she started showing up every morning to roll up her sleeves alongside me. She even scoured the Marie and Nash vendor lists and arranged for some of them to make special products for the gift shop.

I again suggested to her that Jimmy might want to consider working at the safari until he managed his big break, but she insisted equally that he was right on the edge of becoming a millionaire.

How could my daughter be clear-headed in helping me with my business, but so obtuse about her boyfriend's?

I told her the offer would remain open and left it at that.

Dee Dee Boone showed up unannounced again one morning. As soon as I opened the door, I started apologizing. "I never called you with the name. I'm so sorry. I got so caught up in—"

Dee Dee waved a hand. "Not to worry. I saw the sign on Three Notch Road and thought I'd stop in to tell you that the name is brilliant. I love it. I can also see that you took care of the website, also fantastic. Now, what about those billboards?"

I wasn't sure I could afford them. After all, my loan

money seemed to be flowing out of my bank account like feed falling through a granary.

"You really think they'll work?" I asked as I invited her back into the kitchen for coffee. I was still dubious.

"Absolutely. I've been in touch with the billboard people and there are six prime locations I've identified between here and Waldorf that would be perfect for you. Don't think of it as an expense, think of it as an investment in your future." Dee Dee was so animated about her idea as she sat at the kitchen table while I got the coffee going that I didn't have the heart to say no.

Besides, I needed all the enthusiastic help I could get.

"Alright," I said, getting out large, mismatched mugs and spoons, sugar, and creamer. Looking at my "World's Greatest Mom" mug with its layers of staining inside, I made a mental note to have April order branded mugs and glasses for the shop.

I took everything to the table. "How much is this all going to cost me?"

What I can only describe as joy crossed Dee Dee's face. She went into great detail about how different billboards had different monthly rates, each had an installation fee, and that they needed to be up at least three months to do any good but she recommended a package deal to keep them all up for a year.

Yep, I was going to be broke for sure.

Nevertheless, I gave her the green light to arrange it all and she assured me they would be up in two weeks, following my approval of all the designs.

"Now," she added, her hands around her cup, "what are you doing for the grand opening? When promoting a property with an open house—which is really what you're doing—you need to do something to make the property stand out."

"Ummm." I took a gulp of coffee while I thought about it. "I thought I'd have some balloons and streamers and such. Maybe a deejay? Punch and cookies?" Why hadn't I put much planning into it before now?

Dee Dee sighed. "Becca, you need to think much bigger than that. Let's invite some local VIPs to speechify, which will draw the newspapers. Let everyone attend for free that day. And let's see…"

She put her coffee mug down and I saw that it had a small chip on the rim. If I ever made any money at this safari, I was going to treat myself to entire set of matching dishes.

But Dee Dee clearly didn't care about my well-worn cups. "How about a crab feast for a minimal charge, just a few dollars per person?" She clapped her hands together in delight at her own idea. "We could set up long rows of tables in the front yard. That would draw *tons* of people."

"Uh, Dee Dee, you know how much crabs cost, right?" I said, wondering if my money would even last until opening day if all her ideas were implemented.

She held up a hand. "Don't worry about a thing. Kip Hewitt offers the best prices and crabs are running well right now, so they'll be cheaper anyway. I know Kip and I'm sure I can get a bargain. He and his wife, Raleigh, have two young children. Maybe you can offer the family free admission for a year in exchange for a super sweet deal on crabs?"

How could I say no to that?

Dee Dee made a few more minor suggestions to which I agreed, then she signaled a turn in the conversation by pushing her coffee mug completely away from her. I quickly swept it away and put it in the sink with an eye to throwing it into the trash can after she left. I rejoined her at the kitchen table.

"So," she said, and I could tell she was trying to find appropriate words, "how are things going with, you know, Mark? Has he come to his senses?"

I laughed without mirth. "You mean he once had senses? I'm afraid I've only talked to him one time and it ended up in an argument. But I'm fine, I really am."

It was funny how the excitement and busyness of the safari had left me with no room to mourn Mark's departure. Truthfully, I felt more at peace than I had in a long time now that I didn't have to worry about what he was doing—or not doing—all the time.

She nodded. "I'm glad you're doing well. What happened to you must have been very shocking. When John and I broke up, it certainly wasn't the bomb-dropping Mark did on you, but I learned that he had run up a bunch of credit cards on who-knows-what prior to our marriage and never told me about it. He had also told me he had millions in his retirement account and that we would be very comfortable one day. That turned out to be very untrue, he had saved nothing. There was no surviving all that deceit. Once the lies start, you look for them around every corner."

Dee Dee shook her head as if to clear the memory and reached across the table, covering my hand with her own.

"Maybe you think it's too soon," she said, and I could tell she was forming her words awkwardly, "but have you talked to a divorce lawyer?"

I was uncomfortable. I wasn't sure I wanted to discuss thoughts of permanent dissolution with a new friend. "I...um...I don't..." Now I was the one who was awkward.

Dee Dee removed her hand from mine and nodded. "I understand. And I apologize, I was out of bounds to even ask. Not to push my luck with you, but let me offer a piece of advice if I may."

I nodded at her, and she gave me another sympathetic look as if apologizing in advance for what she was about to say.

"My advice is that you need to get legally protected as soon as possible," she said to me. "When things like this happen, it's not likely that there will be reconciliation. Don't leave yourself open to financial hardship."

I nodded, unwilling to think too much about it. After all, Mark had only been gone a few weeks. Wait, had it been longer? I mentally calculated. No, he had actually been in Florida for nearly three months.

It was probably time to start finalizing a relationship that had really been over much longer. I would do so as soon as possible.

After the grand opening.

My cell phone chirped a special signal, letting me know that mail had been delivered at my box.

"Do you mind waiting while I go check mail?" I said to Dee Dee.

"Nope, as long as you don't mind if I have one of these glazed doughnuts." She nodded toward the bakery box on the counter.

"Have as many as you like," I said as I slipped out of the house and walked down to the road to retrieve mail. My box was in the shape of a cow. You pulled its tail to open its mouth to drop in or take out mail. It was a goofy gift Mark had bought after I'd brought home Doodlebug, my first farm animal.

I pulled the metal tail and was shocked to find an entire stack of mail, inches thick. There seemed to be a few bills and catalogs in there, but most of them were cards and letters hand-addressed to me personally. What in the world...?

Maybe they were notes of encouragement regarding Three Notch Safari. I lifted the corners of a few of the envelopes. The postmarks were all from St. Mary's County towns—Mechanicsville, Chaptico, Leonardtown, Lexington Park, St. Mary's City, and the like.

My heart rose in my chest as I considered how perfect strangers were rallying behind me and my enterprise.

I carefully dragged the stack out of the mailbox and carried it back to the house.

Mom had awakened and was eating doughnuts with Dee Dee. Mom's hair was tied back in a ribbon and she wore her long, purple velvet dressing gown. She never looked more like a queen than she did when in that gown.

Dee Dee was in the middle of telling my mother about the plans for billboards in the county. Mom's grim expression as she broke off pieces of her doughnut told me she wasn't impressed with the notion.

Dee Dee stopped her story as I set the pile of mail in the middle of the kitchen table.

Mom's expression didn't change. "Your birthday was in August. When that tiresome man left—"

"I don't think they're birthday cards, Mom. I think they might be notes of congratulations from the community." I pulled the top envelope, which was heart-red. Perhaps it was a Valentine's Day-like message of love.

I slid a finger under the flap and proceeded to mangle the envelope while opening it. Which is what happens when you don't have nice fingernails but instead have ragged-edged, unmanicured fingertips that spend most of their time in hay, feed, or animal hair.

The card had a pretty autumn farm scene on the front of it. What a lovely nod to my own property.

I opened the card to read the message, scrawled in blue ink. I had to read it three times to comprehend the words in front of me.

Rebeckah Garvey,

I heared about your safari. You ain't belonging here if you're going to create such an eyesore and RUIN our county.

Go back to wherever you came from and do sumfin useful with your life.

It was unsigned.

CHAPTER 24

DICKIE WALKER WAS at it again, I was sure of it. I might know who was responsible for it, but it didn't make me feel any better. I stared at the words until they blurred before my eyes, contemplating what I could do to calm the man down.

"What does it say?" Dee Dee asked, interrupting my thoughts.

I read the card aloud, to include the bad spelling. The words hung in the air as Dee Dee gasped.

"WHAT?" Mom demanded, pushing aside the plate containing her doughnut crumbs. "Someone wants you to be his wife? Doesn't he know you're still married to that awful toad?"

Dee Dee giggled involuntarily and quickly bit her lip. "Sorry," she mouthed at me.

I smiled. Dee Dee had lightened the mood, if just for a moment.

"No, Mom, no one is proposing. Someone just isn't happy with my safari."

My mother's self-satisfied smirk wasn't subtle. Nor was the way she now crossed her arms.

Dee Dee seemed to notice it, too. "That was just one card. I'm sure the rest are much better." She took the next one, which was just a regular long envelope.

Her beautifully polished index fingernail slid cleanly under the seal. Dee Dee glanced at the contents of the single sheet of ruled, three-hole notebook paper, then quietly folded it and put it back in the envelope.

"Maybe we should look at another one," she said.

At that point, the two of us began grabbing envelopes and opening them. Every card or letter I touched, and I mean *every single one*, was some sort of attack against Three Notch Safari or me personally.

It was horrifying.

Dee Dee must have been reading the same sort of vitriol that I was for she refused to read anything aloud and instead folded every card or paper back up and placed it back in its envelop. One sheet she crumpled up completely before tossing it onto the pile. That one must've been a doozy.

She stopped and put a hand on top of her pile of opened letters. "Is this the first time this has happened to you?" she asked.

"Yes," I said tightly, caught between fury and dismay. "I've had a little trouble with one of my neighbors and I thought he might have been riling up some of the others along this road, but this looks like he's been waging a political campaign against me."

We returned to the envelopes, but I stopped halfway through the pile. This was insane. "Enough," I said, standing up and tossing my opened envelopes back into the pile before grabbing Dee Dee's stack and placing it with the others.

I pawed through it all. Not a single one of them had a return address. No one was brave enough to put a face on his or her venom.

I sank back in my chair. Was I going to continue receiving mail like this? Worse, would it escalate into something else?

In that moment, I felt even angrier than I had when Mark had made his life-changing announcement.

Mom might not have been able to hear much, but she clearly understood what had just happened and was happy to offer her opinion. "This is yet another omen,

Becca, and the omens are piling up higher than your little stack there. When are you going to listen?"

Dee Dee sat up straight. "Omens?" she asked loudly. "What do you mean, Mrs.—?"

My mother had just been given the opportunity to discuss the dead goshawk and her 'heart attack'. She gave it to Dee Dee in full technicolor detail.

"And now this." Mom waved a hand dramatically over the table. "But Becca won't listen to me. The girl is stubborn."

Dee Dee flashed me a sympathetic glance and I was immediately grateful for her sensitive reaction.

"You've had some harrowing experiences. I know they would have frightened me and so I'm sure they have made you very concerned, Mrs.—"

"You can call me Georgie, dear." My mother actually reached over and patted Dee Dee on the hand. Dee Dee had unknowingly worked her way into Mom's affections by giving credence to her story.

Although I appreciated Dee Dee's intent in indulging my mother, I knew this would quickly head into dangerous territory.

"Mom, you know I'm doing all I can to keep this household afloat, and doing so might mean that I do things that make you unhappy." I knew I sounded caustic, but I couldn't add my mother's superstitions to my swelling list of things to worry over.

Mom bit right back at me. "I'm not *unhappy*, I'm *perceptive*. You should appreciate my warnings more. I've been on this planet far longer than you have and I know bad omens when I see them."

"Omens," I huffed. "You think I—"

"I have an idea," Dee Dee said brightly, preventing me from saying something I would surely regret. "Georgie, I need to stop by a waterfront mansion I've listed so I can put an open house sign in the yard. I could really use your help in sensing whether there are any bad omens in the house. Would you like to go with me?"

Dee Dee surreptitiously winked at me.

Mom sat up straighter. "You need my help? Of course, I'll help you, dear. I'll need my hat."

Mom rose from the table and walked out of the room faster than I had ever seen her do. She re-emerged in mere moments, dressed for the day and wearing her purple pillbox hat, only this time there was a pin in the shape of a rose attached to the side. She also had her purse dangling from her right arm.

"Ready," Mom said and walked to the kitchen door.

"I'll have her home by midnight," Dee Dee told me, winking again. "I know it's a school night."

I played along. "Mom, don't forget you have to finish your homework when you get back."

"WHAT? I have to bet on a jack? Are we going to a casino?" Mom cupped her left ear with her free hand.

"Never mind," I responded, waving her out the door.

Once they left, I scooped up all of the envelopes, dropped them into an old grocery bag, and carried the bag into my room, tossing it onto the shelf above the rack in the closet.

I was exhausted and decided to close my eyes on the couch for fifteen minutes or so to gather strength in the unexpected peace and quiet for all the remaining tasks I had to do.

Naturally, I was just dozing off when my phone rang. My nap was ruined by a very unpleasant caller.

"April tells me that you're opening some sort of fancy safari and I wanted to wish you luck," said the unwanted and unnaturally sprightly voice.

"Yes," I responded. "Thanks."

There was an awkward silence for several moments then Mark cleared his throat. "You must be really busy."

"Yes." Did Mark really believe I was going to get chatty with him about it? I felt a headache emerging near the base of my neck.

"I'm sure it will be a hit. You're so good with the animals. They'll be well-behaved and the guests will love them. Which reminds me, I got a job at the Fairwinds Resort, teaching guests how to surf. I start tomorrow. The management there is already impressed—" I tuned out as Mark waxed eloquent about his surfing and teaching skills.

I returned to my bedroom and fired up my laptop as he continued inundating me with details about his new job. I set my cell phone to speaker and put it on the desk next to me as I got on the internet and idly did a search on Three Notch Safari.

To my surprise, an article popped up on upcoming happenings in the area and my farm—sorry, safari—was mentioned as 'highly anticipated'.

My heart soared. Funny how you can go from a terrible low to an amazing high in the space of hours.

"...so you should be able to turn a profit pretty quickly, right?"

Just like that, my heart plummeted down into my chest.

"Sorry, what?" I said.

"The safari. I'm guessing you didn't have to invest much beyond a few animals, so you should be in the black in no time. That'll be great, huh?"

I couldn't help it, I lashed out. "Great? Great for whom? For me? I'm doing this nearly alone while you're off enjoying sun and sand. I have responsibility for my mother, the farm, and all of the bills you walked away from. Not that it isn't completely worth it to have you gone. I—"

"Hey, hey, calm down," Mark interjected. "I just wanted to congratulate you on what I know will be a great success. I also wanted to point out that because I was willing to take a risk to pursue my dream, you are now able to pursue yours."

I couldn't believe what I was hearing. "Do you ever recall my saying that opening the farm up to tourists was a *dream* of mine?"

"Not exactly, but you must admit that the farm itself was your dream and it was costing me—I mean us—a lot of money every month. Now you have a better way to not just support it but to earn profit. I'm proud of you." His tone was a little too slick for my comfort. I wondered what sort of tripe his smarmy brother, Jake, was stuffing into his head.

"So, you're proud of me. Understood and acknowledged." If he thought I was going to thank him for praising me for clawing my way out of the hole he had tossed me in, he was plumb out of his mind.

"I really am. I just wish you would give me a little credit in return for how I helped make this happen. If not for me, you would still be carrying on in your previously boring routine. Now you will be an independent woman of means."

Now I understood why he had called.

"Are you fishing for money, Mark Garvey? And do you seriously think this is costing me next to nothing? I owe the credit union enough to finance the building of another branch for them."

I was being dramatic, but dear Lord, the man drove me into being someone unrecognizable.

"Of course you do," he replied soothingly, as if I were a toddler who had just fallen and scraped my knee. "But that's only temporary, Reb, and surely you will be profitable within a year. It's only right that I be compensated for my part in your success."

I swear, in that moment I couldn't decide whether to turn on him like a howitzer at the Battle of Gettysburg or to simply start cackling hysterically.

Given that both options would only reflect badly on me, I took a deep breath and went a completely different route, shock and awe.

"Perhaps you're right. Dee Dee Boone has been helping me promote the safari and believes I can be a main tourist attraction in St. Mary's County."

There was dead silence on the other end of the line. I know it was petty, but I felt joy in knowing I had hit the bullseye.

Mark coughed as though he had swallowed something wrong. "You're dragging my co-workers into this?" he choked out.

"Not your co-workers," I replied sweetly. "Your *ex* co-workers. Dee Dee offered to put her realtor skills to use for me. She's a nice gal. I consider her a friend now. She even plans to be at the grand opening."

More silence. I almost felt sorry for Mark as he tried to piece together what had happened in his absence. Whatever it was that he figured out, it made him angry.

"You have no right to drag *my* friends into helping you out. They should be—they should remain—neutral. I don't want you making up stuff about me and then spreading gossip to my friends. You don't—"

"But Mark," I interjected, "I don't have to make up anything. Your own words and actions speak for themselves."

Mark was nearly sputtering in rage. "I'm hanging up and calling Dee Dee right now to tell her to stop working with you."

"What? And have me potentially lose all that profit she will help me earn? Don't be silly."

"You are a horrible woman, Rebecca Marie Garvey.

You deserved for me to leave you. I'm going to make sure your safari belongs to *me* one day."

The line was dead. Maybe Dee Dee was right and it *was* time to call a lawyer.

CHAPTER 25

I PROBABLY SHOULD HAVE been more worried about Mark's threat than I was, but I still had so much to do to prepare for the grand opening that I just shoved him into the tiny recess of my brain I had reserved for him and got back to business.

My miniature cows were so ridiculously cute that I just wanted to cover them with kisses every time I brought them out of their spacious pen in the new barn. The two reds, whom I named Elsie and Babe, were very amenable to training, and I quickly had them adjusted to a lead and harness. Even more quickly, they soon followed me everywhere sans the lead rope. They loved going after my legs with their giant black tongues as though I were a salt lick. That took some training to get them to stop since I wore shorts while working with the animals in all but the coldest months and wasn't going to stop for a slobbery cow.

However, Clarabelle, the Holstein, was more resistant to the training. "Stubborn little mule," I told her one day. She stared back at me as if to transmit I was not going to win the war of wills.

"Little lady," I said, "you are not in charge here."

In response, she walked off, while Elsie showed up from out of nowhere for a quick tongue bath of my right leg.

Clarabelle may have taken a little more time to learn who was boss, but she really was the most adorable of the three. And once all three became attuned to my vocal commands and noises, they quickly learned tricks, such as bowing their heads for applause.

My llamas were already quite pliable and only needed a little bit of coaxing—and a treat or two—to line up in a row along their fence line and perform what I would call some simple dance moves to familiar children's tunes. Buck-toothed Doodlebug really got into it, waving his head back and forth to the music.

What a nut. Nothing—not even family and friends—could bring me peace the way my animals could.

Kenny, Reba, and Randy didn't require much. They couldn't be ridden, but I knew they would be good on leads so I would teach kids how to manage horses by walking them around and giving them treats.

I was a little nervous about some of the goats head-butting people, so I decided that any of them that gave me hesitation would remain way behind their fence line, but I would let a few of them out to be petted by visitors.

It required quite a bit of networking and research, but I found a bird trainer with the Patuxent Bird Club who lived in northern Calvert and was willing to drive down three days a week to work with my new birds.

Simon Rhodes was particularly excited that I was bringing in babies so that he could begin handling them right away.

I concluded upon first meeting Simon that he was a bit of an odd duck—a bad pun, I know. A middle-aged man, he was dressed like a British schoolboy, with charcoal gray shorts and long black socks and shoes, topped by a jacket and a tweed button-top cap.

When I saw him exit his car dressed like that, I was momentarily panicked by his appearance. However, he soon set me at ease with his ready, gapped-tooth smile, gregarious nature, and his expansive knowledge of nearly every known type of bird in the country.

"Let's see our little fellas, yeah?" Simon said.

I took him to the aviary area and he nodded in approval. To my surprise, he went straight into the aviary and began unlocking cages to handle the various birds.

"Ah, you're goin' for the peacocks, yeah?" he said as he opened a cage, not speaking to me but to the mostly featherless birds, who looked like little plucked chickens at this stage.

"These two have names?" he asked me.

When I said they didn't, he asked permission to name everything in the aviary, which I gladly let him do.

Simon may have presented himself oddly, but there was no denying that he understood birds. The chicks were literally flapping and jumping to be closer to him.

I also realized that that jacket protected Simon from drippy bird poop and that he hid treats in the inner pockets of it.

He was quick to advise me on nutritional needs for my little feathered friends and he also provided me with a list of items he needed for training the larger birds.

After that first day, I gave him his own key to the aviary and told him to come whenever he wanted, while also telling him when the safari would open.

He promised to have an educational program ready a month after the grand opening.

I was so busy with everything else that I had left April largely to herself to arrange and stock the gift shop. I went in one day to see what she had done and was amazed. It was so...homey. I was immediately struck by the fragrance of a wood-burning fireplace, which turned out to be wafting from several cleverly hidden air fresheners. Shelves and racks were chock full of both branded and non-branded items, everything from stoneware coffee mugs and t-shirts to baby bibs and tote bags, not to mention party supplies and kids' games.

She also managed packaged soaps, candles, candies, and treats from local vendors. There was even an "all-natural" corner of the shop where she had set up the stuff she liked—crystals, affirmation cards, and the like. For a starting effort, it was amazing.

April blushed at my effusive praise. "You talked about how much you liked Marie and Nash, so I went and got inspiration from them. They really get the credit."

I loved that my daughter was being so modest about her accomplishments. And I truly loved that she wanted to be part of this with me. Having her at my side made me feel like we were on the road to being a dynamic mother-daughter team, like Angie and Tyler at Marie and Nash.

But I asked her about Jimmy, and, alas, she still believed he was on the verge of being a millionaire.

Things had also been going well with my mother. Mom had raved about her outing with Dee Dee, claiming that she had been responsible for letting Dee Dee know that the house she was trying to sell was all clear of omens.

Poor Dee Dee. I appreciated her taking Mom out the way she had.

As modest as April was being, Mom's chest was puffed out like that of my male peacock, whom Simon had named Lapis for his strikingly blue neck. "At least Dee Dee listens to me when I give valuable advice. You would do well to do the same."

"OK, Mom."

The next morning, though, I went on my feeding rounds with Daisy and nearly lost my breath in terror to see a strange figure standing among the llamas in their pen.

As I adjusted my eyes to the early dawn light, I realized who it was.

"Mom?" I asked tentatively. What was she doing with the animals? She detested them.

She clearly hadn't heard me and was now stroking Ladybug's neck and murmuring to her.

Had I entered some strange new dimension where my mother liked farm animals?

"MOM!" I said, much louder this time.

She whirled around, guilt stamped all over her face.

"What are you doing out here?" I asked.

"Nothing, I'm just visiting." Her tone was petulant, but I couldn't argue with what she was doing. If she wanted to interact with the llamas, it was good for both her and the animals.

Mom's expression changed as if she'd thought of something. "I had to come out and visit. I realized you were neglecting your animals and I needed to check them for myself. Shame on you."

"What?" was the only response I could formulate. Not only did she find my farm animals distasteful, but she was also second only to Mark in resenting the inordinate amount of time I spent with them.

Mom nodded. "You need a firm hand, girl. You should listen to your mother."

Giving Ladybug a final pat, she strode past me and back to the house.

What was my mother up to?

Shaken, I spent the next hour in the horse barn, brushing and rubbing them all down until my nerves finally settled down.

I was close to a panic attack by opening day, but the outpouring of help was gratifying. I had April, Bear, Donna, the boys, Michelle, Dee Dee, and of course, Simon, all positioned at various stations. Even my mother, who had refused to say anything further about why she was out with the llamas, had ventured out to assist April in the gift shop.

Dee Dee was true to her word and worked out a deal with Kip Hewitt for crabs, which were stacked in bushel containers at each end of the long set of red-checked cloth-draped tables.

Mr. Hewitt came to me once he had unloaded basket after basket of crabs from his paneled truck emblazoned with *Hewitt's Seafood* down the side to let me know that the bill was all taken care of and that he and his wife would be back later to visit the safari themselves.

Dee Dee had also had a political convention's worth of balloons in every color imaginable brought in and tied to every available surface. If anything shouted, 'The party is HERE!' it was my farm.

By the time the grand opening magical time of ten o'clock in the morning arrived, I was on the verge of tears from both exhaustion and gratitude.

Not only that, by around nine o'clock, cars were lining up on the road leading to my entrance. Billy came running up to me breathlessly. "Aunt Becca, I went to the end of the line. The cars are waiting on the shoulder of Three Notch Road!"

I couldn't help it, the tears started to flow and I dashed into the house to compose myself.

There may have been a jerk or two trying to ruin me, but I could also count on the good people of St. Mary's County to see me through.

At nine-thirty, I decided not to make people wait any longer. Confirming everyone was ready, I signaled to Bear, who was on parking duty and blocking anyone from entering, to let people in.

More than one enormous surprise was waiting for me.

CHAPTER 26

VISITORS BEGAN POURING in and there were myriad problems for me to work out. Among other things, it wasn't obvious that people should enter the gift shop to buy tickets, the golf carts were positioned too far away from the start of the path and there wasn't a clear-cut division between where golf carts should go and where people should walk.

Everything else worked itself out and guests didn't seem to be angry for long.

A fancy, dark blue minibus with tinted windows pulled in and the driver had some quick conversation with Bear, who pointed toward a separate area further down the road.

I watched in fascination as the driver guided the bus away and then pulled off to the edge of the woods, expertly turning the vehicle around so that it was now pointing nose out. The door opened and the occupants stepped out.

I couldn't believe it. Out of the bus came all five of our county's commissioners.

Before I could even take a step toward them, Michelle appeared next to me from out of nowhere, her camera to her eye as she clicked away in a rapid-fire manner, capturing the procession of our county officials toward the gift shop.

Just as I had the notion that perhaps I should give them complimentary admission, I watched as Donna scurried to the gift shop door from where she had been standing with the miniature ponies, showing kids how to lead them.

Donna was vigorously waving her hands "no" at the commissioners and they were shaking their heads just as emphatically as they stepped around her into the shop, with Michelle close on their heels.

They were determined to pay their way.

I forgot about them as I got wrapped up in the happy chaos around me. A child got frightened by one of the macaws squawking loudly close to her ear. I ran to the house and found some cookies, which distracted the child and satisfied her mother.

Kenny pooped a good pile and an adult stepped square into it. With profuse apologies, I had the man remove his worn boots—thank God he wasn't in nice tennis shoes—and hosed them down. Fortunately, he thought it was funny. Another crisis averted.

With the parking becoming a bit more self-organized and running smoothly, Bear had positioned himself with the crab feast table, overseeing it and collecting money from people who were wandering over to it by about noon.

Seeing people snapping open crab shells struck an automatic response of desire in me. I had forgotten to eat in the morning and my stomach offered me a low growl to remind me of my error.

Well, there was nothing to be done for it now. I spent a few minutes helping Bear get people seated and dumping a few crabs on the table in front of them.

I was soon distracted again when a large, white van pulled down the road and into the parking lot. It had what looked to be a satellite dish on top of it. What in the world…?

"Dang, sis, I think your grand opening just got crashed by a television station," Bear said from where he was clearing the table of crab shell remains and dumping them into a trash barrel lined with a thick plastic bag. Crab shells were sharp and could easily poke through flimsy plastic.

"Really?" I questioned. "I wonder where they're from."

Bear squinted at the truck. "Looks like it says 'Channel Four' on the van. That's a D.C. station, right? You go talk to them; I've got everything here."

I couldn't believe I had a television station showing up at my event. How did they even know about it?

It must have been Dee Dee's doing. I made my way to the van, the side panel of which had been thrown open. I could see three people working inside.

"Hello?" I said as I knocked on the side of the van.

From the front seat, a woman opened the door and popped out, literally jumping to the ground she was so petite. "Hi, are you the owner?" she asked. "I'm Jasmine Elliott with Channel Four News."

I nodded her dumbly.

"Great!" Jasmine Elliott was slim and perky, in a form-fitting burgundy-colored skirt and jacket. She fit the stereotype of what the ideal news reporter should look like.

It seemed as though ten seconds later, two cameramen and someone holding a fur-covered microphone on a long pole and popped out of the truck and were setting up around me.

I looked down at what I was wearing. Was I going to be on this evening's news looking like this? I had Old Bay crab seasoning smeared all over me, in addition to a wee bit of horse manure on my shoes.

But Jasmine didn't give me much time to consider my appearance, for suddenly the fuzzy microphone was dangling over me. One camera operator was off to my side with his camera pointing toward Jasmine, while the other was pointing a camera over her shoulder at me. I had no idea what was going on, yet whatever it was, was occurring at lightning speed.

It reminded me of what it's like to be in the hospital and they're about to wheel you back for surgery. Suddenly, a half dozen people are swooping over you, rushing you down a hallway on a gurney, and speed-talking you through whatever is about to happen.

The only difference was that in the hospital they begin turning up the happy juice as you are wheeled to the operating room. Here, it was just a lot of commotion without anything to settle the nerves.

However, the reporter quickly made me comfortable. "Ignore the camera and look only at me," she instructed. That helped a lot.

She went on to interview me for several minutes and she had clearly done her homework on my modest little farm and what I was trying to create.

It was her last question, though, that jarred me.

"What do your neighbors think of your new safari?" Jasmine waited for my response.

How long could I hesitate before it would look awkward on camera? I rattled off the first thing in my head, which was starting to buzz with white noise over the question. "Well, as you can see by the crowd, people are really embracing it."

I hoped she wouldn't catch my sleight of hand in shifting the idea from the neighbors on my street to my fellow countians.

The reporter seemed to think nothing of it. She looked directly into the camera. "Not only are people embracing the concept of this safari, but kids young and old are literally embracing cows, horses, and llamas. If you're looking for a fun day out with the kids this weekend, Three Notch Safari is the place to be. I'm Jasmine Elliott with Channel Four."

The reporter paused for a moment until the camera's

light went out, then she relaxed. "Let's get some B-roll and do some interviews with attendees," she said to her crew, who nodded.

She spoke to me a final time. "You'll be on the five o'clock news unless something else happens to displace you. Then you might go to ten o'clock or we might not use the footage at all. It will be decided later. But thanks for the interview, you did a good job."

I'm sure that was a pro forma statement, but I was grateful for it nonetheless.

My impression was that she didn't want me tagging along as she obtained the rest of her footage and I didn't really want to follow her around anyway, so I returned to helping Bear with the crab feast. He was too busy to stop for more than just a, "Have fun?", to which I nodded and kept pulling crabs out of a basket for people.

About a half hour later, I noticed that Dee Dee was standing nearby. As the reporter and her crew piled back into the van, Dee Dee walked over to me and I stepped away from the picnic tables.

"A news crew. You've hit the big time on your first day," she said with a wink.

"Did you arrange this?" I asked.

Dee Dee shrugged and refused to answer. I didn't have time to pursue it with her because the county commissioners were getting out of their golf carts and heading toward me.

After several surreal minutes of being praised by them, I felt wobbly. It was all just so overwhelming.

The commissioners all shook my hand and departed, stating that they had to attend a ribbon cutting for a new auto parts store in Lexington Park.

I used the opportunity to run into the house and take a speed shower to wash away the crab seasoning and the other assorted smells that had already become embedded in my skin.

Thank the good Lord I had the good sense to do that, what with the next surprise visitor I had as soon as I walked into the gift shop.

CHAPTER 27

I COULDN'T BELIEVE MY eyes. It was Danny Copsey, whose son lost out on the hedgehogs at the Amish auction because of me. He stood there with his son.

He wore a man's standard St. Mary's County attire of a John Deere baseball cap, Harley Davidson t-shirt, faded jeans, and sneakers. "Told you I wanted to bring Christopher for his birthday, which is actually next week. Looks like you've brought much more than a petting zoo to town."

"Oh, yes, sorry I never called," I said. "Someone suggested that I call it a safari and that expanded my plans to the point where, well, just about everything happened so fast that I've barely had time to breathe."

He wore his St. Mary's County attire better than the average man.

Stop that, Becca Garvey. He's your customer, for Pete's sake.

I also didn't want April or my mother to think I was mooning over some strange man. I needed to just move him along.

But Danny wasn't walking away from me. "Don't worry about it. The gal behind the counter says she's your daughter. Told me I could either take a golf cart or walk the pedestrian path through the safari. What do you recommend?"

"Ahhh…" I really wasn't a very quick thinker on my feet today. "There are benefits to both. Why don't you let Christopher decide?"

The boy must have heard me mention his name, for

he came over to his father's side. "Dad, they have chess boards with the pieces in animal shapes."

April had found the whimsical sets in a catalog.

Danny rolled his eyes at me. "You're going to get a lot of money out of me today."

"If I'm lucky," I shot back.

He raised an eyebrow and I realized that perhaps my statement sounded suggestive. Oops.

"I mean, feel free to spend as much money as you want, and I hope you'll feel like you've gotten your money's worth during your visit to Three Notch Safari." Now I sounded like a bored hostess.

But Danny didn't seem to take offense.

"Do you have time to show Christopher and me around?" He put his arm around the boy's shoulder and it was obvious how easy the relationship was between father and son.

The specter of Mark rose in my mind and I tamped it down.

"Sure, I could spend a few minutes with you."

"Great," Danny said, smiling at me once more. "Christopher, what do you think, golf cart or walk the paths?"

"Golf cart, golf cart!" the boy shouted with enthusiasm.

I went with them to select a golf cart, which thankfully now had the correct name on it. Danny drove while I rode beside him and Christopher sat in the back seat facing in the opposite direction. Danny's son chattered up a storm to himself as we took the path around to the llamas.

Fortunately, there were few people currently near the llamas.

I hopped out of the cart and crooked a finger to Christopher. "Come meet Cuddlebug." The boy dutifully followed me.

"Cuddlebug, give Christopher kisses," I said,

surreptitiously reaching for the plastic treat bag nailed to a nearby post. I reached in for a nugget and handed it to the llama. He quickly dispatched it, bent his head down, and pressed his big furry nose against Christopher's face. The boy squealed with the delight of a child much younger and put his hands on either side of Cuddlebug's face, covering his nose with reciprocated kisses.

Cuddlebug did that to people.

Danny laughed heartily at his son's joy. "That's more affection than he gives Radar. Got any other lovable creatures?"

"Sure, he might like the miniature horses. Christopher, would you like to train a horse?"

Christopher was too busy adoring Cuddlebug to even pay attention to me. Danny shrugged. "I guess we're staying put for the time being."

I chatted about nothing and everything with Danny. I told him about April, he told me about Christopher, whom he had recently enrolled at Father Andrew White School for his fifth-grade year.

I told him my mother lived with me, he told me his parents lived nearby and were active in Christopher's life.

I ventured to tell him that I had started the safari because of Mark's departure, he told me that he had been divorced from his high school sweetheart since Christopher had been around sixteen months old.

Danny's ex hadn't wanted children and only reluctantly agreed to try for one after many years of marriage. "When Christopher was born, some of my friends called me Grandpa Daddy."

No one could possibly look at Danny Copsey and imagine him as a grandfather.

After having Christopher, the ex-wife, Bonnie, had decided she enjoyed alcohol much more than she liked being a mother, and it had all deteriorated from there. Last Danny had heard, Bonnie was floating from man to man, having actually amassed some wealth that way.

I suppose both Mark and Bonnie were living their respective dreams.

"I used to be angry about it," Danny said. "I mean, *really* angry. Now, I think I dodged a forty-five-caliber bullet. I got custody of Christopher and that's all that matters. Right, buddy?" he called out to his son, who was still enamored of the llama and ignoring everything around him.

Doodlebug and Ladybug had become curious about Christopher and circled near him. The boy was in his own state of nirvana.

"What about you?" Danny asked, offering me a probing look. "Do you think your husband will eventually return home to—"

Danny was unable to finish his sentence, as one of my goats appeared out of nowhere at a full gallop and butted him from behind, sending the man flying before my eyes. Danny hit the ground face forward with a thud, limbs sprawling, while my goat went scampering off.

As I stood rooted to the spot in complete disbelief, Christopher was jarred out of his llama love-fest. "Dad?" he asked, running and dropping down to his knees next to his father.

Danny groaned as he began stirring. "Hey, buddy, are you okay?" he said as he struggled into an upright position on the ground. His Harley t-shirt was black, but it was still easy to see the grass and dirt stains it now had.

"Yes, Daddy. That goat hit you!" Christopher said.

"That's what it was?" Danny rubbed his neck with one hand. "Damn."

I was torn between concern for him and the fact that my goat had somehow gotten loose and was potentially terrorizing my guests. Danny was still alive so I had to turn my attention to the goat.

"I'll be right back." I took off in the direction the goat had taken. I found him prancing around as several children were trying to chase him. The kids were laughing and screeching as only kids can do, but this was not a funny situation. The goat could easily turn around and ram them.

I sped along faster, yelling at the children. "Stop chasing him," I screamed at the top of my voice. As if that would serve to do anything but make them run toward the goat faster.

Now people were stopping to see what the commotion was. I wasn't handling this very circumspectly, but I had to get the animal penned up.

The goat, one of my larger Kiko bucks, was now behaving strangely, zigzagging as he ran and occasionally turning in circles, but at least he had gotten out of reach of the children.

What was wrong with him? He was acting like a lunatic. I mean, goats aren't always the brainiest of animals, but this was way out of normal behavior.

The buck was finally wearing himself out and I was able to catch up to him. I grabbed his horns and knelt to stare him in the face, but he was clearly too exhausted to fight me.

"Baaaa," he uttered weakly.

"C'mon," I ordered him as I stood back up, giving one of his horns a nudge.

Just like that he obediently walked with me back to the goat pen. To my utter mortification, guests began clapping as though I had conquered a great beast. I held up a hand to acknowledge them, hoping that they would forget what they had seen and return to enjoying the safari.

But the goat wasn't done yet.

CHAPTER 28

JUST AS I was about to open the gate to the goat pen and put the buck back inside, he started prancing up and down and bleating at me.

"What is *wrong* with you?" I demanded. I then dropped my voice to a whisper. "You're embarrassing me."

He didn't care. He butted me, but much more gently than what he had done to Danny.

"Yes, you know who feeds you, don't you?" I said to him. "Surely that isn't your problem, is it? Are you just hungry?"

He bleated plaintively at me again.

I again went to open the gate and realized that it was unlocked. Not just unlocked, but the L-shaped gate latch had been lifted from its hinges and was lying on the ground..

"Someone let you out?" I whispered. Amazingly, he was the only goat who had wandered out. The rest were still in the large pen, although my approach had caused them to walk toward me, no doubt seeking food.

"C'mon," I said again, nodding toward the pen as I opened the gate and clucked at the others to stay in.

As the buck stepped past me to enter the pen, I swatted gently at his rear.

Pain shot through my hand and I yelped as the goat also protested loudly. I examined my palm.

I had a huge, round, chocolate-colored burr stuck in it.

What in the—?

I had no burr plants anywhere on the farm, I was sure of it.

Maintaining my composure, I plastered a tight smile on my face, and replaced the latch.

I walked to the house and straight to the kitchen sink, where I gently tugged on one of the sticker points until the burr dislodged from my skin.

I dropped it into a bowl and ran back to my room to get on my computer and research what it was.

Turns out it was a "sticktight" burr. How aptly named. But it made no sense. This burr—although readily found in pastures and fields—produced bright yellow flowers from summer to fall, which were then replaced by these barbed nuisances.

It wasn't possible that my goat had picked it up anywhere on the property, although no wonder he had gone bonkers over it.

I didn't like the sinking feeling I was having.

Someone had deliberately opened my goat pen and then stuck a goat with a burr to create havoc on my opening day.

It seemed as though Dickie Walker was bent on torturing me. Maybe if I ignored this, he would decide it wasn't worth it anymore. I had no desire to get the police involved with my neighbors, which would further deteriorate things, so this seemed like the best possible option.

With a little antibiotic ointment and a Band-Aid on it, my hand felt much better. I dug around in the house and found another padlock for the goat pen.

The buck had completely calmed down with the burr out of his rump and he was playing around with the others. I was glad he was okay.

But there were still children and adults standing

around, watching me with curiosity. I had to do something.

"Hey, kids!" I said. "Who wants to watch me feed goats?"

That was all they needed to hear. "Me! Me!" they all shouted.

"Follow me," I commanded and about a half dozen children immediately jockeyed for position behind me. The errant goat seemed to be forgotten, at least by the kids and I hoped by the adults.

I led them to the feed shed and gave them each a job. One to open the goat feed bin, one to hold the bucket, one to dip for feed and pour it into the bucket, and so on.

I led them back to the goat pen and took the feed from the little boy bravely carrying the container that was way too heavy for him.

"Watch this!" I exclaimed and went through my feeding routine.

The kids laughed uproariously as the goats sped from one dish to the other. The Kiko buck was right in the middle of the pack, seemingly no worse for his injury.

"Was that fun or what?" I asked them.

Naturally, they all wanted me to do it again. I had to explain that the goats could only eat a couple of times a day. They returned to their parents, disappointment emblazoned on their little faces.

I felt bad about it, but it gave me an idea. Why not let parents sign their children up for a paid slot on evening feedings of the goats, horses, cows, and so on? With a professional photo add-on option. I made a mental note to talk to Meesh about the idea and to add this to the offerings.

From there, I went back to the llama area, but Danny and his son were gone. The golf cart was no longer there, either.

Nuts.

I jogged down to the gift shop. There were plenty of people milling about, a gratifying sight to see. My mother was busy rearranging farm animal books for children on a table. As soon as April was free at the cash register, I approached the counter.

"How's business?" I asked casually.

"Great, Mom. I have to check to be certain, but I'm pretty sure I've sold twenty percent of our inventory in just a couple of hours. I'll tally up the register at the end of the day, but I think you are well on your way to making your first loan payment." April gave me a thumbs-up.

"That's awesome, sweetheart," I told her. "I'm glad I let you run with the gift shop. You've far exceeded my expectations." I really was proud to hear this.

"I even sold some Amazonite, the stone of harmony for animals, and a few pieces of Aragonite, good for animal wellness." April fingered the stone at the end of a silver necklace around her neck. It had wavy blue lines in it.

"Okay," I said. "By the way, did a man in a Harley t-shirt with his young son return his golf cart recently?"

April frowned. "Tall, dark hair? Shirt really dirty?"

I nodded.

"Yeah, he checked out about ten minutes ago. Didn't seem happy and the kid had clearly been crying."

Oh no. My stomach fluttered in anxiety.

From Christopher's perspective, I had stolen his hedgehogs and then gotten his father injured, which had in turn completely ruined the boy's day.

Danny would no doubt steer clear of Three Notch Safari after this.

Not even a word of goodbye from him. I shouldn't have been disappointed, but I was.

I didn't have long to be disappointed, for I suddenly heard a great howling coming from the direction of the horse pasture.

CHAPTER 29

WHAT NEW MISHAP had befallen this day, I wondered as I hoofed over to the pasture. A small crowd was gathered around what appeared to be Randy with Donna frantically pulling on his harness.

The howling grew louder as I approached.

"What's wrong?" I asked breathlessly, pushing through the gathering.

"GET THIS THING OFF OF ME!" shouted a woman in impossibly large, pink-framed sunglasses standing next to Randy and pounding on his backside. For his part, Randy seemed unfazed.

I then saw that he was standing on her foot. Oh no, even a miniature horse has a lot of weight to him.

"Randy!" I intoned in my deepest voice, grabbing the harness from Donna and giving it a good shake. My stern tone startled him enough to step to one side, freeing the woman, who flexed her foot and put it down gingerly to take a few steps. Within moments she was clearly able to walk again.

"I'm so sorry—" I began, but the woman cut me off, her face scarlet red all the way to her blonde hairline.

"Do you not have any control over these creatures? Why haven't you trained them to behave? If I was a child I might have been killed. As it is, I'm pretty sure I've at least fractured my foot. Do you realize I could sue you out of existence? I should—" The woman was going rabid on me.

I wasn't about to begin arguing with her and I needed

to defuse the situation pronto, even though my stupid horse *had* parked his hoof on her. "I'm sure if we just wait a few minutes, we can make sure your foot is fine. Randy didn't mean to harm you. He really is a sweet boy. He—"

But this woman was not about to allow herself to be consoled. "A sweet boy! Lady, you must be out of your mind. Sweet boys don't attempt to cripple humans."

How was I going to get out of this? The worst part was that other guests were standing around, taking it all in. What if they all went and told their friends about how someone got badly injured at my safari?

I needed to have people sign waivers if they were going to enter the pens.

Dee Dee appeared out of nowhere again and stepped in front of me and two steps to the side, as if both blocking me from the ranting woman's view and distracting her.

"Hi, I'm Dee Dee Boone," she said, smiling sweetly and holding out a hand.

The woman took it. "Allison Sebastian."

Dee Dee nodded. "I'm the marketing director for Three Notch Safari and I'm pleased to tell you that you have just won a very special prize."

The woman named Allison frowned. "Prize?" she said suspiciously. "What do you mean?"

"Well, we are instituting a Wall of Shame and Pain in the gift shop, and you are going to be our inaugural entry." Dee Dee was beaming.

"What's a Wall of Shame and—what is it?" The woman was calming down in her curiosity.

"Shame and Pain. We are going to commemorate those who have funny and unusual interactions with the animals here. Randy put you right up at the top of the board. Can we get a photo of you with him?" Dee Dee looked around. "Where's the photographer?"

I held my hand up and waved at Meesh, who was

taking a photo of a couple climbing into a golf cart. She waved back and started heading toward me.

Allison seemed confused by the turn of events. "I guess I could do that," she said.

Michelle ran up with her camera. "What can I do for you?"

"This guest is Allison Sebastian," I said. "She's just won the inaugural spot on the Wall of Shame and Pain."

God bless Meesh, she didn't even bat an eye but instead just ran with it. "Oh, great! Congratulations! Can I get some photos of you?"

Michelle started posing the woman with Randy and pulled out all of the stops, treating Allison like a model and clicking off hundreds of shots.

For her part, Dee Dee acted like the woman's agent, insisting that Allison's right side was her best for photos.

To my great surprise, the woman was soon laughing about the entire situation.

I had to admire Dee Dee's brilliant maneuvering on my behalf.

Once the situation had been resolved and Michelle promised to send Allison a complimentary copy of the photo while Dee Dee waited to personally escort the woman to her car, I heaved a sigh of relief.

Then I turned and saw my mother standing outside the gift shop, arms crossed and nodding knowingly. I swear, my mother was turning into a ghoul. Pretty soon she would be wearing a long, hooded cape, rattling chains and pointing at me.

I waved half-heartedly at her. She turned and went back into the shop.

"Hey, Becca." Meesh was back at my side. "What's this about a Wall of Shame?"

"And Pain," I added. "Dee Dee came up with it on the fly. She probably just saved me from going into bankruptcy on my first day." I watched as Dee Dee closed Allison's car door and waved enthusiastically as the woman drove off.

Meesh nodded. "Quick thinking. Listen, I have an idea."

I gave her my full attention.

"A family with three children watched me taking photos of a couple of other kids with the cows. The mom asked if you could have a princess-themed birthday party for their daughter who is turning five."

"That sounds fine," I said. "I think April bought some princess-themed party-ware and we can have the girl and her friends dress up and play with the cows and llamas." I made another mental note in the growing list that I was never going to remember I should make sure April still had princess party-ware.

Michelle shook her head. "You don't understand. They're asking for some of the animals to be dressed up to fit the theme. They're offering considerable money for it."

I frowned. "Dress the animals up? Like, put Ladybug in a dress? Have the cows wear crowns? I can't imagine them tolerating it."

"I bet you could teach them to tolerate it. Like I said, this couple offered a lot of money." Michelle whispered a number in my ear.

"Looks like I'm going to have a princess party," I said.

Michelle nodded. "There's one other thing. They want the party next week."

I closed my eyes. "Of course they do."

As the last of the guests were leaving at the conclusion of the day, I suggested to Bear that all my family and friends who had helped out stop at the house for supper. He agreed that it was a good idea for everyone to review the day's good and bad points to make corrections for the next day.

There were no leftover crabs, of course. "I got this," Bear said. "We need Chaptico Market fried chicken and JoJo potatoes."

"Bear, no," I protested. "That's way too far a drive."

He held up a hand. "If you're going to celebrate today, you've got to do it in style."

He motioned to his boys to go with him and the four of them got in Brown Betty and took off.

While he was gone, I got everyone settled in the family room and dug out as much soda, bottled water, beer, and wine as I could find.

By the time the boys returned, everyone was in good spirits, but I knew I was starving so surely they all were, too.

We all fell upon the foil trays of chicken-y goodness and soon we all had Chaptico Market grease all over our hands and faces. The JoJo potatoes, thickly sliced and battered as nicely as the chicken, were hot and delicious, as well.

I sighed in pleasure. Totally worth it.

With all our tummies full and everyone starting to slouch down in chairs and on couches, I asked, "So, overall thoughts on how it went today."

Everyone perked back up and offered opinions. Generally, everyone thought that the animals had been pretty well-behaved given that it was their first round at this, that more signage was needed to guide people properly into the parking lot, and that it had been a really great first day. Simon suggested that the aviary and small animal enclosure needed to be expanded soon with more birds and creatures.

Mom must have put her hearing aids in, for she seemed to be tracking on the entire conversation, even if she offered no opinion whatsoever.

I brought up the couple that wanted a princess-themed birthday party for their daughter, next week. No one seemed to think that should be a problem for me. "You'll figure it out," Dee Dee said, to which everyone else nodded.

Except for mom, of course. She sniffed and excused herself to go to her room.

Why was she so cranky about this?

One by one, everyone else rose, yawned, and called it a day. I couldn't thank everyone enough as they went to their cars.

As Bear, Donna, and the boys were leaving, I tried to pay Bear for the food. My brother waved me off. "Our treat. Save your money to pay your loan."

I admit, his ongoing generosity made me a little misty. "Thanks."

April gave me a tight hug as she was leaving. "I'm proud of you, Mom," she said, then walked out the kitchen door.

I was glad she had left quickly, for the mistiness turned into real tears. The sort of tears that come with both exhaustion and joy.

Despite my exhaustion, I still needed to do a round with the animals to make sure they were fed and in their respective pens.

I went outside and only then realized how much my feet now hurt. I whistled for Daisy and she came running. Together we went through the feeding routine, only this time I did extra checks on everyone just to make sure there were no inadvertent injuries on any animals.

Everyone was fine, including the goat who had had the strange burr stuck in his rump until it had transferred to me. I glanced at my palm and slowly peeled away the Band-Aid. It was still a little red and angry-looking, but I thought it would be okay.

As Daisy and I were finishing up, twilight was setting

in. "You ready for your own dinner, girl?" I asked the dog, then noticed headlights coming up the road.

The car turned up my driveway and the driver got out.

It was the county inspector again.

CHAPTER 30

"MS. GARVEY," LESLIE Alexander said, nodding without a smile as she exited her car holding her clipboard. Today's pantsuit was magenta with large brass buttons on the jacket. "I understand you had a pretty full day here today."

I nodded as Daisy went to inspect the inspector, with sniffs at the woman's wide-legged pants. "Have you come to inspect my shrubbery plantings? I bought a magnolia, several tulip poplars, and—"

She cut me off. "I hear you had some problems with your animals. People got hurt." She tapped her clipboard as though it were a police report.

"Not seriously," I said. "Just a couple of instances where...the animals got a little rambunctious. No one needed to go the hospital or even required any medical attention." I slowly closed my fist so that she couldn't see where the burr had impaled my palm.

"Is that so?" Leslie's expression was scornful. "I see here that a woman submitted a report about one of your horses nearly trampling her to death." She tapped the clipboard again and it startled Daisy enough that the dog came loping back to my side.

Allison Sebastian. She must have driven straight home and jumped onto her computer to report me. I couldn't believe it. I would have sworn on stacks of Bibles that she was perfectly happy when she left. So much for the Wall of Shame and Pain.

"That's an exaggeration," I responded. "There may

have been a couple of bruises incurred here and there, but that's no different than what happens on, say, a go-kart track or a putt-putt golf course."

"Hmmm," the inspector said. "Except, of course, that you have unpredictable animals roaming free. It's an added level of risk—bad publicity, if you will—that the county must be responsible for keeping an eye out on. Public safety is our top priority."

My stomach started to do flip-flops. I didn't like where this was headed. Even though I had insurance to cover any mishaps, I certainly didn't want any bad publicity. "Sure. But this was just our first day and we will continue to fix and improve the guest experience as we—"

Leslie held up the clipboard as if to ward off whatever I was saying. "I'm not convinced you are serious enough about your enterprise, Ms. Garvey. You should have had the plantings approved before opening your business."

"I had an overwhelming amount of work to do in preparation for the grand opening," I explained, "but I did do as you required."

My feet were silently protesting in earnest against their overuse as I walked the inspector around the front part of the property to show her the new trees that had been planted.

One of the new tulip poplars looked a little sad, but I imagined it would probably perk up with a little more water and time. Daisy used the moment to squat down next to the tree to urinate next to the root ball. I was mortified, but Leslie seemed to pay no attention.

In fact, she had barely glanced at anything I was showing her, keeping most of her focus on that stupid clipboard. She shuffled pages back and forth and made notes and doodles everywhere. For all I knew, she was playing tic-tac-toe with herself.

We circled back around toward her car and she said, "I should probably see the horse that caused the injury."

"There was no injur—all right, come meet Randy," I said in resignation, leading her off to the horse barn. It was all I could not to let it show that my feet were howling their need to be up in a recliner.

I hated going in and disturbing the horses, too, now that they'd been fed and were in for the evening.

I took her to Randy's stall. He had eaten most of his feed already and gave us a curious glance at the intrusion. Leslie let herself into his stall and began examining him. It was as if she was mentally measuring his height and length. What was up with this woman?

When she was done doing whatever it was she was doing, she strode out of the barn toward her car. I kept up as well as my feet would allow. I was going to need a seriously long soak in an Epsom salts bath tonight.

"That's all for now, Ms. Garvey. I'm approving your plantings, but the county will be keeping a regular eye on your operation here." She scrawled a signature across the top piece of paper on her clipboard then ostentatiously tore the sheet away and handed it to me before getting into her car without another word.

Before I knew it, she was leaving, her red taillights quickly fading as she disappeared down my street toward the main road.

I had no idea why Leslie Alexander held such animosity against me, but I was willing to bet she wouldn't rest until I was shut down for good.

Perhaps it was time to look into Ms. Alexander.

CHAPTER 31

I DIDN'T GET AS long a soak in the tub as I would have liked after returning to the house and finally feeding Daisy, but I did manage to fall unconscious into bed and sleep straight through until just before dawn.

I fed all the critters, then jumped into the shower to get ready for the day. I also cooked some bacon and made fried egg sandwiches, a favorite of my mother's. She hadn't risen by the time I was done, so I made her a plate and placed it in the oven. Mom knew to look in there for food.

I took my own plate back to my room and got on my computer. My first goal was to see what I could find out about Leslie Alexander, inspector extraordinaire. I settled down with the mouse in my right hand and a piece of very well-done bacon in my left. I really couldn't abide bacon that wasn't cooked nearly to a crisp. In my opinion, bacon should be crunchy not chewy, but not everyone agreed with me.

Other than her picture and contact info, there was nothing about Ms. Alexander on the county website. She didn't seem to be on social media either, so I gave up for the time being.

I then clicked my website's e-mail and couldn't believe what I saw there. It shocked me enough to put the bacon strip back onto my plate.

Danny Copsey had e-mailed me.

Was it a rant at me about what had happened with the goat yesterday? Or was it perhaps something worse?

I hoped he hadn't also complained to the county.

I quickly scanned the e-mail and was astounded by what I read. It wasn't a complaint at all. To the contrary, he apologized for leaving abruptly yesterday and wanted to know if I'd like to have dinner with him so he could apologize more appropriately.

My heart beat rapidly and I struggled to catch my breath. Would it be wrong to go? He wasn't declaring it a date and he knew what my situation was.

I finished reading his e-mail. He proposed meeting on Solomons Island on a Sunday afternoon after the safari closed to dine outdoors at the Lighthouse Restaurant. He suggested following our meal with a stroll along the boardwalk and perhaps ice cream cones from one of the frozen treats stands on the island.

It was a perfectly innocent gesture from him but I wasn't sure it would be purely platonic on my part.

I stared at the e-mail for a long time before responding, full of angst as to whether I should do it. Not only was I unsure about it for myself, I also realized that this was St. Mary's County and I was sure to run into at least a half dozen people I knew while out with Danny. It could really set tongues to wagging.

Yes, I stared at the e-mail until my breakfast was cold and inedible, but in the end, I accepted his invitation.

God help me.

The next week at the safari lurched forward. The days were no worse than the first one, and I learned along the way better methods of interacting with my guests, how many hours to let any individual animal be available, and, most importantly, what kind of staff I thought I needed to hire.

I got right to work on placing ads, with a focus on reaching out to local 4-H clubs, veterinarians, stables, and anywhere else I could think of where people from eight to eighty enjoyed working with animals.

Fortunately for me, there had been enough buzz in the community that I was flooded with interviewees and was soon able to replace Dee Dee and my brother and his family, as well as adding additional staff.

April was ecstatic about the gift shop and was officially calling herself the manager of it and, strangely, given all of her bluster about the safari, my mother seemed to like working in there with her.

But other bluster about the safari continued. Dickie Walker walked down to my place again after the safari had closed one day while I was doing the evening feeding to complain about the nighttime noises from the animals, particularly the birds.

"Dickie," I said, not stopping what I was doing and thus forcing him to walk with me, "our entire area is full of a wide variety of birds that caw, coo, crow, and chirp all day long. How are you assigning all the noise to my safari?"

"Because at night I can hear strange bird sounds coming from the direction of your place. Ain't nothing else making noises because they're all tucked in asleep in the trees. Your birds are all…agitated."

I didn't know how to respond. I didn't hear anything from the aviary at night, but I had to admit that the birds were positioned on the property such that it was possible he could hear something that I couldn't.

If he had complained about morning noises, I would have been more likely to agree with him. The macaws did shriek upon waking to let the world know that it was time to pay attention to them.

I had no idea what to do that would satisfy my neighbor.

"Tell you what," I said, "I'll talk to my trainer to see

what he can offer for settling the birds down more at night."

"They're agitated," Dickie repeated. "And the more your animals are agitated, the more likely you are to fail." He nodded with a self-satisfied smirk and strode off into the twilight toward his own house.

The more likely you are to fail. I stared after him, thinking about the unusual burr in my goat's backside and the cut lock on the goat pen. Dickie Walker was clearly very unhappy about my safari and was expressing it in both temper tantrums and mischief.

Once more restraining myself from lashing out in hopes that he would settle down if I just ignored his actions, I made yet another mental note, this time to talk to Simon about how to keep the birds quieter. Things might get worse as the peacocks got older since they were reputed to be screechers. I hoped he could train that out of them.

Speaking of Simon, I did notice one of the hedgehogs curled up in a ball on the ground outside his raised enclosure one day. It was, of course, completely impossible that the little critters could have gotten out by themselves.

Since the small animals were located near the aviary, I asked Simon about it, but he said he hadn't seen anyone near them.

What could I do other than pick up Pop, give it cuddles, and put it away?

Despite my hateful neighbor, there were people who went out of their way to make my day. Many visitors said they had come after seeing my billboards. I owed Dee Dee a dinner for that brilliant idea. Others told me that friends had visited and loved it so it became an immediate "must do" for them. It was very gratifying, given how hard the safari's setup had been.

I contracted with the Amish again, this time to have a

small stage built under an awning. I was nervous about the expenditure, but I agreed with T-Bone that a funny western show would be unique. I contacted a local theatre troupe to see if they would be interested in both decorating it and putting on a few skits on weekends. I had high hopes for it.

So, all in all, the safari was maintaining itself and nothing truly tragic had thus far happened. Score a win for Becca Garvey.

Until creepy things began occurring with the llamas.

CHAPTER 32

I MET DANNY AT the Lighthouse Restaurant late Sunday afternoon. Bear and Donna had happily agreed to watch Mom and the animals for a few hours when they heard that I was going to spend time with a new friend.

"The sooner Mark is history, the better," Bear had growled on the phone.

I wasn't sure what said "not-taking-this-seriously-but-you-should-notice-that-I'm-still-cute-and-fashionable" well enough, but decided on a denim skirt topped with a yellow and white striped short-sleeved sweater that I dug out of a long-forgotten dresser drawer. I slipped into white sandals and tied my hair up in a ponytail to round it out since I knew we'd be walking on the Solomons boardwalk and it could get windy there.

Wind turned out to be just one of my problems.

Danny had left word with the hostess that he was being joined by someone, so I was immediately escorted to a two-top table outside on the restaurant's deck, which overlooked a mass of moored sailboats along the Patuxent River. The day was unusually pleasant and warm, as the sun drifted in and out from behind clouds. There were plenty of boats put-putting and maneuvering in and out of this piece of the river, where the river itself joined with Mill Creek and the Narrows.

Danny stood when he saw me approaching. He wore crisp blue jeans and a light blue button up shirt. I suspected this was serious dressing up for him. Despite his expression being mostly hidden behind sunglasses, I had the sense that he was gazing at me with appreciation, so I figured my outfit was at least acceptable. I smiled back.

"Where's Christopher?" I asked, reaching the table and sitting down across from him. He had been seated at a table with no umbrella for shade, so I kept my sunglasses on, too. "I thought maybe he'd be here to chaperone you."

"He's with my parents. They have a piano that they let him bang on to his heart's content, plus they have a swimming pool, so he won't notice my absence for hours."

I nodded. "When I left my mother, she was watching a game show that was scheduled to run episodes until at least nine o'clock tonight, so she won't notice my absence, either. Besides, my brother and sister in law are going to check in with her and take her something to eat."

We settled down to a shared dish of hot crab dip with flat bread with which to scoop it. It seemed…intimate… to share food like this, although I'm sure I was the only one who felt that way, given my relative inexperience in such activities.

We discussed inanities while waiting for our meals. Danny ordered a crab cake dinner while I chose a grilled salmon filet. He asked for "angry" crab cakes, and when the server left, I asked him what that meant. "Extra spicy," he said, raising an eyebrow suggestively.

"You're a goof," I said without thinking, eliciting laughter from him.

The meals were served and the talk turned slightly more serious. He talked at length about his taxidermy hobby––"because my day job is too boring to talk about"––while I rambled on—for far too long, I'm sure—about the safari.

He at least listened attentively, for which I was grateful. He also asked lots of questions about the operation and how I obtained my animals. I asked him more about taxidermy and then we compared notes on parenting young adults versus young children.

I relaxed enough to order a glass of sangria and he ordered a beer. I was just at the point of thinking this get together was very successful when it happened.

A seagull came flying low over the deck and pooped. On me. The little bugger was low enough that I actually heard him let loose. It hit my shoulder and dripped warmly down the front of my sweater before I could even attempt to get out of the way.

Danny jumped up, dipped his cloth napkin into his glass of water and started to reach over to me to wipe it off. He clearly thought the better of touching me, for he then awkwardly handed me the wet cloth.

I attempted to wipe the disgusting mess off me but only succeeded in smearing it. So much for looking cute and fashionable.

The server returned and expressed horror over what had happened to me. Despite my protestations that it wasn't necessary, she ran off to get more napkins with which to clean me off. This in turn got the notice of other patrons, which made me the center of attention.

I was beginning to feel like a spectacle.

Except that once the server came back with more cloths and I made a futile attempt to clean more of the bird poop off of me, I became the victim of even more unwanted attention.

As can happen when you are along a shoreline, the wind picked up for no apparent reason. Sometimes, the wind was blustery along the shore but non-existent a quarter of a mile inland. Blustery didn't begin to cover what was suddenly occurring. The cloud cover was growing, too, so although my hair was starting to come loose from its band, I was at least able to remove my sunglasses. Danny removed his, too.

I was about to ask him a question about Christopher when a sudden gust blew against us, pushing my half-eaten plate of salmon directly into my lap. I was now wearing the filet, its delicious sauce, rice pilaf, and green beans. The sauce immediately soaked through my skirt.

I wasn't sure whether to laugh or cry.

Danny chose laughter. In fact, he threw his head back and laughed so heartily that the other patrons were again interested in what was happening at our table.

I still had extra napkins at my place so after putting the plate upright on the table, I scooped up food with a napkin and dumped it on the plate. It was impossible to clean myself properly. I had salmon and rice ground into the denim fabric, as well as a stain spread across the entire front of it.

Could this get any worse? Of course, it could.

Realizing that I was now mortified, Danny quickly paid the check and hustled me through the restaurant and out the front door. "Not your day, is it?" he said.

As we walked toward the public parking lot, the wind died down. As I said, wind gusts can come up suddenly and depart just as rapidly.

I indicated to him where my car was parked and we walked in that direction. "I don't blame you if you say no," Danny said. "But would you still like to get some ice cream?"

I looked down at myself. I couldn't believe he didn't want to hustle my disheveled, stinky self into my car and get rid of me. "Okay," I said in disbelief.

We walked to the ice cream shack on the boardwalk and ordered through the window. Danny asked for a chocolate fudge sundae and I ordered a mint chocolate chip cone.

We enjoyed our treats as we walked along the

boardwalk, stopping at points to rest our arms on the railing to watch sailboats go by and herons flying low over the water.

Herons are so tall, graceful, and elegant. Sometimes I wonder if they shouldn't have been named our national bird.

As we continued down the boardwalk, I dropped just behind Danny at one point because a large group with multiple baby strollers was approaching from the other direction. As we passed them, my sandal got stuck on something protruding from a decking board and I pitched forward.

I caught myself, but not before I had sent my green, chip-dotted ice cream flying onto Danny's back. I even managed to grind it into his shirt as I recovered myself.

He yelped, no doubt from the sudden impact of me and my frozen treat.

Still, he retained his good humor. "You couldn't stand it that I was the only clean one, right?" he said turning back to me. I used my cone and napkin to scoop up as much as I could from the boardwalk, then pitched the entire thing into a nearby trash can.

"How do I look?" he asked, posing dramatically with his back to me.

"Like an ogre exploded on you," I told him.

He laughed. "Nothing a run through the washing machine won't fix. Do you want another cone?"

"No," I said, too harshly than I intended. "I don't think I should get near any other food whatsoever for the rest of the day."

"Understood. Walk a few more minutes?" He offered his arm and I took it, startled by how comforting it felt to have him guide me down the boardwalk.

The comfort only lasted a couple of minutes. I thought I saw someone familiar approaching us but didn't realize who it was until it was too late.

Chick Huber, one of Mark's best buddies, was on the boardwalk with his brother, Chip. Strangely enough, their mother really liked the name Charles and had named both of her sons that, then bestowed nicknames on them to distinguish them. Thus, neither one had ever gone by the name she loved so well.

The two men stopped and Chick said, "Becca?"

As I said, it was impossible to go anywhere in Southern Maryland without bumping into friends and acquaintances. This guy was the worst one possible to encounter. Lanky, balding, and always full of over-the-top bravado in any situation, he was constantly challenging others to drinking, wrestling, motorcycle racing, and other contests. He obsessed over winning and was insufferable when he didn't. I never understood Mark's fondness for him.

Chick narrowed his gaze at Danny and me. To my own consternation, I dropped my hand from the crook of Danny's arm and I sensed that Danny was immediately on alert.

"What's happening here?" Chick asked. "Is Mark with you?"

He didn't know what had happened? How that news hadn't traveled to every cove and inlet in the county was beyond me.

"Hello, Chick. Chip. Mark is in Florida," I said, unwilling to say anything I didn't have to say.

"Doing what? With who? When will he be back?" The questions were suspiciously asked and came at me rapid-fire. "And who is this?" he asked with a nod toward Danny.

"This is Danny Copsey, a friend," I said. "Mark has moved to Florida for the foreseeable future and is living with his brother, Jack." I didn't think I owed him any further explanation. I also wasn't going to suggest that he had gone down there with another woman, which would have sounded petulant.

Chick's expression was one of confusion and became even more so as he took in the smeared stain on the front of my sweater and the mess on the front of my skirt. At least he couldn't see Danny's back.

"Is that so? I didn't know anything 'bout that. 'Deed I didn't. Seems to me Mark would have told me he was leaving town. Maybe that's just something you're telling me because you're where you shouldn't be."

Chip nodded in silent agreement.

"I'm sorry Mark didn't tell you. It was sudden for me, too, Chick. You can call him yourself." Danny's demeanor next to me was chilly, but I wasn't sure if it was for me or Chick.

Chick's expression narrowed again. I hoped he wasn't going to challenge me to a crab-picking contest to prove who was right about Mark's departure.

"Maybe I will. He should know what his wife is up to." Chick gave me a curt nod and walked away with this brother.

I would no doubt receive an accusatory phone call from Mark tonight. I'm sure it would also play into his demands for a share of the safari's profits, whenever they should come about.

"Who was that? You didn't introduce me," Danny said, now *not* offering me his arm as we walked away.

"A friend of Mark's. Not someone I'm particularly fond of." I looked over at him.

He nodded, his expression blank. "He seemed to think nothing had happened between you and Mark. Mark really is gone, right?"

I stopped and turned to face him. "Of course he is. Everything is as I said it was."

Danny was pensive and it made me nervous. "I think I'd like to go home now," he finally said.

"Okay." I couldn't believe the extent to which this afternoon had been a humiliating wreck after starting out with so much hope and anticipation.

Danny walked me to my car. He politely opened my door and waited for me to settle in before saying, "Thanks," and then shutting it. He walked away without another word or even a wave.

My innards gurgled and not just because I was now in an enclosed space with the stink of salmon and seagull. This was just like how he had departed from the safari on opening day.

I had the feeling I had blown it and would not be receiving a third chance. This was over before it had begun.

CHAPTER 33

FORTUNATELY, MARK DIDN'T call me. I didn't think I could take another argument with him.

I threw myself into the safari for the next couple of weeks. The Thanksgiving and Christmas craziness was on its way and I tried to focus all of my attention on the season. It helped me forget the one-and-done date I had with Danny.

It also helped that my new employees started filtering in. Bear organized training sessions for them, which freed me to do other things. The Amish also returned to start construction on my stage. I was excited about the design, which looked like an old-time carnival-type stage in two parts that would be separated by curtains so that the performers could change and grab props behind the curtain.

I found red fabric in a kerchief design and made rod-pocket panel lengths to be hung as the stage divider once the Amish were done. Sewing straight lines was about the extent of my sewing skills but I was still proud of what I had made.

My mother surprised me by wanting to go with me as I scoured the county looking for stage decor. With her in tow, I picked up hay bales, a couple of old, round, pine bar tables, and several mismatched chairs. Combined with the red kerchief backdrop, I thought it exuded a cute western saloon feel.

A local theatre troupe that I had reached out to came to discuss ideas for a western show. They suggested something vaudevillian, thus a combination of comedy routines, singing, magic, and storytelling. They already had a script from an old show they had done several years earlier and thus could be ready in weeks for it. I loved the idea.

Somehow in the middle of all of that, I was able to coordinate the princess birthday party. Ladybug turned out to be the most tolerant of a tiara and I managed to get pink and purple capes on all three of them.

The party was set up in one of the barns after the safari was done for the day, and the llamas wandered around freely with about twenty little girls who squealed in delight at the llama royalty walking around with them.

April took care of all the party supplies and seemed to have a great time with all of the children.

After the party was done and the guests were gone, Michelle followed me back to the house to catch up over a glass of wine. My mother didn't exit her room and the television wasn't blaring so I assumed she was napping.

"Becca, I got some fantastic photos out there. Your llamas are absolute camera hounds."

I rolled my eyes. "They're hams for sure. I'm just glad it went well."

"What do you think about doing seasonal photo vignettes? Not just for the four seasons, but for Christmas, Easter, St. Patrick's Day, and so forth?" Michelle drained her glass and splashed a little more Chardonnay into the stemware.

I thought it was a great idea. "What if we also did more obscure holidays, too, like Grandparents' Day, which would enable families to come for multi-generational photo sessions?" I suggested.

Michelle raised her glass to me. "Excellent. I wonder if Ladybug would wear heart-shaped glasses for Valentine's Day?"

I laughed at the thought. "Probably. Maybe the cows would be willing to be adorned for a holiday. I bet Reba would, too." My mind, relaxed from a successful event and a glass of wine, began brimming with ideas. "I wonder if we could have themed costumes made for the animals that parents could buy for their kids in matching versions."

"You mean like Batman masks and capes for the critters, plus the child would get the full body suit, too?"

"Exactly!" I high-fived my friend across the table.

We laughed about it, then I turned serious, needing to unburden myself about the disastrous afternoon I'd had with Danny Copsey.

"You didn't tell me he'd asked you out," Michelle chided me. "But let's face it. You didn't really know him, anyway. Maybe it's better that it didn't work out."

I was taken aback. "You were quite enthusiastic about him at the livestock auction."

"I know. I was blinded by the fact that he looked pretty good and I want you to be happy. But Becca, he's got a son who was abandoned by his mother and might not be so happy to have the woman who stole his hedgehogs be a permanent fixture in his life."

"I'm also the woman who got his dad head-butted by a goat." Was Michelle right? Was everything surrounding Danny Copsey and me ill-fated?

I sighed and stood, taking our wine glasses to the sink, busying myself to cover the inexplicable hurt I was feeling over Meesh's reaction. I also grabbed the now-empty wine bottle and took it out the kitchen door to drop it into the recycling bin.

I gazed out across the property as I nearly always did when going outside. Movement caught my eye in the distance and I had to mentally process what I was seeing. Was that my mother, Georgina Denise LaMotte Manigault Taylor, dancing on my outdoor stage? If I wasn't mistaken, she was doing a shuffling version of the Hustle.

My hurt over Michelle's reaction was instantly forgotten as I stared at my mother, mesmerized. Mom moved into another dance. She held her arms up as she did so. It was as though she had music playing in her head as she waltzed with an invisible partner around the stage in her tan elastic-waisted polyester pants and white button-up blouse.

Was it Dad? Or maybe someone else from her past?

I wondered what was going through her mind at that moment. I also thought about how that could be me one day. And that I could be just as alone as she was.

I left my mother to her private twirling and went back inside. I didn't tell Michelle about it but instead told her that perhaps she was right, Danny Copsey was not a good choice for me and I was too busy with the safari, anyway.

Michelle seemed relieved. "You also haven't been broken up from Mark for very long. You can't possibly know what you want yet."

All good logic that my heart wasn't particularly interested in hearing.

Mom came banging in through the front door. "Rebecca?" she called out.

"In the kitchen with Michelle," I sang back.

Mom entered the kitchen, thoroughly flushed and sweaty, yet beaming.

"Everything okay?" Michelle asked her.

"Yes, yes, of course. I was just...inspecting the grounds. It's too much property for Becca to manage on her own, you know." Mom went to a cabinet and pulled out a glass, then scooped ice from the freezer before pouring sweet tea from a pitcher on the counter.

Michelle had interacted with my mother long enough

to know when a setup statement was being tossed out and wisely said nothing.

"Are the grounds acceptable?" I asked, avoiding her dart about my inability to manage.

My mother sat down and took several gulps from her glass. "Nothing terribly wrong. That stage of yours is ridiculous, though. Who wants to sit outside with the heat and the bugs and watch some silly little play?"

I clamped my lips shut against my instinctive response about her having enjoyed the stage very much just five minutes ago.

She must have taken my silence for well-delivered chastisement, for she went on. "I can't imagine that working. And look at how it's set up. You're going to have another hawk crashing into it. You'll have two bird deaths on your hands. That will be a terrible omen." She took another long drink from her glass.

Again with the omens. I swear, I could never figure out whether my mom was occasionally faking me out with the extent of her Alzheimer's or if she was so far gone that she rambled nonsensically like this. I knew that those suffering from dementia could become obsessed with topics, but Mom seemed a little too... crafty...about it.

Fortunately, my phone rang at that moment. It was Simon Rhodes, who had stayed late and wanted to demonstrate his fully formed bird show for me.

I invited both Mom and Michelle to go with me. Michelle politely declined and took her leave while Mom shrugged and sarcastically said, "Let's hope he doesn't let one get away to crash into the stage."

I sighed. My mother seemed determined to see me fail.

Mom trudged with me to the aviary, complaining the entire way. Simon Rhodes welcomed us and stepped us through his proposed show, which was a combination of talking about bird types and behaviors, showing off the birds themselves, then having them do tricks. He had different birds performing different tricks, although the larger parrots were far better at complicated actions than small birds.

He pulled feathered creatures out individually. All of them paid close attention to Simon's hand signals and simple commands.

Simon had obtained a portable speaker system and lapel microphone, making his voice loud and clear. However, the birds were all fascinated with the mic clipped to his shirt and all in turn tried nipping it away. "I guess I need another sort of microphone," he said.

I nodded. I was getting used to constant, unexpected expenses.

"I guess the peacocks are too young yet?" I asked as he put away a yellow-crested cockatoo—a gorgeous thing with white feathers and an amusing yellow point on the back of its head—and pulled out a military macaw. The macaw looked like a vivid painting, with bright green on the top of its head progressing through shades into olive on its lower body. It had a red splotch at the top of its beak and tail feathers of brown and red.

The birds were growing quickly.

"Yes." Simon's voice boomed through the microphone. "When Lapis is old enough, I'll teach him to spread his tail feathers on command. For now, he just needs to grow."

The trainer held up the parrot on his arm, sweeping the bird gently around so that a future large audience could see him. The bird mumbled something unintelligible.

"Meet MacArthur. Macaws come from Central and South America. Most like tropical rainforests but the military macaw prefers arid land. This fellow will live to be about fifty years old. We must keep his feathers trimmed so he doesn't go anywhere."

Mom shifted uncomfortably next to me.

"What's wrong?" I whispered.

She ignored me and stood to address Simon. "Doesn't that hurt the bird? We've already got one dead hawk here. I don't want you injuring more of them."

Simon smiled. "No, ma'am. You only need to trim one wing to keep the bird grounded and you never trim far up enough to do any damage. Think of it as trimming your nails. You never cut far up enough to cut skin, right? And it never hurts to just trim nails? That's what it's like with trimming a bird's feathers."

Mom seemed doubtful.

"Tell you what," Simon continued, "I was planning to trim this fellow's wing this evening. Why don't you stay and watch?"

"I guess it would be fine if I kept an eye on it. Lots of unfortunate incidents happening around here lately." My mother nodded wisely.

I wasn't sure what to do to derail her from her from this train track to doom she was on with the safari. I mean, sure, a couple of odd things had happened, but it wasn't anything totally inexplicable, nor was it anything over which to call the police…yet.

The graffiti on the barn…I knew *who* had done it, I just hoped he would stop soon.

I was lost in thought but dragged out of it by the sound of wings flapping and air brushing by my face. Simon shouted an obscenity and I saw a blur of green pass by me before I really understood what was happening.

Simon ran past my mother and me, his jacket flapping behind him as he raised his fist in the air and continued yelling at the macaw, who quickly became a little dot of color in the sky.

The trainer returned, his face flushed. "Ms. Garvey, I'm sorry. I—I—I hadn't trimmed his feathers yet, but he hadn't shown any inclination of wanting to go anywhere, so I thought that, well—" Simon visibly gulped.

I didn't like to think of how much money had just been tossed down the toilet. Plus, I'd have to buy another bird. Not only that, would poor MacArthur even survive on its own?

Even worse, Mom found it hilarious. She pointed in the direction of the bird's getaway and cackled. "I told you! You won't listen to me! How many more omens do you need?"

That made me even madder than losing the bird.

CHAPTER 34

A FEW DAYS LATER, I was running around with Daisy, doing an evening feed with the intent of doing a wellness check on the llamas over to ensure their skin, hooves, ears, and mouths were all healthy. After having taken care of goats, cows, horses, and all the little creatures, with Simon having insisted he be solely responsible for the birds each day, I lugged some chow to the llama barn.

"Cuddlebug! Doodlebug! Ladybug!" I sang out, which typically got them waddling over to me. But not this time.

They were congregated on one side of their barn, behind a wood half wall, where I sometimes stored pine shavings for the barn floor.

"Watcha doin', kids?" I asked as I ventured further into the barn. Daisy ran ahead of me, around the wall, and began whining.

Now what? I dropped the bucket of feed and joined the llamas and my dog.

Dear God, my mother was curled up in a ball on the ground with the llamas standing around her. Her eyes were closed and she wasn't moving.

Fear bubbled up in my throat so violently that I felt like I was being strangled. "Mom?" I said tentatively.

When she didn't respond, I cried out, "MOM!", and dropped to my knees next to her rubbing my hand on her exposed shoulder.

Cuddlebug nuzzled my neck and huffed at me but I didn't have time for his cuteness so I waved him away.

"Mom, please," I said, rubbing her shoulder harder.

My mother made a sudden movement—thank God—and her eyelids fluttered open. She turned her head and looked at me in utter confusion. "What? Where am I?"

"You're okay," I said, allowing her to figure out where she was.

She eventually indicated that she wanted help sitting up. Once upright, with pine shavings attached to multiple places on her head, and dirt encrusted under her fingernails, she said, "Why am I here?"

That stab of fear returned. Was mom's Alzheimer's advancing more than I realized?

"I don't know, Mom. Did you come out to visit the llamas?"

My mother looked up and seemed to notice them for the first time. "Why would I do that? These are barn animals and they're filthy. You must have led me out here. Why did you put me down in all of this hay?"

"It's pine shavings, and I didn't—"

"Don't argue with me. What is wrong with you that you dragged me into this filthy place with these disgusting animals? I'm going to my room RIGHT NOW and I expect you to leave me alone." My mother struggled to get up so I stood and offered my hand to her, which she reluctantly took.

I tried to walk her back to the house, but she was having none of it. She shrugged me off with surprising force, leaving me to watch her retreating, pine-shaving-covered back as she made her way to the house.

Maybe I had bigger issues with my mother than I had imagined.

CHAPTER 35

ONCE THE THEATER group was ready to do its performance, which they named the Three Notch Roundup Show, we scheduled a Saturday evening for the show's debut, to be held after the safari part of things was done for the day.

Attendance at the safari had been up and down. Weekends were, of course, the best days for a general audience. I was contemplating closing it down for just private parties and events during the week and then opening up Friday afternoon through the weekend for the community at large. The western show would be a great addition to Saturdays.

My hope was that the incoming money would be more evenly spread that way so I could better manage my finances. For now, I seemed to be writing checks for more dollars than I was taking in, but I was standing—albeit a little shakily—on my own two feet.

I was completely unprepared for what happened with the first Three Notch Roundup Show.

People could pay for pre-set seating near the stage or pay a lower price to be further away and bring their own lawn chairs. It was an idea I'd gotten from the Calvert Marine Museum, which frequently arranged its outdoor concerts in this manner.

There was a decent crowd building as the sun sank lower on the horizon, spreading a gorgeous pink and orange glow across the sky. I would need to put animals away soon but I was excited to see the show first.

A woman in a sequined, violet-colored outfit that I could only characterize as a square-dancing dress on steroids, came out to the floor microphone and welcomed the audience to the show. She promised a "wild, wonderful, and wacky time for everyone," which elicited cheers.

Then she announced her first performer, Cowboy Casey, who came out with a banjo and played very silly tunes. My favorite was one about a horse that went into a saloon and played poker to win money to buy himself some new shoes. The banjo player also did a sing-along with the audience, feeding them lines to sing. The crowd loved it.

After the banjo player, an ensemble cast came out and performed a skit about a man who loses his dog and mopes about town looking for said dog. There was a build-up of all the talents the dog had—shepherding sheep, fetching, pouring beer from the tap for his master, holding reins and guiding his master's horse and cart while the man slept in the wagon—on and on it went until finally the man found the dog, who came out on stage—a man in a dog's costume, walking around on two feet—and shook his owner's hand, thus negating any idea that the dog's abilities were special.

There were more hoots and cheering from the audience and I began realizing that the western show was an excellent addition to the safari.

The emcee returned, this time having changed into a lemon-yellow version of her previous dress, except this one also had green polka dots on it. She also carried a lace fan.

"Ladies and gentlemen, it is my duty to inform you that we have been invaded," she whispered breathlessly into the microphone, waving the fan in front of her. I wondered if she would soon have the vapors.

There were rumbles in the audience.

"Yes, I said invaded. Do you know what cold-hearted villain walks among us?" She crossed her arms in front of her, waiting for an answer.

"Napoleon Bonaparte?" someone yelled.

The emcee arched an eyebrow in the direction of that statement. "No, my little scalawag. Not Bonaparte. Someone *much* more evil. Someone with a heart of coal and the mind of Lucifer. He'd steal candy from a baby just for the amusement of it. He once shot a man for reading a book. He's known as the Fiend of the County. Yes, I'm talking about Bushwood Bart. Do you want to meet him?"

The crowd booed, telling me that they were enjoying this immensely.

"Come out, you scoundrel."

My homemade curtain began rustling as though someone was making his way to the stage. The backdrop suddenly parted and there stood a very large man, wearing an even larger ten-gallon hat, ebony leather boots, and a leather jacket. He carried a prop lasso and wore an enormous holster around his waist.

What was even more remarkable was who it was. My jaw dropped. I couldn't believe my eyes.

The man playing Bushwood Bart was T-Bone, the local radio personality.

There was scattered applause, likely from people who recognized him, but there was also more booing for the "bad guy".

He strutted back and forth across the stage, insulting the emcee as a "strumpet" and asking where he could find some horses to steal.

I couldn't believe what a ham he was. The audience began shouting insults back at him.

"Yer a bunch of lily-livers," he said in an accent that landed somewhere between West Virginia and Texas.

"I'll take ya'll out with my six-shooter and wipe my boots on ya."

"I'm not afraid!" came a male voice from the crowd.

T-Bone—excuse me, Bart—went to the edge of the stage. "Oh, you will be, my boy, you will be. Come up here." He pointed to the stage and the crowd cheered the owner of the voice to go to the stage.

I wondered where this was going.

Turned out it was a teenaged boy. No, wait, he was older than that. In fact, no…it couldn't be.

It was Jimmy, April's genius boyfriend.

He ambled up to the stage, where Bart challenged him to a duel. Except the duel was to be with Nerf blasters. The emcee—who popped Bart over the head with her fan—managed the duel, instructing the participants on taking their paces.

Naturally, as soon as she shouted, "Fire!", Bart was slow to pull and Jimmy got him with a foam Nerf rocket.

Thus began Bart's slow and torturous death as T-Bone overacted his way to his demise, cursing Jimmy and the entire audience along the way before finally flinging himself onto the stage floor.

The crowd loved it.

The emcee escorted Jimmy from the stage then called out, "I need some hands to drag this evil rapscallion away."

To his credit, T-Bone acted like dead weight while four men in western wear came out and hauled him behind the stage.

"Who knew he had it in him?" came a familiar female voice from behind me.

I whipped around to find his wife, Heather. I could see that she was grinning broadly despite the encroaching darkness. I needed some outdoor lights put up around the property if I was going to have evening shows. "He was great," I said.

"You have no idea how long he's been waiting for this evening."

"Perhaps he missed his calling as an actor. Any chance he would leave radio?"

"No way," she said. "It's the T-Bone and Heather Show. I need a T-Bone to make it work."

"True." The emcee was moving on to another skit and I realized that I still needed to do evening rounds with the animals. "Would you like to come with me while I do my evening round-up?"

"Sure, pardner," Heather replied. "I'm interested in seeing your critters for myself."

I smiled myself and we walked companionably together while I did all of my usual chores. Heather asked interested, thoughtful questions about the animals' care and feeding. I loved talking about them and didn't mind sharing what I knew, even though I probably needed to study and work more with some of the animals, namely the birds.

The goats and llamas were last this evening. I dug my large scoop into the goat pellets first and told Heather, "Watch this. Everyone loves watching the goats eat."

I did my usual method of feeding them, and of course, they performed their usual antic of running down the line to the dishes. Except...there was an extra goat and no dish. The goat bleated at me in the darkness. What? It simply wasn't possible that the goats could have skipped over a dish. They were, after all, goats.

I peered closer. "No way," I said in disbelief.

"What's wrong?" Heather asked coming alongside me.

I pointed. "That isn't my goat."

Heather shook her head. "What do you mean, not your goat? It couldn't have just wandered here from a neighboring property, could it?"

"No." I was confused because Heather was absolutely

right. Not only would a goat not have wandered to my property, but it also wasn't likely to have opened the gate by itself.

I had no idea what to do about it in the moment and resolved to find the goat's owner in the morning. I hoped people didn't think I was now a dumping ground for unwanted animals.

"Let's do the llamas," I said, returning to the feed shed for more scoops of food. Heather asked if she could feed them, so I handed the scoops to her and we walked to the llama pen.

"Come on in and meet them," I offered.

Heather reacted as most people do because the Bugs are just so cute. As she poured out their food and told them how adorable they were, I stood to the side so that the llamas wouldn't come to me.

Watching Heather's reaction, I thought that maybe Mom had been attracted to the Bugs because they were so gentle and easy to be around. I was glad that I hadn't found her out here again.

It was while standing off to the side that I heard it.

Bleating nearby. And it was most definitely a goat.

What the—?

With Heather entranced by the llamas and my eyes becoming well-adjusted to the dark, I walked toward the sound of the bleating and came upon another goat here in the llama pen.

"Who are you?" I asked the goat. "How did you get here?"

I reached out and touched the animal, who didn't shy away from me. The goat was a fat little thing.

Wait a minute.

I ran my hand down its side. Or should I say, *her* side. If I wasn't mistaken, this goat was pregnant. Not only could I feel the kid's lump, but Mama's udders were full.

You have got to be kidding me.

Well, I didn't want Heather to know that I had goats dropping out of the sky onto my property. "All done?" I asked brightly.

She hadn't seemed to notice the second goat, so I just led her out of the llama pen, where she thanked me profusely and went to find her presumably revived husband while I returned to coax the goat into the llama barn for the night.

I quickly cordoned off a corner of the barn with sheets of wire pen material, then created a bed of straw for her inside the pen, piling it thick for her comfort and for her kids once she delivered them. I also went to one of my sheds and dragged a large heat lamp back to the pen. Goats, like many animals, handle their own deliveries without the ministrations of doctors, nurses, or midwives. However, having some comforts like a soft bed and a heat lamp helped things along.

Thus satisfied that she was comfortable, I went to the house for some much-needed sleep.

It was restless sleep, as I awoke several times wondering if Dickie Walker dumped goats on me as some sort of protest against the safari.

If so, it didn't make much sense since he was only adding to my collection.

By the next morning, I was in danger of losing one of those additions, for the pregnant mama went into distress.

CHAPTER 36

THE NEXT MORNING, I went out to feed everyone, leaving the llamas for last so I could check on the pregnant doe at length while in their barn. By the time I reached the llamas' barn with both llama and goat feed, workers were arriving to start their day and I could hear the already-familiar crunch of gravel, shutting of car doors, and banter among them. They all sounded reasonably happy.

However, I wasn't hearing the doe bleating. Where was she?

"Becca!" I heard a female voice above the worker noise in the background and the rustling llamas in front of me.

I turned. It was Dee Dee approaching me. "You're up and about early," I said, noticing that she wasn't clad in one of her usual spiffy outfits but was instead wearing old khaki pants with a hole in the right knee and a stained t-shirt.

"I was wondering if you needed any help today. I was supposed to go to settlement on a property but the buyer's financing didn't work out, so it was canceled. I've got time to spare and thought maybe you could use it." Dee Dee had reached me by this point.

"Not sure I need any help, but I do have something interesting to show you," I said. "Come."

I let her into the llama barn to release the goats from their pens. "Here," I said, handing her the giant scoop of llama feed. "This gets split evenly into their troughs."

Dee Dee willingly took the food as I went to check on the doe.

Mama was on the ground, panting and clearly in a wretched state. *Crap.*

Dee Dee joined me with her empty scoop. "What's this?"

"Someone dumped a couple of goats here yesterday, including this mama-to-be. But she needs help delivering and all she's got is you and me."

Thank goodness it was completely light outside now so that I could see what I was doing.

"Um, are you saying you're going to be the goat's obstetrician?" Dee Dee asked.

"Yes, and you're going to assist."

Dee Dee swallowed. "Yes, boss."

I got to work. Most goats bore kids in pairs, so I knew I needed to be prepared to bring two into the world.

The fact that the mama goat wasn't on her haunches trying to give birth, which they did in sort of a urinating position, told me that she had already been unsuccessful at that.

"I'm guessing the first kid is breach," I said. "Can you go into the feed shed next door and open the third cabinet from the left? I should have some gloves and lubricant in there. There should be some old towels in there, too."

"Uh, okay." Dee Dee returned quickly with the items. I snapped on gloves and asked her to do the same.

"Arrange towels beneath her so I can grab the newborns in them," I instructed.

Dee Dee did as I said, although I could tell she was unnerved.

I squirted lubricant all over my gloves and rubbed my hands together. "Mama, I'll work as fast as I can so this doesn't hurt much."

Pushing one of her legs up, I entered the mother with

one hand, feeling for the kid's hooves or his head. I glanced back at Dee Dee. She was a little green but didn't back away.

"It's different when you're on this side of things," I joked.

That seemed to dispel a little of the tension for her.

I was unable to find what I wanted. I pushed the kid further back up into the birth canal. "Sorry, Mama, I'm trying to get him turned around."

I waited a few moments then went back in. Ah, a hoof! I worked my hand around until I could feel his head and the other hoof. Firmly taking both front hooves in my hand, I gently tugged until I felt him moving forward. As he made his way down, I placed my other hand inside to cradle his head.

I brought him out, bending him so that he dropped out like a little comma. He spilled onto the towel.

"Oh my god, oh my god, oh my god," Dee Dee panted next to me in rhythm to the mama goat's heavy breathing.

"Whoa, you're a big fella," I said. Without directly touching it, I instructed Dee Dee to pick it up within the towel and present it to the mama while I handled the next birth. Dee Dee did so, laying the blanket next to the mama and somehow managing to get mucous and blood all over herself.

Mama sniffed but wasn't ready for her baby yet.

I worked to pull the next kid out, but noticed there was far less movement from the baby this time. In fact, this baby didn't seem to be cooperating at all. As with the first one, I pushed this one back into the birth canal. The mama goat struggled hard to launch this one and I really had to help her get it out.

The second kid spilled out and didn't move.

"Ohhh," Dee Dee breathed.

Not sure what to do, I enveloped this kid in another

towel and presented it to its mother. The mama goat completely ignored her stillborn kid. Having apparently regained a little strength with the birthing over, she concentrated on the living one, licking it thoroughly not only to clean it but to stimulate her baby to start nursing.

"Poor little thing," Dee Dee said. "What will you do with him?"

"Bury it. I've got a place deep in the woods that I use for animals that die. It happens with more regularity than you might think."

About an hour later, we had buried the stillborn goat deep into the ground to avoid any predators digging it up. We returned to the barn to find the baby nourished, the mama exhausted, and both of them passed out. Mama had passed the placenta and eaten half of it. I picked up the new kid, who was now fluffy and clean thanks to its mother's ministrations. "You need some cuddles," I said as I held him and breathed deep of his newness. I was suddenly filled with warmth toward these creatures. "Maybe I should name my goats," I ventured.

"Of course you should," Dee Dee said, rising and stripping off her gloves then trying futilely to remove straw and pine shavings from her pants. "Don't you name everything else?"

"Yes, but never the goats for some reason."

Dee Dee gazed down at the newborn. "How about Cuddles?"

I smiled. "Perfect." I laid the kid down at Mama's teat again. Mama grunted as her baby latched on again, but quickly settled in with it.

"If the kid is Cuddles, what about Bubbles for Mama?" I suggested. "It sort of rhymes."

"Sounds great to me. You should name the rest of them later. I can't believe how exhausting that was. And we weren't doing nearly the work that Mama was doing."

Dee Dee exhaled loudly. "Is there a sink nearby?" She pointed down to her pants, which were now drying with the birthing's aftermath on them.

"There's a hose behind the barn." I was a mess, too, but I moved around to Bubbles's head and rubbed beneath her chin. "Poor girl. Another woman who was left by her man," I said, attempting to lighten the mood.

Dee Dee laughed. "I'm glad I didn't have to help deliver a baby for *you*. That would have given me nightmares for months. Besides, there's quite enough chaos going on in your life. Imagine if you were pregnant, too."

That reminded me. "Mark called me recently. He was looking for profits from the safari. As if there are any yet. But he threatened to call you because I told him you were helping out here and he got mad that you were apparently 'siding' with me. He planned to tell you to quit working with me."

Dee Dee rolled her eyes. "Yes, he called me. I wasn't going to mention it to you because it was so ridiculous. I explained that I was helping you, one woman supporting another. He told me that I was, let's see…" She helped up a grimy hand to count off. "A traitor. A backstabber. Oh, and also a Judas."

I was embarrassed on Mark's behalf. "I'm so sorry. You shouldn't feel obligated to do anything else for me if it creates a bad situation for you with him. You've done so much already."

Dee Dee shook her head. "I'm pretty sure the 'friend' ship has sailed off into the Atlantic with him. It's fine. I love your little safari. And now I especially love this little kid. But what I don't love are my crusty hands. I'm going to go find that hose and clean up."

I was becoming very fortunate in my friendships. I wasn't so lucky in my family, particularly at dinner at Bear's house the following evening.

CHAPTER 37

BEAR DECIDED TO do an impromptu dinner at his house, one of his famous "grill fests." My brother was obsessed with smoking food. Turkeys, beef, chicken...if it had once been alive, Bear wanted to smoke it. He had multiple bags of various flavored wood chips—apple, cherry, mesquite, hickory, and he loved mixing them together in different combinations to try and perfect the flavor for various kinds of meat.

Whenever he bagged some new animal, I could be sure he would make some new smoking attempt, and I was happy to serve as one of his food testers.

As Mom and I pulled up in his driveway, I noticed April's car was already there. "I guess this is an all-family dinner," I observed. There were also three cars there that I didn't recognize.

"WHAT?" Mom said, cupping an ear toward me.

I shook my head. "Nothing."

Inside the house was the usual joyous Taylor chaos. Several of Bear's and Donna's friends were also in attendance to partake of whatever Bear had come up with, and the boys were talking at full volume to whoever would listen.

April was standing in a corner, a red plastic cup in her hand, gazing up into Jimmy's face as she hung on breathlessly to whatever he was saying.

Stop being so critical, Becca.

"Gram!" Billy exploded right before us. "You haven't

seen my new bass rod. I'm gonna catch me some catfish." He led my bewildered mother away.

I took the opportunity to say hello to April and Jimmy, schooling my features to be as bright and sunny as possible.

"Hi, Mom!" April was cheerful herself. "Jimmy and I were just talking about ideas for another western variety show at the safari. Remember when you saw him on stage a few days ago and you agreed with me later that he had done a great job? Because he got his target on the first try?"

"Yes, I remember. It *was* very awesome," I agreed and ventured into another territory to show that I was a supportive mom. "How are your new car air fresheners working out?" I asked Jimmy.

He grimaced. "Too much working against me to make the different scents," he said, taking a sip from his own red cup. "Did you know that you hafta work with a chemist to do that? You can't just name a scent and buy it from a distributor. And them chemists are expensive."

Of course you couldn't just "buy a scent" from somewhere. "I'm sorry to hear that. You know, the offer is still open if you'd like to work at the safari. I could use help with—"

"Oh, Mom," April stopped me. "Jimmy never lets grass grow under his feet. He has a new idea that doesn't require a chemist's help. In fact, it's so ridiculously simple that he'll probably have them manufactured in mere weeks."

I braced myself for what was next. Maybe I should have gotten my own red cup full of something clear and strong before coming over. "What's that?"

"Tell her," April urged her boyfriend.

Jimmy went to a nearby occasional table full of framed family photographs and came back with a phone, presumably his own.

"Everyone has one of these, right?" he said rhetorically, holding it up for me to see.

I nodded.

"And we use them in all conditions. In the house, in the car, at work, at the store, whatever."

I nodded again. Where was Captain Obvious going?

"They are perfectly made for all of these locations. But what they are not perfectly made for is the outdoors, especially when it rains. So, I'm going to make portable phone umbrellas that attach by a strap to the upper part of the phone. The umbrellas will be on an adjustable rod so you can tuck under it while using your phone. The phone stays perfectly dry while you use it."

That was Jimmy's longest speech to date. It accompanied what may have also been his dumbest idea to date.

I nodded at him, unsure what else to do.

"I helped him, too," April said. "He was just going to do umbrellas in just blue, black, and white, but I convinced him to do a bunch of other colors and to do some designs. Once they start selling, he could branch out into personalized phone umbrellas and let people upload their own photos and designs for them."

"I see. Are you sure you don't want a job at the safari in the meantime?" I asked, biting my tongue against anything else.

Before April could chastise me, Bear called everyone out into the backyard for meat and fixins.

We all filed out eagerly onto his back patio to sit at one of the three picnic tables he had set up. Red-checked plastic tablecloths adorned the tables. A separate table was loaded with foil-covered side dishes, white foam plates, plastic flatware, more cups, a melting bag of ice, and napkins emblazoned with the Chevrolet logo.

Being in Bear's backyard during a grill fest was like

being transported to Kansas City. The odor of cooking meat overcame you like a lasso and pulled you toward it.

Bear ceremoniously opened the lid of the smoker so that we could all admire the hunk of meat. "Beef brisket, smoked for ten hours with mainly hickory chips with a handful of cherry for good measure," he said proudly.

It could have been an armadillo for all I cared. I wanted some of that delicious smelling meat in my belly.

After we had all loaded our plates with sides of salads—potato, shrimp, macaroni, and crab—followed by receiving slices of tender meat from Bear, who jealously guarded his smoker, I sat at the end of one the tables with Donna next to me and Billy across from me. Bear sat next to his son when he had finished handing out meat portions.

Donna wasted no time inquiring about my personal life. "What's happening with Mark and what about the man I saw following you around at the grand opening?" she asked without preamble.

I took a bite of the brisket. I loved me some crab and generally thought it the tastiest, most versatile food God had ever put on the planet for mankind, but this was running a close second. Kansas City had nothing on my brother. I didn't answer her for a moment while I chewed slowly and swallowed, my taste buds electrified with joy.

But three pairs of eyes were staring at me, waiting for answers. I briefly outlined my interactions with Mark and the fact that he had ranted at Dee Dee over helping me.

"Have you seen a lawyer yet?" Bear demanded.

"No." I lowered my eyes and focused on my plate. Somehow my brother made me feel sheepish that I had not yet done so. Had I not already resolved to contact someone? There just hadn't been an opportunity to do so.

"Becca, it's time," he said. "You can't let him treat you that way—abandoning you and then dictating what you do. You need advice and you need to protect yourself. And the safari."

"Okay, okay," I replied, piercing a final, small chunk of meat with my clear plastic fork and putting it in my mouth. With smoking skills like he had, I would agree to anything as long as I could have seconds.

Bear nodded.

There was an uncomfortable silence for several moments before Donna ventured into asking about Danny again. Not a topic I wanted to discuss.

"He was someone I met at a livestock auction. I beat out his kid on a pair of hedgehogs but when he learned about the safari, he decided to bring his boy, Christopher, to opening day. That's all." A long gulp of iced tea removed the lingering smoke taste from my mouth.

"That's all?" Donna arched an eyebrow at me, putting down her fork.

Someone must have seen me on Solomons Island with him and reported it.

"Well, we also met for lunch at the Lighthouse but it didn't turn out very well."

Bear frowned. "Why not? Did he do something rude to you? I'll find him and—"

I held up a hand. "No, Bear, it was mostly me. I was clumsy and stupid and then we ran into one of Mark's friends who thought I was cheating on Mark—"

Damn, hot tears welled up in my eyes. Where had they come from? Danny Copsey didn't mean anything to me after just one disastrous date.

"Oh, honey." Donna wrapped an arm around my shoulders. "You'll find someone else."

I didn't like that notion, either. I wiped my eyes with

a napkin, shook my head, and smiled. "I know. I'm fine. Really, I am. Just stressed over the safari."

"And that will get better, too." She squeezed my shoulder and released her arm.

Billy was antsy at his seat, no doubt bursting to say something because he had been forced to be quiet for five solid minutes while the adults talked.

"Aunt Becca," he said, clearly sensing that the conversation was dwindling, "I saw the sugar gliders at your safari. I really liked them. Thanks for getting them."

Leave it to a fourteen-year-old boy to make you feel better. "You're welcome, Billy. I got lucky in finding them, but I didn't want you to be disappointed."

"Yeah. I liked the other animals, too. I never cared about them before, but now that they are part of a safari it makes them different." Billy stabbed at a shrimp in his shrimp salad, completely avoiding the macaroni around it.

"I hope you'll come back again and again," I said. He was just a kid, but there was something nice in having your nephew—who had no vested interest in the business—praise what was happening. I knew it was genuine.

"Yeah," he repeated. "I bet you could make the animals do weird tricks, too. Like run around like they're crazy or something. Or jump on top of things and then jump off again. Oh, or chase people. That would be cool."

Bear rolled his eyes. "Really, Billy?"

After the meal, everyone milled around for a while. It was gratifying to have Bear's friends ask after the safari, with all of them telling me they had already visited. Of course, they also wanted to advise me on it, too, on everything from what other animals I should add to what other items I should include in the shop to advertising venues.

"My best friend is starting a new website and you could advertise there..."

"Have you looked into sponsorships?"

"My cousin is making candles. You should carry some of them."

I knew they all meant well, but it was difficult to keep a smile plastered on your face while people offered unsolicited advice about your livelihood.

With twilight setting in, I finally said goodbye to April, then to Bear and Donna, interrupted my mother's Monopoly game with the boys to put her in the truck, and drove home.

Twenty minutes later, we arrived at the farm to find the llama pen open and the Bugs running loose around the property.

CHAPTER 38

I SLAMMED ON THE brakes. "Mom, go ahead on into the house," I said, not bothering to ensure whether she had heard me.

I jumped out of the truck, and quickly corralled the llamas back into their pen.

I also checked on Bubbles and Cuddles. Both were sleeping in their pen in the barn. Giving birth and being born were both hard work.

I went back to the llamas, my hands on my hips. "How did you three get out?" I asked. "Did I leave the latch up by accident? Have you ding-a-lings figured out how to open it? Did someone wander by and decide to visit you on his own?"

Cuddlebug walked up to me, pressed his nose against mine, and huffed. He was so impossibly cute.

"I'm still not happy about this," I admonished him, refusing to succumb to his charm. I was also still confused. It felt like I was being gaslit by someone. So many things happening. Was it possible I had done something wrong or been forgetful? It wasn't likely, was it? It seemed equally unlikely that Dickie Walker was clever enough to do it all.

I wondered for the first time if my mother might be right about the bad omens.

The next morning, I was almost convinced about Mom's ranting of omens, for Leslie Alexander showed up again. Someone had reported my llamas wandering around freely.

"With the animal attacks on your opening day, combined with the animals a neighbor of yours reported were running loose, I have no choice but to shut you down until you can prove that you can exert control over this so-called safari."

I swear she was almost gleeful in her delivery of the news to me.

The inspector was vague in exactly how it was I was to prove that my safari was "under control," telling me that I would have to demonstrate that my animals were not attacking anyone.

How was I supposed to prove they weren't attacking anyone unless the safari was open and people were interacting with them?

Bureaucracy at its finest.

I let the inspector go before I went into a bigger rage than one of my goats. After she drove away, I jumped into my own vehicle and drove down to Dickie Walker's house.

I stopped behind the two cars parked in the driveway and completely ignored the metal sign informing me that I would be shot for trespassing. Instead, I barged right up to the front porch and banged on the storm door, which rattled on loose hinges as I did so. The house was a rambler but set in shotgun style with the length running front to back.

The porch, which ran the short front length of the house, had an old, dusty swing on it. It was heaped with old boxes that had apparently once contained a coffeemaker, a waffle maker, an infant's teething ring set, a car seat, a lamp, and a set of standard pillows. The boxes had never made it to the refuse transfer center. Or even a trash can, for that matter.

No one answered.

Still angry, I banged again. "Dickie!" I called out. "Let's talk about what you've done to my safari."

The front door yanked open, screeching in protest. Dickie appeared, standing behind the glass. I could barely make out his diminutive wife, Nancy, cowering behind him.

He hooked his right thumb into the metal ring of his dungarees near his shoulder and glared at me from beneath the visor of his John Deere cap, which he apparently wore both outside and inside. "Dadgum, woman, what in the name of Sam Hill is the matter with you? Ain't it enough that you've turned our neighborhood into an amusement park?"

I wasn't going to be cowed by him. "Did you let my llamas out of their pasture?" I demanded.

"What? Why would I touch those fool things?" he shot back.

"I don't believe you. Did you also dump two goats on me, including one that was pregnant? She's okay, by the way. I delivered one healthy kid for her. And did you stick a burr onto the behind of one of my bucks? Did you graffiti up my gift shop?" I was really warming up now, thinking that maybe the dead hawk wasn't a coincidence and I should accuse him of throwing it onto my porch.

"'Deed by God you're a crazy one." He turned back to his wife. "Nancy, don't be associating with her anymore. She's cuckoo for Cocoa Puffs. I don't need you in the looney bin, too."

I opened my mouth to respond but he shut the door firmly in my face. I was still furious but realized my approach was probably not the best and I should leave. Especially since I was pretty confident he was already locking and loading.

I jumped back into my car and backed away before I could be the recipient of any warning shots.

As I started toward my own home, already feeling a little ridiculous for my offensive against Dickie Walker, I saw Mrs. Lomax puttering down the road toward me, a red plastic cup in her hand and a cigarette dangling from her lips.

She held out a hand to flag me down. I stopped and opened my window. "Good day, Mrs. Lomax," I said. Up close I could see that her cup was full of something caramel-colored. Could be a soda, was probably something else.

"What's happening with that safari of yours?" she asked, flicking an ash away from her cigarette. "Any problems? Be too bad if you had to shut down too quickly."

I swear she smirked when she said it.

———

Still roiling over the county shutting me down and both Dickie Walker's and Carrie Lomax's comments to me, I decided to do something else to improve my life, which was to finally visit a lawyer.

After calling all my workers to let them know that the safari was temporarily dead and accepting everyone's expressions of outrage and apology, I went to work finding a lawyer.

I literally picked the first attorney I could find who was willing to see me on short notice. Most had waiting lists that were months long, but I happened to call the office of Sue Ellen Armstrong and discovered she had a cancellation for the following day.

Her office was warmly appointed, and the waiting area was full of magazines to read while waiting. As soon as I saw well-worn copies of *Hobby Farms* and *Chickens* among the usual sports, gossip, and home life magazines, I knew I had stumbled into the right attorney for me.

Meeting her reinforced it. The woman was a cross

between a sorority sister and a shark, someone you felt you could tell your darkest secrets to who would then swallow whole anyone who dared to hurt you. I spilled my guts to her, everything from Mark's behavior to my mysterious safari troubles and problems with the county. Sue Ellen arched an eyebrow over the inspector's shenanigans and assured me that I would retain full control of the safari, no matter how many people tried to work against me.

I believed her and left her office feeling lighter than I had in days. I even treated myself to ice cream at Bruster's before heading home, only to find Danny Copsey sitting on my porch, waiting for me.

I pulled up next to his truck and parked. And wouldn't you know, while trying my best to exit my vehicle gracefully, I dumped my mint chocolate chip cone onto the front of my shirt.

CHAPTER 39

"Hey," Danny said, standing up and ignoring the stain on my shirt and the ball of ice cream that dropped to the ground. At least I wasn't dressed in farm clothes.

I side-stepped the blob and stood there with an empty cone in my hand. "Hey," I parroted, my anxieties returning as I wondered why he was there.

"Umm, I wanted to apologize to you. I know our date didn't go very well. Not the food falling on you—that was actually pretty cute—but I got pretty upset when that Chick character started accusing you of cheating on your husband. It made me a little bit crazy in the moment, but I know you aren't cheating on anyone, and I think I was making you pay for the sins of my ex-wife. I'm very sorry about that and, well, I was wondering if I could have a do-over?" He gave me a shy smile. "Maybe something simple, like coffee and a treat? But, not ice cream."

I had to laugh. "I deserved that."

I went into the house to change while he waited in his vehicle for me. Thank goodness I could hear Mom snoring from her room, so I didn't have to deal with that explanation.

Freshened up in a simple floral sundress and sandals with a little spritz of fragrance on my shoulders, I came outside to find him standing by the passenger door, waiting to open it for me.

I was confused by the gallantry since Mark had never done that, not even while we were dating.

I may have been confused by it, but I sure did like it.

Danny Copsey kept the interior of his truck very tidy. I liked that, too. He suggested going to the Flour Donuts in Leonardtown and I agreed to it.

Because they served sandwiches, the bakery was busy even though it was late afternoon. We ordered coffee and chocolate-covered pretzel doughnuts, which were vanilla doughnuts topped with crushed pretzels and chocolate drizzle.

Don't dump this on your lap, I warned myself as I carried mine to an empty table near the window. The shop was on the perimeter of Leonardtown Square and right next to Marie and Nash, where I had gotten valuable marketing advice from the mother-daughter owners.

Both shops were housed in an old automotive dealership that had been in existence through a couple of families for more than a century. Sitting here now, it was difficult to imagine that my table was placed in the middle of what was once a car showroom floor.

"Hope I didn't catch you at a bad time, by the way," he said, blowing on the steam rising from his cup. "It was just good timing for me because Christopher went for an overnighter at a friend's house."

"Actually, I was just returning from visiting a divorce lawyer," I said.

He raised an eyebrow. "Interesting."

"It really was. I think she's going to help ensure that I don't lose everything. Mark is trying his hardest to have it all—a completely separate life and a piece of the action, so to speak." I couldn't even refer to Mark as my husband or even my ex-husband. He was just Mark.

"Sounds like a great guy," Danny said drily. "But let's not talk about him. How is everything with the safari?"

I finished swallowing the chunk of doughnut I had

broken off and once again felt unbidden tears blinding me. "Sorry," I said, grabbing a napkin from the dispenser on the table and dabbing at my eyes. I really had to quit doing that.

Danny remained quiet as I told him about the county shutting me down. In fact, he was paying such close, sympathetic attention to my every word that I found myself telling him everything, from my struggles with my mother and April to the horrible interactions with my neighbors and the bizarre things that had occurred in the opening of Three Notch Safari. However, I couched everything with so many ifs and qualifiers about what may have been an accident and what may have been done on purpose that it was probably impossible to make any conclusions about my situation.

He finished his coffee while listening to me and went back to the counter for a refill before commenting. As he sat down with his fresh cup, he said, "Becca, doesn't it seem to you that the inspector is being overly harsh on you? And you say she is starting her own petting zoo? It seems to me she might be actively working against you."

"My attorney hinted at the same thing. Do you think the inspector painted up my gift shop and is responsible for the crazy things with my animals?" Here was a second person who suggested it was possible, but it just didn't seem like something a county official would do.

Danny shrugged. "She is certainly familiar with the animals you have. I mean, who could possibly think to find some rare burr and stick it on your goat?"

"*If* it was intentional," I reminded him.

"Sure," he said. I don't think he was convinced. "Well, let's say this inspector, Leslie Alexander, or someone else is trying to sabotage you for unknown reasons. It seems to me that you need to accomplish two things. The first is to get the safari opened back up right away. If she says you need to prove your animals can be contained, then contained they will be. Can you put fencing around the entire property such that it isn't just around individual pastures but also encompasses the parking lot, the gift shop, and so forth? With secure gates at appropriate points."

I stared at him. "I have thirty acres. That would cost a fortune. I would need Midas money and the entire Mesozoic period to get it done."

"But you don't need the whole thirty fenced. Just where the animals are and down the driveway aways then end with a cattle crossing grid. What if you had help? I'm not a stranger to the work. I'm sure your brother is handy. I bet you could even get together a group of people to do it very quickly. Sort of like Habitat for Humanity only it would be Habitat for Safari. Or, rather, A Fence in Four Days."

I couldn't help it, I laughed. The idea was completely insane.

But Danny had all kinds of thoughts for getting it accomplished, even flipping it around to sound like it would be a great marketing idea. "Imagine how the community would come together for you, knowing that the only way your safari could reopen is with this impossible length of fence erected partway up your drive. And it would put pressure on that inspector to let you open back up with the public knowing so much about it."

Maybe the idea wasn't completely insane. I tentatively agreed to it. Meesh could take photos and I was sure Dee Dee would be happy to take the lead on marketing the idea.

"What is the second thing I need to accomplish?" I asked.

He raised his cup in salute to me. "The best revenge, as they say, is living well."

I shook my head. "I don't understand."

"You need to do something that will knock everyone's socks off. Don't get me wrong, you've got the aviary, the western show, and the only drive-through petting zoo in St. Mary's County, but you need to think even more outside the box. How about an animal that few people have been up close to before? How about, I don't know, a monkey?"

I went down the list of animals that couldn't be owned in Maryland without special licensing as a zoo, which I wasn't about to dive into trying to do.

"Well, there's got to be some other interesting creature you can find. So, nothing too wild from the Serengeti, like cheetahs or hyenas or whatever, but what about from the Pacific Northwest? Can you have a moose? Or an elk?"

I jumped onto my cell phone to research it. "Well, beyond whether or not they're legal, they are just enormous. As in, the average moose is nearly seven feet tall, has a big antler rack, and weighs about a half-ton. Elks are a little smaller but with more dangerous antlers. I couldn't have beasts that huge wandering around among people in golf carts."

"I guess that rules out a buffalo or a bison. So, you need something more pedestrian that would still give folks a thrill. What's related to a horse or a llama or a goat or to whatever else you have?"

"Well, a wildebeest is sort of a cousin to goats."

"Wait, a wildebeest is an actual thing? I thought it was a made-up animal for jokes. You know, as in, 'When that guy has too much to drink, he becomes a wildebeest'."

I shook my head no. "They're real. But I don't think you can own one. And anyway, I believe they bellow a lot. For llamas the most similar thing would be alpacas, but I'm not sure that they would be different enough from the llamas—other than being a bit smaller—to excite anyone. As for horses, donkeys and mules are related to them."

Danny didn't seem impressed. "Maybe. Still not very exotic, though, are they? Lots of folks would just consider them work animals."

We fell into silence together as we finished our coffee, our doughnuts long gone.

"You bought those mini cows and you have mini horses. Could you get something else that's a miniature version of whatever it is?"

Cows. Horses. Llamas. Goats.
Imagine them all, on parade floats.

I shook my head to clear it from the goofy rhyme. Perhaps I'd had too much caffeine today. Yet when Danny held his cup up and wiggled it, an offer to get me another one, I immediately nodded.

While he was at the counter, I continued scrolling through web pages, looking for animals related to my mini cows and horses. I laughed when I discovered that there were such things as zonkeys and zorses, which were exactly what you'd think they would be—a cross between a zebra and a donkey and a zebra and a horse.

A zebra.

After more research, I was staring down at a photo of a zebra being offered by a ranch in Texas and found myself trembling.

Danny returned with my coffee but I ignored it. I held up my phone to him. "Look at this. Zebras are related to donkeys so I can have one."

"*Very* exotic," Danny agreed.

I was on a roll now, looking up the care and feeding of one of these striped animals. It made me think of that silly old gum called Fruit Stripe that had a cartoon zebra as its mascot. Dreadful taste and texture but it seemed to have lasted on the market a long time.

It looked like I could care for a zebra in a fairly similar way as I did my horses, except they needed their own special feed pellets and I'd need to plant some special long grasses for them to digest. A zebra was expensive, though. And would need a playmate. Should I get two zebras? A zebra and a donkey? The donkey would be cheaper. My fingers were flying across my phone.

"Becca, are you there? Hello?" Danny's voice sounded far away. I looked up and realized that I had gotten so obsessed with the idea of the zebra that I had completely forgotten about him.

There I went, messing up another date.

I quickly tossed my phone into my purse. "I need to go to Texas to pick up a zebra," I said.

To his credit, he rolled with it. "Okay. Do you want some company?"

The thought of traveling with him shot a dart of pleasure through me. However, I was in no position for it yet. Mark was still unresolved. A date was one thing, confinement together for a week was quite another.

Hating my own words, I told him I should probably have Bear go with me.

He graciously accepted my response. "If you need help when you get the zebra onto your property, let me know."

We finished our second large cups of coffee, by which time I was practically humming from caffeine and excitement over my anticipated purchase. I couldn't wait to get home to call the Texas ranch offering the zebras.

As we left the bakery, I remembered that Marie and Nash had planned to do a special on their animal print purses to support an animal charity for me. I told Danny I'd like to stop in there before returning to my house.

"Hey, good to see you," Angie exclaimed from behind the white marble counter. "We've sold twenty purses so far so forty dollars to charity. People love the cheetah-spotted one, although the faux alligator is a close second."

Tyler appeared from a back room. "How goes the safari?"

I briefly relayed to her all of the good and none of the bad that had happened. "And now I'm thinking about getting a zebra," I concluded.

"Both fun and perfect," Tyler replied. "We have zebra print purses, too."

She looked at Danny curiously so I introduced him to Tyler and her mother as my friend. It felt awkward but Tyler just nodded knowingly.

"Nice to meet you," she said before returning her attention to me. "I hope we'll see you more often, although I know you must be very busy at your farm. Visit anytime."

But I wouldn't be back anytime soon. My daughter was about to wreck my life.

CHAPTER 40

INSTEAD OF BEAR going with me to Texas, Donna joined me so that Bear could help Danny lead the effort to construct a property-encompassing fence. I let the men run with it as I was completely consumed with my zebra since it turned out the ranch had a few babies from which I could choose.

"We'll show you how to bottle feed and that will ensure your zebra is tame. You can also order special feed from us," the ranch manager had said. Bottle feed a zebra? I was completely hooked before I left my driveway to pick up Donna and go barreling across Route 301 toward the interstate.

I spent most of the trip chattering about the zebra and what I was going to name it, while Donna was predominantly curious about what was going on with Mark and, of course, Danny.

"With Danny, it feels like I've just obtained a newborn, wobbly foal and I'm not sure yet if it's going to grow to maturity," I said.

I sensed Donna rolling her eyes next to me as I focused on not getting trapped between a tractor-trailer and a concrete barrier in a patch of ever-under-construction Interstate 95.

"Always an animal analogy with you," she said, shaking her head.

"Great alliteration," I shot back, not taking the bait. "Oh! Maybe that's what I'll name the zebra: Allie. No, no, I don't like it."

I had plenty of time to think about it on the drive and eventually settled on Zelda as the zebra's name.

It was love at first sight when we arrived at the zebra ranch three days and 1,500 miles later. The filly was five months old and gazed up at me with winsomely adorable black eyes set against a dark brown muzzle and fuzzy, chocolate-and-cream striped hair that was vertical on her front half, transitioning to horizontal stripes on her rear half.

"Those brown stripes will turn black as she ages," the ranch manager, Clyde, told me as he showed me the ropes on caring for a baby zebra. "And if you're interested, her mama actually had two foals, the other is a colt. Very rare for a zebra to give birth to two, but since they're siblings, you can buy them both if you want."

He took me to where the colt was with his mama. He was just as cute as his sister, and I knew I needed someone to control me from buying them both.

Unfortunately, Donna said, "Wow, they are unbelievably adorable."

Which I took as a sign I should buy them both.

With the deal done, I asked to spend a few minutes with the mare. I put a hand to her neck and spoke low to her, explaining that I was going to take care of her babies from now on and that she shouldn't worry about them.

I know it sounds crazy, but I choose to believe that some animals can understand us when we talk to them. The mare shook her head and huffed a bit before bending down into her feed trough. Whether that was a sign that she was mad at me or a sign that she couldn't care less, I wasn't sure.

The ride back from Texas was stressful since we had to stop a lot for feedings and cleaning of the horse trailer. Yet Donna and I were singing to the radio at the top of our lungs by the time we got back and joking about how jolted the community would be by these two gorgeous creatures.

Oh, and I had named the colt Zeus by the time we hit the driveway. I loved the sound of Zelda and Zeus together.

But I was the one jolted when we reached the house in the early evening of the fourth day after leaving Texas, for, true to Danny's prediction, there was now a gorgeous yellow pine split rail fence around various points of my property, reinforced with panels of chicken wire—nearly invisible to the casual observer but very effective in keeping wanted creatures in and unwanted creatures out.

"I can't believe they did it," Donna breathed, echoing my own thoughts. I stopped in the driveway, which was filled with cars.

I was speechless.

At that moment, people began pouring out of my house. Not just Bear and Danny, but their boys, several Amish men, and people I just flat didn't recognize.

Everyone was smiling and welcoming me home. I just sat in my car, dumbstruck by what had happened for me.

I got out of my truck, trembling like autumn leaves on a maple tree, thanking each person individually and containing my tears of gratitude at knowing I'd be able to open my safari again as soon as I had the fence inspected.

With everyone gone except Bear, Danny, and Donna, I said to the men, "Ready to see the new babies?"

I opened the back of the trailer, and naturally my brother's first words were, "I thought you were only buying one and planned to get a donkey to go with it."

"Bear!" Donna admonished. "Aren't they the cutest things ever?"

"Oh. Yeah. Very cute." My brother wasn't very good at hiding what he really thought.

"They're siblings and I couldn't resist getting them both," I explained.

Danny knelt at the trailer's opening. "Well, I guess you guys need to see your new home." He reached out a hand to Zeus, who was clearly nervous with four pairs of eyes now on him. But the zebra allowed Danny to stroke him a few times, causing Danny to chuckle. "You are going to be a hit with people."

The three of them helped me lead the zebras to the horse barn, where I put them in an empty stall together. I was lucky I had this much empty space but I was going to run out soon.

Once the babies were fed and tucked in for the night, Bear and Donna took their leave to get home to their boys, who had helped with the fence but today had left early for football practice.

"Want to walk with me while I feed everyone?" I asked Danny.

"Sure." He fell into companionable silence as he walked with me across the property to the feed shed. As I had done with others, I had him hold containers after I had scooped them into their respective feed bins.

We went together to feed the sheep—dang, I was realized they were really going to need regular shearing to not become matted masses—then the goats, then finally my beloved llamas. The mama goat and her baby were still there together and doing well, but soon I would move them in with the rest of the goats.

"I presume no one is going to tackle me to the ground this time?" Danny asked. I heard the humor in his voice, so I smiled.

"Only if you've got some molasses cakes that I don't know about," I said. "Doodlebug might slobber his way into your pockets for them."

Danny helped me with feeding the llamas as he had done the other animals, working silently and instinctively next to me. I hardly had to instruct him, he just followed suit to whatever I did. He even murmured pleasantries to Ladybug as he moved about.

Once they were fed, we left the barn and I turned on a spigot next to the barn and lifted the hose attached to it. We thoroughly rinsed our hands and also drank deeply from the hose.

That done, we started walking toward his vehicle. The evening was over and I was secretly disappointed.

To my surprise, Danny took my hand and led me up the path toward the aviary.

I was so shocked to have my hand enveloped in his that I said nothing, just let him lead me.

He stopped in the middle of the aviary. None of the birds were quite settled down for the night and I could feel many pairs of eyes on me. Well, more like single eyes staring at me from colorful, cocked heads attached to bodies perched on branches.

Except for an occasional chirp, the birds were generally quiet over our presence.

In terms of volume, roosters had nothing on parrots, although the parrots at least calmed down after their morning pronouncements. Roosters went on and on all day. It was why I didn't keep chickens in general. Well, that and the getting-eaten-by-other-animals problem that accompanied poultry.

"You've created something really great here for St. Mary's County," Danny said, turning to me.

I warmed at the praise. "Thanks. You really think so?"

"Yes. You are…unique, Becca Garvey. I am—the county is—lucky to have you. I'm not sure anyone else could have created what you have."

His hay-green eyes clouded and his expression became so serious I wondered if I had offended him.

"It started as my brother's idea. I just executed his suggestion and—"

Danny cupped my face in his hands, dipped his face toward me, and pressed his lips to mine.

I think I may have passed out for a few moments because I lost all sense of time as Danny kissed me, softly and sweetly at first, then with more urgency.

Exhilaration shot through me as though I was a teenager again getting my first kiss. I hadn't felt like this in a very long time.

Kissing Mark was sort of like kissing a wet noodle. Bland and tasteless. No enthusiasm or emotion behind it.

This was…explosive. I felt wobbly again, as I had when I first saw the completed fence.

Danny broke the kiss, held me to him, then kissed me again.

This time, we were interrupted by a scarlet macaw, who offered a chiding squawk at us.

Danny pulled away from me and laughed. "You have a chaperone."

"He's jealous."

With one more quick kiss, Danny said his goodbyes.

After he left, I was fluttery inside in a way I hadn't felt in a very long time. I mentally re-lived that first kiss on an endless play loop in my mind as I took another stroll out to visit the zebras one last time for the evening.

They were snuggled together, asleep, no doubt completely exhausted from their trip.

I decided to visit my old friend, John Wayne, humming to myself as I walked to his stall and breaking into full-fledged song by the time I reached him.

John Wayne seemed a bit put out with me.

"I'm a lousy crooner, aren't I? No range at all." I stroked his cheek and he glanced sideways at me, huffing as he did so.

"Be that way," I told him. "You can't put a damper on how I feel this evening."

I continued taking care of him, Annie Oakley, Kenny, Randy, and Reba. The other horses didn't seem to mind my humming and singing.

"You're not nice," I said, returning to John Wayne's stall. The horse completely ignored me. If I didn't realize he was just a horse I would swear he was jealous.

Did I have Danny's scent on me? I sniffed at my sleeve. Yes, his aftershave lingered on me. I liked it. I glanced up at John Wayne, who clearly did not like it.

"I love you, you old coot," I said, taking my leave of the barn.

It took me nearly two hours to go to sleep as I re-lived Danny's embrace. It was weird feeling like a sixteen-year-old again, all a-flutter about a boy. It also made me realize that I had been going through the motions with Mark for years. Yet, after all that had been wrong with Mark, it had somehow required his desire for a beach bum's life to make me completely separate from him. Which reminded me that he should have been delivered the papers by now.

I hoped to God he didn't bother calling me as I was more than done.

I called Leslie Alexander the next morning and, to her credit, she came out right away to inspect my fencing. I knew it would be impossible for her to deny re-opening me based on what had been done and indeed she did revoke the shutdown.

I was so happy that I didn't even care that she did so with clear animus.

I called April, whom I hadn't seen around the house lately. I wanted to share all of my joy regarding the safari and Danny, as well as to tell her she could open the gift shop the next day, but she didn't answer her phone. I texted her repeatedly, too, but several hours later I still hadn't heard back from her. It was very unusual for her to not be all over her phone, but I didn't want to be overprotective and start calling everyone I knew, looking for her.

My pleasant flutters were threatening to turn into a full-fledged panic attack.

Sometimes it seemed like the worst part of being a mother was *waiting* when you were nervous about your children. You can't do anything that calms your nerves, although pacing through the house at least allowed me to burn off energy.

For some reason, the anxiety over your kids didn't get better once they were adults. I think if women knew that going into it, the human species might have ceased existence thousands of years ago.

After I had gone through half a bottle of wine and chewed off eight of my fingernails, April finally called me around eleven o'clock that night with devastating news.

CHAPTER 41

"SORRY, MOM, BUT it's my destiny. You'll find someone to take care of the shop."

I could hardly keep the phone held to my ear without passing out.

April had just announced to me that she was moving to Florida with Jimmy and they were going to move in with Mark temporarily until they got their own place. In fact, she told me, her father had called her to suggest that she move down there.

I'm sure that was *completely* coincidental to Mark being served divorce papers.

It felt vaguely traitorous that she was going to go live with her father but there was nothing I could do about it. And her being mad at him on my behalf months ago didn't mean she would stay mad at him. Mark was, after all, her daddy.

I swallowed and attempted to steel my nerves. "And what is it that Jimmy plans to do down there?"

Shockingly, the cell phone umbrellas had gone nowhere. That boy had a million ideas, none of them worth more than a nickel.

"He read a book on investing. Jimmy says it's pretty easy and he wants to be a financial planner. He says Florida is the perfect place to set up shop because of all the retirees down there. He can really help them live well and get rich himself in the process. And Uncle Jake doesn't mind us camping out with him and Dad temporarily until Jimmy's business gets going. Jimmy wants to eventually buy a house on the Gulf Coast."

I had a thousand caustic comments regarding this stupid and unworkable plan itching to break free from my brain. I had been quiet up to this point, because Jimmy's plans had not involved taking my daughter a thousand miles away to another state. Now things were different.

"Okay," I said. "Does Jimmy plan to become a *certified* financial planner? Does he plan to do more than just read a single self-help guide, which anyone can do?"

"Mom, don't be so mean. Jimmy is smart and picked up lots of good info. Most people can't grasp ideas the way he can. That's why he'll be so good for the seniors. They're vulnerable, you know? He can help them more than those planners with their fancy talk and high fees. Plus, he won't have to invest in any manufacturing. It will be just Jimmy and his brain."

What a thought. "April, I'm sorry, but this is moronic. Those 'fancy' financial planners have years, if not decades, of experience in helping people managing their money, in addition to undergoing rigorous, specific coursework. Most of them also train on issues of social security and other government programs. Jimmy has just read one, single book. Surely you see how ridiculous this is?"

But April was resolute. "Every businessperson has to get his start somewhere. It might take him time to show his customers how much he knows, but then they will be flocking to him for advice."

I wanted to tear my dyed hair out in clumps. How could my daughter be so savvy in some areas and so blind in others?

"Honey, I'm sorry, but this makes absolutely no sense. To date, Jimmy hasn't had a single business idea that has made sense. We've had Snore-a-Gone, fast food scented car fresheners, and cell phone umbrellas. All nonsensical and unworkable. This, too, will collapse quickly. How can you not see that?"

April was silent for several moments and I hoped she had realized I was right. That hope was quickly dashed.

"You know, Mom, I'm glad I'm leaving town with Jimmy. It will be a great fresh start and—"

"Fresh start!" I exploded, knowing I was losing control of the conversation but completely unable to help myself. It was like Dickie Walker all over again. "You're only twenty-one. You've barely started life."

"—and I can get away from your negativity. It really hurts my energy field when you aren't supportive. Dad thinks it's a great idea."

The beach bum thinks the bum's idea is a good one? How shocking.

"April, you can't be serious. This is—"

"Just stop, Mom. My mind is made up. Dad and Uncle Jake are encouraging me and I need to be around people who will brighten my energy field. You aren't one of those people so I need to disconnect from you for the foreseeable future. Good luck with Three Notch Safari."

"Please, honey, don't be so—"

Click.

I sat there, staring at my dark phone screen.

What was I going to do now?

Daisy padded into the room and sat down at my feet, staring at me intently. Apparently, what I was to do now was to let her outside.

CHAPTER 42

THE NEXT MORNING, I was so heart-heavy and sick to my stomach that I could barely make my feeding rounds. Even the new zebras, who were even more impossibly adorable than the mini cows, couldn't lift me out of my funk as I cradled them and gave them bottles. How had I gone from complete euphoria over Danny to the depths of despair over April in a few short hours?

It didn't help that it was raining. It's like we're always either in the middle of a drought or on the verge of needing to build an ark in Southern Maryland. When it rained, it was never one of those Florida rains that gave the plants a nice soak and then passed over in a half hour. No, the clouds liked St. Mary's County as much as we humans did and would linger.

I hoped we weren't in for consecutive days of downpours.

I decided to work in the gift shop myself instead of trying to find someone else to do it on short notice. My mother wandered in just as the gates were opening for visitors. She shook off her umbrella outside the entrance door, then glanced at me curiously as I stood behind the cash register.

"April couldn't be here today," I said, as brightly as I could manage. I'm sure I sounded like a songbird with a clipped wing, able to sing but unable to fly.

Mom approached me, staying on the other side of the counter. "Jimmy won," she said flatly.

"What?" I replied. "What do you know?"

My mother cut me one of her classic sarcastic looks. "How many times do I have to tell you that this safari was a bad idea and that the omens are unmistakable?"

I ignored her and didn't pursue whatever April may or may not have told her. I'd had way too many confrontations lately and my mother couldn't seem to get past her notion of omens, anyway. No doubt April had talked about Jimmy's plans enough with her that Mom had likely had an idea, even in her state, that April was planning to bolt.

And didn't tell me. It was almost as if my mother was trying to help along the omens theory.

My luck turned a little bit during the day when the rain slowed to a light mist, thus the afternoon was almost as busy as usual at the safari. Meesh showed up to pick up some ad hoc photography sessions with visitors and stopped into the shop. With my mother occupied giving a tableful of children crayons and coloring sheets of flying cows and pigs wearing tuxedos, I told Meesh in low tones what had happened with April.

"How awful," she whispered back in sympathy. "So that's why you're running the shop today. Tell you what, why don't I run it until April realizes the mistake she's made and comes crawling back? I'm sure it won't take long."

I wasn't so sure but I appreciated my friend's optimism. "Really? Do you have time to do it?"

"Sure. And I can advertise and book photo shoots while I'm here."

I really did have great friends.

I spent most of the day attending to myriad little issues and concerns that were a daily fact of life for the safari. As the kinks got worked out and the staff got more experienced, it was getting easier.

Toward the end of the afternoon, the rain had

miraculously cleared, leaving bright skies overhead. I visited the zebras again, feeding them, brushing them, and getting them used to being handled. It wouldn't be long before I could put them in a fenced-off pasture so people could see them without getting too close. They weren't quite ready to be touched yet.

I then walked around the property, getting mud stuck in the crevices of my boots as I visited the goats, the cows, the sheep, the horses, and, finally, the llamas.

I confess that Simon Rhodes had the birds and small animals so well in hand—despite the macaw's disappearance—that I didn't even worry about them.

As I neared the llama enclosure, I could hear music and laughter coming from the direction of the stage. The llamas lumbered over to greet me, Cuddlebug pressing his nose against my forehead and breathing noisily against me. I smiled despite myself.

Daisy showed up and ducked in and around the llamas, annoying them to no end.

"Sorry, Cuddlebug, border collies are gonna be border collies."

In the distance behind me, I could hear the front gate being rolled into place, telling me that we were closed for the evening.

I left the llamas to tidy up the stage. There wasn't much to do there and while I did a little sweeping, I made mental note of how fortunate I was in how well this theatre group was caring for my property.

I finally realized it was twilight, not so much because it was getting dark but because the mosquitoes and little no-see-ums were out in battalions to conquer whatever lay in their paths. It was a little late in the season for them but maybe the rain had awakened them.

I was soon slapping at insects on my skin and wondering why I had not yet set up bat houses on the property to combat the bug problem.

Something else for my to-do list.

I walked back to the house to rub some anti-itch cream on my bites. The house was curiously dark and quiet. "Mom?" I called out.

There was no answer, but that didn't mean she wasn't already in bed. She certainly wasn't watching television in her room because I would have heard that as I approached the house.

I quietly opened the door to my mother's room. The room was dark except for a nightlight, which illuminated for me that my mother wasn't in there.

I went to her bathroom down the hall. That was dark, too.

Thinking that maybe she had wandered elsewhere in the house, I hurriedly flipped on lights in every room, calling for her as I did so. No answer.

Where was my mother?

I grabbed a flashlight from the kitchen and went outside to search around the house with Daisy herding me along as I called.

Where in God's name was my mother?

With my anxiety level tripling over what had happened with April, I thought about where to look next. I remembered mom wandering out with the llamas. Was she there again?

I jogged to the llama barn and switched off my flashlight as I flipped the wall switch, flooding the place with light from the huge canister lights dangling from the ceiling. The llamas were once again huddled together in the place where I had found Mom before.

Sure enough, there she was, curled up in a ball again in the pine shavings. Was my farm lifestyle incompatible with caretaking my ailing mother?

"Mom?" I said, dropping to one knee.

Her eyes fluttered open. "Yessss," she replied shakily.

Once more I helped her into a sitting position and

when she seemed steady enough, I helped her up and back to the house. Once I had her in bed, she muttered to me, "Your father might be proud of you, but he doesn't understand that this safari idea means bad things for you. I've had to make him see reason, you know. He understands now and he will talk to you, so I no longer have to convince you." With that, Mom closed her eyes and began softly snoring.

I quietly closed the door to her room and wondered why she was specifically going to the llama barn for her odd naps. It seemed so strange, not just because it couldn't possibly be comfortable to curl up on a barn floor, but because she had never indicated any affection for my llamas.

I traipsed back to the llama barn, which was still lit up. Daisy had kept the llamas cornered in the rear of the barn. "Daisy, leave them alone, girl," I said as I went back there. The llamas broke out of their huddle upon my approach.

I stood where my mother had lain in a ball. I breathed deeply and tried to figure out why she was drawn to this place. Doodlebug placed his nose against my arm and huffed at me. I absentmindedly reached out with my other hand and patted his face.

"Why does Mom like it out here?" I asked aloud.

I looked all around. Up, then forward and around my direct line of sight, and then I swept my gaze across the ground, which is when I noticed something peculiar. The floor was generally covered with pine shavings, plus I had some straw strewn in certain areas to provide spots of animals cushions for sitting or sleeping. But there was a pile of straw neatly pushed up against one section of wall. It didn't look as if the llamas could have moved it like that.

I went to the wall, knelt down, and gently scraped the hay away from the barn's metal wall. When I had almost reached the bottom, my fingers touched a paper. I grabbed a corner and pulled it out, shaking bits of straw and pine shavings from it.

I held an old photo in my hand. I gazed at it and realized it was a picture of Mom and Dad from their youth. They stood together in front of a car so large it looked like it could have floated down the Potomac River as a ferry. Dad wore old denim jeans and a white t-shirt as he leaned against the car, looking at the lens. His arm was casually slung around Mom's shoulders and whoever held the camera had caught him in mid-laugh.

Mom wore a prim and proper skirt, blouse, and sweater. She was leaned into Dad, gazing up at him with a hand placed on his chest.

My heart swelled at seeing my father like that. He appeared to be at least twenty years younger than I was now. This must have been just before he entered military life. He looked ready to take off and travel the world with his best girl at his side.

I brushed away a tear. Life was never really what you planned for it to be. Don't get me wrong, Dad's life wasn't horrible, but I also don't think he woke up every day and bounded out of bed because he still had that girl at his side.

What if he had known at that moment that Mom would end up being bossy and demeaning? Would he have run screaming? Would Bear and I have never been born?

I missed my dad painfully in the moment.

But I also realized that Mom missed him, too. Much more than she had ever let on. Was that something the elderly did? Do we become so accustomed to pain and death over time that when someone close to us dies we are able to compartmentalize the sorrow and just pull it off a shelf whenever we want to look at it and remember what once was?

Maybe the llamas had proved themselves to be as comforting to my mother as they were to me.

CHAPTER 43

AS THE SAFARI flourished, so did my zebras. The more I researched them, the more I was glad that I had picked them up as foals. By being bottle-fed, they were bonding with me. Had I purchased older zebras with an unknown background, I might have been facing wild beasts with a propensity to kick and no desire to be tamed. I read that an angry zebra's kick can kill a lion.

Hard to believe from the cuddly baby with a fuzzy mane curled up on the ground next to me one morning. Zelda's head was in my lap as I sat cross-legged on the ground, bottle-feeding her. I intended to work with both of them to ensure they would be exceedingly tame. In fact, I would soon use the mini cow harnesses to begin working with them, teaching them to follow me when I tugged gently on a lead. It reminded me that it was probably time to visit Mr. Stauffer again at the feed mill because I was running low on—

My cell phone buzzed on the ground next to me.

It was someone from the St. Mary's Animal Welfare League. SMAWL, we called it here. In rescuing about twenty cats from a hoarding situation, the organization had discovered a donkey locked up in a shed. As far as they could tell, the donkey hadn't eaten in some time, would I be willing to come collect it?

I saw red as I became enraged over the idea that a poor animal had been abused. "I'll be right there," I said, typing the address into my phone's notes app.

And that pretty much summed up my hypocrisy, right? I couldn't bear to see an animal hurt in any way, but I would have happily used Mark for target practice if I could have done so.

I finished up with Zelda and quickly fed Zeus, too. "Harness practice next week, you two," I said, planting a kiss on each of their sweet little foreheads.

I changed into my worst rags, boots, and jacket before leaving, not knowing what I would encounter at the property. Mom was already up and seated at the kitchen table, so I even invited her to come with me, telling her she could wait in the car.

She wisely declined.

I filled a plastic bag with horse feed and also grabbed two plastic bowls, several bottles of water, and a rope, hooked up the trailer to the truck, and off I went to a remote address down in Ridge.

I pulled into a gravel driveway and stopped in front of a dilapidated rambler with several outbuildings—sheds, chicken coops, and a single barn.

There were no other cars. Someone from SMAWL should already be here. I waited nearly a half hour then called SMAWL. My contact had been called away to some other animal abuse situation and asked if I would mind just taking care of the donkey myself.

Great. This could be potentially dangerous for me if the owner showed back up, but my greater concern was for the animal, so I agreed and clicked off the call.

I was betting the cats had been scooped up from both the house and the barn. I was told the donkey was in the shed, so I continued around to where the largest one was located and backed the trailer up to it.

I'd picked the correct outbuilding, for I could hear the animal braying weakly inside.

A broken lock lay on the ground next to the shed's door. Presumably, SMAWL staff had cut it off. I opened the door slowly, talking gently as I did so and hoping the daylight wouldn't be too startling for it.

The poor animal was clearly terrified, rolling its eyes up in its head and bearing its big teeth at me. The shed stank of urine and feces. Thank God it wasn't the middle of summer or it would have been unbearable.

"Are you a jack or a jenny?" I asked, slowly kneeling to peer toward the donkey's underside. The animal was thin and had all manner of scrapes and scabs on it. What the hell had the owner done to it?

"Why, you're a little jack. How are you doing, boy? I bet you'd like some food and water, huh?"

To my shock, I realized it wasn't just a donkey, it was a miniature donkey. He also seemed rather young, since I didn't notice any cloudiness to the eyes nor any gray hair or sagging skin. I was really building up a collection of tiny versions of animals. In response to my voice, the donkey took a couple of steps to the side away from me.

"I understand, you don't know me very well. But I've got a peace offering for you."

I slowly exited the shed and returned to my truck, hurriedly dumping some of the feed into one bowl and pouring one of the water bottles into another bowl.

I carefully carried them into the shed and put them a short distance away from him before backing out of the shed again. I sat in my truck for a short while, hoping that he would eat if he thought I was gone.

I flipped through phone messages, handling various questions that staff were shooting to me. Meesh sent me a text indicating that a kids' charity wanted to do a fundraiser at the safari, what did I think?

I was always willing to try anything once, so I agreed.

With work issues finally cleared up, I slid back out of the truck to see how the donkey was doing.

Once again, I approached cautiously and opened the door. The donkey shrank away again, this time almost to the back wall of the shed. "It's okay, boy, nothing or no one is going to hurt you anymore."

His bowl was completely empty. I couldn't see a stray nugget anywhere. Poor fellow.

Apparently completely fortified, the jack responded to me by kicking up his back legs against the wall of the shed. The noise in the relatively small space was deafening. He followed it up with two more kicks.

I went backward one step, hoping that would calm him down. He nodded up and down as though he was pleased with the impact it had on me.

I stayed still for several more moments then tried again.

"I think I'll call you Bam-Bam," I said. "Bam-Bam the Baby Donkey."

"HAWWWW," he exclaimed, offering me a better look at his teeth. They didn't look too terrible, so perhaps his malnutrition was a recent thing.

"But you can't behave like that anymore. You're about to have a much better life, but you must be a gentleman around your new roommates and around people, okay?"

To say that it took me a very long time to convince the donkey to come with me would be a great understatement, but he did eventually come out willingly, blinking his eyes in the glare of the sun. Realizing that he had probably spent God knows how long locked up in that shed made waves of crimson pass before my eyes again.

It may have been early December but the work was still strenuous and I felt my underarms dampen as I finally got him up to the trailer. I had just gotten him loaded and shut the door when a car pulled into the driveway and parked next to the passenger side of my truck. It was an old sedan, probably a pale green but so covered in years of dusty neglect that it was hard to tell.

Duct tape held up one side of the front bumper and a long crack ran across the windshield.

I ran a forearm across my sweaty brow as a rotund woman about my age got out of the car, dressed in a long-sleeved yellow t-shirt over black-and-red plaid flannel pajama bottoms and wearing huge, fuzzy, baby-blue slippers. Her dishwater blonde hair had enormous pink rollers in it and she held a gigantic WAWA drink cup in her right hand, the straw's upper third smothered in her orangey lipstick.

"What do you think you're doing?" the woman demanded, her gaze shifting between the open shed door and me as she took a sip from her drink, the straw filling with the tell-tale hue of a cola drink. "This is my property. You all already took my precious kitties, now you think you can take Gizmo? I need him for my kiddos to play with and ride."

Kiddos? Was she younger than me?

The woman continued, pointing at me with her stubby left hand and maintaining her death clutch on her soda. "I oughta kick you into next week. You ain't been beat up until you've been beat up by Rayanne Johnson. I know my rights and I know that I can shoot you for taking my animal."

Well, she really couldn't, but I wasn't about to pedantically point that out. She might really have a weapon on her.

I remained calm while she continued with her invective, hoping Bam-Bam wouldn't hear her and get upset at the sound of her voice. It was a vain hope, for I could already hear him rustling nervously inside the trailer.

When Rayanne seemed to run out of steam and the barrel of a gun had not been produced, I spoke in my lowest and most dangerous tone, fueled by both the sweat running down my back beneath my shirt and jacket—which was making me cranky—and my anger over how this nitwit had been treating animals.

"Here's how it is," I said. "You are a pathetic excuse of a human being. You shouldn't own animals, you shouldn't have children, and you definitely shouldn't be offering anyone fashion advice. You should be ashamed of yourself but, of course, you aren't. You bet I'm taking the donkey. I'm taking him as far away from you as possible and you'd best hope I never, *ever* see you near this poor beast again. Because *you've* never been beat up until you've been beat up by Rebecca Garvey."

Rayanne was clearly not used to being addressed that way, for she stood there with her mouth hanging open. I noted with satisfaction that her teeth were far worse than Bam-Bam's.

With that, I calmly got into my truck and started the engine.

I gotta tell you, it felt mighty fine to let that woman have it verbally between the eyes, although it did seem like I was making a lot of people mad these days.

I raised the tip of my index finger up to my mouth and blew across it, then briefly holstered my finger gun in the waistband of my jeans as I drove away, hoping that I was scattering dirt and rock against the woman's car but also knowing it wouldn't matter to that decrepit thing.

The safari was in full swing for the day when I returned, now calmed down from my interaction with the odious Rayanne Johnson. I smiled and waved to guests as I drove slowly around to the horse barn with my precious cargo, avoiding golf carts and people walking the paths as I did so.

Bam-Bam was going to be a good companion for the zebras, but not yet. He was still too skittish and they were too young. Fortunately, I still had one horse stall left open. Visitors gathered to watch as I coaxed the donkey out of the trailer and into the barn. They all seemed to think it was part of the safari's entertainment, so once I had him settled into a stall, I went back outside and addressed the gathering, briefly outlining for them how I had been requested to rescue the donkey from a bad situation. I left Rayanne's name out of it.

Embarrassingly, the visitors praised me for rescuing the donkey. I didn't deserve praise—what else would any normal person do in the situation?

I tended to other duties before wandering over to the small animal and aviary area, hoping to catch Simon to see how everything was going.

He wasn't there, but thoughts of him fled my mind as I happened upon the small animal enclosures. On the ground below its cage was one of the hedgehogs, curled up in a tight ball. "Hey, Pop, how did you get out again?" I scooped a hand under it. There was no response at all to my touch.

"Wake up sleepy," I said, a knot of dread forming in my stomach.

I put my other hand under it and examined its little body, which was when I realized my hedgehog was dead.

Tears sprang up hot and instantaneously. I hated losing an animal despite knowing that they died often and sometimes without notice. Nevertheless, I sniffed and swallowed my grief lest any visitors see what had happened. I quickly carried him to the feed shed to get him out of anyone's view and laid him gently on a hay bale so I could take care of burying him once everyone was gone.

How had this happened again? Had a child gotten into the enclosure and removed him? If so, did that mean Simon hadn't had all the small animals properly locked up?

Christopher was never going to forgive me for this.

CHAPTER 44

SIMON INSISTED THAT all of the small animal enclosures had been very well secured, and I didn't want to belabor the situation, instead resolving to personally check every enclosure every night, including the aviary.

Doing so didn't add that much time to my nightly rounds and made me feel like I was being more proactive about protecting my flock.

I received a call from my shark sorority sister/attorney, updating me on where things stood on my separation agreement. Maryland had eliminated any waiting period years ago so from the separation agreement we could go to court and the divorce would be final. "The state finally figured out that no one was getting back together at the end of the one-year separation. It was just dragging out bad relationships," she told me.

My gut suggested my bad relationship was going to be dragged out. "Your husband sent me a document I can't make heads or tails out of. I'm going to forward it to you and maybe you can summarize for me what it says. I should let you know that I've already spent several billable hours on it."

Great. Hundreds, if not thousands, of dollars for my attorney to figure out Mark's mind, an impossible task.

That night, with the animals fed and mom ensconced in front of her television, which was blaring out some old western series, I sat down at my computer with a steaming mug of tea to steady myself while I clicked open the attorney's e-mail.

I downloaded the attachment, which turned out to be a multi-tabbed spreadsheet.

Each tab contained the name of some account or asset. Inside the tab were long explanations about what the asset or account was about, including rants about how I hadn't appreciated him enough during the marriage. Was this information my attorney required?

He also included his determined value of the asset or account, and how he had derived some sort of percentage split for it, resulting in arrows showing a random amount to come to me or him.

It was a Jackson Pollock interpretation of finances, just a spattering of multiple colors against a spreadsheet canvas.

It took me more than an hour to figure it all out, and I knew the man, so I can only imagine how frustrating it was for my attorney. The doozy was how he had approached the safari. Apparently, since he was the catalyst for my beginning this money-making venture, Mark felt that the lion's share of it should go to him.

I closed my eyes, envisioning him before me, holding a surfboard and bragging about a wave he had ridden. *"C'mon, Reb, follow me. It'll be fun."*

I was very glad he wasn't in front of me in the moment. I'm not sure what I would have done.

I raised the mug to my lips and took a sip to steady my nerves. I must have been sitting there for some time because the tea was already lukewarm. I glanced at the computer's clock. Remarkably, more than two hours had already passed.

No wonder the attorney was billing me so much.

I created another spreadsheet. On it, I made a simple list of our assets and accounts—less anything concerning the safari—then just added them up and split them in half. Easy peasy. One page, a half hour of work. Did Mark really have to make every bit of my life difficult after having left me to fend for myself?

I dashed off a note to my lawyer and included the new spreadsheet, indicating that she could send it to him for review and suggest to him that we work with what I had done.

I fell into a fitful sleep, wondering what Mark might do next.

CHAPTER 45

A COUPLE OF WEEKS later, Meesh told me that a church group that didn't have its own building wished to have a week-long, evening Christmas event at the safari. Would I consider creating a manger scene with my animals if they provided the nativity players—Mary, Joseph, the shepherd boy, three wise men, and a doll as the baby Jesus? And would I mind if it started in a few days' time?

It sounded like a really fun idea and I quickly agreed to it.

The days were going by in a blur. I barely had time to catch my breath at the end of the day—a fact my mother regularly pointed out and bitterly complained about—but I made as much time as possible for Danny, as well as friends and family. It frequently resulted in group dinners and hangouts, which were great opportunities to release pressure at the end of a hard week at the safari. Occasionally I bought dinner for all my staff members, too.

Much to my relief, the strife with Dickie Walker seemed to have abated. I hadn't had any problems with him in weeks. Perhaps all would be well, after all.

To my surprise, I went out to feed the animals one morning and realized that there was chilly air nipping at my skin, my zebras no longer required bottles and were ready for visitor interaction, and not only was Bam-Bam's skin completely healed, but he had turned into a perfect gentleman.

Time was racing away from me.

On the other hand, April was still not communicating with me. Whenever I thought about that, time slowed to a crawl.

Simon Rhodes had developed a series of shows, targeted at a variety of age ranges. He now referred to it as Professor Finegan's Fantastic Feathered Friends. He asked for money to build a small stage set within the aviary and I gave it to him.

I even sat in on his latest show, meant for elementary school children. In the show, he brought up a little boy and gave him a giant plastic clothespin and said, "This is what a parrot's beak is like. Let's see if you can pick up this ring and carry it over there, putting over that small post in the ground." He pointed to a spot about twenty feet away.

While the boy struggled to grab the ring with his clumsy "beak," Simon set a cockatoo on the ground next to a second ring. Naturally, the bird picked it up and waddled straight over to the post and dropped the ring over it while the boy was still trying to figure out how to get the clothespin to work properly.

The boy had been so absorbed in his activity that he hardly realized that the bird had beaten him handily. The other children in attendance loved it.

While they all laughed, I heard a familiar noise in the air from somewhere behind me. Before I could figure out what it was, a flash of green went whizzing by me.

Unbelievable. It was the lost macaw, returning to the aviary as though nothing had happened. The bird landed on Simon's shoulder. I thought the man was going to break down into tears in relief and joy.

The children knew no better and assumed the new bird was part of the act, thus began clapping at the "trick" the macaw had performed.

MacArthur had come back to me. It somehow felt like a sign, but I wasn't sure what that sign was.

Turns out it was the sign of the devil.

I went back to the house to do some paperwork. I had quickly learned that paperwork was something that never ended for a business and all I could do was avoid drowning in it.

As I opened an e-mail from the state reminding me that I would soon need to file an annual report, there was a staccato rapping at my front door. I jumped at the sound and hopped up to answer it. Dee Dee stood there, her eyes wide in fright.

I invited her in.

"Becca, you won't believe who is down at the gift shop. It's Mark."

"*What?*" I was in total disbelief. "How can that be?"

"I tried to chase him off, but he was insistent that he come up here, that it's his house, too, and he can't be prevented from entering. The best I could figure out was to tell him you were on a conference call and that I'd see if I could interrupt you from it. I'm so sorry."

I held up a hand. "Don't worry about it. I should have known something like this would eventually happen."

I surmised that he had gotten so mad about my spreadsheet edits that he had hopped into his car in a blind rage to drive up here and let me know how brilliant they were.

How would the surfing world survive without him during his time in Maryland?

"Also, umm…" Dee Dee hesitated, "I may have, er, bragged about how well the safari is succeeding, just to show you in the best light. But as soon as I said it, I realized how stupid it was to imply so much value in your farm. Like I haven't been through enough real estate transactions between splitting couples to know better. I'm so sorry," she repeated.

I put a hand on her shoulder. "Seriously, it's okay. With the divorce proceedings, something like this was bound to happen no matter what."

I didn't feel nearly as confident as I sounded, but I didn't want Dee Dee to feel guilty for blurting out in my defense. I also had no intention of feeling guilty about Danny, who had become a much-desired presence in my life.

Dee Dee walked back toward the gift shop, shoulders slumped.

I waited on my front porch until she disappeared into the gift shop, to be replaced by my errant, soon-to-be ex-husband climbing up the grassy expanse to the house.

I didn't give Mark any opportunity to make cajoling small talk with me. "Did my attorney send you my simplified spreadsheet?" I asked. "What you did was ridiculously confusing."

Mark offered me a pout. I could barely remember when I used to think it was an adorable pose. "It's only fair that my side of things be thoroughly explained."

Beaten to death, then turned over to be beaten again was more like it. I sighed. "Mark, your side doesn't require any explaining. We just need to come to an agreement on the total value of our assets—less what I have created here without any help from you—and then split it in half."

He frowned. "No, I don't think I can agree that you created the safari without *any* help from me. I was the inspiration for it."

"You mean...you were the inspiration because you abandoned me?"

"Don't think of it like that, Reb. I pursued my professional dream which enabled you to pursue your passion for animals."

I swallowed every sarcastic comment roiling in my mouth, banging against my teeth to be let out.

Instead, I asked him how April was doing.

"She's great, she's great," he said. "You know our girl, always into something."

I narrowed my gaze. That was a stupid answer. "What is it she's into? Is she working with Jimmy on his financial planning idea?"

"Oh, yes, yes. They're doing a great job, I can tell you." Mark's head bobbed up and down.

He was lying about it, but why?

As if to attempt to gain control of the conversation, Mark turned back to our financial impasse.

"I think you should buy me out of the farm to include the value of the safari."

"Mark Garvey, you are out of your mind if you think I'll do that." I did feel a prickle of fear in his suggestion. Would a judge possibly agree that Mark was entitled to some of the value of my safari? I didn't have the money to buy him out. I was barely making loan payments and feeding everyone, animals and humans alike.

Moreover, the man was not ever taking any part of the safari. I would move the animals elsewhere and burn the place to the ground before I allowed that to happen.

Mark must have taken my silence for reconsideration of his demand because he said, "You could take your time in paying me. I'm not heartless, after all. I'll give you three or four years to buy me out. That way you don't have to sell the farm."

I mentally zoomed back to the day I had picked up Bam-Bam and encountered his arrogant owner. "So I don't have to—*what?*"

He held up a hand as if to calm me. "Reb, there's a better solution. Let's just skip the divorce. I'll spend half the year in Florida on my own pursuits and come up here on special occasions and when the family needs me. And of course I'll be here for Christmas. We can have a long-distance relationship. It might spice things up, you know?"

I couldn't decide whether to slap him or spit on him.

"Too late, Mark. The divorce is nearly final." *And I'm happier without you,* went unsaid.

"Aww, c'mon, honey, we have such a long history between us."

Fortunately, I didn't have to make the decision to slap or spit, as a male voice called from behind me, "Hey, Becca."

I whirled around. It was Danny walking toward me with his son. "Christopher hasn't visited the hedgehogs since the first time we were here so I told him we could come back to do that and catch your stage show." Danny's expression was one of great joy at seeing me. It made me shiver with expectation even as I trembled at the thought of telling him about poor Pop.

Mark must have sensed something between Danny and me, for he walked up next to me and casually slung his left arm over my shoulders. "How ya doing?" he asked Danny.

That expression of joy went to one of complete confusion as he glanced back and forth between Mark and me. I tried to casually step out of Mark's clutches, but he was holding on tight.

I decided that I was beyond being polite, particularly where Mark was concerned. I stomped on his foot, which caused him to immediately release me with a strangled squawk. I moved outside his reach and glared at him.

However, Mark was quickly all smiles, acting as though nothing had just happened. "I'm Mark Garvey, Becca's husband. She and I have recently been through a misunderstanding, but I'm ready to shout from the rooftops now that we have reconciled and, brother, you are the first to hear it. Fantastic Christmas present for the family, right?" He stuck out his right hand and Danny reluctantly took it, staring at me quizzically.

"No, we are not reconciled," I said, rolling my eyes. "Hey, Christopher, how would you like to see a pair of baby zebras? No one else has seen them yet."

Christopher beamed and I hurried away with him. Danny was just going to have to fend for himself with Mark for the moment.

Christopher was completely enamored by Zeus and Zelda, especially when I gave him treats to feed them. Relieved that the hedgehog visit was at least temporarily forgotten, I returned him to Danny, who was now sitting alone on my front porch.

He stood as we approached. "That's some ex you've got there."

"What did he say?" I asked, dreading the answer.

Danny merely shook his head. "Nothing to worry about, I promise."

"Where did he go?" I couldn't see him anywhere nearby.

"Off the premises," Danny said. "Ready to see the show, son?"

"Yeah, Dad! Can I get a bag of kettle corn at the gift shop first?"

Danny rolled his eyes. "Sure. Join us?" he said to me.

I could think of nothing better to take my mind off my myriad of problems. "I'd love to, but, um, about the hedgehogs…"

Danny covered his disappointment well at the news. Christopher imitated his father and acted unconcerned, but I could tell the boy was also greatly disheartened by it.

I seemed to be incapable of avoiding falling flat on my face in front of them.

CHAPTER 46

THE BAPTIST CHURCH'S live nativity proved to be very popular in the community. The church made special invitations to disabled children throughout the county to visit the nativity on a special opening night that was crystal clear—if chilly—with stars twinkling their approval over the event.

The children, accompanied by caregivers, were given battery-operated candles to hold while Silent Night and other noels were sung around the nativity.

It was breathtakingly beautiful.

I used the llamas as camel substitutes, throwing blankets over them for their own warmth. They behaved like angels, not the least bit fazed by the adoring crowd and the music. They even stood still later for photographs.

However, it got me to thinking that maybe I should buy a real camel, if the state would allow it. It would require another barn, for sure.

I had a couple of sheep wandering around the event at will, too. All in all, I thought it was one of the most perfect vignettes the safari had ever produced. And the church planned to return every night for the next two weeks for nativity visits by the general population.

On the last nativity evening, it occurred to me that this was something special that should be held every year. I told the church's pastor that I wanted to host Nativity Week every year if he was interested and that perhaps we could theme each night to address some segment of the local population.

I didn't care about making any money as it could be my way of giving back to community members at the end of the year. I suggested that we not worry about an admission fee during Nativity Week, but that we just set up a donation box and the church could take whatever people put in the box.

He agreed and we struck a verbal deal on it.

I was so happy with this outcome that I nearly floated down to the gift shop, which Meesh was running just about full-time by herself in April's absence. She had insisted she was fine with it, that she was picking up more business than she could handle in her off time just by talking to visitors, but I still wondered if she was just being kind to me.

Michelle brought a maturity to the role I didn't have with April, but I had to admit that my daughter had a wildly creative streak that had really imbued the gift shop with fun. Michelle was also creative and the shop was maintained well by her, but it didn't have that unique panache that April had sprinkled into every corner of the place.

I even missed the crystals, which Michelle hadn't reordered after they had sold out.

When I entered the gift shop, I came to a standstill, struck dumb by what I saw. It wasn't the arrangement of products or anything to do with Michelle.

It was my mother.

She had an entire group of her Ladies with Hats sitting at one of the craft tables, all in their social finery. Mom had her own favorite hat on, too, and was giving them a big talk on the safari.

She was going on about how much there was to see at the safari, the best times to visit, how easy it was to drive the golf carts, how friendly all of the animals were, and how much she loved being part of it all.

Had I just entered crazy world?

Mom had not yet noticed my entrance so I hung back near the door, thanking people as they left.

The hat ladies started asking Mom questions about the safari, and I was absolutely astounded by how much she knew. I mean, it was like she had been paying attention to everything that had gone on and was the safari's greatest fan.

I also noticed that Mom had not said, "WHAT?" a single time during the ladies' questions. She must be wearing her hearing aids.

WHAT?! I thought to myself.

I had a million questions for my mother, not the least of which was, 'What changed?'

As I continued to stand there, though, I figured it out for myself. Her friends were hanging on her every word in a way that I never did. She was an expert in their eyes and their attention was laser-focused on her.

I felt that stab of guilt that seemed to be more common these days where Mom was concerned. Just as quickly, I decided what to do about it.

I walked back outside and milled around until the ladies left to go up the hill to see the nativity before it closed.

I then entered the shop again as though for the first time and pulled Mom aside, asking her if she would consider being the safari's new concierge, answering questions and providing directions to visitors.

Mom positively glowed at the suggestion.

"I think we should come up with a uniform for you, too. I would ask that you wear your hearing aids each day, though," I said.

Mom gazed incredulously at me. "I always wear my hearing aids. I have to be able to hear, don't I?"

And just like that, Mom was back to her normal, caustic self.

I discussed the day's sales with Michelle then went

to do my nighttime feeding rounds. The nativity was breaking up, so I herded the llamas and sheep back to their barns before scooping food for each of them.

By the time I got to the horse barn, everyone else was gone and the safari entrance was locked down.

John Wayne and Annie Oakley huffed noisily as I entered. "I guess I'm a little late. My apologies," I told them.

After feeding them and doing a quick once-over of their bodies, I went to the zebra stall.

"Are you hungry, Zeus and Zel—" I started but stopped in my tracks in front of their stall.

They were gone.

CHAPTER 47

I TRIED NOT TO panic. At first, I concluded that the zebras had wandered off through a gate that was accidentally left open. I raced out and checked all of my gates. Not a single one was open.

Okay, maybe someone had left a gate open and later closed it, not realizing that the zebras had wandered out.

I knew I was grasping at straws. Both of my striped companions stayed very close to me whenever I let them out. I didn't think they would take it upon themselves to wander away even if the gate was open and someone had installed runway lights and placed neon arrows on the field to show them the way out.

I closed my eyes, trying to decide what to do next.

Finish feeding everyone.

I went to the horse feed area, where I realized that the new pellets I had ordered from the Texas ranch where I had purchased the zebras were missing, too.

Well, given that my zebras had hooves and not opposable thumbs, I didn't think it likely they had run away from home and taken a food supply with them.

Someone had stolen my zebras and intended to keep them. A trip to Dickie Walker's house quickly demonstrated that he didn't have them.

My next thought was that it was Mark, but stealing zebras seemed like too complex a plan for him to have concocted.

Was someone else persecuting my safari?

It was a dreadful Christmas, to say the least. I was so upset over the loss of my zebras that I was hardly eating and rapidly dropped five pounds.

Bear and Donna invited me, Mom, and Danny and Christopher to their house for festivities, but I mostly sat on the couch, smiling weakly at the boys opening gifts and offering perfunctory noises of appreciation over Donna's stuffed ham, which I normally loved.

I had reported the loss of the zebras to both the police and animal control, both of whom told me they would be on the lookout for my animals, but I didn't sense any urgency from either of them.

Can't say I blamed the police, given what they dealt with on a daily basis. And what was animal control ultimately supposed to do? Go door to door asking residents if they had seen a zebra wandering through their neighborhood?

I placed some "lost" ads but they resulted in nothing, either. Hence, I was morose by Christmas Day.

Danny gave me a gorgeous Cloisonné pendant necklace, over which everyone *oohed* and *ahhed*. It was in the shape of a giraffe and worked in what appeared to be semi-precious stones like turquoise, lapis lazuli, garnet, and tiger's eye, outlined in gold.

I was touched by it and the thoughtful gift almost lifted me out of my funk. Almost. Not even his sweet kisses were bringing me any joy.

The day after Christmas, there was a folded, typed note in my mailbox.

Your zebras are fine.
I'll bring them back when you
close down your safari.

I had to presume the zebras were being kept locally and it would be rather hard to hide the fact that you had two zebras.

Unless they were locked up in a shed, like Bam-Bam had been.

I shivered at the thought.

I couldn't shut down the safari though. Maybe my best course of action was to continue sending up digital smoke signals that I wanted my zebras back and offer a reward to whomever found them for me. I also sent the note to the police, hoping—but not expecting—that something would come of it.

Meanwhile, I just soldiered on with life.

To my surprise, the safari showed no signs of slowing down in early January, despite how cold it was. It helped that we had not yet had snow.

Being busy helped me get through the days of contemplating where the zebras were and wondering if April would ever talk to me again.

The march of time also resulted in pleasant news. A court date was arranged for my divorce settlement to be hammered out. Mark pled his case to the judge for why he deserved more than half of the safari. To my great satisfaction, the judge sternly rebuked Mark for his greed and awarded me sole right to the safari as well as ownership of the farm with only an equity payout in the house to Mark.

I nearly wept with relief.

A week later, I had my divorce decree in hand.

I invited everyone out to Southern Trail Distillery in Mechanicsville on a Friday evening after the safari closed to celebrate my newfound freedom.

Arriving there first, Danny and I pushed together several bar-height cocktail tables and soon I was sitting on one end, talking to Bear, Donna, Michelle, her husband Jack, Danny, and Dee Dee.

Even Mom had wanted to come along, although while the rest of us were drinking Southern Trail specialties like their key lime coconut crush and redneck margarita, Mom sipped on unspiked lemonade.

Only April was missing.

After a couple of drinks and a barrage of Jack's dad jokes that had everyone laughing uproariously, I rapped on the table to get everyone's attention. "I have an important announcement to make."

"Wait, let us guess," Bear said. "You're building a bonfire of Mark's things and we're all invited to throw matches on it. I'll bring a blowtorch."

I shook my head.

"You're going to write a book about the safari and sell it for a million dollars to a New York publisher?" Michelle asked.

Again, I shook my head although that sounded like a great idea if publishers were actually handing out million-dollar checks these days.

Donna was laughing so hard that she could barely gasp out, "You're getting remarried?"

The table went silent and as all gazes turned to me, I watched a flush creep up Danny's neck.

"Oops," Donna said. "I think I need another bourbon smash to get over this awkwardness." She signaled to a server.

Danny had recovered himself. "No, she's not getting remarried. At least, not yet." He flashed me a smile and saluted me with his glass.

Now I was the one feeling flush, although his comment pleased me inordinately. However, this conversation was going way out of bounds of where I had been originally headed.

"No more guesses," I said. "My announcement is that I've decided to buy myself a present. I'm going to buy—"

Dee Dee stopped me. "No, let us guess! You're going to buy a Mercedes and drive around town with one of the cows belted in the passenger seat."

The table broke up in laughter again.

"No," I said, rolling my eyes.

"You're going to put a llama in the passenger seat? No, no, I don't think any of them would fit." Dee Dee dissolved into a fit of giggles. She had clearly had one too many.

I shook my head. "Again, no. But you're correct that it's about animals. I'm going to buy a camel."

The table went silent again but only for a moment. Most of the table broke out in a clamor over it.

"How big is a camel?"

"Will it get along with everything else?"

"Don't they stink?"

I held up a hand to quiet everyone. "The camel will be even more unique than the zebras are—were, and it can be an authentic part of the Nativity set each year. It can be trained for rides, too. The camel will be my last animal purchase for the foreseeable future."

Laughter erupted again. "Sure, sis, that will most certainly be your last animal," Bear said, shaking his head.

"If a llama won't fit in your Mercedes, a camel definitely won't. You should think about that." Dee Dee grinned foolishly and took a sip from her nearly empty glass.

As my group had sat there, a local band had been setting up along the far wall of the distillery, beneath a sign that read: *DRINKING RUM BEFORE 10 AM MAKES YOU A PIRATE, NOT AN ALCOHOLIC.*

Once they began playing, we all seemed to just slide off our bar chairs in one motion and got up to dance as a block, one person trading off with another in rapid succession. It was like dancing musical chairs.

When the band struck up a ballad, Danny sought me out. I was sweaty from all of the wriggling and bopping from fast dancing but so was he, so I ignored however I might look or smell and immersed myself into the moment with him.

He hummed along to the tune as we swayed together. Near the end of the song, he drew his head back from mine and said, "A camel, huh? I have to admit, I've always dealt in small, um, deceased animals with my taxidermy, but you've made me much more interested in living creatures. Want some help getting the camel? You can teach me what you know about training, too. I'm an obedient student, I promise." He arched an eyebrow at me.

There seemed to be a double entendre in his statement and I giggled.

"I'd love the help. But you must pay very careful attention to my instructions." I also arched an eyebrow. Well, I attempted to do so. I'm sure I looked like a dork because he laughed in response.

The entire evening was so nice I nearly forgot about my stolen zebras for a little while.

Later, Mom and I arrived home and I held open the kitchen door for her. I was still amazed at how spry she was when it came to stairs. I followed into the house and nearly ran into the back of her when she stopped short in the kitchen. "Oh," she breathed.

I stepped around her and realized why she had stopped.

April was sitting at the breakfast table.

CHAPTER 48

THE FIRST THING I noticed was that April had dried streaks of tears on her face. Should I be furious with Jimmy or Mark?

Mom must have noticed it, too, because she went straight to April, put an arm around her shoulders, and kissed the top of her head. "Want some tea or coffee? Some sweet tea?" Mom asked.

April shrugged. "Coffee, I guess."

My mother busied herself in the kitchen with a coffee setup while I sat at the table with my daughter.

I said nothing, just waited for April to tell me what was wrong. It wasn't long in forthcoming, as tears sprang anew within moments.

"It's over," April said, swiping at her face. Mom appeared with a box of tissues for April, who grabbed one, dabbed at her eyes, then twisted the moistened tissue within her fingers.

"What's over?" I asked gently.

"Jimmy and me. Oh, Mom, he turned out to be worthless. He got some clients down in Florida and began cheating them. It was terrible. I thought he was so ambitious. So entrepreneurial. So intelligent. But he wasn't. He was just a run-of-the-mill loser. How could I have been so blind?"

Don't say anything sarcastic, I admonished myself.

Nothing pulls at a mother's heart like her child's unhappiness. Even knowing that she and Jimmy were likely to end up this way did not make it any easier to witness the pain. And hadn't I been blind in my own relationship, as well?

Mom brought a tray with a thermal carafe on it, two cups, spoons, sugar, and creamer. She set it down and quietly left the room.

I poured April a cup and said, "Honey, you can't be too hard on yourself. We all make bad decisions, and we all have moments in our lives where we swirl around in bad situations despite what evidence might be all around us. I don't mean to speak ill of your father, but my situation with him wasn't exactly a garden of lilies and sunflowers."

April offered an unhappy laugh. It came out like a puppy's bark. "Dad. Jeez. He's just as bad as Jimmy. You should see how he flirts with and chummies up to women on the beach to get them to buy surfing lessons. Uncle Jake thought it was funny. I thought it was totally gross. I'm so sorry I left you to go down there, Mom. I was an idiot."

I didn't want to get into a Mark-bashing session with my daughter, especially since she was now back home.

"Don't give it another thought," I said, reaching out to stroke her hair. I paused with my hand on her neck. "Why don't you move back home for a while as you decide what you want to do next? You can rejoin the gift shop, or—" I had to think about whether it was fair to nudge Michelle out, plus April might need a complete change of scenery. "—or maybe you'd like to help me with some of the costuming and scene sets for the animals. You can develop new ideas for that."

April's eyes grew large and she smiled tremulously, so I knew I had hit her creative nerve with that suggestion. She nodded at me.

At least this part of my life made sense again.

CHAPTER 49

APRIL NEVER MENTIONED Jimmy again. I decided it was wise to never bring up her father either, except to tell her that the divorce had come through. April had just nodded and said, "Good for you and good for Danny."

The Amish community visited one Tuesday morning. The long line of carriages was both touching and amusing. These visitors all paid cash and refused to take golf carts, instead walking through the safari.

Mr. Stauffer, from whom I bought much of my feed, was among the visitors. He found me near the miniature horses and nodded at me kindly, the skin around his eyes wrinkling beneath his wire-framed glasses. "Now I see where all your purchases go. You have a nice farm here, although I still can't imagine keeping work animals as pets."

I held up a finger. "Ah, but they do perform work for me. As attractions for visitors."

Mr. Stauffer frowned as he contemplated that. "Perhaps there is a ring of truth to that," he said.

Later, a couple introduced themselves to me as Jacob and Hannah Zimmerman. Hannah shyly handed a quilt to me. "We hear you lost a pair of zebras. Thought you might like to raffle this off to raise money to buy another pair."

With Hannah's help, I unfolded the quilt, done in a gorgeous large diamond block design in blues and yellows against a cream background. Inside each diamond was a farm animal appliqué in complementary calico fabrics. I knew that every stitch had been done by a loving hand.

I was once more overwhelmed and speechless by the county's generosity.

I decided that the third Tuesday of March would forever be Amish Day, dedicated exclusively to these hard-working people to have a day of fun at the safari. I resolved to have my theatre group develop a special show for them, as well.

I felt loved by my community. Until the day someone reported to me where my zebras were.

After the safari's closing one day, I found a note tucked inside the kitchen door.

Your zebras are at Hollywood Hills Farm
~ A Friend

It took just a little bit of searching to learn where the farm was, just a few miles away, off McIntosh Road in Hollywood. Ownership of the farm was a little fuzzy. It was owned by the Hollywood Hills Corporation, which was in turn part of the St. Mary's Field of Dreams Corporation, but I couldn't determine an actual owner's name.

I made some calls to friends to see if anyone had knowledge of the farm, but no one seemed to have even heard of it.

I decided to be a little more cautious this time than I had been when rescuing Bam-Bam. Someone who wasn't transparent about property ownership and had the audacity to steal two zebras from a farm might not be entirely…friendly.

I went down to the sheriff's office in Leonardtown to show them the note, and the officer on duty promised that someone would go over there when there was time. I knew that meant they would go when they had a break in controlling crimes involving humans.

I wasn't mad at the police, just disappointed.

Dee Dee had stopped by with some advertising receipts so I told her about having found the zebras' location and my concerns about going there. "I went to the police but, as you can imagine, this isn't high on their priority list," I said.

"Did you really think they were going to help you load zebras up in your trailer?" Dee Dee asked.

"Well, no, but maybe they would have arrested the farm owner."

"Sure, and then you'll have some protracted court case after you just finished one with Mark. I have a better idea. Let's go steal your zebras back tonight. That way you don't even have to have a confrontation with the lunatic who took your striped babies." Dee Dee's eyes gleamed at her own idea.

"Ahhhh, I'm not sure that's a very good idea," I said. "The farmer likely owns a big shotgun."

"That's why we will do it secretly. You've got dark clothing, right?"

I must have been out of my mind, but I agreed to Dee Dee's plan to get my zebras back, mostly because I thought it would be the fastest thing possible and she was right that it kept me out of legal wrangling. Unless we got caught.

It didn't prevent me from having a knot in my stomach as we drove to the farm around midnight. I was silent the entire drive, thinking about everything that could go wrong. An impenetrable lock. Animals waking up and squawking, mooing, or bleating. A vicious guard dog.

What loomed largest in my mind, though, was the idea of a barrel-chested, full-bearded farmer holding a gun. I wanted my zebras back but not at the expense of my life and Dee Dee's.

I glanced over at her in the passenger seat. She seemed to be anticipating our adventure with relish. She wore her hair tucked up in a black ski cap and was clothed entirely in black, down to her stylish military-like boots. She'd even gone as far as putting black grease paint on her face.

I was dressed just as warmly but a little less dramatically. I hoped I couldn't be recognized.

The night was still March-cold but clear, with a full moon to illuminate everything. I drove slowly down McIntosh Road, attempting to keep the horse trailer rattling to a minimum. As I turned onto the farm's dirt road, I turned off my headlights and continued my slow creep.

I stopped my truck a short distance away and shut off the engine. Fortunately, the farm's residence was a considerable distance away from any of its outbuildings.

"Which barn do you think holds the zebras?" Dee Dee whispered.

"I don't think they can hear us," I said in a normal tone.

"Oh, right."

I contemplated the farm and its buildings, which admittedly looked inviting and pastoral under the low-hanging moon. Unless the farmer was a complete butthead like Bam-Bam's previous owner—and I instinctively doubted that—the zebras should be in reasonably comfortable accommodations.

I noticed that one large structure seemed to be a building that could contain stables. There was also a horse trailer parked near it. I pointed toward the building. "They are probably in there."

Dee Dee clapped mittened hands together. "Let's do it."

I turned off the overhead light so it wouldn't illuminate as we got out of the truck. I opened the back door and grabbed a pair of harnesses and leads, as well as a small flashlight, then went to the rear of the horse trailer to open the door and let down the ramp. If the zebras remembered me, they should come willingly.

Please let them remember me.

We walked in silence up to the stables.

Up close, the building wasn't as nice as it looked from a distance. Even in the murky moonlight, I could see peeling paint, rusted hinges, and rotted bales of hay piled up nearby. It possessed an overall air of neglect.

There was no lock on the dusty, red-painted door. One good sign. Surprisingly, the barn was held shut by a simple hook-and-eye latch. I pressed lightly on the door and lifted the metal hook out of the eye. The door easily and quietly gave way and I entered the stables with Dee Dee so close to me I could hear her breathing.

I flipped on the flashlight, which had a narrow, focused beam. "Where do you think—" Dee Dee started to whisper but I held a finger to my lips.

I crept forward past individual stalls. The place smelled like it wasn't getting mucked as often as it should have been. One horse huffed at our entry but none of the animals seemed overly upset. I counted eight stalls.

We reached the end of the building, which was where I found Zeus and Zelda sleeping in a stall together, Zelda's head resting on Zeus's back.

My heart swelled just at seeing them there.

"Hey, kids," I whispered.

Zelda changed position but didn't wake up. I unlatched the stall door and pulled it open. My entering their stall awakened them. To my delight, they weren't afraid of me at all. They each pulled themselves up to standing.

"You've grown so much," I whispered, as though I

were encountering grandchildren after having not seen them since their previous summer visit.

I rubbed them each down. They seemed relatively healthy if a little thin.

"C'mon, let's go." Dee Dee was restless behind me.

I quickly put a harness on each zebra and then attached leads to the harnesses. The zebras stood patiently for it, as if they were ready to go, too.

I led them out and handed one of the leads to Dee Dee. "Follow me," I said, throwing the flashlight's beam to the ground to illuminate our path.

Zeus and Zelda were as docile as lambs as they readily walked with us. I wondered if they were actually happy to be with me again.

We were nearing the door when I heard the sound of something connecting with metal, then Dee Dee cursed.

"What happened?" I hissed as I stopped.

"A bucket or something. Ow, that hurt my foot."

Unfortunately, the noise agitated the other animals. To my horror, one of the horses whinnied loudly and bobbed his head up and down at us. This got the other horses even more upset.

"Crap." Should I stay still and hope they settled down or just flee as quickly as possible?

Dee Dee was breathing heavily behind me. "Sorry," she said.

I hesitated only a moment more, then made my decision. "C'mon, we're getting out of here before we get caught!"

I continued walking as calmly as I could, fearful that the other animals were going to get the zebras worked up, which might result in them refusing to budge any further.

By the time I had two humans and two zebras outside and the door latched, there was near pandemonium inside the stable. Worse, I saw a light flick on up at the farmhouse.

I didn't point that fact out to Dee Dee, whom I think already felt bad enough for being the cause of the ruckus. Instead, I just kept moving. We were halfway down the driveway when I heard shouting behind us.

"What do you think you're doing? Are you stealing my animals? I will fill you with lead."

I knew that voice. Dear God, it was Leslie Alexander. The kidnapper really *was* a butthead.

I heard the tell-tale explosion of a shotgun up in the air, briefly deafening me, but I kept going, picking up the pace and forcing the zebra to trot next to me. I didn't turn around, just trusted that Dee Dee was right behind me with Zelda.

As I neared the truck, another shot rang out. I heard it lodge into a nearby tree. We were now beyond the warning stage.

I tore around to the back of the trailer, thankful that I had opened it up earlier. I led Zeus to the ramp and he ran up, as though he understood that time was of the essence. Zelda quickly followed behind. I didn't bother taking off leads and furiously slid the ramp into its slot and slammed the door.

Dee Dee was already in the passenger seat when I got behind the wheel.

BOOM. An enormous, leafless branch fell off a tree.

Leslie meant business. I started the engine and did a wide turnaround as fast as I could. Thank God there was plenty of open land around the driveway.

More shots rang out behind us, but Leslie had terrible aim and nothing even struck my truck or trailer. Next to me, Dee Dee was screaming, "Go! Go! Go!"

I was going as fast as I could, the trailer bouncing behind me. *God, let the zebras be okay.*

I got back out onto McIntosh Road and sped up.

Dee Dee laughed, the sound nearly hysterical. "Holy crap! That was unbelievable! I've never been shot at before. Woosh!"

My hammering heart didn't calm down until I entered my driveway. By then I'd had time to think. I had my zebras back, but what would Leslie do to me next?

CHAPTER 50

WITH BOTH APRIL and my zebras back in the fold, I was content enough that I didn't even want to bother suing Leslie Alexander for kidnapping my animals. I didn't like the negative publicity a legal battle with a county employee might bring, and I wasn't really sure what sort of penalties there would be against her anyway for all of the trouble that would be stirred up. Plus, I had no doubt in my mind *she* would counter-sue me for trespassing when I 'took' them back. No, security cameras around the farm were the way to go for any future visits from Leslie—or any other mischief maker.

So, I just threw myself into the daily routine of the safari. Animal feedings, grooming, shearing, hoof and tooth inspections, vet visits, stall mucking, training, and, of course, petting and cooing at them all.

I even found time to ride John Wayne and Annie Oakley on occasion to keep them exercised and to keep me sane. There is nothing more mind-clearing than to be at one with a half-ton creature, gripping its muscular sides with your knees as you move together fluidly across a field. It never mattered to me whether it was warm or cold out, I loved being on my horses.

When not riding or caring for my animals, during regular safari hours I could be found bouncing from location to location, ensuring things were working properly and solving problems. Those problems had, fortunately, reduced dramatically as I continued perfecting the visitor experience at Three Notch Safari.

Speaking of the visitor experience, the zebras were a total hit. Visitors told me it felt like a "real" safari experience to get up close to touch them and give them treats.

I'd also had a couple more buildings constructed to hold more animals. I ensured one was large enough for the camel I still intended to purchase.

I saw Danny when I could, but between his job and its non-negotiable hours, plus his side taxidermy business and caring for his son, he didn't have lots of free time, nor did I. We tried to hold Sundays sacrosanct for church, and either lunch or some other play date together.

I had re-titled April as my Show Manager. She had taken to making animal costumes more readily than I had even dreamed she would. She had plenty of unique ideas for dressing them up—especially the llamas, who tolerated everything from hats to giant plastic sunglasses—and I just let her run with everything.

It was so good to have my daughter back. Mom had perked up even more with April home, too.

The spring turned into summer, as it always does without fail. On a Thursday afternoon in late June, the sun had just come out after a soaking morning rain. We had needed the rain and it had cooled things off considerably. June tended to be unpredictable—chilly one day and boiling hot the next.

I was in the middle of watching Simon work with the peacocks, teaching the male to spread his new tail feathers on command, when Meesh came and found me at the aviary. "Visitor at your front door," she said and disappeared again back to the gift shop. Her photo work at the safari had been exceedingly busy with kids now out of school, and she probably had had just enough time to find me and let me know without even bothering to tell me who it was.

I stopped short as I realized Leslie Alexander was

standing on my doorstep. She held up her hands, palms toward me, in a surrender gesture, so I assumed she didn't have any loaded weaponry tucked away in her waistband. Today she looked like a bumblebee, with a yellow pantsuit trimmed with a black belt and an ebony-and-gold beaded necklace.

Still, I didn't trust her. I opened without preamble. "They're mine, you know they are, and you aren't taking them."

"Yeah," she said. "I know you don't believe me, but I really am sorry about that. I—er, you were on the right track when you asked me what I was doing beyond an alpaca farm. I wanted to create a landmark farm in the county, too, but you came along and did it so *fast*. I couldn't keep up. You seem to have all the help in the world, and I only have my cousin Lyle and his family. I had to do something to slow you down." She put her hands down but continued flexing her fingers, telling me how tense she was.

I really did have great support and the safari had rocketed off much quicker than I could have ever imagined, despite Leslie's interference.

"Couldn't you have just hired people to help you get off the ground? Why did you think stealing my animals made sense? How did you imagine you suddenly having zebras when my safari had been advertising them was going to work?" Leslie Alexander wasn't getting off that easy.

"I—I don't know. It was sort of a spur-of-the-moment decision to halt your success. I would have returned them eventually. Once my own business got off the ground."

If there was anything I was certain of it was that Leslie was never planning to return my zebras.

I kept my expression stony. "So, you've been behind all of the bizarre incidents that have been happening here over the past nine months or so? You graffitied my gift shop, killed my hedgehog, tossed a goshawk on my porch, stuck a burr into my goat's backside—"

Leslie shook her head violently. "I don't know what you're talking about. I didn't do any of those things. I don't mistreat animals."

I gave her a look to let her know how little I believed her.

"All I did was take the zebras," she insisted. "Oh, and I dropped off some goats. I didn't have time to deal with having babies around and the other one was obstinate. Kill a hedgehog? What would be the point of that?"

"Because of how much you despise me," I said. What kind of farm owner doesn't want to deal with new life on the farm? And who told her that goats were anything but obstinate?

Leslie gazed at me with what I swear was almost pity. "If all those horrible things are happening to you, then you have to face the fact that you have really made someone mad for more than just having a successful business."

CHAPTER 51

I DIDN'T HAVE MUCH time to consider what Leslie had told me, because her next pronouncement was that she had decided to give up her own safari dreams. Oh, and did I want her animals?

I most certainly did not, but I wasn't about to let them go God knows where. Looks like I was expanding again.

Within a week, Leslie had brought several trailers full of animals, finally confessing with the last delivery that she had been fired from her job and was leaving the area to go live with relatives in Virginia.

I never did learn who had ratted her out to me.

I increased my holdings by two more miniature horses, a scary-looking pig that turned out to be both gentle and a clown, four alpacas that badly needed grooming, and, to my utter dismay, a bunch of exotic ducks.

I had a pond and had tried a few ducks years before but couldn't keep a flock intact.

Ducks, like other fowl, need a lot of work to ensure they don't get picked off by hawks, foxes, and the occasional stray dog. They are also notoriously messy, their webbed feet trampling over grass and creating muddy flats everywhere. They also tend to die suddenly for no apparent reason.

Most disturbing to me about ducks, though, was that males wanted to mate all the time. You had to feel very sorry for the females, who received ten seconds of a male's most sincere attention at least ten times a day.

I now had some Orpingtons, notable for their black

bills and feet, as well as some gorgeous, emerald green Cayugas, and a couple of Cresteds, which were hilarious with their cotton ball-like topped heads.

Off they went to the pond, which they all immediately dove into with great relish.

I hoped they would last.

I also hoped my troubles with the safari were over with Leslie Alexander's departure, but her parting comment stayed with me like a tiny splinter buried in your finger. It's annoying but you can't quite dig it out.

One day near closing I was outside, waving to departing visitors. I had noticed that people—especially kids—liked it when I waved goodbye to them as they left, so I did so as often as I could.

After visitors departed, so did the staff, and I waved to them, as well. As the last car left, I pulled the long iron horse stall gate shut and flipped the sign that dangled from one post: **WE'RE CLOSED—PLEASE VISIT AGAIN.**

I had let April take my truck to run up to G Street Fabrics in Rockville. She wanted to visit this sewing mecca for costume inspiration and planned to stay up in that city for a couple of days, so I was stuck at home until she returned. I busied myself with animal care, particularly with my llamas and new alpacas.

Although llamas and alpacas are very similar, the alpacas were far smaller than my llamas and their ears were spear-shaped, as opposed to the llamas with their curved, banana-shaped ears.

The alpacas, whom I had named Sheldon, Leonard, Howard, and Penny, also tended to cluster together, whereas the llamas strutted around independently.

However, my new alpacas were sweet and gentle with very little training from me. Leslie had actually chosen these animals well.

Thus, I was concerned when I noticed that Howard

had separated himself from the others in the field. I ran my hands over his body, noticed the lump on his neck, and realized he had an abscess. "Poor baby, wait here," I said.

I went to the llama feed shed and retrieved vinyl gloves and a syringe. I had just drained the pus from the abscess when I noticed movement in my peripheral vision.

A familiar form was trudging up my driveway in the dusky light of sunset. It was Carrie Lomax.

I patted the alpaca and stripped off my gloves, then rolled up the syringe inside of them, stashing it all at the base of a tree near the llama enclosure gate. "You should be feeling better very soon," I said and walked down to meet my neighbor in the driveway.

Carrie was shuffling along in ill-fitting pants topped with a T-shirt large enough to be a nightgown and emblazoned with *I got Crabs at Seabreeze Restaurant*. It looked as though she had upended a tableful of the crustaceans on herself at some point, with old red and orange stains all over it.

She carried her trademark red cup and had a cigarette in her mouth, an impossibly long ash dangling from the end. She was moving along without her cane today. As she neared me, she pulled the cigarette from her mouth and flicked the ash onto my driveway. "How's it going? Working hard or hardly working?" Carrie laughed hoarsely at the pun, one that was well-worn in the county.

I smiled weakly. "What can I do for you, Mrs. Lomax?"

Her face was pinched as if she had swallowed a gnat. "Just...erm...wanted to see your herd of llamas. I hear tell they kiss people. Wouldn't mind seeing that for myself."

I crossed my arms. "I thought you were unhappy about my safari."

"Yeah. Still bad for the neighborhood. But I guess you ain't going anywhere so I might as well make the best of it."

Was this Carrie Lomax's version of an apology?

I relented. "Come on back. The safari has both llamas and alpacas now. I was just treating one of my alpacas before herding them all into their barn."

She trudged behind me, clutching both cigarette and cup. By the time we got to the gate, she had discarded the cigarette.

After the fiasco with the llamas escaping, I had installed a more complicated latch and lock system on the gate, one that would be difficult for the average child to figure out and probably even the average adult.

Next to me, Mrs. Lomax tilted her head, watching intently as I undid the latches. "That's crazy," she said.

"They tend to wander off," I said without offering details.

"That so?" She coughed. It was deep and phlegmy. I shuddered.

"Here we are," I said, inviting her into the enclosure. "Can't stay long because I need to get them put up before dark. Cuddlebug!"

My favorite llama came lumbering over.

"Meet Mrs. Lomax."

Cuddlebug was now so used to visitors that he went right to the woman and huffed against her nose.

To my surprise, Mrs. Lomax actually smiled. That smile turned into a laugh. Which then turned into another cough. Cuddlebug waited patiently while she finished hacking up and then swallowing whatever was in her lungs, then huffed in her face again.

The other llamas surrounded her, while Sheldon, Leonard, and Penny stood nearby. Mrs. Lomax seemed delighted by the attention.

Maybe I should have been more attentive and kinder to this woman, who appeared to just be sick and lonely.

"It's nearly dark. Want to help me put them away?" I asked.

Mrs. Lomax perked up at the idea. I clucked my tongue at the animals and started walking across the field toward their barn, Mrs. Lomax trailing behind me. I could also hear the hoofbeats of my llamas and alpacas following me, too.

I had installed the same complicated latch system on their barn to be doubly sure of no escape, so once I had let Mrs. Lomax guide the animals to their appropriate stalls and she once more stood outside with me, I refastened everything. I was proud of my new latch system, particularly because I had recently oiled up the door's hinges, so the door moved as smoothly as melted butter on a biscuit.

"Hope you enjoyed the visit," I said, ready to get inside the house to have dinner with Mom and catch up my never-ending stack of paperwork.

Mrs. Lomax didn't budge. "Thanks for stopping by," I tried again.

"Yeah, so, I might notta told you the truth on something," she said.

"What's that?"

"Yeah. I mighta painted your building over there. I won't do it again."

I knew it. Now all I had to do was figure out who killed my hedgehog, stuck a burr on my goat, dropped additional goats onto my farm, let out my llamas, and potentially threw a dead hawk onto my front porch.

"Wanted to send a message to you about the safari. Might not have been my finest Christian moment."

Indeed not. "But you couldn't possibly have done that by yourself," I said.

"No. Dickie Walker helped me. He had paint and ladders and brushes and all."

I set my lips in a grim line. "Mrs. Lomax, are you sure Mr. Walker didn't put you up to it in the first place?"

She wrinkled her nose. "I don't think so. No, I think it was my idea. He thought it was a good one, though. His wife didn't like it, but he don't listen none to her."

I started walking toward the driveway to get Mrs. Lomax moving. The sun had sunk below the horizon and it was going to get dark quickly.

"Were you also responsible for the other bad things that have happened around here?" I enumerated them as I had done for Leslie Alexander.

"Why would you think I did anything like that? I already told you I painted your building. Ain't that enough confessing for you?" She was strangely indignant over the accusation.

I didn't care much for her response. However, I realized that that was indeed as close to an apology as I was going to get.

"Do you think Mr. Walker is also done with antagonizing me?"

Carrie Lomax shrugged. "No one controls him, 'specially not me." She walked away, clutching her red plastic cup. I watched her retreating away. She paused at the bottom of my driveway and somehow managed to hold onto that cup while digging both a cigarette and a lighter out of her pants pocket. I admit I was impressed that within seconds I could see the glow from the cigarette as she continued wandering down the driveway and toward her own house.

I turned away, hoping that marked the end of the bad occurrences at Three Notch Safari. I retrieved the used syringe and gloves so I could dispose of them and went to the house.

Mom was waiting for me at the kitchen door. I entered and could smell ground beef simmering on the stovetop. A giant jar of spaghetti sauce was open on the counter next to the pan.

"Like I told you, this place is full of bad omens."

I closed my eyes. "Mom, please, not this again. You've been so happy at the safari lately."

My mother ignored me. "That woman is bad for you. I've seen her around the llamas before."

CHAPTER 52

IT WAS OF no surprise to me that Mrs. Lomax was behind the other events at the safari. It had probably taken a lot of pride-swallowing for her to admit to spraying graffiti on my gift shop. But I just wanted it all to be over and done with, and I wanted to trust that she and Dickie Walker, and whatever other neighbor might have been involved, were done attempting to ruin me.

Besides, business was booming gloriously and so was my life. Leslie Alexander and Mark were permanently out of my life and April was back in. Mom was flourishing in her new role, my relationship with Danny was turning serious with him making subtle hints about the future, and Christopher had even forgiven me for the dead hedgehog. And the number of visitors—and staff—for my safari was growing. I was even turning a small profit.

I was happy to have all the sordidness behind me. I just wanted to enjoy my new circumstances.

About a week or so after my encounter with Mrs. Lomax, I had had a particularly busy day with the safari. The theatre troupe's manager had the idea to incorporate some of the parrots into one of their skits. The manager had worked with Simon Rhodes and this was the debut of the skit, which involved having the parrot serve as the "sheriff" in the act.

It had all gone well in their multiple rehearsals and then not so well during the live performance. The scarlet macaw must have eaten something that didn't agree with him—or maybe it was stage fright—do birds get stage fright?—for he pooped non-stop on stage. The white and green slime made its way down the front of all the actors as the bird went from shoulder to shoulder during the performance. The actors did a great job ignoring it until there was enough on the stage floor itself that one of the actors slipped and fell in it.

Fortunately, the audience thought it was a slapstick comedy show and laughed uproariously. However, it required my smoothing over some very hurt feelings between the theatre troupe and Simon.

I went to bed that night with a book I had ordered on dromedary behavior and care. I'd found bottle-fed, year-old camels for sale in Texas, which seemed to be my go-to state for exotics, and planned to pick up a weaned youngster in a couple of weeks. This particular breeder also had kangaroos for sale, which I considered for a hot minute but decided I needed to honor my promise to make the camel the last acquisition for a while.

I drifted off to sleep while brushing up on one-hump camel genetics and their reproductive systems and was soon dreaming about what I would name my new camel and fantasizing about how well he would get along with the llamas and alpacas since they were all related creatures, even sharing the distasteful habit of spitting when upset.

Aladdin? Sinbad? Babar? Ali Baba? My dreaming mind settled on Aladdin. Who knew, maybe one day there would be a Jasmine to join him.

I became restless in my sleep, feeling overcome by strange yet familiar noises. I tossed back and forth, waking up slowly to the realization that I was hearing actual noises from outside.

It sounded like all the birds were agitated. Sounds of frantic honking and cheeping wafted over me. What had them in a tizzy? Maybe a fox or even a coyote.

I threw the covers back and jumped back into the previous day's clothes, then pulled my shotgun out from under my bed and loaded it—grabbing some extra birdshot shells for good measure and shoving them into my jeans pocket—before quietly leaving my room. The shotgun was an old one my father had given me years ago, but he had always kept it clean and in pristine condition, and I had tried my best to follow suit.

As expected, I could hear Mom snoring through her door, oblivious to the growing pandemonium outdoors. Unusually, Daisy was asleep on the living room sofa, kicking one leg in a doggie dream.

I slipped out the kitchen door, carrying the shotgun in my hand. The shells were uncomfortable in my pocket but I might have to use them in quick order depending upon what was getting to the birds.

Birdshot shells have tiny pellets in them that spray out when firing a shotgun, making it easier to hit a flying target, like a bird. My quickly moving target might be any sort of wild animal and I would take no chances.

I moved as stealthily as I could toward the aviary but soon realized the rustling noises weren't coming from there. They were coming from the llama barn. I changed course and headed toward the building, the anxiety emanating from there pulsing to a fever pitch.

Llamas make a funny sound when distressed, sort of a cross between a donkey's bray and a duck's quack. As near as I could tell, all of them were distressed. The alpacas, though, were quieter in their anxiety with noises that sounded like frantic birds.

I approached the llama barn gate and realized it was open.

That wasn't possible. My new latching system couldn't ever be undone by one of my animals and the only person who had ever witnessed me undo it was—

My heart sank. Carrie Lomax had fooled me, hadn't she?

I pulled on the door's latch and it gave way silently. Not that it would have been heard over the racket going on in the barn.

In the dim light of the barn provided by a single bulb nearly twenty feet up in the rafters, I saw Mrs. Lomax crouched down, her back to me, near one of the feeders I had placed along their stall fences. Her telltale red cup sat on the ground next to her.

It was eerily reminiscent of my mother going to the llama barn to lie down with them, but I didn't sense that Mrs. Lomax was indulging in something so innocent. She reached down for her red cup, and instead of sipping from it herself, she poured some of its contents into a water trough.

What in the—? Was she intentionally trying to make my llamas and alpacas drunk? Or sick? What possible reason could she have for doing so?

I propped the shotgun against the outside of the barn as I did not intend to shoot my neighbor, no matter what she was doing to trouble me.

I rapidly crossed the distance between the barn door and the llama stall where the woman was still crouched, pouring something from her cup into the feeder.

Reaching her, I grabbed her shoulder and spun her around, causing her to lose her balance and drop the red cup. Mrs. Lomax let out a string of invectives against me.

Except...it wasn't Carrie Lomax's shoulder in my death grip.

CHAPTER 53

"I DON'T UNDERSTAND," WAS all I could manage, releasing her.

Dee Dee Boone got her feet under her and rose from the ground, crossing her arms as she faced me. She wore ratty clothing and her hair was mussed. Had she been trying to look like Carrie Lomax? When had she even met Mrs. Lomax?

I noticed that Dee Dee wore the same grease paint on her face she had worn when we had rescued the zebras.

How was it even possible that this woman who had accidentally come into my life and had been of such great help to me in making my safari successful, was suddenly working against me?

I reached over the fencing and removed the doctored feeder. I probably didn't need to bother, since both llamas and alpacas were off to one side, cowering, spitting, and shrieking, with no interest in their water feeder.

In one fluid motion, I dumped the adulterated water over Dee Dee's head and tossed the feeder behind me into the center of the barn.

"What are you doing?" I demanded as she sputtered and wiped her soaking her hair away from her eyes.

That resulted in another cursing stream from her. I'd never heard such language come out of her before, as she always presented herself as polished and warm-hearted.

As she stood there yelling at me for *daring* to throw water on her, I grew exceedingly impatient.

In fact, I got irritated enough that I stopped her cold by slapping her across the face as hard as I could. My palm stung from the connection with her cheek, but inwardly I glowed with warmth at the satisfying *smack* that hung in the air.

The animals even ceased their anxiety-ridden clamor, seemingly fascinated by what I had just done.

"Why are you in my barn poisoning my animals, *friend*?" If Dee Dee were smart, she would have heard my tone going low and slow. It felt like I was confronting Mark for stupid behavior. Except his behavior was just stupid—Dee Dee was trying to cause death and destruction for no apparent reason.

Dee Dee raised one hand to her cheek. "You hit me."

I needed answers. "The next one will be a knockout blow if you don't explain to me what you are doing in my barn, trying to kill my animals." Thank goodness the llamas and alpacas had put up a fuss. I might still be sleeping right now otherwise.

"It was just some grub control solution I used on a client's lawn to get her property ready for sale. It wouldn't necessarily have killed off your herd, just made them sick for a while, so don't worry."

Don't worry.

"I swear to you, Dee Dee, this is the last time I'm going to ask. WHAT. ARE. YOU. *DOING*?"

Dee Dee held up both hands, palms toward me. "Calm down. I've been your friend for a long time, haven't I?"

I was silent, refusing to acknowledge anything.

"But I've been Mark's friend longer. And Mark has been a good friend to me, ever since he took the blame for the secret leak at Globotechnico. Only a good friend will take a hit for you like that. He hadn't quite realized yet what a good friend I am to him, although he started figuring it out the day he visited the safari."

I remembered Dee Dee had been mortified that she had revealed to Mark how successful the safari was. Was that a lie?

And what did she mean by being a "good friend" to him? They were just co-workers. Except apparently Dee Dee was the criminal, not Mark.

I said nothing, waiting for her to tell me more. Dee Dee glanced from side to side, as if wondering whether she could get past me. I wished I hadn't left my shotgun outside the barn.

"You have to realize that I've always been in love with Mark," she continued with a sigh. "When I found out he'd gone to Florida, I knew I'd found my chance."

I looked her incredulously. "You have a boyfriend. Jason."

Dee Dee airily waved a hand. "Not anymore. We broke up long ago. Didn't you ever notice that I never brought him with me to your farm?"

I hadn't noticed that at all. I had been far too consumed with my own situation to even give hers a second thought. But she was right, I'd never even met her boyfriend at any point since starting the safari.

"When Mark called me to chew me out for taking your side in things, I explained my feelings for him and we came to…an understanding. Especially when I told him everything I had done for him. He let me into his life and that's when I knew he and I were soulmates."

"Everything you had done?"

At this, Dee Dee's lips curved into a smile. "Yes. You know, the mailbox notes, the dead hawk, the goat with the burr—that was my personal favorite—letting the llamas escape, dropping your hedgehog…it was so much fun deciding what to do next. You have to understand, Becca, I needed to ruin you so that Mark wouldn't ever want to come back and I could have him for myself. After all he and I had sacrificed for one another, it was destiny that we be together. And being near you was the best way to implement that destiny."

I imagined she was unaware that her soulmate had briefly attempted a reconciliation with me.

I was speechless. Was Dee Dee Boone standing before me, telling me that she had attempted to ruin my safari while she was helping me with it, in order to make my ex-husband fall in love with her? I shook my head to clear the thick cobweb forming over the preposterous idea.

"But Carrie Lomax confessed to me that she had painted up the gift shop," I said. "What part did she play in your scheme?" I asked.

"That old bat? She was just a useful idiot to me. So easy to convince her and that other neighbor—what's his name—to help me a little by telling them that if you got run out of town the ensuing fire sale of the farm would result in a good deal for them."

"But it wouldn't have happened that way."

She shrugged. "I'm a realtor. They believed me. Plus, a case of bourbon for her and a dozen boxes of chewing tobacco tins for him and they paid close attention to whatever I had to say."

I realized something else. "So, your quitting Globotechnico was because—"

Dee Dee shrugged again. "The secrets I lifted from Globo were for another company promising me a high-paying position if I delivered them. Once Globo discovered the theft, though, the other company and I parted ways to avoid any problems and I switched careers pronto. I thought the coast was clear but after a bunch of Globo bellyaching, the government got involved and latched onto Mark for some reason. If he knew it was me, he never let on. He's a wonderful man." Dee Dee had a dreamy look in her eyes.

Blech.

"Did Carrie Lomax help you with all of those threatening letters and notes?"

Dee Dee's expression was bemused. "No, I spent two days writing them all myself. It was all I could do not to laugh as we sat and went through them together. The look on your face was priceless."

I had thought Mark was out of his mind but I realized now that he was a lightweight compared to Dee Dee Boone's insanity.

I was still so completely gob-smacked that all I could do was repeat my own thoughts. "You helped me in order to ruin me? You even risked your life to help me rescue my zebras—all the while planning to destroy me."

"Eh, it was a fun time," she replied carelessly.

I'd had enough. "You two deserve each other," I told her. "You're like two pigs, flopping in filth together and loving it." Well, the two of them plus whatever woman Mark was currently flirting his way into buying surfing lessons.

"You mean it as an insult, but I'm flattered. Mark is handsome, fun-loving, and clever. Of course, he wasn't interested in your farm, it was beneath him. Once he decided he wanted to get financial benefit from the safari, I even helped him work up his spreadsheets for splitting everything, but you were so disagreeable about that."

"Those spreadsheets were ridiculous," I spat. "I can hardly believe that was the work of a supposed realtor."

Another lift of her shoulders. "I knew they were getting complicated but Mark insisted on putting his spin on them. I also knew they would cost you a fortune in legal fees to get them interpreted, so that was okay. Especially since you talked the judge into giving you everything."

"But *you* suggested that I see a lawyer. To protect

myself, *you* said." How had I been so taken in by this woman?

"Well, sure I said that. I really just wanted you divorced from Mark. I knew I could figure out the details later."

The sun was rising, its rays just starting to peek up and shine in my face through one of the barn's windows.

"I could go to the authorities about you right now," I said.

That didn't intimidate her at all. "Sure, tell them that the woman your husband has taken up with is actually a super-secret spy and that although you have zero proof of it, you are positively convinced it's true. Don't worry, Becca, you won't get laughed at one bit."

Was she right?

I had to know more. "What, exactly, is your plan now?"

"Well, you catching me in the act wasn't really on my agenda. But from here I'm going to go to Florida, of course. It's a more advantageous place for two people as bold and resourceful as Mark and I are. I was going to wait until you got unnerved enough or went into the hole enough to get rid of the place, of course, but plans change."

"What gave you any indication that my safari was failing? It's doing better than ever."

"Yeah, I was leaning more toward you being unnerved. Your mother was very helpful in that regard, too."

So, Dee Dee was behind Mom's intonations about bad omens. I remembered Dee Dee had taken Mom out for an afternoon to look at a property. I wish I had known that Dee Dee's goal was to influence my mother's thoughts and ideas, but who could have predicted it?

The rising sun's beam momentarily blinded me and I couldn't see Dee Dee properly. I put up a hand to shield my eyes.

She took her advantage and rushed me, knocking me to the ground before taking off through the barn door.

The llamas and alpacas started honking and cheeping again.

"It's okay," I called out to them as I struggled to sit up. I wobbled up to my feet and loped out of the barn to follow Dee Dee, shaking my head once more to clear it.

Dee Dee must not have noticed Dad's shotgun leaning against the barn as she took off. I grabbed it and kept going, soon getting within thirty feet of her in my long driveway.

I shouted at her to stop and fired up in the air.

As expected, she ignored me and kept moving. I was glad the sun was no longer in my eyes. It made it easier to reload another shell.

Now I could hear Daisy barking from inside the house.

I continued firing in the air and re-loading shotgun shells as I made progress toward Dee Dee. Leslie Alexander wasn't the only one passionate about protecting her property.

I pulled the last shell from my pants pocket. I kissed the ribbed, fire engine red shell for luck and loaded it into my shotgun. This time, I aimed.

Dee Dee howled as I blasted her rear end full of birdshot.

I cupped a hand around my mouth. "Don't worry," I shouted to her. "It won't kill you, you'll just feel sick for a while."

Dad would have been proud of my dead-on aim.

Was it wrong of me that I laughed while Dee Dee continued howling as she stumbled, grabbing her butt as she fled up the road to wherever I was sure she had hidden her car? I mean, it was a deep, pressure-releasing belly laugh. As I carried on with myself, tears streaming down my face, I felt all the stress about my divorce and the worry about the safari attacks fade far back into the distance.

It felt *great*.

And now Dee Dee had been shot at twice in a short time, only this time she had had the experience of a stinging backside.

I marched back to the house with the shotgun slung over my shoulder like a Marine returning from guard duty. Mom was at the kitchen door again. "Got rid of her, did you? Good."

"It wasn't Carrie Lomax," I told her as Daisy raced out the door toward 'her' llamas and the rest of the herd to protect them.

"So I saw. Bad omens started right around the time you met that cheap, disgusting harlot."

Leave it to Mom to characterize people in such vulgar terms. But in this case, she was right.

CHAPTER 54

DEE DEE SEEMED to make good on her promise to go to Florida, for I never saw her again.

It had been fairly easy to replace her, as the safari was becoming a desirable employment location for high schoolers, college students, and retirees. Who wouldn't jump at the chance to work with animals all day? Except for the mucking part, which I made sure every employee had to participate in so that it didn't seem like there were certain "dirty" jobs that employees could refuse to touch.

Mom was quite proud of her prognostications, claiming to all who would listen that she had been right all along about the bad omens she was seeing, that she had effectively known Dee Dee Boone was causing trouble for the safari.

She was having such a good time with her role as oracle that I didn't have the heart to tell her that Dee Dee had planted thoughts in her mind and that it had been Dee Dee she had seen skulking around the property, not Carrie Lomax.

April had clucked in disgust over her father, hugged me, and never spoke of it again. She was completely consumed with scene sets and costumes for the animals. I also noticed one of the young men who helped with parking and general groundskeeping was occupying some of her attention.

Danny had been inordinately proud of how I had

handled Dee Dee. He began referring to me as "Bird Shot Becca."

Interestingly, my other family and friends expressed initial shock over Dee Dee's perfidy, but quickly forgot about her. "Good riddance, focus on success," Bear had said, which seemed to be the general message from everyone.

So that's what I did, concentrating on Danny and Christopher, my family and friends, and my lovable collection of animals.

I even got the camel, who was even more ridiculously cute than the llamas, alpacas, and miniature cows. Aladdin was a dark, cinnamon brown with impossibly long eyelashes, which were intended to protect against sand in desert environments.

He wouldn't be full grown until he was seven years old, but he already looked plenty big to me.

True to his word, Danny had driven to Texas with me to pick up the camel and had then gotten involved with Aladdin's care and training. One day, Danny showed me a trick he had taught the camel. Aladdin didn't just reach across to rub noses with people, he reached over and wrapped his long neck around people's shoulders in an affectionate camel hug. He even instinctively knew to maintain the pose when Michelle's camera was clicking around him.

I couldn't believe what a natural Danny was with my animals, given that he was used to primarily dealing with the non-living kind.

Kids and adults alike went nuts for Aladdin. Especially Christopher, who had taken to joining his father after school to groom and train Aladdin. I confess it made my heart grow two sizes to watch them together with Aladdin. They were becoming an inextricable part of my world.

Between the camel and the zebras, the safari really was turning into a bit of a wildlife preserve. Life was good.

Early on a Wednesday morning, I waved goodbye to my mother as she hopped into the Ladies with Hats van. They were off to visit the National Zoo in D.C., where I was certain my mother would hold everyone rapt with her opinions on the zoo's layout and animal care approach.

I stood on the porch, watching the van grow smaller as it drove away, and was shaken out of my reverie by the sound of my phone ringing from inside the house.

I rolled my eyes when I saw that it was Mark calling me. *Now* what did he expect from me?

"Hey, Reb," he said when I answered. "How's it going?"

"What do you want?" His voice was an intrusion on my happy life.

"Um, just wanted to make sure you're okay."

"Why wouldn't I be?" I knew Mark well enough to know that his hesitancy meant he was hopping around a distasteful subject.

"No reason, no reason. Glad to hear all is well. Yep. April's enjoying herself?" He was just dangling on the line.

"Mark, I'm busy today. What can I do for you?"

"Yeah. So, look. I just wanted to let you know that, er, some things have happened. I'm, well, I'm remarried. To Dee Dee."

No surprise there.

"I moved out of Jake's condo and we got an apartment in Port St. John."

I frowned. "That's not on the ocean, is it?"

He cleared his throat. "No. It's about a half hour from Cocoa Beach but it's where Dee Dee wanted to live. She says it's an up-and-coming place. Good real estate prospects. She says we will eventually buy a house here."

"What about your surfing instructor dreams?"

"I'm still going to give lessons and hang out at the ocean. I'll just be commuting a bit."

A commuting beach bum. Made perfect sense.

"Well, as long as you're happy, I'm happy. Thanks for call—"

Mark interrupted. "Um, I wanted to tell you something. Dee Dee told me about everything she did to you. I swear, Reb, I had no clue what she was doing."

"Of course not."

"I mean it. Uh, well, not at first, anyway." He was hopping again.

"Did you figure it out before or after she helped you with your spreadsheet initiative?"

Mark laughed nervously. "Oh, that was her idea. She wanted to help me get my financial house in order, and she proposed that I make my case to your lawyer. But I regret it, I really do. I—I think I fell under her spell, Becca. Dee Dee can be very…hypnotic."

Blech. These two were making me nauseous.

"Good for Dee Dee. And for you." I wanted the call to end. I knew exactly what sort of creatures both my ex-husband and my ex-friend were and I had no desire to travel over the road that included the two of them again.

Mark, though, still had more on his mind. "When I came up and visited the safari was when we, uh…"

"Sealed the deal?" I offered.

"Reb, don't be like that. I was going to say that that was when I realized she had feelings for me and let's face it, who doesn't want to be with someone who cares about you passionately?"

Was that how Mark and I had ended up together? Had I been passionate about him way back when? It was already difficult to remember the good times.

I didn't respond.

"I mean, you were the love of my life, but Dee Dee was there for me. She pursued me, respected my dreams."

I rolled my eyes. "Okay. Dee Dee Boone Garvey is a saint who happens to poison farm animals as a side gig. Got it. Just don't make her angry, Mark. She's got a spiteful streak and I'd hate to see it turned on you. Anything else?"

There was silence for a few moments. "I guess not. But Reb, you shouldn't have shot her, even if it was just with birdshot. You could have really injured her."

"Nah," I said airily. "I had no intention of killing her, just getting her attention and letting her know that she is no longer welcome at Three Notch Safari."

"Don't say that. When we come back to Maryland to visit April, won't we be invited to the house?"

How much stupider was this conversation going to get?

"No, Mark! You married the woman who was trying to ruin my safari and who nearly ruined Globo. If either of you set foot on my property, I've got a birdshot welcome for both of you. It's a double barrel, you know. As I told her, you two are like pigs rolling in filth together. Have a great rest of your life."

"Reb, wait. Tell April—"

I clicked off before he could finish his sentence.

I laughed long and hard after the call ended, almost as much as I had when I had filled Dee Dee's butt with birdshot.

CHAPTER 55

THE DAY OF my wedding, October 19th, was perfect. It was as though God had put me through the trials of Job, found me to be faithful, and was now rewarding me with twice all that I had lost.

Danny had agreed that getting married at the safari was perfect. We decided to let the animals roam free before, during, and after the morning ceremony, and they were already taking that duty seriously, wandering up the center aisle under the white tent to inspect our guests. We had only invited close family and friends, plus all of the neighbors, so everyone was well-steeped in my "safari culture" and took the attention of the animals with great aplomb.

I even noticed my mother scratching an alpaca behind the ears.

The priest from St. Francis Xavier Church agreed to come there to marry us and had two of my sheep by his side. With his beard and robe, Father could have been the Good Shepherd milling around.

The sky was clear and few bugs were out. We had decided on a late morning ceremony while the animals were fresh from sleep.

Danny had proposed to me while we were at Calvert Cliffs State Park one day with Christopher. We had decided to go the day after I had been bestowed with an Entrepreneur of the Year award from the Chamber of Commerce, a totally unexpected honor.

The three of us walked the trail all the way down

to the Chesapeake Bay, then Danny and I sat on an old, petrified log at the water's edge while Christopher went off to practice skipping rocks on the water. We applauded his efforts.

Eventually, Danny made a slow, long whistle. Christopher stopped what he was doing and returned to us, digging something out of his shorts pocket.

It was a complete oyster shell.

"Where did you find that?" I asked. Oysters didn't exactly just lay around on the seashore.

Christopher glanced at Danny, who nodded at him. The boy dropped to one knee and presented it up to me.

I looked at Danny. "What is happening here?"

Danny pointed to the oyster shell. "Open it."

I did. The oyster had long ago been discarded and the shells thoroughly scrubbed. Inside lay a perfect diamond ring set in platinum.

"Will you be my new mom?" Christopher asked.

Never had I cried so hard from joy before.

Not wanting to wait any longer than necessary, we got right to work planning a wedding to take place three months later. Michelle had insisted on doing photos gratis for us, and the waterman, Kip Hewitt, created a sumptuous seafood feast of crabs, shrimp, oysters, and side dishes under a separate reception tent.

April was my maid of honor. Having her with me in that moment, smiling with her hair splayed about her shoulders in curls, made me want to cry even harder than I had at receiving the engagement ring.

I'd asked Mom to be a bridesmaid, which might seem weird to some people, but it just seemed appropriate, given that I was getting married at the safari and she had ultimately been a big part of it.

Danny had Christopher as his best man. In a surprising twist, he decided to have Aladdin as his other groomsman. And wouldn't you know, he trained the camel to walk in from the side and stand next to Christopher all on his own. Danny even attached a top hat to the camel's head and a black bow tie around his neck.

Aladdin behaved like a perfect gentleman throughout the ceremony. He even waited to poop until after Danny and I were pronounced husband and wife and I became Becca Copsey.

Simon had arranged a parrot flyover as Danny and I walked back down the aisle together, which everyone cheered.

The reception was a peculiar old-fashioned hoedown. We had a local band play a blend of popular and country music for dancing. Miniature horses and cows, sheep, llamas, alpacas, and pigs, all wandered about at will among the guests and Michelle was firing off her camera as fast as she could.

Somehow, it all seemed normal at Three Notch Safari.

Carrie Lomax, the Walkers, and several of my neighbors who had expressed displeasure over my safari showed up halfway through the reception and asked to speak to me. I stepped out of the tent with them, lifting my dress as I walked and thus exposing my white, crystal-studded cowgirl boots. I just couldn't imagine wearing heels anywhere on the farm and so this had been my best compromise on comfort and dignity. I followed them to the back of a truck with its tailgate down. Daisy was hot on my heels, guiding me along as she always did. On the bed was a large, flat package, just a few inches thick.

Dickie Walker spoke for the group. "We know that you got taken in by that Dee Dee Boone. We all did, I guess." He cleared his throat. "Thought you might like a peace offering. Call it a wedding present."

The package was too heavy and I couldn't lift it. Dickie stayed my hands. "I'll open it."

He pulled a Leatherman multi-purpose tool from the chest pocket of his dungarees, found the knife on it, and slid it through the tape on the box. He pulled the flaps open to reveal what lay in the box.

It contained a stack of metal signs, each one personalized to one of my animals with an adorable, cartoony picture of the type of animal it was above the name. They had managed to remember every single beast that I had named. I bet they had talked to Bear or Donna to collect the names. What a thoughtful gesture by my once-antagonistic neighbors.

Carrie Lomax coughed her wet, syrupy cough and said, "We won't never again do you no harm."

I cried yet again and vowed that I would hang the signs in their respective stalls and pens as soon as Danny and I returned from our honeymoon.

We were planning a cruise to the Caribbean that sailed in three days. I'd never been on a cruise before but was looking forward to a "running of the pigs" excursion at one of the islands we'd be visiting, as well as a swim-with-the-dolphins adventure.

I returned to the reception, famished from the morning and ready to break open some Old Bay-seasoned crabs, my ivory silk dress be damned.

Sitting down next to Danny, I prepared to eat from my new, complete set of matching dishes, which I had sworn to buy myself if I ever made money from the safari.

In truth, I had bought three sets.

I leaned over to plant a kiss on Danny's cheek and pledged silently to myself that if I was miraculously able to have a baby at my age with this wonderful man, I'd buy three more sets.

AUTHOR'S NOTE

THE IDEA FOR this story came from Sarah Copsey, who owns Keep it Simple Stables in Hollywood, Maryland (https://www.keepitsimplestables.net). Sarah is a dynamo who started her little ten-acre, spotlessly clean, hobby farm from scratch more than a decade ago.

When Sarah and her husband, Jae, decide to purchase the property, the seller had his own horse there. What Sarah and Jae didn't realize until they took possession of the house was that the seller was planning to include the horse with the property.

Although she had ridden horses as a child, Sarah knew nothing about the actual care and feeding of such an animal, but she learned quickly.

Keep it Simple is in no way a traditional farm, as Sarah doesn't grow any produce whatsoever. Instead, Sarah, with the help of her ever-patient husband, began clearing land, building fencing for small pastures, and erecting barns, stalls, and other structures to accommodate her slowly growing collection of horses, goats, and other animals.

Her animals—and let's be serious, they are all pets—have come to her in various ways. Sometimes she has rescued animals, sometimes they have been dropped on her doorstep, and sometimes she has actively pursued a purchase. At this point, I think Jae just sighs with each acquisition and asks, "What do you need built now?"

Like Danny in the story, Jae is a taxidermist on the side and does call his business "Copsey's Critters."

Several years ago, a photographer friend suggested that

Sarah let her do a children's photoshoot there, offering to pay Sarah for her time.

This gave Sarah an idea: what if she created her own seasonal and holiday-themed vignettes for people to use as a backdrop for people to use in taking their own pictures of their children and other family members?

An idea was born.

Sarah is a "horse whisperer" type of person, so all her animals are quite tame. In fact, one of her llamas—animals known to spit when agitated—will approach complete strangers to "kiss" them by placing his furry nose against them. Visitors go wild for all her patient and friendly creatures. As do I.

Over time, Sarah has added a bouncy house, props for children to use, picnic tables, a porta-potty for visitors, and, of course, more animals.

As of this writing, she has three horses, two miniature horses—one of which once stepped squarely on my foot, pinning me to the ground in immense pain—a donkey, three llamas, about a dozen goats, two pigs (that she didn't want), and four miniature cows, which are quite possibly the most adorable things God ever created. This, of course, doesn't count the three dogs, one cat, and a parrot that live (mostly) indoors.

Sarah has experimented with fowl such as geese, but the hawks kept spiriting them away, so no more birds.

To date, she hasn't purchased any zebras or camels, but who knows what she will do in the future?

Sarah spent an inordinate amount of her own precious time with me in the writing of this book, showing me how her animals are fed, how she cares for them, where she buys them, and how she tames them. I don't know she does it all, but I greatly admire the life she has built.

Although Three Notch Safari is built upon the idea of Sarah's lovely animal ranch, Becca's story in no way reflects Sarah's life.

Also, for what it's worth, Keep it Simple is *not* a drive-through safari, but you can go there for picture-taking and to be kissed by a llama.

I do realize that constructing a tourist attraction of Three Notch Safari's magnitude would have required more than a few months. However, in the interest of story pacing, I chose to present it as something that could happen quickly. And the Amish do work at the speed of light.

Local readers will also observe that Becca has a conversation with "T-Bone" and Heather. That conversation reflects an actual discussion I had with the two local radio personalities. When I sat down with them to discuss radio advertising and my book plots for this series, I expressed frustration in developing a title for this novel, because the words "Farm" and "Ranch" really didn't seem to fit what Becca's property was. It was T-Bone who suggested naming this book *Three Notch Safari*.

Thanks, T-Bone!

READER QUESTIONS

- Under what genre would you classify Three Notch Safari? Romance? Mystery? Women's Fiction? All of the above or a different genre?
- Do you think that using her farm to earn money was a wise idea on Becca's part? What were the risks she ran to do so? Would you have done it if placed in her position?
- Did you feel any empathy for Mark Garvey? Did he have qualities with which you could relate?
- Did Becca's story strike a particular emotion in you? What emotion and why?
- Becca's relationship with her mother has its ups and downs. In what ways were Becca's interactions with Georgie like yours with your own mother?
- Could you identify with Becca's struggles with her daughter? In what ways were her struggles similar to yours with a child or other close relative?
- In the blockbuster movie based on this book, whom would you cast to play Becca Garvey? Danny Copsey?
- Were you surprised by who ended up being the person "whodunnit"? If not, what was the biggest clue that made you realize who it was? If you were surprised, who did you think it was going to be instead?
- Did Becca's love for animals resonate with you? What exotic animal would you like to own if you had a thirty-acre "safari"?

- How did you the secondary characters in Three Notch Safari contribute to the story? Who was your favorite side character? Least favorite?

Bonus questions for St. Mary's County residents:

- Were you able to identify local places mentioned in the book? Were any of them near where you live? Which place gave you the biggest "aha!" moment of recognition?
- Did the descriptions of local places and culture ring true to you? What stuck out in your mind the most?

SNEAK PEEK

RALEIGH SAT UP in bed, completely disoriented as usual. She blinked several times in the dark as she regained her senses and forced herself to breathe normally.

She was alive.

She was also drenched in sweat, despite being clad only in one of Grant's old cotton t-shirts and a pair of his dark blue silk boxer shorts. Neither felt particularly good against her clammy skin.

Raleigh looked down to her left at the spot where her husband should be. The bed was still made on his side. Each night, when she reluctantly crawled under the covers, she was careful not to disturb his side, and she invaded his space only enough to throw an arm over his pillow. She had never told anyone, but she was superstitiously terrified that if she were to roll down the covers or otherwise muss them up, his scent would be forever released from the bed, never to be recaptured.

It was why he had been gone months now and she still refused to change the sheets, despite how rank her side was becoming. It would be like throwing Grant into a laundry tub, an unbearable thought.

Instead, she chose to live out this equally unbearable Groundhog's Day, in which she perpetually reenacted her husband's death.

Raleigh was not a pilot and had not been in the cockpit with Grant that day—that seat had been taken by an experienced colleague of Grant's, Mateo Martinez, the flight officer who had also been killed in addition to Crunch and the flight officer of the other plane.

Wasn't it ironic that the impact of two aircraft wing tips touching mid-air was nothing like, say, two vehicle side view mirrors knocking against each other as two cars passed each other on a highway? Whereas the side view mirrors would be demolished, the cars would continue with barely an impact to their forward motion. The aircraft, though, with just a whisper-touch of their wing tips, could spin, crash into one another, and erupt into fiery balls of jet fuel.

Martinez's wife had been a statue at the joint funeral held for all four men at the base chapel. Sofía had hardly spoken to anyone, instead staring straight ahead with one child's hand clutched in each of hers as each man received an honor guard rifle salute and a flyover. Martinez's body was then shipped off to his family's home in Arizona, and Sofía left for her own family in Texas.

She hadn't even said goodbye to Raleigh, which was particularly painful not only because of their shared loss but because test pilot wives tended to stick together.

Raleigh had heard that Jasmine Green, who had been engaged to Crunch's flight officer, was striving to remain part of the test pilot community. She was trying to make some sense of how her rose petal-strewn future path had been destroyed, as if a tornado had violently appeared from nowhere and laid a dystopian waste to it.

Good for her if she could manage to make some sense of it.

Raleigh picked up her cell phone to look at the time. It was just past four in the morning. Too early to get up, too late to get any sort of real sleep before she actually had to get up and start another tiresome day.

Must this happen every night? Couldn't God just for once be merciful and let her go to sleep so that she never had to wake up trembling again?

Her dreams took different forms. Sometimes she was in her office, reliving the moment that she had received the call, and other times she imagined she was on the ground on Solomons Island, watching the planes' wing tips nick each other. The worst dreams, though, were when she imagined being in the cockpit with Grant as his partner on the flight. Although she wasn't a pilot, Grant had described it all so vividly before that her traitorous mind was able to conjure up the smell, feel, and muffled noise of the cockpit.

The other dreams left her unsettled and crying, but this one went deep into horror territory, mostly because it made her question, for the millionth time, what it was like for Grant when he realized his life was over.

"Accidents happen in the blink of an eye and your husband probably experienced none of the drawn-out terror of your dreams, Raleigh," the therapist had said. "Rest in the comfort that he felt no pain," blah blah blah.

Therapists. How could they possibly understand her pain?

Raleigh hardly remembered the funeral. There were just bits and pieces that periodically passed before her eyes. Sofía Martinez, emotionless and fragile. The pastor offering forgettable words of comfort. The American flag folded tautly by Grant's comrades and offered to her with a salute. Friends asking, "What can I do for you?" to which she wanted to scream, "How do I know? I am just trying to get through the next five minutes!" but instead smiling and accepting their sympathetic, fierce hugs. Her mother and sister, trying desperately—and futilely—to make Raleigh smile.

Then there were Grant's parents, David and Margaret Bishop, so broken themselves they could hardly speak to Raleigh. The Bishops had lived in St. Mary's County since the 17th century and had a proud lineage that stretched back into Merrie Olde England.

The family had had its share of tragic accidents over the centuries, all documented in voluminous heritage scrapbooks, but never anything as high profile and public as this. Raleigh had even had a condolence call from the governor, and both she and Grant's parents had received letters from the president.

As she considered it, Raleigh hadn't talked to the Bishops since last week, when they had suggested she finally open Grant's will and begin taking care of his estate. As Raleigh recalled, she had snapped something about not picking at Grant's corpse like beady-eyed vultures.

Not her finest moment.

So the Bishops had retreated from their daughter-in-law of seven years. Raleigh knew she owed them an apology, but for now, she just wanted to be left alone in her ongoing misery.

Realizing she was fully awake now, Raleigh slid out of bed, her feet gently hitting the oak floor.

Routine and habits—like being quiet so as not to wake Grant when he had been out all hours on night flights—were staying with her.

As if they would ever leave.

Raleigh stretched and yawned, then realized that the bedroom was very chilly. Time to adjust the thermostat, for she certainly wasn't going to switch out for flannel pajamas. Not while she had so many of Grant's clothes to keep close to her skin.

Her cell phone buzzed on the nightstand. It was her boss, Bert Mattingly, Director of the St. Mary's Historical Museum.

Raleigh contemplated ignoring the call, but Bert had been so understanding of her situation—allowing her nearly an indefinite period of leave after Grant's death—that it seemed churlish not to answer.

"Mornin', Raleigh," Bert said with excessive enthusiasm. "Just wanted to let you know that we finally received the state grants for both the new colonial farming display and the Yaocomico village exhibit you applied for last year. You're welcome to start on it whenever you'd like."

Guilt nipped at Raleigh's innards, tearing away at the grief she had been nurturing for so long. "I guess I should think about returning to the office…"

Bert seized on her doubt. "Of course, you should. We haven't touched your office so it's just as you left it."

"That's nice of you," Raleigh said noncommittally.

Bert took it as enthusiasm. "It would be good for you to spend a day or two a week in the office. I hear people say they see you jogging through your neighborhood with your dog, occasionally stopping to pick at a bag of green grapes for sustenance. You need more than that."

"Oh, that," Raleigh laughed weakly. "I don't quite have my appetite back."

Bert was silent for a moment. "After over a year?" he said quietly.

The guilt chewed at her more. "I know, I know. Look, I'll think about it, okay?"

"Okay." Bert sighed in resignation. "But remember

that you don't have to immediately come back full-time. Spend Mondays in the office."

"I promise to think about it," Raleigh repeated, now anxious to end the call.

Raleigh glanced back down at the bed. She was fully awake now, but it was tempting to scurry back under the covers and inhale as deeply as she could of Grant's lingering scent, which was all she had left of him.

No, she may as well start the day, such as it was. Besides, Lindbergh's nails were clicking up the stairs, a sign that he was ready for his morning walk.

Raleigh hadn't wanted a dog, not with Grant's postings so unsure all the time and the time commitment of a pet, but her husband had found their Chesapeake Bay Retriever through a local rescue agency. In no time, Mutt Boy—as Raleigh frequently referred to their water-loving beast—had become Grant's best pal next to Crunch.

Lindbergh sat in the bedroom doorway and glanced up at her with quizzical eyes. "Good morning, Mutt Boy," Raleigh said. The dog's tail thumped twice then he rose and walked over to Raleigh, leaning against her bare legs, another one of his customs. It could be hard to maintain balance against all eighty pounds of chocolate-colored, rumple-furred pooch. She reached down and scratched him behind his ears, to which Lindbergh leaned his head back to more fully enjoy her attentions.

"Tonight maybe, Lindbergh?" she asked the dog. Lindbergh hadn't slept on the bed since Grant had died. Instead, he spent his nights downstairs, curled up on the braided rug by the front door, as if still expecting that his master would be back at any moment. If she thought it might work, Raleigh would have joined him there.

Lindbergh offered no response except a quick whine and two wags of his tail. "All right, give me a minute."

Raleigh brushed her teeth and washed her face, trying

to avoid looking into the bathroom mirror, which she knew would reflect red-rimmed green eyes and tousled ash-blonde hair that had once been as straight as a field of straw.

She changed into a pair of gray sweats with the words "U.S. Navy" running down the left leg in large blue letters and the round Navy seal across the sweatshirt front. Then, following her ridiculous superstition, she tucked Grant's t-shirt and boxers down at the foot of the bed and drew the covers up. She could still get more wear out of them before it would be time to open his dresser drawer and pull out a new shirt and pair of boxers, treasuring the smell and feel of them.

What was she going to do when she ran out of his clothes?

Raleigh took a brisk jog with Lindbergh around the neighborhood, thankful that it was still early enough that there were no neighbors out to offer her sympathetic glances or words of encouragement. She and Grant had purchased their home in a new development built to look like a quaint town, despite it having been erected on two hundred acres of fallow farmland that had likely been abandoned when the owner died. Selling farms could result in huge cash payouts to heirs who wanted nothing to do with tilling the soil.

Raleigh had stacks of digitized records at the museum, showing the trend of farm sell-offs that had occurred over the decades. She hated to see the landscape lose its rural flavor, yet she and Grant had also benefited from having this particular farm made over into housing, so it was hard for her to criticize the changes.

Their cool-down was a brisk walk up the driveway to her house with its dark blue siding, bright yellow door, and white trim. Grant had picked the house's shades as a nod to his beloved Navy's colors.

Releasing the dog from his leash inside the house,

she fed him some kibble and prepped the coffeemaker with her favorite French roast. Although she had been repulsed by food since Grant's death, she was able to down copious amounts of coffee. She figured that if she loaded it occasionally with sugar and cream, it counted as nutrition for those inquiring minds, like Bert's, who seemed determined to ensure she was eating right.

She poured a little more cream into her cup, stirring it listlessly as she stared out the window at a squirrel raiding the bird feeder. The little thief had chased all of the birds out of their small, fenced-in yard. Raleigh shrugged. It was a dangerous world out there. Sometimes the squirrels won and the birds lost.

Raleigh was like a fledgling baby bird these days, up against a band of squirrels.

She spent the next few hours lying on the couch, idling flipping through channels while she drank more coffee. A sweet Hallmark movie with its true-love-found-against-all-odds theme did little to improve her mood.

Lindbergh hefted his big carcass onto the couch and laid his length along her body, snuffling his snout under her chin. Raleigh wrapped an arm around him and cried silently against his fur. Everything had fallen away from her.

"Everything except for you, Mutt Boy," she whispered, wishing she had something—anything—to lift her out of this constant gloominess. He licked her cheek and huffed before putting his head down for a nap. Raleigh fell into a fitful sleep with Grant's dog—now her dog— until late afternoon. At least she didn't have any of her usual horrifying dreams.

Raleigh awoke to Lindbergh whining by the front door. Time to take him back out again.

Was the rest of her life going to be like this? One awful day melding painfully into another, with no relief from the sorrow and the grief? Was she going to withdraw to the point that she completely disappeared? On one hand, it sounded preferable to living without Grant, but the deep, primal instinct of her soul protested the idea.

Perhaps it was time to take Bert's suggestion to return to work and to listen to her in-laws' urging to open Grant's will. That's what she'd do, get a good night of sleep, actually take a shower and wash her hair in the morning, apply a little powder and lipstick for the first time in months, then go to the bank to get the will out of their safe deposit box.

THE NEXT MORNING, she had the large, sealed envelope containing Grant's will in her hands by half past ten. She hurried home with it, deciding that she would read it from bed so that she could feel as though she was reading it with Grant next to her. More ridiculousness, she knew, glad that no one knew about all of her strange behaviors.

Oddly enough, when she sat cross-legged on top of the covers, Lindbergh came clicking into the room and jumped onto the bed for the first time since Grant had died. He immediately curled up in a giant ball and stared up at Raleigh expectantly.

"Shall I read it to you, Mutt Boy?" she asked, breaking the seal on the envelope and removing the document. Lindbergh whined and reached out a paw to her. Feeling silly, she took the dog's paw, as if she could draw strength from it.

Raleigh Bishop began reading her husband's will. The words were utterly inconceivable… *To my beloved wife, I leave —*

Available at your favorite online retailer.

Acknowledgments

First and foremost, I'd like to thank YOU, dear reader, for your ongoing passion and support for my books. I do believe I am blessed with the most loyal and enthusiastic readers in the world. I've loved meeting you at signings and book clubs. Your excitement for the *Heart of St. Mary's County* series is what keeps me motivated to dive into a manuscript every day.

Real people in this book include Angie and Tyler from Marie and Nash, as well as radio personalities T-Bone and Heather. I'm very grateful to all of them for their help in promoting my books. Additionally, Ronnie Farrell is a well-known auctioneer in the area.

I also have a fantastic team that brings my books to market. From my developmental editor, Sue Grimshaw, to the experts at Killion Design—Kim Killion, book cover designer extraordinaire, and Jennifer Jakes, formatter, copyeditor, and all-around good egg—I am surrounded by amazing professionals with whom I couldn't live without.

I'm also grateful to Alessandra Torre, Terezia Barna, Eva Frediani, and the entire Inkerscon team for creating the Masterminds concept that enabled me to write this book in half the time it would normally take. You ladies rock!

Finally, I would be nowhere without Don, the best thing I never planned.

Dominus illuminatio mea.

BOOKS BY CHRISTINE TRENT

HEART OF ST. MARY'S COUNTY
St. Clements Bluff
Three Notch Safari

THE ROYAL TRADES SERIES
The Queen's Dollmaker
A Royal Likeness
By the King's Design

THE LADY OF ASHES MYSTERIES
Lady of Ashes
Stolen Remains
A Virtuous Death
The Mourning Bells
Death at the Abbey
A Grave Celebration

FLORENCE NIGHTINGALE MYSTERIES
No Cure for the Dead
A Murderous Malady

SHORT STORIES & ANTHOLOGIES
A Death on the Way to Portsmouth (eBook only)
A Pocketful of Death (The Deadly Hours)
Mrs. Beeton's Sausage Stuffing (Malice Domestic Presents Murder Most Edible)

About the Author

CHRISTINE TRENT IS the author of the *Royal Trades* historical series, the *Lady of Ashes* historical mystery series, and several other historical novels.

Her new series, The Heart of St. Mary's County, is set in her beloved, wonderfully history-rich home community in Southern Maryland.

Visit her at *www.ChristineTrent.com*

Made in the USA
Middletown, DE
11 July 2024